Caribbean Counterstrike

Caribbean Counterstrike

A Coast Guard Cutter *Kauai* Sea Adventure by

Edward M. Hochsmann

E-Book ISBN-13: 978-1-956777-98-7
Paperback ISBN-13: 978-1-956777-95-6
Audiobook ISBN-13: 978-1-956777-04-8

Edward M. Hochsmann
PO Box 286
Shalimar, Florida 32579-0286
https://www.edwardhochsmann.com/

First edition
Cover art by SpudzArt©

Table of Contents

Dedication

This book is dedicated to my wife and sons, who provide the love and support that gets me through each day and every effort I face. It is also dedicated to the Armed Forces of the United States, whose men and women strive and sacrifice in every corner of the globe to protect and defend our nation.

Semper Paratus

Main Characters

Benjamin "Ben" Wyporek, Lieutenant Junior Grade, U. S. Coast Guard. Ben is the Second-in-Command or "Executive Officer" of the Coast Guard Cutter *Kauai*. He is young for an officer, but his demeanor and experience have earned the respect of the professionals around him, and although he is firm in his job, he never lets his position go to his head. Ben is currently in a long-distance relationship with Victoria Carpenter, the beautiful Defense Intelligence Agency analyst he met during a mission a few months ago.

Victoria Carpenter is a mathematical genius employed by the Defense Intelligence Agency as a Data Scientist. Her talents for "connecting the dots" in large databases and Internet searches have proven invaluable to the organization. She suffers from a mild form of autism that makes relationships and some life activities challenging for her. Her relationship with Ben is warm and durable.

Dr. Peter Simmons is a field agent with the Defense Intelligence Agency. He has a talent for deception, which has led to his success as a DIA field agent but is the antithesis of Ben's ethos. Simmons also has a risk-seeking bent that borders on pathology. He shares a cordial relationship with Ben and is supportive of his relationship with Victoria, his protégé and sister of his beloved late fiancée.

Samuel "Sam" Powell, Lieutenant, U. S. Coast Guard. Sam is Ben's boss and Commanding Officer of the Coast Guard Cutter *Kauai*. Sam is one of those people who is the total package - knowledge, judgment, experience, and "people sense." He was raised in a wealthy family and was being groomed to become another Wall Street "Master of the Universe" when a clash with his father led him to abandon that path and enlist in the Coast Guard. He is over ten years older than Ben, but despite this and their different backgrounds, they are best friends.

Emilia "Hoppy" Hopkins, Chief Operations Specialist, U. S. Coast Guard. She is close in age and a lot like Sam in terms of competence and professionalism, and they have as strong a friendship as people in their respective positions can. She has enormous respect and an exasperated affection for Ben, who reminds her of her late husband. Although a straight arrow, she is not afraid to forego convention in highly unusual circumstances.

Shelley Lee, Boatswain's Mate Second Class, US Coast Guard. The premier small boat driver of the crew is more rough-and-ready than Hopkins and a solid, courageous performer. She and Ben are close in age, similar in personality, and share a strong mutual respect and trust bond.

James "COB" Drake, Chief Machinery Technician, U. S. Coast Guard. The senior enlisted member of the crew and the classic father figure among the enlisted and, to some extent, Ben. He is the quintessential "operator" and has what amounts to an underground network of fellow CPOs from whom he can acquire technical assistance, materiel, and "intel." His background is somewhat mysterious, but he is "connected" up to the senior officer level of the Coast Guard.

Horatio "Harry" Pennington, Rear Admiral, U. S. Coast Guard. Pennington is the Director of the Joint Interagency Task Force South, responsible for coordinating all law enforcement activity within the United States Southern Command. *Kauai* and her crew are under his command for the operation depicted in the story.

Joana Mendez Powell. Wife of Sam and unofficial "First Lady" of *Kauai*. She is a former navy petty officer and work-from-home computer graphics artist who looks after the crew's families while they are at sea. She is close friends with Ben and Emilia.

Military Ranks

Commissioned Officers		
Coast Guard/Navy	**Army/Air Force**	**Characters**
Admiral	General	Miller (USA)
Vice Admiral	Lieutenant General	Irving (USN)
Rear Admiral	Major General Brigadier General	Pennington, Brown (USCG)
Captain	Colonel	Mercier (USCG)
Commander	Lieutenant Colonel	Keener (USCG)
Lieutenant Commander	Major	Becker (USCG) Roberts (USA)
Lieutenant	Captain	Powell, Holmgren (USCG) Davis (USN) Landry, Fergus (USAF)
Lieutenant Junior Grade	1st Lieutenant	Wyporek (USCG)
Enlisted		
Coast Guard/Navy	**Air Force**	**Characters**
Master Chief Petty Officer	Chief Master Sergeant	Shipley (USAF)
Senior Chief Petty Officer	Senior Master Sergeant	D'Agostino (USN)
Chief Petty Officer	Master Sergeant	Drake, Hopkins (USCG)
Petty Officer First Class	Technical Sergeant	Bondurant, Williams (USCG) Parker (USN)
Petty Officer Second Class	Staff Sergeant	Lee, Guerrero, Brown, Hebert (USCG)
Petty Officer Third Class	Senior Airman	Bunting, Jenkins, Lopex, Zuccaro (USCG)

Select Technical Terms

1MC	Ship's internal announcement system
252s	Transnational Criminal Organization
AUTEC	Atlantic Undersea Test and Evaluation Center
Bridge	Control center for the ship
Captain	The title for a commanding officer when aboard their ship, regardless of nominal rank. Also, a Coast Guard and Navy rank at paygrade O6—equivalent to a Colonel in the Army, Air Force, and Marine Corps
CO	Commanding Officer
COB	Chief of the Boat
Conn	Position controlling operation of the ship
Coxswain	Position controlling the operation of a small boat
DIA	Defense Intelligence Agency
EO/IR	Electro-Optical/Infrared
FC3	Fire Control/Command and Control system
Helm	Position or station controlling the ship's rudder
Knots	Nautical Miles per Hour
"Light Off"	Start or activate an engine or device
Main Control	Control station for the ship's main engines
NVG	Night Vision Goggles
OOD	Officer of the Deck
PB	Patrol Boat
Port (side)	To the left, when facing the bow aboard a ship
RHIB	Rigid Hull Inflatable Boat
RJ	Rivet Joint Electronic Warfare Aircraft
Salinas Cartel	Honduran drug gang

SEAL	SEa-Air-Land – U.S. Navy Special Warfare Operators
Starboard (side)	To the right, when facing the bow aboard a ship
WILCO	Brevity code for "Will Comply."
XO	Executive Officer—second-in-command of a ship

Prologue

Fifteen months ago, Captain Jane Mercier, U.S. Coast Guard, Chief of the Office of Response for the Seventh Coast Guard District, received a phone call she had been dreading for several weeks from Captain Nathan Worley, Commander of Coast Guard Sector Miami. The patrol boat USCGC *Kauai* was en route to her homeport in Miami; her Alien Migrant Interdiction Operations patrol cut short by a fatal mishap. Two migrants were dead, several injured, and the boat's second-in-command and senior boatswain's mate were also severely injured and medically evacuated.

"Jane, I have no choice. I have to yank him," Worley said, referring to the cutter's commanding officer. "Is there anything you can do to help me with a quick replacement?"

"What about the XO?" Mercier asked, referring to *Kauai*'s second-in-command, or Executive Officer.

"We had to medevac him for a head injury. Besides, you know he isn't up to it."

"Yes, I know," Mercier said. *Kauai* had been on their mutual radar for several months, with materiel discrepancies and adverse personnel actions well above the norm. They had sent a "fixer", a Chief Machinery Technician named James Drake, known for his ability to ferret out and solve problems, to replace the chief on board and privately provide a report on the command. Drake's account had been shockingly frank—the boat was in a downward spiral only a change of command could fix. Mercier and Worley had been working through the administrative details to make that happen quietly when the incident had forced their hand.

Kauai was an Island Class Patrol Boat, 110 feet long and displacing 168 tons, with a crew of fourteen enlisted and two officers. The last of her class built, and among the last few still serving with the Coast Guard, *Kauai* was scheduled for decommissioning within two years. The issue with the command presented a dilemma—should they invest in repairs and the disruption of a relief for cause, or just call it a day and move up the decommissioning?

Drake's report also said the hull was in good shape, and he could turn around the engineering department with a bit of help. Mercier was reluctant to throw *Kauai* away early because the boat had been upgraded with a prototype of the automated main gun installed on the new patrol boats and the hull had plenty of life left. For a replacement commanding officer, she had her eye on a lieutenant in her department named Sam Powell, who was working through the command center controller syllabus after a very successful command tour on a smaller eighty-seven-foot coastal patrol boat. The need to replace the injured executive officer was unexpected, and she would have to scramble through the recent list of screened officers to find an available replacement.

Sam was stunned when Mercier pulled him into her office a few minutes later and ordered him to report to Base Miami Beach and assume command of *Kauai* as soon as the Sector Commander relieved his predecessor. But, like any officer of his high caliber, he said "aye, aye" and carried out his orders. Within two weeks, Mercier had identified and transferred in the new second-in-command, Lieutenant Junior Grade Ben Wyporek.

Sam and Ben's job was to restore the ship and crew to operational readiness as soon as possible. This they did within a few months, despite the damage from mishap and the critical morale problems their predecessors had left behind. After the restoration period was complete and a few operational wins were under their belt, Sam and Ben pivoted to building the crew's esprit de corps.

Kauai's crew became Mercier's special project, and even Sam was surprised with the ease with which they could swap out the few irredeemable troublemakers and slackers for top performers. Given their proximity to decommissioning, he had feared *Kauai* would become a dumping ground for malcontents. Over time, the combined efforts of Mercier directing top-notch personnel into the crew, Drake's wheeler-dealer skills with maintenance and parts, and Sam and Ben's leadership acumen brought *Kauai* to a peak of operational competence and readiness unimaginable a year earlier.

Kauai was about halfway through a routine law enforcement patrol when she encountered a derelict sailboat laden with illegal narcotics, wrecked and devoid of a crew except for a single corpse trapped inside the cabin. Within hours of reporting their unusual find, they were detached from their normal operations and assigned to a national defense mission under the control of a mysterious Defense Intelligence Agency officer, Dr. Peter Simmons. After a couple of days of being kept in the dark about their purpose, ending in a deadly car chase that nearly cost Ben his life, the two officers confronted Simmons with a "come clean" or "abort mission" ultimatum. The answer they received was astounding—they were actually searching for a stray nuclear weapon believed to have landed in the area.

The search had begun five days earlier. A U.S. fighter intercepted a Russian Backfire bomber on the edge of U.S. airspace and they collided, triggering a nuclear-tipped hypersonic missile's uncommanded launch. Contact was lost almost immediately after the launch and never recovered. Despite the relief that the warhead had not detonated, the peace of the world depended on locating the weapon and keeping it and the circumstances of its launch under wraps. The government had performed those search actions that could be completed covertly, without result. *Kauai*'s discovery of the wreck and Simmons's confirmation that the damage was consistent with what would be expected in a near-miss by a hypersonic vehicle had opened another avenue of opportunity for covert search.

After a few days on the search, Ben, ashore at the time with Simmons assisting his team in their land-based efforts, deduced the warhead's location. While investigating, they drew in a heavily armed seizure team from the same criminal organization that owned the derelict drug vessel. Ben and Simmons engaged the criminals and held them off. Both were wounded, and without *Kauai*'s arrival, literally at the last second, they would have been killed. Or worse.

After being "honorably acquitted" in the formal, but highly secret debrief of the mission for a committee of senior officials in the U.S. intelligence community, Mercier pulled Ben and Sam aside for a private chat. She explained to the two officers that she had taken advantage of the replacement of *Kauai*'s former command to experiment with building an elite crew that could be used for complicated and sensitive missions like this one. Because of their excellent performance, the patrol boat was given a new lease on life, with additional training and crew and an upgrade of her electronics and propulsion systems paid for by the Director of National Intelligence. The Coast Guard would retain and use *Kauai* as it saw fit, with the caveat she would be made available immediately should the DNI need her for any sensitive missions.

Kauai was transferred from Sector Miami to work directly for the 7th District Commander. Her homeport was moved from Miami to Port Canaveral, ostensibly to serve as the permanent range safety cutter for Cape Canaveral rocket launches. In fact, it kept her mostly out of sight, avoiding awkward questions of why the Coast Guard was retaining and upgrading a nominally obsolete patrol boat. She continued performing standard patrol boat operations when not offline for upgrades or special training, but was kept close at hand to respond as needed for DNI-assigned missions.

The true nature of their fateful mission remained unknown to *Kauai*'s crew, other than Ben, Sam, Operations Specialist Hopkins, and Drake. For the rest, the action was a lethal encounter with a vicious transnational criminal organization, and their prompt intervention prevented Ben and the DIA officer from being killed, which was factual as far as it went. Still, the crew was sharp and knew the upgrades conveyed a special status that recognized their high performance, leveling-up the pride they already enjoyed.

"There are no great men; there are only great challenges, which ordinary men like you and me are forced by circumstances to meet."

Attributed to Fleet Admiral William F. Halsey, Jr., US Navy

Part I

Pre-Mission

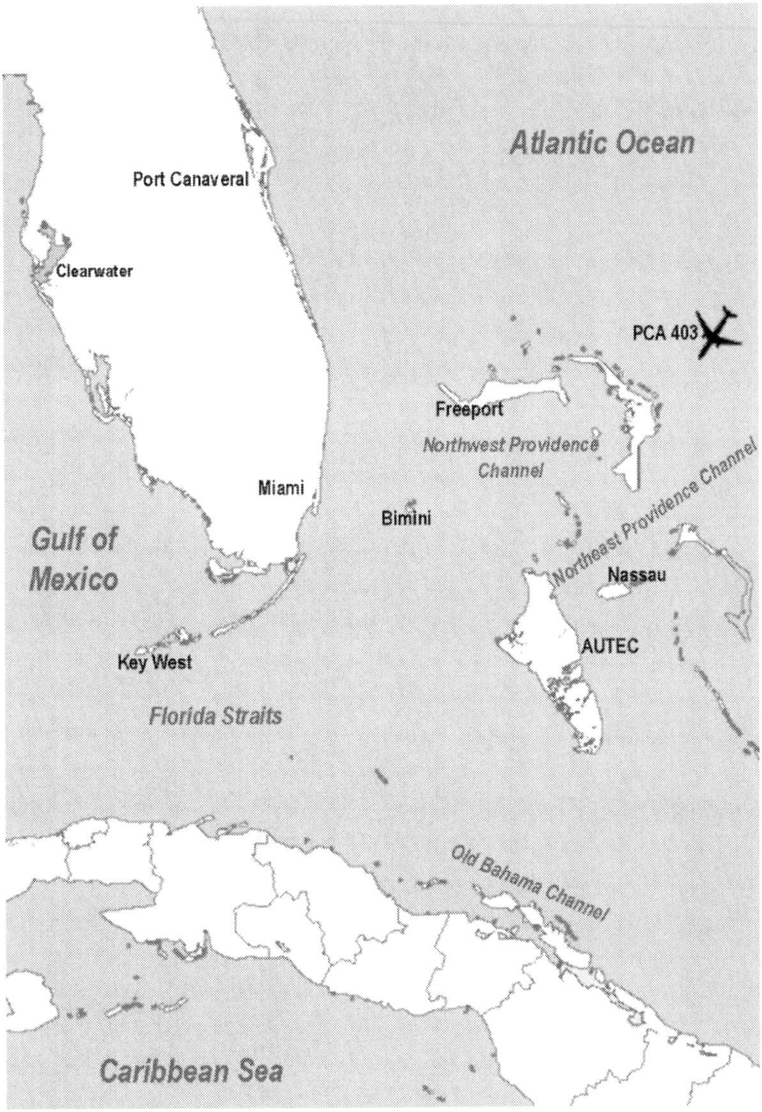
Atlantic Ocean
Port Canaveral
Clearwater
PCA 403
Freeport
Northwest Providence Channel
Northeast Providence Channel
Miami
Bimini
Gulf of Mexico
Nassau
AUTEC
Key West
Florida Straits
Old Bahama Channel
Caribbean Sea

1

The Crack of Doom

USCG Cutter *Kauai*, Atlantic Ocean, ten nautical miles east-southeast of Hollywood, Florida
02:27 EDT, 11 March

Sam

Lieutenant Samuel "Sam" Powell watched the image of the "go-fast" boat on the right-hand multi-function display of the Bridge's Fire Control/Command and Control or FC3 station. The ghostly green image was transmitted from a Customs and Border Patrol DHC-8 maritime patrol aircraft, flying at a minimum speed at two thousand feet, zigzagging back and forth to avoid overrunning the target. The aspect of the speeding boat's image gradually changed as the plane traced a broad S-shaped pattern behind it while the data display overlaying the bottom of the screen showed its latitude, longitude, heading, and speed. An open forty-footer with three large outboard engines and eight people on board, the boat was on a course leading slightly ahead of *Kauai's* current position on this heading, but the latter's slow motion would bring the two vessels to the same point in the ocean in about five minutes.

It was the darkest of nights, a solid overcast blocking out both moon and stars. The only light was the glow of the Miami-Ft. Lauderdale metroplex stretched across a broad arc of *Kauai's* starboard beam. Sam would have preferred meeting the target boat further offshore, where the city light would not silhouette his patrol boat, but this was the only place the intercept geometry worked. Both seas and winds were very light, making for a comfortable ride. The only sound was the low and steady hum of the three diesel engines. All things considered, they had a pretty good chance of catching the incoming smuggler by surprise.

It was *Kauai's* first operational mission after completing an extensive rebuild and a few weeks of shakedown training. They should be heading for the Atlantic Undersea Test and Evaluation Center, better known as AUTEC, at Andros Island in the Bahamas, to complete testing and evaluate the new gear added to the cutter. However, the Coast Guard had hard intelligence; the boat racing toward them carried a high-ranking member of an Eastern European human-trafficking gang, whose notoriety prevented travel to the U.S. by conventional means. He was a high-value target, or HVT, armed and dangerous, and had to be stopped. But the boat also held other people, illegal immigrants, yes, but people undeserving of being caught in a lethal crossfire between a dangerous sociopath and law enforcement. Sorting out this dilemma was the type of mission for which *Kauai* was rebuilt and her crew retrained.

"Target still constant bearing, decreasing range. Range now two-point-four, ETA four minutes fifty," said Electronics Technician First Class Joe Williams. He sat in the center position at the FC3 console, the tactical station controlling the cutter's 25-mm main gun, the automated searchlight, and the new "entangling weapon" mounted just forward of the main gun they had spent the previous week testing. Operations Specialist Third Class Natalia Zuccaro sat to his right, monitoring navigation and radar, and Electronics Technician Third Class Darryl Bunting sat on his left, tending to systems and communications.

"Very well," Sam replied. "Warm up the Squid and start the targeting feed." "Squid" was the nickname for the entangling weapon, essentially a three-barreled recoilless cannon shooting encapsulated nets that popped open at the end of their flight and landed in a pre-set pattern. The launcher took target and environmental data from Williams's console and adjusted the firing bearing and elevation to deploy the nets in a pattern a speeding boat could not avoid. The boat would overrun a net, foul the propellers, and be stopped without using lethal gunfire. Hopefully.

The sad fact was a lot had to go just right for this device to work. The target needed to be within two hundred meters of *Kauai*, with both vessels on parallel courses in calm seas. It was a calm night, and Sam had absolute confidence that his Officer of the Deck, or OOD, Chief Operations Specialist Emilia Hopkins, would bring *Kauai* into position in the minimum time possible. The rub was their opponent—success depended on him turning to the left to avoid *Kauai*. If he turned right, he would scoot past their tail and be out of range before they got the heavier patrol boat turned around. Sam had positioned the cutter's Rigid Hull Inflatable Boat, referred to as "the rib" for its acronym RHIB, two hundred yards to seaward and slightly behind to counter this possibility. The RHIB's crew would unmask their floodlight as soon as *Kauai* illuminated the target with her searchlight, which should persuade the incoming boat to turn left to escape. Of course, he could also turn back to Bimini—not as good as a seizure, but it was still a win.

Using the RHIB was a calculated risk—the target could try to force past it using ramming or gunfire, but the odds against that were long. The HVT might be armed and dangerous, but the smuggling crew's priority was to stay alive. They knew if they assaulted law enforcement, the response would be both lethal and instantaneous. Far better to turn tail and outrun the plodding cutter, which they could easily do with their five-knot speed advantage.

"Captain, I have target lock and tracking now on EO," Williams announced, referring to the cutter's electro-optical camera. Although his nominal rank was lieutenant, Sam was addressed as "Captain" aboard *Kauai* by service tradition as her commanding officer. "Laser rangefinder is active, feeding data directly to searchlight, fire control, and the Squid. Range now one-point-nine, ETA three minutes fifty-two seconds." As he spoke, the unlit searchlight swung out onto the bearing of the incoming target.

"Roger that," Sam replied, then keyed the radio transmit button for his headset. "*Kauai* One, *Kauai* Actual, target in sight, ETA three forty-five."

"Roger, sir, standing by," replied the RHIB's coxswain, Boatswain's Mate Second Class Shelley Lee. Lee commanded the RHIB as the coxswain, even though her passengers included her immediate boss, Boatswain's Mate First Class John Bondurant, and *Kauai*'s Executive Officer, Lieutenant Junior Grade Ben Wyporek, who would lead the target's boarding once it had been disabled.

Hopkins keyed the intercom connecting the Bridge to the engine control station deep in the cutter's hull. "Main Control, Conn, take engine control, expect Emergency Full Ahead in three minutes."

"Conn, Main Control," Drake's baritone voice replied. "I have engine control, maintaining three knots, standing by for Emergency Full Ahead in three minutes." "Emergency Full" was a command to route power from the battery bank and three diesel generators for rapid acceleration of the cutter's two electric motors from a full stop or their current slow speed to maximum thrust, either ahead or astern. It required the transfer of engine control to Drake's station, where he could watch the generator and motor instruments and achieve the highest acceleration with the safeties bypassed.

Sam watched the two screens on the FC3 station, one now showing the approaching boat from the view of the EO camera alongside the full-motion video feed from the plane. Williams had selected the boat's range in yards, bearing, and ETA for the data display. Even at full zoom, no boat details were visible in the darkness, just the spreading white "mustache" of the bow wave. "Chief, we are at two thousand yards now. I'm going to light him up at two hundred yards. You are cleared to maneuver as required."

"Very good, sir," Hopkins replied. Emilia "Hoppy" Hopkins was a fast-tracker in the Operations Specialist rating and a twelve-year veteran of the Coast Guard. Thanks to Sam's request to his superiors after their last mission, they upgraded her billet to E7 so she could stay on board *Kauai* while advancing to the coveted rank of chief petty officer. The tall and fit thirty-three-year-old widowed mother of twelve- and nine-year-old sons, Hopkins shared a house with her mother, who looked after the boys when she was at sea. Both Ben and Sam shared considerable respect, affection, and trust for their new chief, and she felt the same for them.

Sam watched the range readout tick down and, at three hundred yards, announced, "Stand by searchlight."

"Searchlight ready, sir," Williams responded. Then he leaned slightly to the right and nudged Zuccaro, then whispered, "Watch the EO screen when I light off the searchlight."

"OK." She nodded vigorously. Zuccaro had only been aboard a few weeks, an addition that came with the added functionality of the new FC3 console. She looked up to Williams as a mentor and with a bit of awe over his role in *Kauai*'s dustup last January—he had controlled the main gun in that engagement, and his shooting had saved the XO's life.

Hopkins smiled at the interplay between the two petty officers and then keyed the intercom. "Stand by, Main Control."

"Main Control ready."

At 210 yards, Sam leaned over and put a hand on Williams's shoulder. "Illuminate target."

"Illuminate target, sir," Williams responded as he punched the light on/off button. In the same motion, he punched on the floodlight illuminating the Coast Guard "Racing Stripe" painted on *Kauai*'s hull and the cutter's running lights.

"Main Control, Conn, Emergency Full Ahead," Hopkins ordered.

"Emergency Full Ahead, aye!" Drake replied as *Kauai*'s engines roared, and she jumped forward into the darkness.

The searchlight flickered on and directed a fifteen million candela beam directly into the approaching boat's cockpit. Williams smiled with satisfaction, watching the driver's eyes widen and jaw drop in shock on the EO display, then turned to Zuccaro. "Ah, the 'Oh, shit!' moment. Now THAT never gets old!"

As Williams chuckled, the RHIB's floodlight came on to the target driver's right. He glanced in that direction for half a second and then spun his steering wheel to the left, nearly capsizing the speeding vessel during the turn. The boat steadied on a southerly course and picked up speed rapidly, slowly drawing ahead about sixty yards away from *Kauai*'s port bow.

"Conn, Main Control, that's all I can give you right now," Drake's voice came up from the intercom.

"Conn, aye, hold that." Turning to the helmsman, Hopkins ordered, "Left five degrees rudder."

"Left five degrees rudder, Chief," the helmsman replied. "Chief, my rudder is left five degrees."

When Hopkins was satisfied the vessels were running parallel, she turned to the helmsman. "Rudder amidships."

"Rudder amidships, aye. Chief, my rudder is amidships, heading one eight three."

"Very well," Hopkins responded, then turned to Sam. "Target aspect and relative motion stable, Captain."

"Very well. Williams, prepare to fire Squid."

Williams noted the yellow "Solution" light on his panel, showing that the projector's control system had locked onto the fleeing target boat. Its internal artificial intelligence had calculated the required azimuth and elevation to lay down an optimal pattern of the three nets. "Targeting solution achieved."

"Match generated bearings and shoot."

Williams hit the activation switch. The projector pivoted to match the generated azimuth and elevation angles, resulting in a green "Ready to Fire" light on the panel. Williams announced, "Firing Squid." Then he pressed the trigger.

Ben

Ben sat on the RHIB's left side and glanced across the water at *Kauai*, visible in the city glow two hundred yards off the boat's starboard side. He looked back into the boat. Lee was sitting at the helm, making minor adjustments to keep station on the larger cutter as they crept through the water. Lee was single, twenty-five years old, and on the short side for a boatswain's mate, barely five-foot-three, but very athletic. Ben liked Lee; besides being close to his age, she was competent and dependable. She was also the finest coxswain he had ever known—she *lived* for driving the RHIB.

Ben's gaze moved to Bondurant, sitting on the opposite side of the boat, holding the floodlight. He was a full foot taller than Lee and powerfully built. The thirty-four-year-old father of two high school-aged boys, Bondurant was Ben's choice for known hostile boardings. Not that Lee couldn't handle herself, quite the contrary, but violent idiots were discouraged from trying anything physical by the size of the hulking Bondurant. Better to avoid the fight to begin with, a philosophy with which Lee heartily agreed—she couldn't drive the RHIB if she were in the boarding party.

"*Kauai* One, *Kauai* Actual, target in sight, ETA three forty-five," came over Ben's headset, followed by Lee's acknowledgment. Ben smiled as he pictured Sam calmly walking around the Bridge two hundred yards away. To Ben, Sam had the total package: knowledge, judgment, experience, and "people sense." He considered him a model officer and his closest friend. He was about an inch taller than Ben and similarly slim and athletic.

Ben himself was a little over average height at five-foot-ten. At twenty-four, he was also among the younger members of *Kauai*'s complement. Although somewhat awed by his fight with the drug gang a few months previously, the crew appreciated his cheery demeanor and the respect he showed them as valued professionals. His close brush with death dispelled whatever boyishness he had, but he kept his bright wit and approachability.

Ben gazed out to seaward. Not long now. They would hear the incoming boat long before they saw it and act when *Kauai*'s searchlight activated. In the meantime, they were to hold station on the cutter. Ben's thoughts returned to the worst case, the boat turning right. If they tried to ram and Lee wasn't able to evade.... He glanced at Lee and noted her rapid visual scan and cool look in the soft light of the RHIB's instrument panel. Ben smiled to himself and looked out to sea again. *Yeah, as if!*

Across the boat, Bondurant stirred. "I hear them!" He brought the floodlight to the ready and unlocked the shutter. The light was already turned on, so it would be instantly available. Both men kneeled and braced themselves for a quick start. Ben could hear the roar of the target boat's engines now, coming from left to right across RHIB's bow. Almost simultaneously, *Kauai*'s engines roared to full power, and the cutter's searchlight settled on the incoming boat.

"Light him up!" Ben shouted.

Bondurant dropped the shutter and trained the floodlight on the boat. The driver glanced their way momentarily, then swung the speeding boat into a hard left turn.

Yes! "Go, Shelley!" Ben shouted.

Lee slammed the throttle forward, and the RHIB seemed to leap ahead after the speeding target. Bondurant struggled to keep the floodlight on target as the RHIB thumped across the target boat's wake. Lee pulled the RHIB into a parallel track about fifty yards away on the target's port quarter as briefed. The RHIB had the speed to overtake the target, but Lee knew her job tonight was herding.

A minute into the pursuit, Ben heard three bangs in quick succession from *Kauai*. The three Squid canisters arced invisibly over the speeding target vessel in the darkness, with small fins spinning them at fifteen revolutions per second to provide stability and help spread out the nets when their internal charges detonated at the end of their flight. Sam's voice came over Ben's headset. "*Kauai* One, Squid fired, break left in three, two, one, NOW!" Twenty-five feet above the water, all three capsules fired within a second, dropping an unavoidable Kevlar trap forty yards ahead of the target boat as the RHIB and *Kauai* sheared off to the left and right.

The boat narrowly missed the right-hand net but ran straight through the center one. When its propellers contacted the netting, two engines sheared their driveshafts and oversped, triggering the automatic shutoff. The third engine ground to a stop with its propeller wrapped up in the net. The boat lurched to a quick halt, throwing all occupants but the driver onto the deck. As the RHIB swung around through the turn, Ben watched the driver hang his head and beat on the steering wheel with his fist in frustration as his crew and passengers began standing up in dazed confusion.

"All right, Shelley, let's heave to until *Kauai* gets into position," Ben said. He didn't want the RHIB to overrun a net in the dark—it had a propeller too and was just as vulnerable as the target boat. As Lee closed the throttle and brought the RHIB to a halt, Bondurant shut off and secured the floodlight.

Kauai took five minutes to complete her turn and edge into position—she also had propellers plus stabilizing fins on her bilge turns, which could suffer severe damage if fouled on a net. Sam's voice came over the headset again as the cutter stopped about fifty yards west of the disabled boat with her searchlight locked on. "*Kauai* One, *Kauai* Actual, start a slow approach. Nets one and three are behind us. Net two is fouled on the target."

"*Kauai*, *Kauai* One, roger, sir, starting approach," Lee replied as she moved the throttle off idle.

"LE-One, *Kauai* Actual, believe the HVT is the individual conversing with the helmsman. No weapons are visible, but the threat level is still red. Overwatch is in position and ready. We will make initial contact now." Ben had his own callsign, LE-One, on the comms net since he would act independently of the RHIB during the boarding.

"Roger, sir. Continuing," Ben replied. This was the hard part. Somehow, Ben had to talk down a dangerously excited murderer and convince him to surrender. He saw two men arguing in the boat's cockpit, one black and the other white. The black man had to be the boat's Bahamian master, and the other, the HVT, undoubtedly pushing for a more satisfactory outcome than his arrest. At least no guns were out. *Overwatch is in position.* Overwatch was Gunner's Mate Second Class Deke Guerrero, positioned with a fifty-caliber sniper rifle on the Flying Bridge above *Kauai*'s main Bridge. Guerrero could deliver a kill shot reliably from a mile away—fifty yards on a calm night was point-blank for him. If Sam, Ben, or Bondurant uttered the word "Yankee" on the radio, Guerrero would fire that kill shot as soon as he had a clear target.

As the RHIB edged toward the target boat, Williams's voice came from the loudhailer on *Kauai*. "Master of the disabled vessel, this is the United

States Coast Guard. Your vessel is forfeit under Title Eight of the United States Code, Section 1324. All persons on board will be placed under arrest. You will muster all persons on board aft of the cockpit, where they will be seated with their hands on top of their heads. All persons on board are to discard any weapons in their possession. Any person on board observed holding a weapon after this announcement will be subject to lethal force. To repeat…" The announcement was repeated and ended with: "You will comply at once. Start mustering all persons now."

The master lowered his head, then gave an order. As the other six people started moving aft, the HVT began an argument. When the RHIB pulled within earshot, Ben could hear the final statement of the master: "It's broken, man! We are done."

The HVT started looking back and forth, then reached for something in the cockpit. He rose, placed a pistol against the master's head, and pulled the man between himself and *Kauai*.

Shit! "Gun!" Ben shouted as he and Bondurant crouched and pulled their pistols. Lee brought the RHIB to a halt and crouched behind the helm console. One woman screamed on the disabled boat, and all but the HVT and his human shield immediately laid down. "*Kauai*, LE-One," Ben said into his headset. "HVT has a handgun and has taken the master hostage. We are stopped with sidearms ready. Recommend I try to negotiate surrender from our present position, over."

After a brief pause, Sam's voice came over the headset. "LE-One, *Kauai* Actual, approved. Do not continue the approach without confirmed surrender and disarming of the suspect. Go on hot mike, and keep it open during negotiations."

"*Kauai*, LE-One, WILCO." Ben moved the transmit switch to Hot Mic. Both he and Bondurant brought up and aimed their pistols. "On the disabled boat, this is the Coast Guard! Put your weapon down immediately!"

The HVT turned his head in surprise and adjusted to make himself a smaller target for Ben and Bondurant while still shielding himself from *Kauai*. "Screw you! You are going to let me go, or this man dies!"

Ben lowered his voice to be inaudible on the target. "Overwatch, LE-One. Do you have a shot? Over."

Guerrero's voice responded at once. "Negative, LE-One, no clear shot."

"Roger." Ben resumed his interchange with the HVT. "Sir, that is not an option! Your vessel is disabled and cannot be repaired! It's over! Please, no one has to die today!"

"Fine! Then I take your boat!"

"Sorry, sir, we can't do that! Even if we could, you wouldn't have enough fuel to get anywhere!"

"Then get me a boat that can! I'm not fucking around! I will kill this man!"

The master's eyes, which had been flitting back and forth in terror, fixed on Ben. Ben took his support hand off the pistol and made a slow, down-waving motion until the master nodded slowly, then placed his hand back on the gun. He whispered into his microphone, "Yankee." Then more loudly. "That is not going to happen! There are only two possible outcomes here—you drop that gun, and we arrest you, or you get killed!"

"Then I'll see you in Hell!"

What followed happened in under one second. The HVT took the pistol's muzzle off the master's temple and started to draw on Ben. The master immediately twisted and bent over, disrupting the HVT's aim. There was the loud "Crack" of a large-caliber rifle shot. Then the pistol dropped to the deck, followed by the HVT, who crumpled like a marionette with the strings cut. The former hostage kneeled and put his hands on top of his head.

"Suspect down, repeat suspect is down," Ben said. "Hostage is safe and signaling surrender." Then, he remembered to take his transmit switch off Hot Mic. And to breathe.

"LE-One, *Kauai* Actual, roger, approach with discretion, over."

"WILCO, sir." Holstering his pistol with a trembling hand, he turned to Lee. "Shelley, move in dead slow, please. If anyone else pops up with a gun, duck and haul ass."

She flashed him a relieved smile as she moved the throttle out of idle. "Sir, I'm the *quintessence* of discretion."

Ben smiled warmly in return, then turned to Bondurant. "Boats, how about I go on first with you covering, then I'll cover you when you board?"

"Sounds right, sir. You want me to do the hook-ups?"

"Yes, let's start with the skipper and move aft from there. Stay alert, although I'm pretty sure they've had enough excitement for tonight."

"Let's hope so."

As they approached the boat, Ben called out, "On the boat, this is the US Coast Guard. Remain seated with your hands on top of your head. Do not stand or make any sudden movements. Comply with the boarding officer's instructions completely and immediately." Ben stepped aboard and drew his pistol as the RHIB contacted the boat with a soft nudge. *Kauai*'s searchlight lit the scene, and the only sounds were the low growl of the RHIB's engine, the gentle lapping of small waves on the hull, and the soft sobs of a woman, presumably the one who screamed at the incident's outset. After a quick visual sweep and count of seven people seated with hands visible, he felt for a pulse on the downed suspect. Nothing. The man was dead before he hit the deck, his spine severed just below his skull. Ben stood and nodded to Bondurant. "Now, Boats." The big boatswain nodded, holstered his pistol, and stepped on board. Ben motioned him over and whispered, "Leave the woman for last. We'll need to swap Shelley in for that pat-down."

"Yes, sir." Bondurant turned and went straight to the kneeling master and whispered, "Are you the

Captain?" After getting a nod in return, he continued, "Please stand up, keeping your hands on top of your head, sir." The man complied, and Ben was startled to see he was as tall as Bondurant.

Bondurant completed a pat-down for weapons and said, "Right hand, please." He attached a zip cuff. "Left hand, please." After securing the other cuff, he said, "Please, sit down." After helping the man to a sitting position, Bondurant moved on, and the man turned to Ben and mouthed, "thank you." Ben returned a nod.

After servicing the remaining six male prisoners, Bondurant re-boarded the RHIB to relieve Lee, who completed the female prisoner's pat-down and handcuffing. When she rejoined Ben near the cockpit, he called over to the cutter, "*Kauai*, LE-One, vessel and prisoners secure. Just the one fatality, over."

"LE-One, *Kauai*, roger, well done. I'll need you to send back the RHIB so we can retrieve those nets. Do any prisoners need immediate evacuation?"

"Negative, sir. They're all OK for now."

Lee looked up at Ben. "OK, sir. I'll just be going then…."

"Sorry, Shelley." Ben shook his head. "A female prisoner means you get to stick around."

"Yeah, I figured as much." She looked sadly on as Bondurant steered the RHIB back to *Kauai*.

2

Reap the Whirlwind

Los Robles La Paz, Departamento del Cesar, Colombia
06:27 COT, 17 March

González

This would be a textbook annihilation operation—swift and complete. *Teniente Coronel* Óscar González, *Ejército Nacional de Colombia*, bent over a map table, making notes in various locations as the updates came in via encrypted radio. His short battalion of *Brigada Especial Contra el Narcotráfico*, or BRCNA, was deploying into launch position for a full-on armed assault on a large supply depot for the cocaine cartel known as La Cantaña. He had every enemy strong point zeroed in for mortar fire and every route in and out covered by anti-tank and heavy machine guns. Half a dozen snipers occupied elevated positions in the area. González was confident of success. His troops were the elite of one of the finest armies in South America and, at least in counterinsurgency operations like this one, among the world's best.

This operation and the circumstances were very unusual these days. Large, heavily armed quasi-armies that characterized the cartels running the Colombian drug trade had mostly disappeared. The army pivoted and broke up the larger gangs after defeating the *Fuerzas Armadas Revolucionarias de Colombia* or FARC rebels. What remained usually followed such a low profile they were known as "the Invisibles." Not that the trade itself subsided, quite the contrary. But these organizations had abandoned trafficking cocaine to the United States in favor of the more lucrative, and less risky and violent markets of Europe, China, and Australia. *Plata no Plomo*: Silver, not Lead, was the new business model. As long as these groups kept the violence among themselves and at a low level, the government was content to leave them alone.

La Cantaña was an exception. They had established a tightly coupled relationship with one of the European syndicates, whose increasing demand for product pushed the organization into a larger logistical frame. The more massive stockpiles and shipments and concomitant security escalated violence that moved beyond their competitors. After the ambush and murder of two police patrols that stumbled onto active operations, La Cantaña was no longer an “Invisible.” They broke the rules and would now pay the price.

Man-for-man, there was no comparison between his troops’ quality and their opposition this morning, but González took nothing for granted. These were his boys, and he wouldn’t waste one of them because of miserly allocation of force or shoddy preparation. His troops knew this and reciprocated confidence in the man whose martial skill and coolness under fire garnered the nickname *Coronel Relajado*. Most of the gunmen in these cartels were former FARC members, at liberty because of the Colombian government’s peace deal. González understood, in principle, the need to break the cycle of violence after fifty years of civil war. Still, he hated the idea that some of the most sadistic murderers in history had escaped justice. He smiled to himself. At least these three dozen La Cantaña murderers would meet God for judgment in about fifteen minutes, and his men would conduct the introductions.

González looked over at the American intelligence agent following the operation. Usually, he would not have had any *Nord Americano* anywhere near his headquarters. The duplicity and arrogance of the American Drug Enforcement Agency and Central Intelligence Agency men displayed in joint operations with the Colombian Army during the 1990s and 2000s cemented his resentment and contempt for those organizations.

This Defense Intelligence Agency man was different. He brought the first intelligence that contributed to the localization of this drug cache and much more about La Cantaña's activities. Despite himself, González had become personally fond of the younger man in their two weeks together. Besides his "How can I help?" attitude, his Castilian Spanish was impeccable, and his knowledge of Cervantes and Unamuno, González's favorite authors, led to several spirited and enjoyable discussions. The American would return to Washington this evening—González would be sorry to see him go.

"Any thoughts, professor?" González asked.

Peter Simmons smiled at the Colonel's use of the nickname. It was not far off—Simmons held a Ph.D. in Astrophysics from Princeton—but he had done nothing professorial in the six years he had been with the DIA. "Ah, *señor*, this is one area I would not dare to offer critique. I just create messes—it's up to you professionals to clean them up."

González chuckled. "Very well, my friend. Watch and learn."

The last reports came in two minutes later: all units were in position and ready. González took one last, long look at the map and dispositions, then turned and picked up his rifle and helmet. "OK, let's go," he said as he climbed into his command vehicle with his radioman and Simmons. A short, five-minute drive later, they pulled up on one of the follow-on units. González wanted to lead the first assault troops into the compound personally, but accepted that it was no longer his place as a senior officer and commander. His men understood.

He stepped out of the vehicle and walked up to his second in command, Major Enrique Moreno, who turned and said, "All ready and awaiting your order, *Coronel*." There were no salutes, standing at attention, or any other parade ground crap in the field. Not that BRCNA was an egalitarian unit, it was that such displays just made it easier for enemy snipers to pick who to shoot first.

"Thank you, *Mayor*," González replied. He looked up at the clear, early morning sky. In a few minutes, the sun would clear the Serranía del Perijá mountains to the east, and soon after, it would become a typical, scorching hot lowland Colombia day. "Let's get on with it. Wake up the bastards."

"*Si, señor*." Moreno held the handset to his ear and pressed the transmit button. "Mortar teams, on designated target, five rounds high explosive, commence, commence, commence!"

Six soldiers each dropped a twenty-seven-pound, 4.2-inch round down the barrel of an M30 mortar at virtually the same time. In the twenty seconds it took this first salvo to reach their targets, a second had been fired, and a third was in mid-launch. After the fifth distinct set of "crumpf" sounds from mortar explosions, Moreno turned to González and, after receiving a nod, pressed the transmit switch again. "Mortar teams, check, check, check! Assault teams, advance!"

Within half a minute, the sounds of distant automatic gunfire filled the air. After about two minutes, this tapered off to sporadic single shots.

Moreno's handset buzzed, and he put it to his ear, "*Commandante. Si*, stand by." He looked up at González. "All objectives secure, *señor*."

"Excellent! Pass on to all commanders well done and to remind their rookies to watch out for booby traps." Turning to Simmons and the radioman, he continued, "Let's roll." The three mounted the Colonel's vehicle and headed for the La Cantaña facility half a kilometer distant.

By the time the vehicle arrived at the target, the shooting had stopped, and soldiers were collecting the bodies at a central location. After the three had dismounted, a junior captain ran up and, in his excitement, barely stopped himself from saluting. "*Coronel!* We've just done a preliminary assessment of the amount of product in storage, and it's three thousand, not one thousand tons!"

"*Maravilloso!*" González smiled. "This might break the back of La Cantaña—they'll have the devil's own time trying to recover. Well done, *Capitán*!" The smile then disappeared. "What are our casualties?"

"Three wounded, *señor*, none seriously. Our mortars really pasted them. The survivors were still stumbling around in shock, looking for their weapons, when our assault troops hit them. Only a few got shots off before being cut down."

"Thank God for that!" The smile returned as he turned to Simmons. "An outcome far better than even I had hoped, my friend!"

"Indeed. Congratulations, *señor*!" Simmons nodded. "What will you do with all this product?"

"We were going to burn it in situ. Capturing three times the amount in the intelligence brief was not a situation I expected. I must arrange for transport and disposal now, dammit!"

"I'm sure your men will figure it out. There seems to be nothing they can't do. With your permission, *señor*, I would like to go over and collect biometrics from the corpses."

"Granted, with pleasure, but I caution you like my rookies—don't go poking around the camp and take extreme care rifling the pockets of the dead. These bastards love leaving behind surprises."

"I'll be on my guard. *Gracias, Coronel.*"

As the American turned and walked toward the lengthening row of bodies, González motioned over Moreno and the young captain. "Gentlemen, let's get the wounded evacuated and bring up the trucks for the dead. I want the *Sargento Mayor* and one officer supervising the contraband until we can get it transported away. In the meantime, set up a perimeter; I don't want any survivors of La Cantaña or their competitors getting any bright ideas."

"Si, *señor*," both men replied, then turned to their duties.

González removed his cap and wiped his forehead. It was already getting uncomfortably hot, and, with the sun almost directly overhead this time of year, it was going to be miserable by noon. He watched as Simmons moved from corpse to corpse, taking electronic fingerprints and cellphone photos of faces, for those that still had hands and faces, that is. He

The man shifted again and looked at Holtz with a pained expression. "There is no replacement. They got everything."

Holtz could not believe his ears. "Everything? Did they raid your entire export network? How did they track all your locations? Your security must be shit!"

"We had it gathered in a single depot just over the border. It was too difficult to disperse and secure that much product. We didn't have enough men. We had a secure place—it was one of our bases during the war. No one knew about it."

"Stop!" Holtz interrupted. "I told you I wasn't interested in excuses. What is your plan to fix this?"

"Um. We know most of the product is still there. With your help, we can launch a raid...."

"WHAT? You want us to invade Colombia and attack the best combat unit they have to fix your fuck-up? Are you insane? What else do you have?"

The man looked down and shook his head.

"Alright, here's the deal. The only reason you are still alive right now is I need you to carry a message to your bosses. They will return every euro of our down payment within two weeks, plus twenty percent. Fifteen days from now, if we don't have every bit of that sum, we will issue irrevocable hit contracts on every member of La Cantaña and their families. Questions?"

The man looked up in horror. "I don't know if we can gather that amount. We have obligations...."

"I'm not interested in excuses. If you don't have the cash handy, get it. Hit your competitors, rob banks, whatever. This is not negotiable. Pay us or die, you and your families."

The man said nothing, just blinked and nodded.

Holtz turned to one of his men. "Show this piece of shit out." After they had left, Holtz turned to his assistant, Fedor Dorshak, who was knowledgeable about the local drug trade. "Start a sweep. We need to get what we can together for the next rendezvous. Then I need options for future deliveries. We'll be paying through the nose for this one, and that will lessen any negotiating power we have in Venezuela, at least for now. Is there anything we can work on in the north?"

"There are the Mexicans. They have the product and complete control of the supply chain."

"No, not the damn Mexicans! We can't go cap-in-hand to them—they're too powerful already. What about Guatemala or Honduras, anyone young and hungry there?"

"I'm not sure. I've heard of a few, but they're not the sort of people we normally deal with."

"These are not normal times. Look into it."

"Yes, Boss." Dorshak got up and left.

Holtz was the head of the first large-scale operation in South America by the 252 Syndicate, a diverse criminal enterprise spread across much of the former Warsaw Pact countries of Central and Eastern Europe. The syndicate was founded by the worst of not only the Soviet KGB, but the East German Stasi, Romanian Securitate, and Bulgarian State Security. Named for the Warsaw Pact's disbanding date, 25

February 1991, the 252s built a criminal empire of drugs, prostitution, extortion, and murder for hire throughout Eastern Europe in the decades following the collapse. Ironically, these former communist henchmen became some of the most aggressive entrepreneurs the continent had ever seen, recruiting former spies, counterintelligence agents, and mercenaries to increase their reach and power.

The 252s were the leading broker in the illegal opiate trade east of the former Iron Curtain—no one operated in the trade anywhere in the region who was not either a client or had reached some manner of reciprocity agreement with the syndicate. Their supply chains through Afghanistan were productive and resilient, secured by alliances with local chieftains and bribery of what passed for the government in the country. The cocaine trade was considerably more challenging, with the supply points laying over twelve thousand kilometers to the nearest seaport servicing 252-controlled territory. Just as critical, unlike Afghanistan, Colombia was not a geographic free-for-all with no effective government—the 252s could not just walk in and set up a supply depot.

Fortunately, Colombia's neighbor, Venezuela, was an economic basket case approaching Afghan anarchy levels. Holtz had led the setup of a mobile headquarters aboard the *Carlos Rojas*, safe from the crime-ridden streets and focusing the overhead of bribery on a relatively limited set of port and customs officials. The ship herself was not used for smuggling—she was too small and slow for economic shipments. But, being a converted offshore construction vessel, she had plenty of space for staff and abundant internal electrical generation capability that made her ideal for coordinating the transfer of illicit cargo to larger ocean-going vessels.

The 252s had a preferred contractor for cocaine within Colombia, the La Cantaña organization, who could arrange for the short cross-border shipments required. Quantities needed were an order of magnitude higher than any set before, but the organization was confident they could meet the demand. The first shipment went as planned, but even with heightened security precautions, the movement of so much product drew the Colombian government's attention, with the inevitable result.

Holtz was worried—the syndicate had made enormous investments in infrastructure and bribery to prepare for the large influx of cocaine. That La Cantaña was his boss's choice, not his, would not count for much if the 252s fell behind in deliveries to their downstream suppliers and dealers. He had to find another source and get things up and running again before the boss found out. He grimly shook his head again when he considered what the alternative would mean: it would be a quick and relatively painless bullet in the back of his head if he were lucky.

Then there was his other problem: the mad scientist downstairs. The *Carlos Rojas*, besides providing a mobile command-and-control hub for the 252s, also contained a laboratory to support their research into exotic poisons supporting their murder-for-hire business. The security provided by having a tightly accessed, mobile platform with self-contained power and the ability to dispose of highly toxic waste without documentation outweighed the inconvenience of shipboard life. And the organization needed to keep this work a closely guarded secret.

Since their founding, the 252s operated a lucrative murder-for-hire business around Europe and Western Asia, eliminating anyone, men, women, even children, if the price was right. The organization's reputation for brutality was supported by the remorseless pursuit of targets, regardless of the opposition or collateral damage. Gradually, civilization returned to former soviet block countries. The randomness of drive-by shootings and car and airliner bombings became too difficult for even the most corrupt officials and politicians to tolerate.

Like all successful organizations, the 252s adapted to the new reality. Impressed by the effectiveness and selectivity of the poisons developed by the former Soviet Union's Foliant program, the syndicate hired several chemical researchers associated with the Russian intelligence services' weapons development programs. Before long, 252 killers were equipped with the latest nerve agents of the Novichok family, and their targets started dropping dead without the headline-generating acts of explosive mayhem and gunfire.

The Russians were not amused. Their intelligence services used the Novichok variants sparingly since the West had obtained samples and knew what to look for when someone opposed to Russian interests suddenly and mysteriously died. They were reserved for the highest-value targets only. The application of 252 knock-offs for mere "thuggery" that left evidence pointing to Russia was an alarming development requiring corrective action. When ten 252 operatives met a violent demise at the hands of the Russian GRU within days every time a knock-off was used, the 252 senior management got the message and stopped their Novichok program. But the attractiveness of this assassination mode generated a new research and development effort for similar quick and clean weapons, so they built the lab aboard the *Carlos Rojas*.

The man running the lab, Dr. Piotr Gronkowsky, was probably among the top five biochemists globally. He was a genius in organophosphates and other nerve agents and was well along in developing a new line to replace the Novichok knock-offs. His history was mysterious—Holtz suspected the Russian GRU had recruited him as a student. Given that, it was somewhat surprising he was working for the 252s. Holtz suspected money was probably a factor, but he could see why the GRU was glad to see him go after meeting the man.

Gronkowsky was the creepiest man Holtz had ever met. He was utterly unemotional, dead-eyed, and laser-focused on whatever research occupied his attention at the time. Holtz's charter was to keep him and his lab secret at all costs and otherwise provide him with whatever he needed, be it power, chemicals, or test subjects, including human ones. Gronkowsky was not a sadist—he derived no pleasure from the suffering and death of his human victims; he simply did not care about them. He was, by definition, a psychopath. Even Holtz, who had known some of the most ruthless killers in history, was chilled by his presence.

Holtz gathered himself together, then stood and headed down to the lab on the lower decks. He found Gronkowsky seated at his desk in the lab, typing furiously on his computer workstation with several machines humming nearby. He stopped and looked over when Holtz knocked on the bulkhead.

"Yes, Holtz?" he asked.

Holtz shivered as the cold, dead eyes fixed on him. "We will need to move the ship to another location. Our source of supply for cocaine has been disrupted."

"How unfortunate for you. When do you plan on moving?"

"I don't know. Probably between one and two weeks from now."

"Make it twelve days."

"Why twelve days?"

"Because I will complete testing and be ready for production by then. The testing requires a stable platform, whereas the production of the binaries does not."

"You are ready for production?" Holtz asked in surprise.

"No, I am still testing. I expect to be ready for production in twelve days."

Holtz blinked and smiled at the possibility of good news to help offset the setback with La Cantaña. "Well, this is great! How will it compare to Novichok?"

Gronkowsky tilted his head without changing his expression, as if he was confronting a stubborn problem. "Testing is required, but I expect it to be between three and five times more effective, with an environmental half-life an order of magnitude less."

Holtz asked, "I don't understand what half-life means. Is this a significant improvement?"

"Definitely. The biggest drawback of chemical weapons is their persistence in the environment and the difficulty of completely cleaning up. An area subjected to a chemical attack is uninhabitable indefinitely without an enormous effort to remove every trace of the agent from all surfaces. If this agent performs as expected, it would be self-cleaning to a safe level within days." After a few seconds of silence, he continued. "This agent could revolutionize chemical warfare, making it a practicable alternative to other means of eradicating enemy forces that leave behind widespread destruction or contamination of infrastructure. The profits from marketing it could be immense."

Holtz struggled to keep the horror from his face. He had grown up in what was then East Germany and was an apprentice with the Stasi when the Warsaw Pact broke up. Everyone in the Stasi knew the use of chemical weapons was assumed in a conflict with NATO and what that would mean for the population of East Germany. The costs of this outcome, like that of nuclear war, had kept the peace for decades. The idea that weapons of this lethality could be used without lasting consequences by anyone.... *Not even the syndicate would market something like that, would they?* Holtz honestly didn't know. "I see. Well, the boss will be pleased."

"I should hope so. Now, I need to return to my work. I have emailed you a list of my requirements for the testing and setup of production." He turned back to his screen and began typing again.

Holtz turned and trudged back to his office. His sense of dread had returned, greatly magnified now as he contemplated what *supplies* would be required for testing. He was sure these would include a variety of human test subjects. It would not be easy, but he had contacts within the local law enforcement and criminal gangs he had used before for this sort of thing. *Hopefully, this will be the last time,* he thought as he stepped into his office and closed the door.

3

Dead Stick

Pan-Commonwealth Airways Flight 403 (G-PCAD), Airborne over the North Atlantic Ocean, 208 nautical miles northeast of Nassau, Bahamas
14:57 EDT, 26 March

Taylor

Captain Emma Taylor worked through the stretching exercises she always performed before an approach to landing. This day was long for her and her crew, a flight from London Heathrow to the Lynden Pindling International Airport in Nassau, Bahamas, with an intermediate stop just past the midpoint at the L. F. Wade International Airport in Bermuda. The first leg to Bermuda had taken just over three hours, and after an hour-and-a-half to refuel and swap out a few passengers, they took off for the remaining two-and-a-half hours to Nassau.

Taylor loved flying in general and the Airbus 321 LR in particular. The plane was the latest in the narrow-body family of Airbus airliners, with increased fuel capacity for over-water flights—"LR" meant Long Range. She was delighted working for the relatively new airline Pan-Commonwealth, built to compete with the UK state airline British Airways using more economical, smaller cabin planes for routes between the UK and Commonwealth Nations in Africa and the Western Hemisphere. This particular route was her favorite this time of year—nine hours of work, then two days off in a lovely beach hotel in Nassau before another two legs back to London's dreary cold and wet.

Her co-pilot, First Officer Samesh Patel, handled the flying on this leg, although he was doing little more than monitoring the plane's performance with the autopilot engaged. She liked Patel and the four flight attendants servicing the cabin, and they regularly flew together. PCA was founded by an eccentric billionaire, but run by some old-time Royal Air Force and Fleet Air Arm fliers. They firmly believed in crew integrity and teamwork and kept crews together for scheduling whenever practicable.

Taylor was a statuesque five foot eight, and at forty-two, her shoulder-length blonde hair was just starting to show hints of gray. She was ex-RAF, a squadron leader tanker pilot who opted to leave the service for the higher pay and politics-free world of commercial aviation. Her application to British Airways was met with marginally polite disdain, which led her to PCA—a far better deal in her mind.

She was still recovering from the breakup of a childless marriage to another RAF officer—she was happily single with nothing in the works but her current job.

Patel came through the commercial pilot route, working several jobs to pay for the training and qualifications to get him an airline transport pilot license. Then he slogged through the grueling pace of working up through the commuter lines after moving to the UK from Australia, finally landing a coveted major airline job with PCA. Patel was devoted to his wife and two children. Although he was not very outgoing, Taylor liked him personally and admired his diligence and dedication to the craft. Unlike some of the other pilots she had worked with in the RAF and PCA, she had complete confidence in Patel.

Chief Steward Richard Burgess led the crew in the cabin. He was a seasoned flight attendant with twenty-two years at British Airways before coming over to PCA. He was consistently cheerful and patient and had a fantastic sense of humor. His safety briefs were more like standup comedy routines that never failed to engage the passengers. He was celebrating his fifteenth wedding anniversary tomorrow, and his husband Gerry was among the passengers on this flight.

The only rub on this trip was the weather. A rare early Spring depression was moving through the northern Bahamas, generating an unusual amount of thunderstorm activity at the tail end of their route today. Taylor could see build-ups in the distance, which boded for a bumpy ride ahead. It was time to check in with approach control. With Patel on the controls, Taylor's job was communications, and she handled the radio call to the oceanic air traffic control center.

"Miami Center, Peregrine Four-Zero-Three, two hundred to Nassau, ready for approach, over." PCA's company callsign Peregrine was another subtle jab at their rival British Airways, whose callsign for international flights was "Speedbird."

"Peregrine Four-Zero-Three, Miami Center, roger. Information India current, runway one-four in use at Lynden Pindling, expect visual approach, altimeter two niner eight three. Descend and maintain flight level two four zero."

"Miami Center, Four-Zero-Three, roger, two niner eight three, leaving three eight zero for two four zero. Are you showing any convective weather? Over."

"Four-Zero-Three, Miami Center, affirmative. Satellites and PIREPs show medium to heavy convective activity, from three-three-zero to zero-two-zero out to one hundred fifty miles from Nassau. Airfield and approach are clear within sixty miles. Over."

"Miami Center, Four-Zero-Three, roger, we may need to maneuver. Over."

"Four-Zero-Three, Miami Center, no traffic in your area. Maneuver at discretion, over."

"Miami Center, Four-Zero-Three, roger, out." She turned to Patel and added, "Let's cruise down to twenty-four thousand, Sami."

"Roger, Boss," Patel dialed in the new altitude and selected a constant speed descent.

Taylor picked up the intercom phone and pressed the call button. After a minute, Burgess picked up and said, "Cabin here."

"Chief, we are starting down now. Looks like some rough stuff ahead, so get everything tied down, please."

"Oh, Skipper. You always have to make things interesting, don't you?"

"It's what I live for," she said with a smile as she pressed the "Fasten Seat Belts" announcement button. She hung up the handset and selected the weather radar on her main cockpit panel screen. The multicolor display was ominous, almost a continuous line of heavy rain cells stretching across the sixty-degree scan ahead. As they got closer, she saw a gap opening slightly to the right of their current course. "Sami, looks like a hole to the right. I make it around two-three-zero. Let's slow to two-seventy."

"Roger, coming right to two-three-zero and two-seventy." As Patel dialed in the new settings, the aircraft responded with a slight bank to the new heading while the thrust levers pulled back to slow the plane. Taylor wanted to stabilize the altitude before they got near the weather ahead, and two hundred seventy knots was the recommended airspeed when dealing with turbulence.

As they approached the weather line at a little over seven miles per minute, Taylor was distinctly displeased to see the "gap" she had picked out was closing. It was still the best route in sight, but they were going to take a beating. "Better go on manual, Sami."

Patel grasped the sidestick control with his right hand, laid his left on the thrust levers, and punched the autopilot release button. "Autopilot off."

"Right," Taylor said, scanning back and forth between the dark gray mounds of cloud approaching fast and the increasingly red trace of the weather radar. Her stomach flipped, as it always did when they first punched into the solid-looking cloud wall. Almost immediately, the eighty-seven-ton aircraft began bouncing as it passed through the alternating up- and down-drafts in the center of the cloud. After a few seconds, the plane broke into clear air and steadied down.

"So far, so good," Patel said.

"Hold on. We're not through yet," Taylor replied. "Come about fifteen degrees to port," she ordered, selecting the least red-looking path ahead. They punched into another boiling gray cloud a few seconds later, and the change was immediate. The A321 entered a period of violent bucking that only grew worse with time. When she began having difficulty reading the instruments, Taylor had had enough. "Start a climb, Sami!" As Patel pushed the thrust levers forward, she pushed the radio button and said, "Miami Center, Peregrine Four-Zero-Three, we are in severe turbulence at flight level two four zero and need to climb, over."

"Four-Zero-Three, Miami Center, approved. Climb at discretion. Are you declaring an emergency? Over."

Taylor was about to reply when the sound of rapid-fire hammering nearly made her jump from her seat. *Hail!* She did not have time to press the transmit switch before a series of sharp gunshot-like sounds came from behind. Her eyes immediately went to the center screen of the cockpit panel, flashing emergency and displaying turbine temperatures in the red. "Bloody Hell! Compressor stalls—reduce power!"

It was too late. Large hailstones and rain flooded both engines, blocking airflow and allowing the burning combustion gases to backfire into the compressors, spiking the temperature and damaging the rotating and stationary vanes. Taylor watched in horror as the engine speed and torque plunged, first on the right engine, then the left. "Flameout number two, flameout number one! I have the controls!"

Instinct and training immediately kicked in for both pilots. As Taylor grabbed her sidestick and pulled the thrust levers back to idle, Patel reached up and punched the button to deploy the Ram Air Turbine. A small pod holding an emergency generator locked into a position where the aircraft's slipstream could spin its propeller, providing electrical and hydraulic power lost when the engines shut down. "Your controls, RAT deployed!" Patel announced. He reached down to the pocket beside his seat, drew out the emergency procedures book, and ran through the checklist.

They were punching out of the storm, at least, as the clouds fell away and bright sunlight illuminated the cockpit. Taylor set the optimum glide airspeed using the pitch attitude, then keyed the radio transmitter. "Mayday, Mayday, Mayday, Peregrine Four-Zero-Three has dual engine flameout, total power loss, over."

"Peregrine Four-Zero-Three, Miami Center, roger. Say number of souls and fuel on board and position."

"Center, Four-Zero-Three, one two six souls, twenty-four thousand pounds, zero two four and one hundred fifty-three from Nassau, over."

"Peregrine Four-Zero-Three, Miami Center, copy one two six souls, twenty-four thousand pounds, zero two four, one hundred fifty-three from Nassau. Nassau has you radar contact but stay with me. We are standing by this frequency, out." The air traffic controller knew the crew would have their hands full and cleared off to let them get to work.

They were dropping fast toward the bright blue Atlantic. Patel was running through the main engine restart procedure, having already started the auxiliary power unit to supplement the RAT. They would have time for one restart attempt on each engine. If they could get one relit, it would provide enough thrust to keep them in the air. While there was always hope, Taylor geared herself for the most likely outcome, that neither engine was salvageable. With eight miles of travel possible before they ran out of altitude and over fifty to the nearest land, they were going to end up in the water, a nightmare scenario for a fully loaded airliner.

Taylor grabbed the intercom handset and pressed the call button. Burgess answered immediately, "Cabin, here."

"We're going in, Chief. Get them ready for it. We're going to try for the Hudson River scenario, so keep the aft doors closed."

"Understood, Captain. I have two burly beauties from the RN on guard in the last row. You worry about bringing us in safe. We'll be alright back here."

Taylor smiled slightly. *I might have known. God bless you, Richard!* "Well done! I'll ring the bell five seconds before contact. Get them moving as we come to a stop."

"WILCO. Godspeed, Captain. Out."

The scenario Taylor referred to involved the ditching of a similar Airbus in New York's Hudson River when bird ingestion knocked out both its engines shortly after takeoff from La Guardia airport. The flight crew executed a masterpiece of judgment and skill, saving everyone on board. *Not so easy this time. They landed in the sheltered water of a river—we'll have waves and swells to deal with.*

"Peregrine Four-Zero-Three, Miami Center, Nassau is losing radar contact. Observe you heading two one five magnetic, over." Surveillance radar was limited to line of sight, and at this distance, the aircraft dropped below the radar's horizon at around thirteen thousand feet. The controller would use the aircraft's last heading, descent rate, and speed to estimate the impact point to be passed to rescue forces.

"Center, Four-Zero-Three, roger, estimate six miles to contact, over."

"Four-Zero-Three, Center, copy. Best of luck, Captain. Out."

"No joy, Captain," Patel said as he took his hand off the starter.

"Right, leave it. Give me flaps four at one thousand." Taylor had held off the flaps until the last possible moment. They would reduce the aircraft's touchdown speed dramatically, but also added significant drag. "Ring the cabin bell once you position the handle."

"Will do, Captain."

They were passing through two thousand feet now, and Taylor could see the swells clearly. Stirred by the prevailing east-northeasterly trade winds over thousands of miles of ocean, the waves were running roughly in a direction aligned to their present heading. She began a ninety-degree turn to bring the aircraft heading parallel to the swells, rolling level as they passed through one thousand feet, and Patel dropped the flaps and rang the bell. She knew Burgess and the other flight attendants were shouting at the passengers to brace for landing, gripping the seat or bulkhead in front of them and bending over at the waist.

As the water rushed upward toward them, Taylor pulled back on the sidestick, trading airspeed to arrest their descent in a flare maneuver. The tail section contacted the water first with a growing tugging sensation. *Stay level, you beauty!* The wings quickly lost lift, and the aircraft settled into the water. Taylor held her breath as an on-coming swell caught the left wingtip and engine nacelle, yawing them abruptly to the left and her eyes grew wide as the nose plunged into the water with a loud thud. She released her breath when the cockpit windows emerged from the water. *Thank you, God!* She pressed the transmit switch on the radio one last time. "This is Peregrine Four-Zero-Three in the blind. We are down in the water, commencing evacuation." She took off her headset and turned to Patel with a sad smile.

"That one was a bloody beauty, Captain," Patel said with a nod.

"Thanks, Sami. Let's get moving.

The evacuation of the passengers was orderly, with less hysterics than one would typically expect in a situation as dire as they all faced. Filing out the forward cabin doors and four over-wing exits, the passengers made their way to the large life rafts inflated alongside. Taylor and Patel watched from the cockpit door, and when Burgess, the last person in the cabin, gave them a thumbs-up before going out one of the wing exits.

It was understood in these situations that the captain would make one last check for stragglers, if practicable. There was already flooding visible at the opposite end of the aircraft, but Taylor had to concede that a final tour was feasible, as frightening as it was to go deep within a sinking plane. *Lovely.*

Patel sensed her anxiety and said, "I can go walkabout, skipper."

Taylor shook her head and said, “Skipper’s job. Off you go, Sami. Get a count. I’ll be along straight away.”

“Very good, Captain. Be careful,” Patel said, then stepped through the door.

Taylor walked aft down the passageway between the seats, checking each row. As she passed the middle rows with the over-wing exits, she was already knee-deep in water and anxiously looked out onto the wings. The plane was pitching up and down slowly with the passing of the sea swells, as the last-second pivot had turned the aircraft’s nose into them. *Four flight attendants have already checked. Do I really need to do this?* Taylor swallowed hard and continued down the aisle.

She was almost waist-deep in the rapidly flooding cabin when she reached the rear and, after peeking in both lavatories, turned and hurried forward. She climbed out through one of the wing exits, walked to the nearest raft, and jumped in, to the cheers of the passengers. Taylor looked around and spotted Patel in another raft. “Report, Number One!”

“All present and correct, Captain! No deaths, thirteen injuries, none serious!”

“Good! Let’s cast off, but we need to tether the rafts together!”

“Very good, Captain!”

Progressive flooding claimed the Airbus five minutes later, which sank upright, her white tail painted with the PCA falcon logo finally disappearing into the blue Atlantic. “Alfa-Delta was a good ship, Captain,” Burgess said softly, referring to the aircraft's tail number G-PCAD. "And a proper lady—never once showed her knickers."

"She was that," Taylor replied, brushing away a tear. *So much for my airline career. Still, thank God I didn't kill a hundred-odd people in the process.*

She caught Patel's eye in the adjacent raft and gave him a rueful smile. His face was grim, and he silently mouthed, "Check your six," then nodded past her. Taylor turned and saw clouds building to the west, as ominous as those they had come through in the northeast.

I spoke too soon.

USCG Cutter *Kauai*, Northeast Providence Channel, twenty-one nautical miles northeast of Nassau, Bahamas
15:23 EDT, 26 March

Ben

They had just made the turn into the Northeast Providence Channel for the last leg in their journey to AUTEC for a few weeks of testing on the squid and other new equipment. Ben was wrapping up some paperwork in his stateroom when Bondurant's voice boomed from the 1MC, "Captain to the Bridge!"

Ben grabbed his cap, bounded to the ladder, and was on the Bridge within twenty seconds, with Sam right behind him. "Captain on the Bridge!" Bondurant said.

"Carry on. What's happening?" Sam asked.

"Big-time SAR case, Captain. A commercial airliner is down one hundred and ten miles northeast of here. Our orders are to proceed there at max speed. I have changed course toward the approximate position, and Main Control is bringing the third main online," Bondurant said.

"Well done! Carry on." Sam replied.

As Ben stepped over to the communications position, he could hear the whine of a diesel engine starter as the remaining two increased speed. The message on the chat from the Rescue Coordination Center in Miami was terse:

CGC KAUAI proceed at max speed for mayday-downed aircraft in position 27.0N 77.4W. PCA flight 403 reported total power failure, radar and radio contact lost. Position correlated with EPIRB signal on 406 MHz. Casualties UNK, reported 126 POB. CGNR 6017 ENR from Nassau, ETA 1.5 hrs. CGNR 1718 ENR from Clearwater, ETA 1.3 Hrs. KAUAI assume OSC on arrival.

An icy ball formed in Ben's stomach. His father was an airline pilot with United Airlines and a former naval aviator. Ben had once brought up the possibility of being involved in a rescue effort for a downed airliner, and his father just shook his head and said, "Bring a lot of body bags."

The message showed a Coast Guard MH-60T "Jayhawk" helicopter was launching in response from the forward base in Nassau, and an HC-130H "Hercules" Long-Range Maritime Patrol Airplane was underway from Air Station Clearwater. Neither would be of much help in recovering one hundred twenty-six people, but they would hopefully eliminate the need for *Kauai* to search for the survivors. That the rescue system was picking up an Emergency Position-Indicating Radio Beacon, or EPIRB, suggested they got at least one raft launched.

Ben looked at the electronic navigation page—even at their best speed, it would be almost four hours before *Kauai* could reach the crash site. Ben checked the astronomical display on the adjoining screen—sunset at 19:23, right about when they got on the scene. *With luck, we can get them on board before we lose all the light.* He stepped over to where Sam was on the intercom to Main Control.

"Captain, I'm pulling every trick I know that won't melt down the rotors. I think I can get you thirty-two knots, at least for a while," Drake's baritone voice intoned from the speaker.

"Do what you can, COB," Sam responded. "Every minute counts."

"On it, sir."

Sam turned to Ben and Bondurant. "Guys, the upside of our ETA is we have some time to prepare. Best case, everyone is in rafts, and we can come alongside for a direct pickup. Even then, though, a fair number of them won't be in any shape to climb a Jacob's ladder. We need some way to hoist them up to the main deck. Thoughts?"

"We can rig a davit with a block and tackle, sir," Bondurant said. "We'll have to jury rig some sort of Bosun's chair."

"I like the davit, sir," Ben piped up, "But I'm not a fan of any jury-rigged chair. Maybe we can get the helo to leave their rescue basket for us.

Sam nodded and said, "That would be great. I'll certainly ask, but I wouldn't count on it. XO, let's get Chief Hopkins up here to take over OOD so you guys can get to work. Besides finding them and getting them on board, we have to find a way to get them all inside the hull."

Ben was flabbergasted. "You're kidding, Captain! A hundred twenty-six people? No one could even sit down."

"You're probably right, but consider that storm brought down a commercial airliner. Between the wind and the lightning, we can't leave anyone on the weather decks while we get clear. Get with COB and Chef and come up with a plan to maximize interior floor space and get the people inside fast. We won't have time to stand there scratching our heads."

Ben nodded. "Understood, Captain."

envied that the young man would be on his way back home to the United States by nightfall while he would be here, guarding this poison. Still, the unexpected need to safeguard and transport the cocaine was a minor annoyance compared to the brilliant victory they had achieved. González was looking forward to getting home and telling his wife and children that the world was safer today than yesterday, thanks to his men.

He could not have been more wrong.

OSUV *Carlos Rojas*, Moored, Berth 142, Port of Maracaibo, Venezuela
11:32 VET, 18 March

Holtz

Anton Holtz was a very unhappy man, but not as unhappy as the man sitting before him. It was bad enough to be cooped up in this stinking tub with lousy food, cramped quarters, and no entertainment of any kind. Dealing with this sniveling brown wretch was just too much. Holtz slammed a fist on the table. "I don't want to hear excuses. You promised us this product today! Where the hell is it?"

"It, it's still in Colombia." The man looked down and shifted in his seat. "The BRCNA raided our depot."

"That's unfortunate for you. When can you reroute the replacement product?"

4

Salvation

Atlantic Ocean, 128 nautical miles north-northeast of Nassau, Bahamas
16:51 EDT, 26 March

Taylor

The Coast Guard Hercules aircraft had arrived overhead twenty minutes previously. The initial excitement among the passengers quickly subsided when they realized the plane could not land in the water to pick them up. Still, it was good news that they had been found, and the aircraft would linger to vector in the ships and other aircraft that could rescue them.

The appearance of the Coast Guard helicopter brought similar optimism, also quickly dashed when everyone realized it could pick up only a few of them at a time. Taylor could imagine that the conversation within the aircraft as it circled their position was some variation of “Holy Shit!” After two circles, it came to a hover about fifty yards away from Taylor’s raft and lowered a crewman into the water with its hoist cable. Even from this distance, the downdraft was noticeable—it would be a difficult situation if it had to hover directly over the rafts.

The crewman swam quickly to Taylor’s raft, took off and tossed his fins in, then climbed in using the ladder and pulled up his swim mask and snorkel. He was not a large man, but his short wetsuit made no secret of a highly athletic physique. He scanned the raft and, seeing the four stripes on Taylor’s uniform shirt, said, “Petty Officer Sean Moran, U.S. Coast Guard. Are you the pilot, ma’am?”

“Yes, Captain Emma Taylor.”

“Glad to meet you, ma’am,” the young petty officer said. “Can you tell me how many people you have here?”

“Yes, one hundred twenty-six.”

The young man grinned. “You got everyone off safe? That’s fantastic! Hell of a job, ma’am.”

“Thank you, petty officer.” She glanced at the helicopter circling the rafts. “Somehow, I don’t think we’ll all fit on your bird.”

“No, ma’am, we might get six or seven, depending on how large they are. But the good news is a cutter is headed this way balls-to-the-walls and should be here in about two hours.” He looked around in surprise when most of the people on the rafts started clapping and cheering. He struggled to make himself heard. “Ma’am, ma’am!” The crowd quieted down when he whistled. "As I was saying, ma'am, we can take a few earlier if we need to get them urgent medical attention. But it will be pretty rough on everybody if that H-60 has to do any hoists, so I wouldn't recommend it unless we really have to."

Taylor shook her head. There were two physicians and one registered nurse among the passengers who had checked the injured. The two with broken bones had those splinted, and the other eleven had only minor complaints. "We have thirteen injured, but none seriously. I think we can all wait two hours, petty officer. But several might have problems scrambling up ladders."

"Got it covered, ma'am," Moran said. "My crew will transfer the rescue basket to the cutter just before it gets here. They're rigging a davit to hoist up anyone who can't climb."

Taylor smiled with relief. "I am glad to hear that."

Moran nodded. "If you'll excuse me, ma'am, I have to report in." He drew a handheld radio, pressed the button, and said, "Six-Zero-One-Seven, swimmer."

"Swimmer, One-Seven, go ahead," said a voice from the radio.

"One-Seven, swimmer, all POB accounted for. Repeat, one-two-six survivors. Pilot says thirteen, that's one-three injured, but none require medevac, sir."

"Swimmer, One-Seven, roger. We'll go with Plan A, then. Keep us posted if anything changes.

"WILCO, sir." Moran tucked the radio back into his vest.

"Plan A?" Taylor asked.

"I wait here with you all, ma'am, and help with the on-loading. The helo will maintain contact for as long as possible."

"Is he running short of fuel?"

"No, ma'am," Moran answered and nodded to his left toward the weather building in the west. Lightning flashes were now clearly visible among the clouds.

"I see," Taylor said. "Well, I'm sure you have plenty of interesting stories from your line of work. We would certainly be grateful if you could regale us with a few while we wait."

"Really?"

"Yes, indeed. What do you say, folks?"

After a chorus of "yes," "give it up, mate," and the like, Moran nodded and said, "OK." Then he adopted a fierce expression and said with a mock dramatic tone, "There I was...."

USCG Cutter *Kauai*, Atlantic Ocean, one hundred twenty-three nautical miles north-northeast of Nassau, Bahamas
19:02 EDT, 26 March

Ben

It had already started raining, cutting visibility in half and making deck activity more hazardous and unpleasant. Ben could see many heavy rain cells marching west to east across the screen displaying

Kauai's weather radar, each of which held the potential for heavy rain and lightning. *It just couldn't be easy*, he thought ruefully.

The HC-130 had to pull back because of severe turbulence and was orbiting to the southeast. The MH-60T helicopter was doggedly hanging on over the rafts—it worked far lower, at levels not prone to turbulence—but it could not risk lingering much longer with the threat of lightning and wind shears building. The helicopter had ducked out briefly to rendezvous with *Kauai* to drop off the rescue basket before returning to the scene. The basket was necessary, being the only safe way to hoist untrained, infirmed people. The risks were too high to use a bosun's chair or horse collar to lift people out of the rafts, particularly if they were injured.

Every crewmember that could be spared would be on deck, helping to get the survivors on board and safely tucked inside the shell of *Kauai*'s hull and superstructure. Only four would be on the Bridge: Sam, Hopkins as OOD, Williams handling the entire FC3 console, and Pickins on the helm. Ben would head down as soon as they had visual contact with the rafts to supervise the operation and provide an extra set of hands. Lee and Fireman Connally would be underway in the RHIB, stationed outside of the rafts, in a position to respond to anyone falling overboard. The remaining eight crew, including Ben, would work the operation on the main deck.

Speed was of the essence, given the thunderstorms in the area. The cutter was an inviting target for lightning, being the tallest object within 50 miles, but her hull would act as a Faraday cage and protect anything inside. The rub was that it was a deadly risk to anyone caught outside during a strike, and both the crew and survivors were highly vulnerable during the recovery operation.

"I'm picking up the scene on IR, sir," Williams said, pointing at one of the display panels showing the output of the Infrared camera on *Kauai's* mast. Something that looked like a tiny comet blazed horizontally across the screen. "See? There's the H-60's exhaust."

"I got that. Still don't see the rafts," Ben said.

"Wait a sec for the helo to clear," Williams said, then pointed at some hazy glows below the helicopter's path. "See? There and there."

"Roger that." Ben plugged his headset into the radio console and selected the helicopter's frequency. "Six Zero One Seven, *Kauai*, over."

"*Kauai*, One Seven, go ahead."

"Can we talk directly to your swimmer?"

"Affirmative. He's on channel eighty-three."

"Roger, out." Ben switched his selector and dialed up channel 83 on the cutter's VHF-FM radio. "Swimmer, *Kauai*, on channel 83."

After a brief delay, Moran's voice answered, "*Kauai*, Swimmer, got you Lima-Charlie."

"Roger. We have you on infrared about three miles out. We should be alongside in about five minutes. We have two ladders and a davit rigged out on the starboard side with the basket. Do you feel comfortable working all three at once? Over."

"Affirmative. I've briefed everyone on what to expect, and I have the flight crew plus two Royal Navy guys who will be assisting. We are in four rafts, all lashed together. I recommend we do one at a time and take people directly from their current raft rather than having them cross over. I'll transfer to whichever raft we are working to supervise."

"Sounds like a plan. Our RHIB will stand by to pick up any leakers. Explain to the survivors that we have to get everybody inside out of the weather, and it will be a tight fit. They must follow our crew's instructions and be patient with the cramped quarters. Also, if there's anyone with a serious claustrophobia problem, we'll take them last." Ben had a touch of claustrophobia and knew the cramped quarters they planned to pack everyone into could be a trigger. The last thing they needed was someone having a meltdown inside the ship. The nervous folks would go on the messdeck, a larger space with windows.

"WILCO."

"Right. We'll be standing by on this channel. Out." Ben unplugged and turned to Sam. "Captain, request permission to lay below."

Sam clapped him on the shoulder. "Go. Please be quick and careful, XO."

"Will do, sir." Ben turned and hurried to the port-side door in the rear of the Bridge, then down the ladders to the main deck. The rain had already soaked him to the skin by the time he arrived. The RHIB was at the port rail, ready for Lee and Connally to jump in and launch—they would do so when Hopkins slowed down to approach the rafts. It was only a six-foot climb from the water level up to the main deck, which all but the infirm should be able to manage. Bondurant already had the two Jacob's ladders attached to cleats on the deck and a small davit rigged with a block and tackle and the rescue basket. He and Machinery Technician Brown would work the davit while Ben oversaw the ladders during the onload. The other five crew were standing by, ready to lead people to the interior spaces where they would wait out the storm.

Although it was still twenty minutes to sunset, the clouds and rain made it seem more like twilight. "Conn, Main Deck, could we get the deck lights on, please?" Ben asked over the intra-ship radio. Within seconds, the white deck lighting along the sides of the ship and the large red floodlight on the mast came on, compensating for the fading daylight.

"*Kauai*, Swimmer, we have you in sight. You're getting a big applause over here, sir!"

Yeah? We'll see how much they love us after they're stuffed inside like sardines in a can! "Roger. Just a couple of minutes now," Ben replied on the radio. The diesel engines slowed a few seconds afterward, and *Kauai* settled into the water from planing to displacement mode. "Boats, let's get the RHIB ready," Ben said.

As Lee and Connally jumped into the boat, Ben transmitted, "Conn, Main Deck, RHIB ready for launch."

"Main Deck, Conn, cleared to launch," Williams's voice replied.

Ben leaned over to Lee and said, "OK, keep it tight, Shelley. Any questions?"

"No, sir!"

"Right. Good luck!" Ben turned and gave Boatswain's Mate Third Class Jenkins on the crane a thumbs-up, and the RHIB was motoring twenty yards off the starboard quarter ten seconds later. Ben could barely make out rafts now through the fading light and rain about a quarter-mile distant. Hopkins was maneuvering to put the rafts alongside to starboard in *Kauai*'s lee, a challenging task given the visibility and variable, gusty winds. At least they didn't have to contend with heavy seas—that would be a nightmare. Ben could make out people on the rafts now and see an individual standing in one of them. *That must be Moran.* Ben keyed his radio microphone and said, "Swimmer, *Kauai*, is that you standing?"

"Affirmative, sir," Moran replied.

"OK, we will take your raft first. Stand by for a heaving line. We'll be passing a sea painter, but I want you to pull to us and hold the raft to our side—don't tie off the line. That way, we cut the risks of dragging the raft, and you can just carry it to the next one. Got it?"

"WILCO, sir."

Ben turned to the other crewmembers on deck. "OK, put over the ladders. Jenkins, come over here and bring the heaving line," he said.

The young boatswain stepped forward as the crew hung the ladders off the side. "Yes, sir."

"OK, you see that raft with the guy standing?"

"Yes, sir. I've got him."

"Good. When you're confident you can reach him, let fly with the line."

"Yes, sir!"

The rafts slid closer as Hopkins used rudder and asymmetric thrust from the engines to walk *Kauai* sideways. Jenkins was staring intently at Moran's raft, unconsciously bouncing up and down on the balls of his feet. Finally, he nodded and cast the line with a sidearm throw. The line stretched out and draped across the raft just to Moran's left, and he grabbed it and started pulling in.

"That was a beauty of a throw, Brian. Nice job," Ben said.

"Thanks, sir," Jenkins replied as he fed out the line.

The end was tied to a thicker line better for handling and supporting the raft's weight. Soon Moran had the line, and he and two large men Ben presumed were Royal Navy sailors pulled it until the raft was snug against *Kauai*'s side with the ladders dangling inside. A woman wearing a white shirt, tie, and epaulets with four stripes was first up the ladder, and Ben took her hand to help her on deck.

"Captain Emma Taylor," she said with a smile.

"Lieutenant J.G. Ben Wyporek, ma'am," Ben replied. "Would you care to stay and observe?" he added as more survivors followed up the ladder, helped by other crewmembers.

"Yes, indeed. Thank you for coming so quickly."

"Our pleasure."

The unloading of the rafts proceeded quickly. A line of wet and bedraggled people rapidly formed into the door leading inside as *Kauai's* crew tucked them wherever there was space. They were about one-third of the way through the on-load when lightning struck close by on the starboard beam with a bright flash, followed by a loud boom a second later. Almost everyone instinctively ducked, and several people on the rafts started screaming and scrambling toward the ladders. It was what Ben feared—a contagious panic that would kill dozens while they were helpless to stop it.

"KNOCK IT OFF!" Bondurant bellowed from his position at the davit, shocking everyone into motionless silence. He then nodded to Ben. "All yours, sir."

"Thanks, Boats," Ben whispered and then shouted, "We're OK! One spot's as good as another out here! Just stay calm, wait your turn, and we'll wrap this up quicker!"

The procession up the ladders from the rafts resumed, and Taylor whispered to Ben, "This spot includes a rather tall object, *Leftenant*."

"You'll be safer inside, ma'am, if you'd like," Ben whispered back.

"No, I'll stay and grin like an idiot. 'Keep calm and carry on,' as they say."

"That's why they pay us the big bucks," Ben said with a smile.

An older woman stepped up and embraced Ben. "Thank you, sir!"

"Our pleasure," Ben repeated, patting her on the back. "Please move along, ma'am."

The woman rejoined the line leading into the ship. It took around thirty minutes before the last passenger climbed the ladder to the main deck, followed by Patel, Burgess, and Moran. There were several more lightning strikes, but none were as close as the first nor caused any pause in the operation.

Ben gripped Moran's hand as he came up and said, "Nice job, Petty Officer Moran."

"Thanks, sir."

"Head inside. If you need anything, just grab one of the guys."

"Roger that. See you at the other end, sir."

As Moran walked off toward the door, Ben turned to Taylor. "Would you follow me to the Bridge, ma'am?"

"Of course." They had climbed the ladder and nearly reached the bridge door when a second close lightning strike shook the ship. "Bloody Hell!"

Ben smiled as he held the door for her. "I couldn't have said it better, ma'am!"

Bondurant's voice came over Ben's headset on the intra-ship radio as they stepped into the Bridge. "Conn, Main Deck, RHIB cradled and secure, ready for maneuvers."

"Conn, aye," Hopkins replied. "Left full rudder," she said as she pushed the thrust levers forward. "Steady on two-one-three."

"My rudder is left full, coming to two one three, Chief," Pickens repeated.

As Ben and Taylor stepped up to the command chair, Ben said, "Captain, this is the pilot, Captain Emma Taylor."

Sam climbed from his chair and shook Taylor's hand. "I'm sorry about your bad luck, Captain."

"Thank you. It turned out to the good in the end, I'm happy to say, thanks to you and your crew."

"Part of the job. Is there anything we can get for you?"

"A large Tanqueray gimlet would go well about now."

"I'd keep you company. Unfortunately, we're as dry as the Navy here, and water or some pretty bitter coffee is the best I can do."

"A coffee is second in the heavenly queue, Captain. May I ask where we are heading?"

"Nassau. It's the closest port."

"Well, that's convenient for everyone. Do you have an ETA?"

"We are figuring that out right now. Our maximum sustainable speed is twenty-eight knots, but I need to make sure I don't have over a hundred people throwing up on each other down below."

"I'm grateful for that, Captain. I'm no stranger to *mal de mer* myself."

"Same can be said for anyone assigned to a patrol boat. Chief Hopkins will find a sweet spot for us, and we'll make as quick a trip as possible."

"Thank you, Captain. Now, if practicable, I need to rejoin my crew and passengers."

"Sure. XO, can you handle that, please?"

"Absolutely, Captain," Ben replied. "Would you follow me, ma'am?"

"Certainly." As they stepped to the rear of the Bridge and headed down, Taylor said quietly, "I'm afraid we are likely to have some motion sickness issues, based on my experience with air travelers."

"I know, ma'am," Ben replied. "We have trash cans in every room, and our Health Services Technician can administer Dramamine in severe cases."

Taylor sighed. "It's going to be a long night, *Leftenant*."

"Yea verily, ma'am."

USCG Cutter *Kauai*, moored, Prince George Wharf, Nassau, Bahamas
02:29 EDT, 27 March

Ben

Ben was exhausted, his eyes burning and legs aching with fatigue as he scanned the dock. It was crowded with news crews and other people striding purposefully among the milling passengers. *Probably scum-sucking ambulance-chasers looking for a payday,* Ben thought with disgust. *Kauai* was almost surrounded by towering cruise ships in the busy port, and a port authority official had already paid a call to inquire when they would be sailing so he could clear the dock for more arrivals. The last survivors were moving ashore to the waiting buses the airline had chartered to take them to hotels. Soon after they departed, *Kauai* would resume her journey to AUTEC.

The trip had been mercifully uneventful, with no serious illness or injuries. Ben had spent six hours moving among the survivors, consciously suppressing his claustrophobia while inquiring about their health and jotting down their names for the report. Taylor accompanied him and proved to be a very calming influence on the crowd throughout the journey. Their joy at being pulled from the water and delivered to their original destination certainly helped. The conversation snippets with the pilot were also interesting and reminded Ben of his many aviation discussions with his father growing up.

Ben had tremendous sympathy for Taylor, whose ordeal was only beginning. A one-hundred-thirty-million-dollar aircraft entrusted to her care now lay at the bottom of the Atlantic. The reckoning for that was likely to be severe, regardless of the circumstances. When the last passenger departed, Taylor turned to Ben and said, "I guess this is goodbye, Ben."

"You have a hotel room, ma'am?"

"Yes, indeed, checking in a bit later than planned. Later still, if I can find an open pub to get legless in."

"I'd love to join you," Ben said. Then, sadly added, "Captain, I wish you the best of luck. Please get in touch with me if there is anything I can do to help."

Taylor stepped forward and hugged him warmly. Then she stepped back and said, "That's from all of us. Please take care." She turned and walked off the ship, then disappeared into a swarm of media people.

Ben had turned to walk to the Bridge when Bondurant called out, "XO, there's a gentleman from the embassy here to see you."

Ben sighed, turned, and followed the big boatswain to a thin, average-sized, balding man wearing a suit and tie standing on the quarterdeck. "Lieutenant Junior Grade Wyporek, Executive Officer, how can I help you, sir?"

"Hello, Lieutenant Junior Grade. I'm Frederick Gianni, the ambassador's deputy for public affairs. I would like to speak to the captain."

"I'm sorry, he's not available. Perhaps I can be of assistance."

"When will he be available?"

"Not today. The Port Authority has requested we vacate this berth as soon as practicable, and he is engaged in sailing preps."

"Oh, well, I guess you'll do," he said, oblivious to Ben's icy stare. "Several camera crews from the major networks are here and would like to do some interviews."

"No."

"I beg your pardon?"

"I said no. As I told you, we have been asked to depart, and all of us will be heavily engaged in making that happen."

"Well, perhaps one or two of the crews could ride with you...."

"Are you serious? Absolutely not."

"Well, what's your next port? They can meet you there."

"Ship movements are classified, Mr. Gianni. I'm sorry, I can't help you."

"You are being most uncooperative, Lieutenant Junior Grade. That will not reflect well on you in my report."

"I am doing my job, sir. Speaking of which, all of us are pretty busy right now, and I am sure the news networks can get all the information they need from the Seventh District Public Affairs Office. So, if you don't mind, please leave the ship."

"And what am I supposed to tell the news crews?"

"Tell them to go to Hell."

After Gianni turned and stormed off the ship, Bondurant said, "Missed opportunity, XO. Wouldn't your folks like to see you on TV?"

"My mom would be pretty upset hearing me using the kind of language I would direct at those bastards, Boats."

As they turned and headed for the Bridge, Bondurant chuckled and said, "Your stock just keeps going up, sir!"

5

Rogues Amongst Themselves

Suite 224, La Paloma del Mar Hotel, 43 Ave. Dionisio de Herrera, La Ceiba, Honduras
08:53 CDT, 1 April

Holtz

Holtz knew the news was bad when the satellite phone buzzed this early in the morning, but he had no idea how bad it could be. The first words out of Dorshak's mouth once the phone connected were, "Boss, they are killing our men!" After half a minute of shouting and shooting in the background, Holtz heard a banging sound, a crash, then muffled voices.

"Holtz?" a fresh voice said.

"Yes?"

"We have your boat, your crew, and your lab workers. Pay us twenty million euros, or we kill them all." Holtz knew the voice. It was the cartel's lead man, whose face was a mask of tattoos. The one Holtz believed was thoroughly intimidated by the power and reach of the 252 Syndicate.

"Do you know who you're talking to, asshole?"

"*Tráelo*!" Holtz heard a scuffle and then two shots, followed by a shriek of pain. "I just blew the balls off one of your guards, *bendejo*! Maybe I should do that with one of your pretty boys next!"

"No, no, wait!" Holtz temporized. These sub-humans had him cold. The guards were one thing—losing them was the cost of doing business. The same went for *Carlos Rojas*'s crew. But Gronkowsky? If he let anything happen to him.... "OK, I don't have that much with me. It will take time."

"How much time?"

"Two weeks."

"One week."

"I can't get that much in seven days!"

"Then call someone who can! *Comprende*? In one week, I cut pieces off your pretty boys here." The line went dead. Holtz stared at the phone for about half a minute before putting it aside.

It was not supposed to be this way. He had landed this contract and arranged all the logistics. The possibilities for future purchases of cocaine were unlimited, and Holtz's star would rise high in the organization. Even with the misfortune of their original cocaine source in Venezuela drying up, he found a satisfactory solution at a lower cost. Or so he thought.

The first meeting carried a warning. Holtz flew into Barbello, an island about ninety miles off Honduras's coast, in his chartered seaplane. Barbello was nominally part of Honduras but was effectively ruled by the Salinas Cartel, an ultraviolent death cult financing themselves through drug trafficking. Holtz was not concerned—the reputation of his organization was such that he expected to roll over the negotiations quickly and easily. And so it seemed, with the head man, a rather frightening figure with his tattoos, piercings, and twin forty-four-caliber Auto Mag pistols, nodding in sullen acceptance to Holtz's terms.

Holtz activated one of his burner phones and dialed his control number in Bucharest. After several rings, Holtz was greeted with the deep baritone of his superior's voice. "Yes?"

"Boss, this is Holtz."

"Yes, Holtz, what is it?"

"We have a problem with the cocaine delivery."

There was an audible sigh. "What sort of problem?"

"The suppliers have seized the vessel and everyone on board. They've shot several of our men and are threatening our researcher if they aren't paid twenty million euros within one week."

"I don't believe it. La Cantaña wouldn't dare fuck with us like that."

"It's not La Cantaña, boss. They got rolled up by the BRCNA a couple of weeks ago. I went with a new supplier in Honduras, the Salinas Cartel."

"You *what*?" came the incredulous reply.

"I set up with the Salinas Cartel. They had the product, the transshipment point, and the cost was right." Holtz said defensively.

"You did a deal with those animals? Idiot! Did it occur to you that there might be a reason we *haven't* dealt with them? Alright, where is the ship?"

"It's in the harbor at Barbello. I thought moving to the source was prudent...."

"Stop! Let me get this straight. You took it on yourself to set up a new supply chain without clearing it through us. Then you set up a deal with the worst, most insane gang in the Western Hemisphere, bringing their shitstorm into our business. Finally, you sail our ship, with our scientist and his equipment, into the middle of their stronghold. Am I missing anything?"

"Um...."

"Never mind, that question was rhetorical. Where are you now?"

"L-La Ceiba. The La Paloma del Mar."

"Good. At least you weren't stupid enough to put yourself in their hands."

"What should I tell them? When can we get them the money?"

"Are you insane? We aren't paying them to screw with us! We're going to cure this cancer before it gets out of hand. One week, you said?"

"Y-Yes."

"Fine, if we bring everything else to a halt, we should be able to concentrate there in time." The voice softened. "I need you to stay where you are and brief the team when they arrive. We'll need your insights if we are going to unscrew this thing. Clear?"

"Yes, boss."

"Fine. Out." The phone call disconnected.

Anton, you are a dead man. His brain reeled briefly over the realization, and then his survival instinct awakened. Holtz was a despicable human working for one of the world's most evil organizations, but he was a survivor. He quickly stuffed his cash, passports, and gun into the shoulder bag he carried for just such an occasion, leaving the satellite phone and his still turned-on cell phone behind under his underwear in the drawer. His only hope at this point was to convince his former associates that he was still lounging in the room while making his escape. Holtz didn't know of any other 252 men in La Ceiba. Regardless, they had connections and would use them to close his case quickly.

He glanced at the closed bedroom door and paused for a second. Rosita was still asleep in the bed they had shared. She would suffer a very unpleasant death if they caught her. Ordinarily, he wouldn't have wasted a single thought on another human being, but Rosey was something special. He slammed open the door, shouting, "Get up!" The woman groaned and rolled over. "Get up if you want to live!"

Rosita's eyes opened wide. "What?"

"Here are your wages," He dropped a hundred euro note on the nightstand. "Grab your stuff and get out. Don't follow me or try to contact me. Get out of this place and run!" He turned and ran out the door, tuning out her cries of "Anton!" Well, he had given her a chance. Hopefully, she had enough brains to use it. He eschewed the elevator and flew down the stairs to the exit.

Leaving the hotel, he merged into the sizeable crowds heading for the beach. Traffic was far heavier than usual in the Semana Santa, as the Holy Week was known here. Holtz worked his way through and picked up a cab. Once well clear of the hotel, he pulled out one of his burner phones and dialed his pilot.

"Yeah?"

"I need you at the plane now."

"Are you fucking kidding me? There's nothing scheduled today."

"We need to leave now. I'll tell you where we are going once we're in the air."

"Man, I can't fly! I'm too hungover. Call me in six hours."

"Look, asshole, if I don't get out of here, they'll kill me. While they're at it, they will wring out of me the names of everyone I've associated with here, so they can run them down and clean up any loose ends. Get down here now if you want to live!"

"Shit! Alright, alright, I'll be there in half an hour. Stay out of sight until I get there."

"I'll be watching." Holtz hung up the phone and tossed it out the cab window. While he believed it would be almost impossible for his associates to trace him this soon, he took no chances. Holtz had the cab driver drop him at the bus station, where he picked up a second cab to the marina. While considering his situation, he strode to the seaplane slip and hid behind a storage building.

Fleeing La Ceiba provided temporary safety at best. Holtz knew his former employers would relentlessly track him down to eliminate any potential threat he posed. He had to find someone who could help fix this mess or give him the means to fade out of sight. If he could reach the Americans.... Holtz knew they were becoming troublesome—his boss had complained enough about them. Maybe he could work a deal with them, trading knowledge of the organization and the threat posed by Grankowsky's gas for immunity, or at least a new identity and safety. The Americans were well known for that.

He tensed when a local police officer arrived and stood about fifty yards from his hiding place behind the building. Holtz flattened himself against the wall and drew the 9-mm pistol out of his shoulder bag before placing it aside. The officer was standing still and talking into his hand—Holtz couldn't tell if it was into a radio or a mobile phone. *Move along, son. Nothing to see here!* He didn't want to shoot a police officer. Not because he had any affection for the police or any other person. He just knew shooting a cop would only bring all hell down upon him and likely prevent his escape. He almost cried out with relief when the man pocketed his phone and walked off in the other direction. There were no other encounters before the pilot arrived.

"You better be right about this," the bleary-eyed pilot grumbled. "If we run into any trouble, I'll probably get us both killed."

"If we don't leave now, we're both dead for sure. So, let's go."

"Okay, take in the aft mooring line and get in." Holtz complied and climbed into the cockpit of the seaplane, a trim Lake Buccaneer. The pilot unhitched and stowed the forward line, then staved off the dock with an oar. The engine fired at once, and within three minutes, they were airborne, heading east.

"OK, now where the hell are we going?" the pilot asked.

"Can you make it to Grand Cayman and back without refueling?"

"Barely, but I won't be flying into any airport without a flight plan."

"Not a problem. You'll be dropping me off at a secluded beach I know and return to La Ceiba with no one the wiser."

"Fine. You realize there will be a significant surcharge for this premium service."

Holtz smiled. "If we live through this flight, you'll go back with double the usual rate."

The pilot nodded. "That works for me."

The three-hour flight was uneventful, almost boring, and the pilot made a reasonably smooth landing, given his condition, in the cove Holtz had directed. They pulled within fifty feet of the waterline, and Holtz grabbed his bags and hopped out to wade ashore. He did not look back as the plane turned around and made a hasty departure.

Holtz made his way to a nearby road, then over to one of the less-frequented public beaches, where he turned on another burner phone and called a cab. While waiting, he called American Airlines and booked a round-trip flight from George Town to Miami under an alias he had kept secret from the syndicate for just this sort of emergency. Not that Holtz intended ever to return here, but he knew a one-way booking would arouse suspicion. He had fabricated an entry stamp on the passport bearing his alias, which would hopefully escape scrutiny at George Town. Once the plane had taken off, Holtz would carefully remove the adhesive patch bearing the exit stamp and paste it into his genuine passport. He could not take a chance on using an alias coming through American customs, and even if the syndicate learned of his arrival through some leak, he would be long gone before they arrived at the airport.

After the cab dropped him off at the Owen Roberts International Airport terminal, Holtz went in and picked up the ticket, paying in cash. Then he hurried to a nearby pub to nurse a drink until he saw a crowd building up at the customs exit. Taking advantage of the hurried state of the agent, he breezed through with only a cursory glance at the entry stamp on his passport. So far, so good. An hour later, he was in the air, heading to Miami.

Holtz had no illusions that the entry into the United States would be as easy as his exit from Grand

Cayman. He bought several of the mini bottles of gin during the drink service. They weren't for fortification during the flight—he intended to rinse his mouth with it and sprinkle a bit on his clothing to complete the effect of the boozy tourist when he arrived. Holtz did not draw any added attention to his arrival; they just captured an entry photo while stamping his passport and moved him along.

Leaving the terminal, Holtz grabbed a cab for the cut-rate hotel he had booked using the flight's Internet access, arriving just after nine p.m. local time. Only when he reached his room did Holtz relax. He had escaped to the temporary safety of the United States. He would present himself at the local FBI field office and work out a deal the following day.

****

Holtz was jarred awake by the crash of the chair and wastebasket he placed in front of the door. He could do nothing to stop the three hooded men wearing the night-vision goggles from entering the room, and he was seized immediately and shoved face-down into the bed.

As he felt the needle prick into his neck, his final thought was, *Almost, almost!* Then his vision and consciousness closed down.

5 Intrarea Florilor, Snagov, Romania
16:13 EET, 1 April

Crețu

Dragoș Crețu jammed the disconnect button on his desk phone, then swept the phone and most of the items on his large wooden desk off to the floor with a primal growl. His secretary came into the room at once. "Yes, sir?" she asked fearfully.

"Get out!" The secretary quickly fled and shut the door, leaving Crețu to his rage. "Damned paper-pushing imbecile!" He stood, walked over to the bar, poured himself two fingers of Stolichnaya Vodka, and gulped it down. *The damned Salinas Cartel! If that fool Holtz had done scientific research, he could not have found a worse business partnering option!* The syndicate had an unbelievably profitable opportunity with Gronkowsky's product, now and in the future, and Holtz had pissed it away in one stroke.

He looked out the large windows of his office across Snagov Lake to the trees on the other side. As he felt the rage subsiding, he poured himself another portion of vodka and took a measured sip this time, pulling out a cell phone and selecting a saved number.

"Yes?"

"This is Crețu. I have a job for you."

"Yes, boss?"

"Liquidate Holtz. He's staying at the La Paloma del Mar Hotel in La Ceiba, Honduras."

"Um, we don't have anybody there, boss."

"GET somebody there on the next flight! Or hire a local! I want him dealt with before he gets any bright ideas about cutting a deal with the police."

"Yes, Boss!" The call hung up, and Crețu pocketed the phone.

"Angelika!" he bellowed.

Within three seconds, his secretary was back in the room, trying not to shake badly enough for it to be seen. "Yes, sir!"

Crețu's face softened when he saw her fear. "I'm sorry for yelling. It's been one of those days. Find Stefan and Grigore and get them up here at once."

"Yes, sir," the woman said with palpable relief.

He liked Angelika. She was an efficient secretary and as pleasing to look at as she was in bed. He tried to keep his temper when she was around—it made things more comfortable after work. Ten minutes after summoning them, Crețu's business and military operations chiefs were sitting with him at the table in his office.

"Where in the hell is Barbello?" Grigore asked.

"Off of Honduras in the Western Caribbean," Crețu answered. "We obviously can't let this go unanswered, and we need to know everything we can before we hit them. Get your people on it."

"Putting together a rescue will take time."

"We have seven days. Whatever it takes, we have to get that ship and Gronkowsky back. And when our men are done, I don't want a single Salinas left alive on that island. Clear?"

"Clear."

"What's our personnel status?"

"Still recovering after the Florida deal and that cock-up in Cyprus. If you want to go within a week, we must strip men off other jobs."

"I feared as much. Do it. As soon as you figure out your personnel needs, see Stefan here to arrange it." He turned to the other man. "Before you say anything, we must recover that boat before the Salinas animals learn what they have. And they will learn it, believe me, as soon as they start working on those eggheads. We have less than a week. Get moving."

"Yes, Boss," they both said as they got up from the table and left the room.

Crețu stood and walked back to the bar for another vodka. He was drinking too much these days, he knew. It was not only bad for business; it was personally dangerous. If word got out that he was a drunk, the other senior council members would green-light his elimination, and then who would sit in this office? Probably Grigore. Stefan was the better manager and more profitable. But Grigore had an edge in terms of cold ruthlessness.

Crețu was a former junior thug in the Internal Security Directorate of the Securitate, as the Romanian secret police were known in the days of the Communist Dictator Nicolae Ceaușescu. Before they were disbanded a few days after Ceaușescu's death, the Securitate was one of the most brutal secret police forces in the world, and the Internal Security agents were the most vicious of the lot. After the collapse of the Soviet Union and its communist satellites in

Eastern Europe, many secret police murderers had to flee for their lives. Some less widely known ones could carve a niche in the underworld that sprang into place as the totalitarian governments collapsed. A select few joined into crime syndicates that soon exerted influence over broad geographic areas and segments of individual economies.

The 252s had a central committee of the founders, of which Crețu was one, each holding an underworld fiefdom controlling the syndicate's activities in a particular geographic area. In Crețu's case, this was Romania, Moldova, Bulgaria, North Macedonia, and Albania. With profits shared centrally, each fief holder was free to work outside his territory, even within another's territory, using an "Eat What You Kill" business model. They were almost invulnerable within their domains, working mostly below the local government radar when possible and readily applying bribery, intimidation, and murder to stay free to operate otherwise.

The deal with La Cantaña was a remarkably profitable enterprise—very high income, at almost no risk. That it was run efficiently by a former low-level Stasi clerk like Holtz was amazing. Holtz was a plodder who thought he was James Bond, almost laughable among the organization people who knew him. Crețu chided himself. *You were complacent. He was operating out of his depth, and you should have put one of our more intelligent people with him. Too late now.* He shook his head and took another drink.

6

The Recollected Choice

USCG Cutter *Kauai*, Moored, AUTEC, Andros Island, Bahamas
18:53 EDT, 1 April

Ben

Ben finally finished securing classified publications, zeroing out the codes on various pieces of cryptological and other gear, filing paperwork, and planning and preparing the next day's activities that went along with a vessel availability at a test range. Executive Officer, or XO for short, on a Coast Guard patrol boat as small as *Kauai* also meant Operations Officer, Engineer Officer, and [Fill in the blank with anything other than Commanding] Officer. Hence, his days were long and full at even the quietest times, and workups and test and evaluation periods were the opposite of the quietest times.

He looked across at Hopkins, sharing the final wrap-up activities. *Thank God! I'd be working straight through until the whole damn thing began tomorrow if it weren't for her.* "Come on, Chief," Ben said. "Let me stand you to the best three-course meal that fits in a microwave."

"XO, you sure know how to treat a girl," Hopkins said and followed as Ben led the way to the messdeck.

After their successful mission in January, it had excited Ben when he learned of the upgrades and the new purpose for their ship. He rued that day when he learned of the added security burdens these would entail. They had gained another Operations Specialist petty officer in Zuccaro and Electronics Technician in Bunting, which helped but did not eliminate the extra load Ben and Hopkins had to bear.

When they reached the messdeck, it surprised Ben to find Sam, Chief Drake, and Culinary Specialist Second Class Thomas "Chef" Hebert standing near the stove. He was even more surprised to smell what had to be Chicken Crepes and Cilantro Lime Rice, one of Chef's specialties. "Captain, COB, have you held up your dinner and Chef's liberty just for us?" Ben asked.

"Not at all. COB and I just got back from our nightly harangue at Harbor Ops Office, and Chef was just making sure we didn't screw up the new chafing dish he's breaking in."

"Now, Captain, you know that's not true," Hebert said. "I know y'all were working late, and besides, it's not like there's anywhere to go on this sand heap." Hebert was one of Sam's aces in the hole in terms of morale. Born and raised in New Orleans, Hebert apprenticed in a small family-owned and run restaurant in the Vieux Carré before enlisting in the Coast Guard. Besides the service's regular commissary support, Sam and Drake contributed funds and scavenging to provide for his more "exotic" condiment and equipment needs. The result was superb meals for the crew when underway, a significant plus in a patrol boat's otherwise spartan existence. As for Hebert, he loved the work, relished the appreciation he received, and, best of all, got to shoot a fifty-caliber machine gun in his general quarters billet.

"You'll go to Heaven, Chef," Ben said as he and Hopkins took the proffered plates of food and walked to the mess table to sit with Sam and Drake. "Captain, what's going on with this harangue stuff? Did I mess up something?" Ben asked after he sat.

"Seems we missed our dockside time by thirty-eight minutes, which apparently poses a significant threat to the republic. I pointed out things happen on shakedown, in this case, that phasing problem we had to fix while underway, but the dockmaster wasn't having it. Said a navy ship would have sent a proper notification, and he would have to consider reporting whoever was responsible in a letter to our chain of command."

"What did you say to that, sir?" Ben asked with concern.

Sam smiled. "Nothing. I took out my notebook, wrote 'LT Samuel Powell, CO (i.e., Officer

Responsible), USCGC *Kauai* and Captain Mercier's name and address, tore out the page, handed it to him, and then walked out."

"Oh, Captain, My Captain, you're such an evil influence on us." Ben shook his head in mock disapproval. "What am I to do with you?"

"Mmmm, yeah. As I think about it, I guess I should have been more circumspect, but I was too tired and fed up. I hope it doesn't come back to bite us."

"Captain, I'm sorry," Hopkins interrupted. "I'll get Joe Williams onto a go-no-go alarm on the FC3 panel. It won't happen again."

"Don't worry about the navy, sir," Drake said. "I'll tell the kids to stay on their toes when they're ashore." Drake was the senior enlisted member and the oldest man on the boat at forty-four. Since Hopkins's advancement to the same rank, the crew informally called Drake "COB" for "Chief of the Boat" on *Kauai*, a tradition borrowed from navy submarines. He was the best chief petty officer Ben had ever known because of the mastery of his trade and his leadership among the crew. Six-foot-four and physically imposing, he needed just to lean in to get someone's attention or administer a well-deserved dressing-down. Still, he quickly found an opportunity to work with the individual and give quiet encouragement.

Drake was also a master "wheeler-dealer" who worked an extensive network of connections among fellow chiefs and officers up to Captain's rank to keep *Kauai* well-supplied and running. Somewhat concerned about his "Don't worry, sir, I know a guy…"

activities earlier in their tenure, Sam and Ben had learned not to ask too many questions, just sit back and enjoy what happened next.

"Anyway, I was just telling the skipper we're pretty much there with the new plant," Drake said to Hopkins and Ben. "One more day, maybe two, and we'll have the data those geeks need." The "geeks" Drake referred to were the scientists from the Defense Advanced Research Projects Agency, or DARPA, on board to observe and record the post-shakedown tests of *Kauai*'s new diesel-electric drive and stealth features.

Drake himself was learning plenty. His love/hate relationship with the original aging engines on *Kauai* was over. He now was getting to know the ins and outs of high-efficiency generators, electric motors for propulsion instead of direct-drive diesel, and a high-capacity battery bank for near-silent operations. Drake considered retirement after twenty-four years, going out with *Kauai* when she decommissioned. Her new lease on life changed everything. Despite her engineering make-over being more aligned with Chief Electrician's Mate than Drake's rating, he had pressed hard to stay on board to see things through. Sam was relieved and delighted to make that happen.

Sam's face brightened. "And the good news is our shooting case is officially and favorably closed."

"That's a relief," Ben said. "Although he doesn't show it, I know Deke was worried since he's the one who pulled the trigger." It had been a sticky situation. The FBI wanted that suspect alive for interrogation and was after a pound of flesh. With senior Coast Guard backing, Sam arranged for one of his father's high-powered lawyer friends to represent anyone from *Kauai* called in for an FBI interview. Given that and the fact the full-motion video from *Kauai*'s and the Customs plane cameras and the body cameras on the boarding party made it one of the most documented justified shootings in human history discouraged further interest. Besides, even the FBI had no stomach to go after a Coast Guardsman who put down a murderous sex slaver and child rapist.

The technical discussion continued as Ben ravenously attacked the chicken—he had had nothing but coffee and water since his breakfast at 05:00. He ached with fatigue, having stood on the Bridge on OOD watch continuously since that time except for bathroom breaks. It had been his lot on this trip, with Sam and all other qualified OODs tied up with test events. He wanted to savor Hebert's cooking and then grab some sleep, but he had a date of sorts. When Ben finished, he would call Victoria, a moment he anticipated all day and would not miss for anything.

****

Victoria Carpenter was the greatest surprise of Ben's life. A twenty-three-year-old Data Scientist and Mathematical Analyst for the DIA and protégé of his erstwhile shipmate, Peter Simmons, they had met during the search for the lost nuke. The two men left *Kauai* to focus on the hunt ashore with Simmons's DIA associates. En route from Key West to a hotel in Marathon, where the team had set up shop, Simmons described Victoria as a mathematical genius with a "neurodiverse" streak. It was a warning for Ben not to be surprised by eccentric behavior. The image that formed in Ben's mind as they drove through the night was a plainer, geekier, neurotic version of Velma from the Scooby-Doo cartoons. This image shattered the instant the door to the hotel room opened.

Victoria, who led the greetings, was the most beautiful young woman Ben had ever seen—petite, with long auburn hair pulled back to reveal large aquamarine eyes, high cheekbones, and full lips in a heart-shaped face. Contrary to the frumpy dress that Ben expected, she wore a loose-fitting top and jeans that hinted at a smashing figure. She hugged Simmons and said in a husky voice with a midwestern accent, "Hello, Peter! I am pleased to see you." She turned to Ben with a smile that made him melt. "You are Lieutenant Junior Grade Wyporek?"

Holy crap! Even her voice is incredible. Breathe, boy! Ben took a breath and played it as cool as he could. "Yes, I am. I am very pleased to meet you. You can call me Ben if you like."

"Why would I like to do that when your name is Benjamin?" Her smile faded.

Oops. "Well, some people prefer to call me Ben because it's shorter to say, but I like how you say 'Benjamin,' so I would be happy if you called me that." That lovely smile returned.

"Good. We have been working all day and ordered pizza. Mine is a thin crust with pepperoni and green peppers. Would you like some as well?"

"Victoria, I can't think of anything I would rather do more right now."

"That's good." She then pivoted and walked behind the table holding a large computer monitor and keyboard, sat, and began typing, gazing at the screen. *OK, there it is.* Ben was thankful for Simmons's heads-up, as otherwise, he would have been shocked by the apparent rudeness of the gesture. After the introductions, the team settled into a planning session, with Victoria engrossed in her computer work and Ben munching pizza and stealing looks at her whenever he could. As the team conversation ended with a decision to send Victoria and her programmer partner, Steve, back to Maryland the next day, the analyst opened another door to Ben.

"I wish we had more time to work together, Benjamin."

Ben's heart leaped. "Well, Victoria, we have a few hours, don't we? Can I pitch in?"

"No." Victoria glanced back at the computer work area. "Everything is batch processing right now. However, I read your paper on the SAROPS project that provided the basis of your search strategy. There were several flaws and shortcomings. Would you like me to tell you about them?"

Ka-thunk! Ben blinked and opened his mouth in surprise, then noticed over her shoulder that Simmons was watching him with a slight smile. He consciously dialed down his ego. "Of course, Victoria. I'm always looking for ways to make progress." He then rolled through the most thorough intellectual beating of his life as she listed every flaw in the paper, from basic principles to punctuation errors. She was entirely correct—when he completed that project, he was sick of school and just shooting for "good enough." He found it ironic that his intellectual laziness would come back to haunt him with the most attractive woman he had ever met. "I hope you aren't disappointed in me, considering I'm not the mathematician you are. Also, there were many demands on my time when I wrote that."

"I'm not disappointed." She nodded. "Very few people are as intelligent as I am. I hope you are not sad; sometimes, it is hard for me to tell."

Hope sprung anew, and he smiled. "On the contrary, you can never go wrong being honest with me."

"Oh, good. In that case, I like you. Very much."

Ben's heart skipped a beat. *OK, careful now.* "Despite my inferior scholarship compared to you?" he teased with a smile.

"I am not bothered by that. You are very handsome and a hero." She smiled at him.

The knowledge that was a frank statement threw Ben for a moment. He blushed and said, "Oh, ah, thank you, I'm not a hero."

"I do not understand." The smile disappeared again. "You received the Coast Guard Commendation

Medal for saving three lives last year, and you just arrested a dangerous criminal."

Ben had started stammering, then saw Simmons over Victoria's shoulder, giving a thumbs-up and mouthing, "Take the Win."

Suddenly, a couple of things were obvious. First, Victoria must have researched his background—he wasn't wearing his uniform, so there was no other way she could know about his medal. Second, she was utterly honest and literal without nuance. Her critique of his report was not an expression of disappointment; it was a statement of fact, like identifying the color of paper on which it was printed. Likewise, the "aw shucks" modesty normally expected had no place here. There was no need to downplay actions or achievements; just lay out the facts. It was unique and the most delightful situation he had ever found himself in with a woman.

He described his life in the Coast Guard for almost two hours at her request. Despite the concentration required to make sure everything he said was logically consistent and idiom-free, he enjoyed this first conversation with the beautiful and attentive woman. They parted that night with a warm hug, and it delighted Ben to find Victoria even more beautiful the following day.

"Will you come and visit me in Bethesda?" she said to Ben after he placed her case in the car.

"Yes, I'd like that very much. But it might be some time. I can't leave the area while *Kauai* is operational or in readiness, you understand."

"Yes, I know," she said and then kissed him on the cheek before driving off. The encounter left Ben reeling—even Simmons could see the young woman's effect on him. As they continued on the search, he had a frank discussion with the young officer, pointing out the issues associated with carrying on a relationship with someone with even a mild form of autism, like Victoria's. Not that he had any question of Ben's integrity or other personal qualities. It was just the challenges that went with her condition. He had seen Victoria in other relationships, which had failed when what her partners initially regarded as eccentricities morphed in their minds into annoying tics. He was highly protective of her—she was the younger sister of his beloved late fiancée, and he didn't want to see either of them hurt.

Ben took Simmons's caution to heart. He had never known, much less been in a relationship with someone on the spectrum, and did not know how he would feel over time. He also appreciated that relationships with Coast Guard junior officers like himself brought plenty of their own challenges, even for someone without special needs. Then there was the distance—her duties with the DIA and challenges with public transportation limited her to the DC area. Finally, he was slammed with the demands of *Kauai*'s rebuild and the special training their new role required. As interesting as she was, Ben set out carefully. The last thing he wanted was to hurt her.

They settled into a comfortable friendship supported by phone whenever he had the time and connectivity. He loved listening to Victoria's voice's deep and plummy timbre and the precision in her language as she excitedly described what details she could of her work. He wasn't sharp enough to follow along with all the big-brain math she talked about, but he could hang in there enough to be a valuable sounding board.

On the other hand, he could talk about anything with her, and she listened intently, fascinated by his experiences with his job and coworkers. Whenever he called, she was there and thrilled to talk to him. She also understood the demands of his position and did not resent that sometimes there would be several days between phone calls and things he couldn't discuss with her for operational security reasons. More than one of Ben's earlier relationships had foundered on that very issue.

Over the two-and-a-half months since their meeting, their conversations became more and more precious for him. He missed them terribly whenever he was underway or otherwise tied up with an operational demand. He had never felt this way about anyone else and began thinking he might be falling in love with her.

****

The conversation was winding down as Ben finished the last of his supper. Sam concluded the impromptu dinner meeting with a positive thought: "A couple more days, guys, and then we're off for home. No more speed runs, sound runs, turning around, and heading back to start because some egghead had the green-with-white wire patched into the white-with-green plug. Just good ol' drug and migrant blockade for us, with the occasional rocket launch from the Cape."

"Amen to that," Hopkins said as she wiped her mouth. "I shudder, thinking what my boys have put over on their grandmother since we left."

"Aw, MOM!" Ben said, getting hearty, tired laughs from the others, with Hopkins good-naturedly shaking a finger in his direction. He turned to Sam. "By your leave, Captain?"

"Off for the nightly call, Number One?" Sam asked.

"You know it."

"Good on you. See you in the morning, everyone."

They pushed away from the table, and Ben patted Hebert on the shoulder as he left the messdeck. "*Merci beaucoups, Maître Cuisinier*!"

"*De rien, mon lieutenant*!"

Ben shuffled up to his stateroom, closed the door, and sat at his mini desk. He looked longingly at the two pictures fastened securely to the ship's bulkhead above his desk. Ben had taken the first one with his cell phone after he and Victoria dined at a pleasant restaurant on their first date. He was in a jacket and tie that night, while she wore a gorgeous green cocktail dress with her hair up. The second picture was a candid shot of Ben and Victoria strolling on the Washington DC Mall, taken by an aspiring photographer about a month ago. She held Ben's arm and looked up at him with a bright smile as he looked at her, both in light jackets and jeans. In those everyday clothes, so different from the green dress, she conveyed a wholesome beauty every bit as alluring.

The pictures were artifacts of the only visits he had been allowed with her. He was going through an intense combat training course in Quantico, Virginia, preparing for *Kauai's* new special operations role. It exasperated Ben to be so close to Victoria, a mere hour-and-a-half drive away, yet unable to pry out the time to be with her.

Finally, Ben had wrangled an evening off. It was the first time he had seen her since the Florida Keys operation, and as lovely as he had remembered her then, Ben was unprepared for what awaited him in Bethesda. Ben had always thought the expression "Breathtakingly beautiful" was hyperbole until experiencing it himself at his first sight of Victoria that night. She had to call his attention to the flowers he had bought for her, which snapped him out of his paralyzed state, starting the babbling phase, leading finally to a simple, "You look wonderful" after he pulled his head out of his ass. Not his smoothest moment, but she didn't seem to mind—quite the contrary. After the awkward beginning, they recovered to their usual banter as the evening wore on over dinner. As pleasant as it was just hearing her voice, it was magic when combined with that gorgeous face and lovely eyes as emerald green as the dress. When they returned to the apartment at the end of the evening, Ben asked if he could take her picture.

Victoria was terrifically self-conscious, and it took all the persuasion he could muster to get her to agree to pose. It was worth it, this and every time he could look at the picture and remember that first night.

The second visit occurred a couple of weeks later, an entire Sunday off, and Ben was determined to make the most of it. He drove up early in the morning, and they went out for breakfast and then spent the day at the museums around the Mall. Ben remembered little about the exhibits. He just enjoyed being with Victoria and seeing her fascination with them. He was surprised at the breadth of her knowledge and tastes—his previous experience with mathematical masters was confined to his professors at the academy, most of whom were one-dimensional people barely able to converse with someone outside their specialty. Unlike them, Victoria never held her encyclopedic knowledge over him. She didn't seem to care a wit about how much he *knew*; she was just intensely interested in what he *thought*. It was a marvelous experience. The second picture happened afterward when they strolled on the Mall in the beautiful sunshine.

The day had a hiccup as they were leaving. They had taken the Metro subway system down to avoid wasting time on driving and parking. Metro traffic was light in the morning, and although Victoria was silent during the trip, Ben did not give it any thought. The trip back was a different story. The crowds were heavy and loud, and Victoria was clearly affected. It was the first time her condition had become an issue, and Ben was in a terrible plight. He had mild claustrophobia himself, and the noise and pressing in of the crowd was getting to him—it had to be far worse for her. He wanted to suggest they get off and take a cab, but was afraid of embarrassing her. Finally, her severe reaction to a child's scream jolted Ben out of his indecision, and he immediately asked her if they could get off at the next stop. He was kicking himself on the inside all the way out of the station for letting her distress go on for so long, and was terrified that he had destroyed their wonderful day with his indecision. He was almost giddy with relief when Victoria hugged him gratefully after they got outside.

They had a wonderful dinner at an Italian restaurant across the street from the station. They completed the rest of the journey to the original Metro station by cab, with Victoria snuggled under his arm, her head on his shoulder. Then back to her apartment in his car. Unlike their earlier outing, Ben did not have to report back for training in Quantico until the following day. He desperately wanted to stay with her, but got hung up on how to ask. After the Metro near-miss, Ben was unsure how she would react and rationalized that he shouldn't be pushing in just to take off in a few hours. After a very awkward goodbye, he was almost halfway to his car when he realized he could not just leave it like that and went back. Her joy when she opened the door was apparent, and their night together was warm and tender.

It was the most beautiful day of his life, and when they parted with a passionate kiss early the following day, he realized he was in love with her. Yet, he couldn't find it in himself to tell her. Victoria was so honest with him about everything; he felt sure she would have shown some sign if the feeling was mutual—but she had not. Ben had decided it wasn't fair to lay that on her on the way out the door. He had already pressed his luck and was afraid to risk driving her away and ending what they had.

He had accepted the satisfying but static relationship since, but having a gun pointed at him by a murderous criminal a week ago had changed the calculus. Ben had resolved to press his case to her directly, admit his love for her, and see where it led. But he needed to do it in person rather than by phone. Fortunately, Sam had agreed to cut him loose on several days of leave once they returned home from AUTEC—provided they received the promised operational stand-down.

He retrieved his cell phone from his desk and dialed Victoria's number after turning it on and syncing to the patrol boat's off-network Wi-Fi connection. As usual, she answered after two rings.

"Hello, Benjamin."

Ben smiled, as he always did at her use of his full name and the quiet cheeriness of her greeting. "Hello, Victoria. How was your day?" It was the standard exchange at the beginning of their phone calls. Ben knew Victoria liked things a certain way and enjoyed obliging her.

"Oh, it was an exciting day. First..."

****

"... and so, seems we may wrap things up and head home in a couple of days," Ben said.

"That is excellent news. I am concerned about your workload while you have been there. Do you think you and your crew will be granted relief when you return to Port Canaveral?" Victoria asked.

"Hopefully. That's another thing I wanted to talk to you about. Sam has agreed to give me a few days of leave if we stand down. I would like to fly up there and spend it with you. Would you be agreeable to that and able to take leave yourself?"

"Oh, yes, that would be wonderful! I have an abundance of leave accumulated, and I am sure my supervisor would not object when I tell him it is for you."

I *am known around there? That's an interesting revelation.* "I'm glad to hear that. I'll let you know when I can nail down the dates."

"Oh, good. I am very excited to be able to see you again. I hope it will be soon."

"Me too. Well, I'm pretty tired, Victoria, and I have another long day tomorrow. Would it upset you if I asked to make this one of our shorter phone calls?"

"Of course not, Benjamin. I am very concerned you are not getting enough rest. Will you be able to call me tomorrow night?"

"If we are not on our way home, then definitely. Otherwise, I'll call you as soon as I can."

"I am looking forward to that. Goodnight, Benjamin."

"Goodnight, Victoria," Ben said, hanging up the phone.

He looked at the pictures again, managed a wistful smile as he remembered the details, then turned off the phone. "Goodnight, my love. I'll hold you again soon."

7

The Blue Swan

USCG Cutter *Kauai*, Moored, AUTEC, Andros Island, Bahamas
08:13 EDT, 2 April

Ben

"Take in Line Three!" Ben shouted, giving a thumbs-up to Bunting as soon as the dockworkers cast the line into the water.

Bunting picked up the 1 MC public address system microphone, blew a short "tweet" on the whistle he was holding, and announced, "Shift Colors."

Ben watched with satisfaction as Lee snatched the U. S. Flag from the flagstaff on the stern, Fireman Sean Connally did the same with the Union Jack on the bow's jackstaff, and Zuccaro ran up the U. S. Flag on the mast halyard, all within one second. As he moved the thrust levers ahead to an eight-knot setting, he said, "Helm, right ten degrees rudder, steer zero-eight-five. Bunting, sound one long blast."

"Right ten degrees rudder, steer zero-eight-five, sir," Seaman Pickins, the helmsman, replied.

"Sound one long blast, sir," Bunting said, pushing and holding the button for *Kauai*'s horn for five seconds. The long blast was an aural signal indicating a vessel getting underway. It was of little utility in the bright sun and clear visibility of the harbor that morning, but by the book. And after Sam's run-in with the Harbor Master yesterday, Ben and Hopkins were determined that *Kauai*'s sailing this morning would be an exemplar for everyone present in the harbor. As the patrol boat hurried out to the test area, Bondurant relieved Ben of the OOD to allow him to supervise the morning series of tests from the boat deck.

The morning activities were a series of test runs for the Squid. *Kauai* had been very fortunate to surprise the villains off of Miami, and more so that they turned in the right direction and held a straight course. A few days before, Ben had sat down with Hopkins, Bondurant, and Lee to "war-game" workable tactics for targets that were not so accommodating. They had come up with a series of scenarios for live testing, with the RHIB standing in for the target. Rather than shoot off actual net canisters, which were expensive and hazardous to the boats, the contractor had developed color-coded "paint rounds" with identical ballistics to those containing nets. They had internal charges that would fire at the end of the flight, but instead of a net, a harmless paint pattern would deploy into the water to allow observation of the tactic's effectiveness.

Of course, Lee was the coxswain and very excited to "go tactical" with the RHIB. Although Hopkins was the most skilled OOD on board, Sam wanted a more "average" person at the conn to provide a realistic assessment, so Bondurant got the nod. Hopkins was still present on the Bridge, directing the test. The contractor who developed the Squid insisted on having an observer in the RHIB, a youthful engineer named Paul DeChamps, whose thick round glasses had earned him the nickname "The Owl" among *Kauai's* crew. Connally was the last member of the RHIB's crew, added as a safety crewman to watch over the contractor.

Ben gathered the crew of the RHIB and delivered a safety briefing. With ballistic projectiles being fired over the boat, even benign ones like the paint rounds, the crew was equipped with battle helmets and standard life jackets. At the end, he drew Lee and Connally aside for a private chat. "OK, Shelley, where is it?"

"What's that, sir?" She asked innocently.

"The coffee can with dish soap you intend to tell The Owl is 'prop wash' so he can furnish some hilarious cell camera footage moving back and forth in the boat."

"Why, sir, I'm *shocked* you think me capable of such tomfoolery!" There was a scraping sound as she tried to move the can out of sight with her foot.

Ben reached down, picked up the can, and sniffed it. "Ahem. Well, at least you used biodegradable soap." He put the can aside and continued. "OK, I appreciate that you'd like a little payback for having a civilian perched on your shoulder on this ride, but with ballistic rounds flying around, we need everybody's head in the game. So, besides no prop wash, I don't want to see him manning the mail buoy lookout or rummaging through the toolbox for a left-handed screwdriver or any more boot camp tricks. Consider that an order. Clear?" he said with a grin.

"Yes, sir. Very good, sir," Lee replied with a mock sad look. "You know, I bet you were a lot more fun at the academy!"

"Nope. I was hanging on by my *fingernails* there. I couldn't afford to get caught screwing around," he said with a wink. "Look, it's DeChamps's first time in the RHIB. Show him a good time rather than hazing."

Lee smiled in return. "You've got it, XO."

"Thanks, Shelley. Off you go. Good luck!"

Lee

The RHIB launched shortly afterward with its crew of three, and it and *Kauai* went into the test range. Each test comprised the RHIB moving out to a half-mile distance, barreling in at thirty knots, and executing evasive maneuvers. Bondurant, guided by Hopkins, maneuvered *Kauai* in response. Williams activated and fired the projectors on Sam's command if the Squid got a firing solution. The projectiles fired paint charges into the water, resulting in either a "Hit with Net X" or "Clean Miss All Nets" report from Lee. Wash, rinse, repeat.

They had repeated the cycle enough times to get a reasonably rich dataset when something went awry. A defect in one canister's fins created a "wobble" in flight that caused it to fall behind its companions. When the dispersing charge fired, it was just forward of the speeding RHIB and doused it and its occupants with two-and-a-half gallons of bright blue paint. Lee closed the throttle slowly to bring the boat to a smooth stop, took off her paint-coated sunglasses, and said, "Everybody OK? Give me a thumbs up!"

After getting a thumbs-up from both passengers, Lee shook off her hands, put them on her hips, and glared at DeChamps.

"I think some of our projectiles might need adjustment," the engineer said, squinting up at Lee while holding his paint-fouled glasses.

"Ya think?" Lee replied.

"*Kauai*-One, *Kauai*, report!" her radio barked.

"*Kauai*, *Kauai*-One, direct hit by blue paint, no damage or casualties," Lee replied.

"*Kauai*-One, *Kauai*, roger, cancel operation and return to ship."

"*Kauai*, *Kauai*-One, WILCO, out." Lee took a deep breath and turned to Connally. "Sean, *carefully* help Mr. DeChamps with his glasses." She swished her sunglasses clean in the water beside the RHIB, then sat back down at the helm. Once Connally had helped DeChamps with his glasses and both were seated again, Lee opened the throttle and headed back to the patrol boat. *I'll bet the cameras got an awesome shot of this. I'm SO looking forward to seeing it again, and again, and AGAIN!*

While operating the boat crane, Jenkins left the RHIB at the deck rail after the crew climbed out so the paint could be hosed off before returning to its cradle. The XO met them there with an armful of sodas—he knew they would be dried out after a couple of hours in the sun. He was always doing thoughtful things like this, unlike any other officer she had ever served with, and it was the thing she liked most about him.

"So, Petty Officer Lee," he said with a perfectly straight face as he handed her a can of Coke. "I think we need to get you some vacation time. You're looking mighty blue."

Ha, ha, ha! So, it starts already! Lee paused after taking the Coke and replied, "Thanks, sir. You know, XO, you're wasting your talents here on the bounding main. You should run a comedy podcast!"

"OK, OK, but I have to get a selfie with you guys," he said, holding up his cellphone.

"Alright, sir, but it will cost you," Lee replied with a smirk. *This is going to be good!*

"Name it."

"You have a blue pirate mustache in the selfie."

"Done!" The XO swiped some blue paint off her helmet with his finger and painted on a curly-cue mustache. "Sean, come on. You get in this too!" With the XO grinning, they crowded together, Connally in a "smirky" shrug and Lee with her best "Oh, No!" pose, and the XO snapped the picture. "Thanks, guys. Now you hit the shower and then see Doc. We'll handle the cleanup."

"Aw, come on, XO. It's just paint," Lee sighed.

"It's a chemical, Shelley. No discussion."

"Yes, sir," she said, taking a swig of Coke as she started forward. As she walked, she grumbled, "If I hear a word that even sounds like 'Smurf,' somebody's gonna get their ass thrown overboard!"

Interrogation Room B, Security Division, U.S. Army Garrison-Miami, Doral, Florida
11:47 EDT, 2 April

Holtz

Holtz opened his eyes, then quickly shut them again, almost crying out from the pain in his forehead. Wherever he was, it was deathly quiet, brightly lit, and white. Holtz was sitting in a hard chair, head resting on his folded arms on a table. He slowly opened his eyes, allowing them time to get used to the bright light. Once his eyes were fully open, Holtz sat up slowly in the chair. His left hand was manacled to a rail stretched across the empty table, which had an empty chair sitting on the other side. He looked around the room, which was painted white and featureless other than a single door and a mirror across the room. Someone had dressed him in orange, one-piece coveralls and laceless, slip-on cloth shoes—*a prisoner's uniform.*

Through the fading headache, Holtz experienced a glimmer of hope. He had not been taken by the 252s from his hotel room last night. *Was it last night?* His watch had been removed, and there was no clock in the room. The 252s would not have bothered with torture or interrogation; they would simply have shot him and left his body in the hotel room. This was a government facility, probably American, he reasoned. The Russians could not have tracked him down so quickly, even if they were interested in him. "Hello?" he asked, gazing at the mirror. "Is anyone there? I have information you'll be interested in."

Silence. Wherever this room was, it was isolated from anything else going on in the building. After what seemed like hours, but was probably only minutes, the door opened, and a slender thirtyish man of medium height entered, walked to the table, set down the leather case he was carrying on the far side, and sat in the chair across from Holtz. He was dressed in a plain blue suit, white shirt, and red tie, dark brown hair cut medium-short above a plain face with a close-cropped anchor beard and brown eyes. The man said nothing, just stared expressionlessly at Holtz without moving.

After an uncomfortable period of silence, Holtz could not take it any longer and asked, "Do you have questions of me?" No response. "You must want something. Why am I here?"

After a few more seconds of silence, the man finally spoke. "You are Anton Holtz, correct?"

Whoever had taken him had obviously grabbed his passport. “Yes.”

“Late of the 252 Syndicate?”

Holtz was shocked by the question. Nothing he was carrying had any reference to the syndicate. “I’m unfamiliar with that term.”

The man leaned back with a slight smile. “Oh, come now, Holtz. You have been a member of that organization for at least twenty years. I’m not sure right now why you came to the United States, but I am sure you must be in a hell of a jam with your employers to do so. What you do not want to do is lie to me. Doing that would prove you are of no value whatsoever. If that is the case, I’ll have you turned over to the FBI for a very public tour of our criminal justice system.”

Just the thought of what the man was threatening chilled Holtz to the bone. He knew that any public tour would be a very short one—his erstwhile comrades would make sure of that. “Alright, yes, I have been a member of the 252 organization.”

“Good answer. So, Holtz, what brings you to Miami? It can’t be the sun and mojitos. The evident lack of preparation leads me to believe you are fleeing something. What did you foul up that convinced you to run to us?”

Frightened as Holtz was, he knew better than to offer what he had for nothing. “I need a guarantee of my safety first. You don’t really expect me to give you everything so you can then cast me aside, do you?”

The man leaned forward. “I’ll give you one guarantee, Holtz. If you don’t tell me the whole truth and nothing but the truth when I ask you a question, you get dumped into the system forthwith. On the other hand, if you cooperate fully and without hesitation, I *may* find your information interesting enough that I'll want to keep you alive. Now, what's it going to be?"

Holtz was familiar with interrogation tactics from his apprenticeship in the Stasi and his years rising in the 252 organization. This man was not bluffing. If Holtz didn't offer something up now, he would not get another chance. "The organization is on the verge of marketing a weapon of mass destruction." Holtz knew he had scored a hit when the man suddenly leaned forward.

"What kind of WMD are we talking about, Holtz?"

"Chemical weapons, a carbamate-based nerve agent."

The man sat back disgustingly and scoffed, "Oh, come on, Holtz. There's nothing new there. VX? Novichok? It's all been done."

"Not like this one."

"What, you're going to tell me this one is *deadlier* than the others? We are well beyond the threshold of that making any difference."

"Yes, it's much more lethal, but that is not the important thing. It is also self-cleaning." The man's expression changed, as Holtz knew it would. He had experienced the same shock when Gronkowsky had revealed this to him on the *Carlos Rojas*.

"What do you mean, self-cleaning?"

"It breaks down on exposure to moisture and oxygen into innocuous inert compounds. The half-life is such that applications at a level that ensures death to everyone not in full chemical gear will be down to a safe level within a few days, with no clean-up effort. It is also a binary, with indefinite shelf life and safe handling characteristics. You can set it up to self-mix in an artillery shell or bomb and eradicate everyone in a village or small town, leaving nothing to clean up but the bodies."

The man's expression returned to its previous nonchalance. "I don't believe you. Our intelligence would have picked up on something like that. They couldn't hide it, even in Eastern Europe."

"It's not in Europe. It was developed aboard a repurposed petroleum support ship."

"Alright, let's say I believe you. What difference would it make? If the 252s are producing and getting ready to market it, there's not much we could do to stop it."

"You're wrong. The lab, materials, production facility, data, and even the developer are all still aboard that ship. And the 252s don't have it anymore."

"What do you mean, they don't have it anymore?"

"A drug gang from Honduras seized it."

"A Honduran drug gang seized a 252 ship? You don't expect me to believe that." He paused, tilted his head, and smiled. "Ah, now I think I see. You were working a drug deal that went south. Whether it was bad faith by you or them is not really important. You are the one that will hang for it. Am I correct?" After

Holtz looked down without speaking, the man continued. "I'll take that as a yes. Did the cartel offer terms?"

"They want twenty million euros within a week, but the organization won't pay. It would set a dangerous precedent."

"I can't say I blame them. So, I presume they will mount a retrieval and punitive operation?"

"Yes, within five days."

"Five days? Rather longer than I would expect."

"The ship is in Barbello. It takes time to gather and position a sufficient force to overcome the resistance without wrecking the ship."

The man nodded. "Holtz, you have just bought yourself some consideration. I'm done with you, but I'll send in some experts to debrief you on the ship, the 252s, and their opposition. Keep talking, and you might just live through this." The man stood, put the leather case under his arm, and left the room.

Holtz released the breath he was holding. *Well, the die is cast.*

USCG Cutter *Kauai*, AUTEC Weapons Range, off Andros Island, Bahamas
13:17 EDT, 2 April

Ben

The rest of the day involved a trip to the gunnery range to test and exercise the new targeting system for the 25-mm gun that aimed at specific Global

Positioning System coordinates. Williams's reaction in the briefing was the same as Sam's and Ben's when they first heard of it. "Why do we need something like this? We're not shooting over the horizon with this thing, and it's less accurate than visual or infrared targeting."

The contractor's response mainly was unintelligible gibberish and the fact that they had been hired to do it by the people paying for *Kauai*'s upgrades.

"So, in other words, 'cause," Williams finished with a smirk.

"Joe...," Ben said warningly.

"Sir, I'm sorry, but I'm worried it might mess up the electro-optical or infrared systems. We need those, unlike this thing. Could we put a few rounds through the tube at the end to make sure the others still work?"

Ben looked at Sam and nodded. Sam said, "That's a good idea. We'll hold on to a couple of targets, and you can tear them up at the end."

"Thank you, Captain," Williams replied, directing a scowl toward the hapless contractor.

The gun exercise proceeded as planned, and the new system performed as advertised, with rounds landing within thirty feet of the target, a steel buoy with a shielded GPS receiver attached to the top. *Kauai* engaged the target at various speeds and bearings with the same results.

"Well, it's reliable anyway," Williams grudgingly acknowledged after the last test run.

They continued on the range for about half an hour to run the other targeting systems through their paces and then turned back toward the harbor. Ben looked at the bridge clock—16:47—and nodded to himself. *An early day. With any luck, we'll be in by 17:30, buttoned-up by 18:30, and I can have a nice, leisurely talk with Victoria and get some decent sleep tonight.* He couldn't wait to share the selfie and story of the Great Paint Deluge with her. As interested as she was in the significant events that made up his day, she always seemed delighted to hear about the little ones, particularly if humor was attached.

****

"XO, we're headed for the Thousand Fathoms Club for beers. Want to come along?" Williams asked as he poked his head into Ben's room. "It's Karaoke Night!" Ben could see Lee, Bunting, and Jenkins waiting in the hallway.

"Alas, Joe, I have tons of paperwork and a phone call to make. I'm sure sorry I won't get to hear Shelley's version of 'Song Sung Blue,' though."

Lee gave him a scowl while the others laughed. "You're not going to let that go, are you, sir?"

"Sorry, Shelley, this one's got legs like Eliud Kipchoge. You guys have fun but drink responsibly, don't drink and drive, practice safe sex, stay in school, um, and all that other dad stuff."

"You're an inspiration to us, sir," Lee smirked. She looked at the pictures on Ben's bulkhead with a slight smile. "Tell her we said 'Hi.'"

"Will do. Have fun, guys." Ben smiled as he listed to their conversation fade as they walked down the passageway.

"Who the hell is Eliud Kipchoge?" Bunting asked.

"He's a marathon runner, you idiot," Lee replied.

8

Only the Important Words

4527 Sangamore Road, Apt. B23, Bethesda, Maryland
18:47 EDT, 2 April

Victoria

Victoria had just completed her nightly dinner routine that involved cooking the main course, then the vegetable, and eating them on separate plates with separate dinnerware. It entailed extra effort in the cleanup phase, but it was well worth it to avoid the stress of keeping the food items separate on a single plate. She washed, dried, and put away everything before settling with a glass of wine and, hopefully, a phone call from Benjamin. They agreed such calls would happen between seven and nine p.m. to preserve her dinner and sleep routines. Benjamin had accepted that rule with his usual good-natured acquiescence—his understanding of her peculiar needs was one of the many things she loved about him. Of course, if the phone rang at 6:45 pm or 9:30 pm with his callback number displayed, she would pounce on it like a cat on a helpless mouse.

Victoria's apartment was a small but fashionable one-bedroom, practically across the street from her workplace, the DIA's Data Analysis Division within the National Intelligence University. It was pricey but affordable on her GS-12 pay since she did not travel and had no family and few interests outside of work. It was great to be home after a ten-minute walk without the stress of Maryland driving or the horror of the DC Metro subway system with its crowds, confined spaces, and the noise and all those people *touching* you. She had a car, useful on weekend shopping for foodstuffs or, on rare occasions, drives on one of the parkways in the area when the leaves were changing or the cherry blossoms bloomed. The apartment was not spartan but sparsely decorated with books, no knickknacks on the shelves, and just a few impressionist landscapes decorating the off-white painted walls.

Victoria sat at her computer desk to pull up Scholar Google and check for any new data science papers while waiting to see if Benjamin would call tonight. Although work-related, she preferred to do her academic research at home—her system was far faster for Internet searches than her work computer behind the government firewalls and other security protocols. She looked at the two framed pictures on her desk as her computer booted. One was the picture of her and Benjamin on the Mall. The second was Benjamin, alone in the same setting, and he was beautiful. Victoria knew that was the wrong word to use for a man, but it was the most accurate in his case, with his short sandy brown hair mussed by the breeze, the deep azure color of his eyes matching that of the sky, and the delightfully warm smile on his lightly tanned face. It was a treasured artifact from the full day they had together a month ago, the second of their two dates, and as perfect a day as she had ever experienced.

Benjamin was as surprising to Victoria as she was to him. After receiving their first report of the derelict drug vessel last January, Peter had asked her to pull data for a quick brief on *Kauai*'s command. Samuel Powell's record was very unusual: the elder child of a wealthy family dropped out of the prestigious Wharton Graduate School to enlist in the Coast Guard? She dug deeper and found an arrest for felony assault with charges dropped a couple of months before he enlisted, the victim now a fugitive from justice believed to be living in Serbia. Interesting. Digging deeper into that man, she found a contemporaneous guilty plea for reckless driving with injury, victim Gabrielle Powell—aha! Samuel's younger sister. That explained the anomaly of the arrest in an otherwise flawless personal record. Still, the decision to enlist was strange. Quick advancement to chief petty officer, selected for officer candidate school, followed by tours of duty on Coast Guard cutters in Boston, Honolulu, and now Miami, several personal and unit awards.

Benjamin's record was lean by comparison. He was a mediocre performer at the Coast Guard Academy, had an uneventful tour of duty aboard Coast Guard Cutter *Dependable* in Little Creek, Virginia, then was assigned to *Kauai* as second in command. There was something unusual—he had been awarded the Coast Guard Commendation Medal for heroism in saving three lives after a traffic accident. She had noted this with approval and pulled the men's official photos. They looked like they could be brothers. All official military photos looked the same to her, like instead of "say cheese," the photographers said, "Now, give us your most menacing scowl!"

Victoria was very excited the next day when Peter included her in the scratch team of agents and technicians deployed to the Florida Keys to process Unmanned Aerial Vehicle data. She enjoyed the challenge of the austere information technology environment, and the Florida Keys were not the worst place to be in the middle of January! After a few days on-site, Peter left *Kauai* to join the search team ashore, bringing Benjamin. Victoria expected little from the association. She had downloaded a report of Benjamin's academy project that served as their search strategy and was not impressed, even considering it was undergraduate work. She hoped to avoid engaging in deep technical conversations with him while they were together. Still, there was that medal for bravery, and the day before, he had arrested a dangerous criminal on a boat rigged to explode. She wondered what a hero might be like in person.

The young man who arrived with Peter for the team meeting that first night was nothing like she expected. Some height, but not overly tall, with a slim, athletic build and the most captivating blue eyes she had ever seen. He was not the militaristic buffoon she took him for after reading his personnel file, but a modest, almost shy, and intelligent young man who provided fascinating conversation. She suspected he was attracted to her as well—she had caught glimpses of him looking at her while she worked at her computer during the discussions.

She would have welcomed such attention at one time, but then her self-doubt kicked in again. *I like Benjamin, and I must not drive him away by being too clingy.* Too clingy. That was what her last love interest had said to end their relationship. She knew she had difficulty reading people's feelings—it was a fact of life for someone on the autism spectrum. But the thought she could make herself repellent to someone she loved had been emotionally devastating, and she resolved never to make that mistake again. Hence, as attractive as Benjamin was, Victoria was very cautious in revealing her interest in him.

Victoria opened the door to Benjamin at the end of the team meeting, offering some helpful critique on his report he took in stride. She then expressed admiration for his heroism, which he tried to brush off. Victoria supposed there was a military code of modesty that expected such things. It was strange, but she accepted they must have a reason for it. She finally connected with him by asking about his life in the Coast Guard. Among the other exciting elements, she persuaded him to tell how he got his medal—crawling inside a car about to fall off a cliff to pull out an unconscious woman and her two young children! *And he was shy talking about that? Why?*

After two hours of conversation, mainly Benjamin answering questions and telling anecdotes about his job and himself, Victoria could see the fatigue taking its toll. His descriptions of operations on patrol boats conveyed a general state of sleep deprivation, along with the more exciting aspects. She also noted he had quickly adapted his conversation style to remove the jargon and idioms. Victoria appreciated his thoughtfulness, but realized it required him to put particular effort into almost every sentence. She was sure he was struggling but soldiering on in deference to her, so she offered him a graceful exit.

"You look exhausted, Benjamin. I am tired too. I think it is time we went to bed."

"What?" Benjamin sputtered, eyes wide.

Oh no! No, no, no! He thinks I am inviting him to have sex with me right now! How could I be so stupid? So clingy?

Fortunately, Peter was still present and came to the rescue. "You're right, Victoria. Why don't we all head to our rooms, and we'll pick it up again in the morning?"

The shock on Benjamin's face retreated, and the warm and tired smile he had before her blunder returned. Victoria stood and, after going through the motions of checking her computer for progress on the automatic computations, took a chance and gave Benjamin a warm hug. For the first time in a long while, her last thoughts before falling asleep did not focus on mathematical algorithms. As they were saying goodbye the next morning, she to return to Maryland, Benjamin to continue the search with Peter, she took another chance and kissed him on the cheek. The smile he returned made her tingle and gave her hope.

She spoke to him that evening after she had returned to Bethesda, and he had completed the search activity for the day. This time Benjamin was the receiver, and she was talking. It thrilled her he was interested in what she did, and although she suspected he did not quite understand it all, he still seemed to hang on to every word. It was several days before they spoke on the phone again after Benjamin returned home. Something had happened during the mission, but he could not discuss it. Working in the world of classified information and secrets, she understood. However, whatever happened must have been extraordinary, for both he and Samuel received the Coast Guard Medal, a top award for heroism.

They settled into a routine of nightly phone calls whenever Benjamin had the connectivity. They were a welcome distraction at first, becoming an increasingly important part of her day as she got to know him. He was interesting, charming, and funny all at once, and unlike anyone she had ever met, she could discuss anything on her mind with him. Given this, she was puzzled that he was not married or had a steady girlfriend. When she finally asked why that was, he went silent, and she quickly tried to withdraw the question.

"No, it's OK, Victoria. I've asked myself that a few times. The only answer I can come up with is I haven't met anyone who needed what I could provide." Then he quickly changed the subject, and she was careful not to raise it again. Benjamin's answer created a paradox for her. She often could not connect with people she liked and felt much closer to him, knowing he shared this experience of loneliness. On the other hand, it made her even warier of making any "clingy" blunders. It was a specter hanging over their early conversations, fading over time as she became more comfortable with him.

Between the distance and the relentless demands of Benjamin's job, the conversations were all they had. Benjamin had hoped they could get together when he was close by in Quantico while completing his combat training in February and March, but the short time and large volume of training requirements extended through the weekends. During his course, the only free time allowed was just one evening that served as a somewhat awkward first date and one other full day together, and they seized on those opportunities.

Their first date had been a maelstrom of emotion for Victoria. They had arranged it a week in advance, and Benjamin could only get off for the evening, so they planned for him to pick her up for dinner and return her to her apartment before he had to report back to Quantico. Victoria was terrifically anxious about making a good impression, so much so that she let it slip to Debbie, the office administrative assistant, the next day. Debbie was one of the few people who could see past Victoria's idiosyncrasies and was the closest thing she had to a good friend. When Victoria confessed her anxiety, the middle-aged woman's maternal instincts kicked in at once, and she took Victoria shopping for a suitable dress that afternoon.

"I am not sure I like this one. It is not the style I normally wear," Victoria said as she checked herself in the mirror. The green dress fit snugly and left little to the imagination.

"Trust me, dear." Debbie smiled admiringly. "The color is perfect with your eyes and hair, and the fit is perfect for everything else. This one will knock him for a loop. And before you ask, yes, that is what you want to do."

When the big day came, Debbie stopped in to help her get ready. She knew Victoria found the subtleties of makeup particularly challenging. "Dear, you are beautiful without makeup, but this is one of those times when you need to have makeup, but not look like you're wearing makeup," Debbie explained. Victoria's head spun at the contradictions, but decided it was not prudent to overthink the process. The last rub was her hair. She always wore it pulled back, but Debbie insisted it needed to be up.

"Why?" Victoria asked.

"Sweetie, I don't know how to tell you other than this is a hair-up dress," Debbie explained.

Victoria deferred to the expert on the subject, which proved to be a sound decision. When she answered the door an hour later to Benjamin's knock, he stood transfixed with his mouth hanging open. The uncomfortable moment lasted until she asked about the flowers he was holding. "Those flowers are lovely, Benjamin. Are they for me?"

He broke into an embarrassed smile at the question and said, "Yes, they are. Excuse me, please, but you are just so much more beautiful than I expected. I mean, I expected you to be beautiful, but not…." He stopped, took a breath, and said, "You look wonderful, Victoria!"

"Oh, what a nice thing to say!" Victoria replied. *This brave, intelligent man reduced to babbling by a dress? OK, now I know what "being knocked for a loop" means. And I like it!* "Shall we go?" she said as she took her coat off the hook.

"Yes, indeed," Benjamin had replied as he helped her put on her coat.

The dinner began a little awkwardly, with Victoria asking the server many questions and giving detailed instructions on how the meal should be cooked. Benjamin simply ordered a steak, cooked medium, which worried her. *Does he think I am too obsessive with all these specifications?* She was sure he must have noticed after their food arrived when she tried as subtly as possible to separate the various food items on her plate so they would not touch each other.

Benjamin did not display any reaction she could observe, but she did not trust her ability to tell. Before long, they were just eating, wrapped up in their usual banter, and her worries faded. It was the same comfortable conversation as their phone calls, with the bonus that he was gazing at her with those lovely blue eyes.

The one tricky part of the evening came at the end when Benjamin asked if he could take her picture. Victoria hated getting photographed. She was always conscious of everything that was not just right with how she looked, and a picture would preserve those flaws in vivid detail forever. However, when he prevailed upon her and explained how much it would mean to him to have this memento, she could not deny it to him. In the end, even she admitted to being pleased with her appearance on seeing the picture on his phone.

Overall, it was a satisfactory first date.

****

For the second date, Benjamin had driven up from Quantico early on a Sunday morning and picked her up at her apartment. After a lovely brunch at a Bethesda café, they took the Metro to the Smithsonian. The Metro system was lightly traveled on Sunday mornings, not as terrifying as usual. They had strolled through the National Museum of American History and the West Building of the National Gallery of Art. As they walked along the Mall afterward, Victoria noticed and pointed out a middle-aged man taking their picture. Benjamin took her hand gently off his arm, patted it, and said, "Wait here." The man looked concerned as Benjamin approached and began the conversation with, "Hello, friend. What are you doing?" After a few moments of quiet discussion, the man began showing his pictures, stopping on one when Benjamin smiled and beckoned to her. "I like this one, and he has agreed to sell me a digital copy. What do you think?" he said, showing her the image that became the picture on her desk.

"I like it, too," she said.

"Twenty bucks, and I have full rights?" Ben asked the man.

"Certainly. I'll IM it to you now. Would you like more?"

"Yes," Victoria interrupted. "I would like one just of him, please." She recognized the man had an excellent sense of lighting and pose.

"Done. Could you stand over here, please?" he asked Benjamin, who awkwardly complied. The comical expression on Benjamin's face led her to suppress a laugh—the situation discomforted him for some reason she could not fathom. Finally, the frustrated photographer said, "Relax, man. Think of how much pleasure your girl will get from this." Benjamin looked at her, she smiled at him and his face thawed. Click! She nodded her approval when the photographer showed her the result. "OK, now how about one of you?"

"No! No, no, no." She shook her head firmly. What would he do with her image after he had it? The thought of it spreading over the Internet filled her with horror. *No wonder Benjamin had been so nervous. I should never have asked him for that. What a clingy thing to do!*

"These two will do, thank you," Benjamin said as he stepped over and gave her a brief hug across her shoulders. He paid the man $40, and they resumed their walk.

After a couple of minutes, she worked up the nerve to tell him. "I dislike strangers taking my picture. That is why I was so upset."

"You don't need to explain it to me. I don't like having my picture taken at all. That's why I behaved like a doofus when he was lining up mine. He won me over by reminding me it was for you." Benjamin squeezed her hand, and with palpable relief, she leaned into him and rested her head on his upper arm as they walked. She had never felt this way with anyone and had difficulty identifying the emotion. Safe, that was it. She felt safe when he was with her, despite being in this frighteningly public place with its crowds and noise and disorder. None of the terrors could touch her while he was with her.

They continued their walk for another hour, ending at the Smithsonian Metro station. The ride back was far less peaceful than the ride down. Weekend sightseers crowded both the stations and the trains at this time of day. Their car seemed filled with screaming, unruly children by the second stop, and

Victoria could do nothing but face downward with her eyes closed, trying at least to reduce the visual stimulation. She felt the oxygen being depleted in the car, her chest tightening and heart-pounding, despite Benjamin's presence. Victoria desperately wanted to flee, but was afraid Benjamin would be disappointed in her lack of fortitude. Then there was a spine-tingling child's shriek, during which her grip on his arm reflexively tightened so much she feared she had caused a bruise. He leaned over at once and whispered, "Look, I'm embarrassed to admit this, but my claustrophobia is getting to me. Do you mind if we jump at the next station and take a cab the rest of the way?"

"No, not at all," she replied. They rose at the next stop, and Benjamin positioned himself between her and the little demons as they left. A short walk through the station returned them to the sunshine and air one could breathe in safety. They stopped outside the station entrance, and she hugged him and buried her face in his chest.

He stroked her back and said, "Thank you for being so understanding. I can usually keep it together better than that. I don't know what came over me."

You are lying, Benjamin. You noticed I was nervous at the station, but you did not want to embarrass me by asking if we should leave. You held out as long as you could without intervening until you saw I was about to break down, and you saved me from that. Now you are worried I will be humiliated, so you are trying to save me from that too. Are you doing this because you feel something for me? Or is it because you are a good and kind man and feel sorry for me? She looked up at him and forced a smile. "That is alright, Benjamin. I am nervous in confined spaces too and was relieved you suggested we step out."

"No harm done then," he said with a wink. "It's been hours since brunch. Would you like to grab dinner here before we get that cab?" He motioned toward an Italian café across the street.

"Yes, I would like that very much."

"*D'accordo, andiamo, la mia bella signora!*"

"Do you speak Italian, Benjamin?"

"Only the important words, Victoria."

The dinner was delicious, and Victoria regained her feeling of complete safety as they rode in the cab back up to Bethesda station, her head resting on Benjamin's shoulder as he held her close. After the short ride in his car, they were back at her apartment door, and he looked into her eyes tenderly as he held her hands in his. *Ask me if you can stay. Please, Benjamin! I do not want this day to end!*

"Victoria, I, um...." He gazed longingly at her for a few seconds, then looked down. After another moment, he held her eyes again. "I had a great time today. Thank you."

"Yes, I did too." She willed herself not to cry. "I hope I can see you again soon."

"Yes. Definitely. As soon as possible. Goodnight, Victoria."

"Goodnight, Benjamin." She reached up and kissed him fully on the lips. After a few seconds, Victoria pulled back, then stepped inside the apartment and closed the door. She sat on the floor, oblivious to the fact that you are not supposed to sit on the floor, pulled up her legs, and put her chin on her knees. *OK, he* was *just being kind because he felt sorry for me. I will not cry!* And then, of course, she cried. About half a minute later, a knock on the door startled her. She stood slowly, reeled to the door, and looked out the peephole. She gasped and fumbled with the lock and wrenched the door open. "Benjamin!"

He stood in the doorway with a serious expression on his face. "Victoria, I'm sorry, but I can't leave it like this. I want to be with you. I know it's unfair to lay this on you so late at night and then run out at oh-dark-thirty tomorrow. But after today, I want to have every moment I can with you. If you don't feel the same, I'll understand, and I'll go, but I had to tell you."

She stepped up to him, put her arms around his neck, and pressed her head onto his chest, listening to his deep breaths and pounding heart while blinking away her tears. After a minute, she hugged him tightly, then took his hand, led him inside, and closed the door.

It was the most perfect of days.

****

She almost jumped out of her seat when the phone buzzed on her desk. She checked and made sure it was Benjamin's number, then waited. It would appear clingy if it seemed like she was waiting by the phone.

After the second ring, she waited three seconds, took a deep breath to steady her voice, and punched the "Answer" button. "Hello, Benjamin," she said calmly.

"Hello, Victoria. How was your day?"

Part II

The Mission

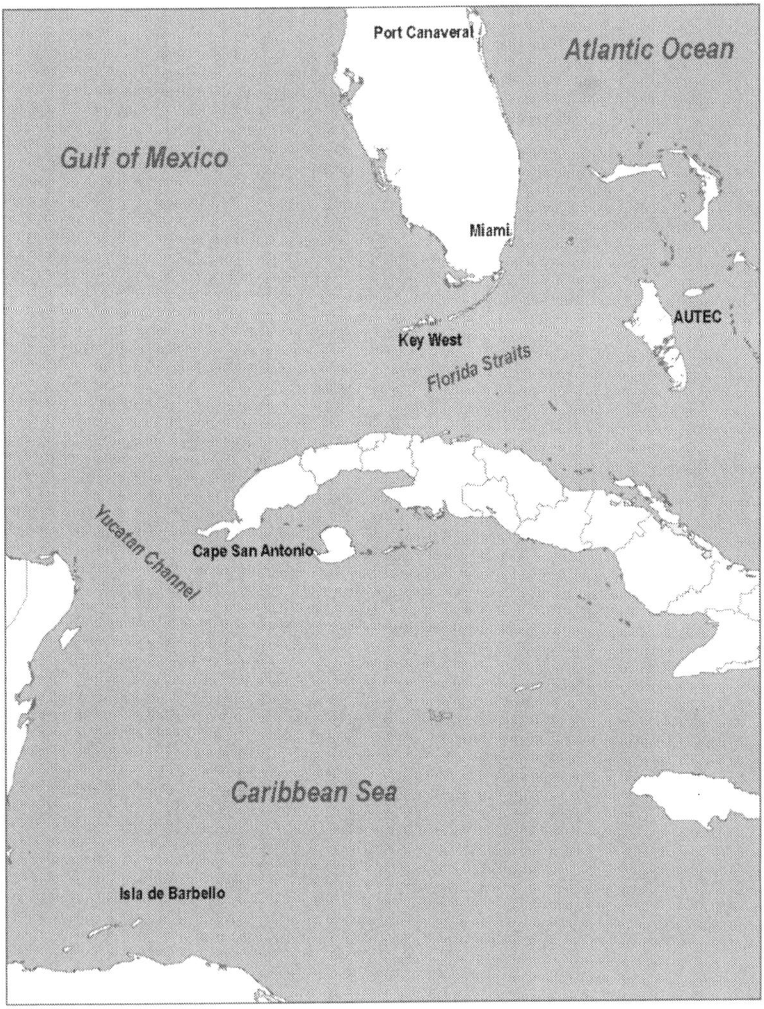
Port Canaveral
Atlantic Ocean
Gulf of Mexico
Miami
AUTEC
Key West
Florida Straits
Yucatan Channel
Cape San Antonio
Caribbean Sea
Isla de Barbello

9

The Offspring of Necessity

Office of the Commander, US Southern Command, Doral, Florida
08:17 EDT, 3 April

Pennington

Rear Admiral Horatio "Harry" Pennington, USCG, Director, Joint Interagency Task Force South, had just arrived in the office with his Executive Assistant, Commander Daniel Keener, USCG, after the three-and-a-half-hour drive from Key West. Air Force Chief Master Sergeant Charles Shipley, who served as SOUTHCOM's administrative assistant, stood and saluted smartly, with Pennington nodding in return. "Good Morning, Admiral," he said. "The general requests you go right in, please." Turning to Keener, he continued, "I'm sorry, Commander, but it's principals only for this meeting."

"Sorry, Dan," Pennington said. "I'll back-brief you when we're done."

"Yes, sir," the officer replied.

"Please come with me, sir," Shipley said. He walked over to a set of heavy wooden double doors, knocked, opened the door, and stuck in his head. "Admiral Pennington is here, sir."

"Bring him in, please."

Shipley held open the door as Pennington entered the room and then closed it behind him as he departed. Pennington snapped to attention at the sight of his superior and said, "Good morning, General!"

"Good morning, Harry! Relax, please," General Lamont Miller said as he came around the table with his right hand outstretched. The army four-star general leading Southern Command was six-foot-five and 245 pounds of solid muscle. The only difference between his appearance today and thirty-six years before as a middle linebacker on the University of Tennessee Volunteers was his shaven head and the wrinkles gained from years of standing in the sun in the commander's cupolas of M2 Bradley Fighting Vehicles and M1A1 Main Battle Tanks. "I'm real sorry to drag your ass all the way up here on no notice. How was the drive?" he continued with a noticeable Tennessee accent as he warmly shook the admiral's hand.

"No problem, sir," Pennington replied. "It was long but productive. Although I'll need a wrist brace—I haven't signed that many papers since the last time I bought a house!" The physical contrast between the two men was notable. At five-foot-ten and 175 pounds, Pennington was not a small man but seemed so next to the big general. His full head of short-cropped graying brown hair and round metal-rimmed glasses provided more of a professor look than an athlete.

"Yea verily, bubba," Miller chuckled. "Come on over here, so we can read you in on JUBILEE," he said as he put an arm around Pennington and guided him to the large table where four people were standing. "You know Fred, of course." Pennington recognized the Coast Guard Seventh District Commander, fellow Rear Admiral Fred Brown, but was unfamiliar with the female Captain at his side or the two other people, one female and one male, both in civilian clothes. The female was older, about his age, and her face seemed familiar, but he could not put the finger on where he had seen her. The younger man was unfamiliar to him.

"Hello, Fred," Pennington said, shaking the man's hand. "It's good to see you."

"Likewise, Harry," Brown said. "This is Jane Mercier, my Response Chief."

"Captain, I'm glad to meet you." Pennington shook her hand. "I've heard lots of good things."

"Thank you, sir," Mercier replied.

"OK, on to the new folks," Miller said, steering him down the table. "I don't believe you know Vice Admiral Jennifer Irving, Director of the DIA?"

"How do you do, ma'am," Pennington said, shaking her hand. *Aha! That's where I've seen her.*

"Pleased to meet you, Admiral," Irving replied. "May I introduce one of my DCS officers, Dr. Peter

Simmons? He'll be providing the Flag Brief this morning."

"Doctor," Pennington said, shaking Simmons's hand. *DIA? Holy shit, what the hell is going on here?*

"OK, let's get started," Miller said as he and everyone but Simmons moved to sit down. "Harry, you're both the last one to the table on this and the guy carrying the ball. Sorry about that." As Pennington nodded, Miller turned to Simmons and said, "Take it away, Doc."

"Thank you, sir," Simmons said. "Admiral, we have a situation involving a WMD falling into the hands of a Central American drug cartel."

Pennington's eyes widened, and his mouth opened in shock and then closed. He looked at Irving and Miller, receiving a nod from each. "Well, Doctor Simmons, it looks like nobody will accuse you of burying the lede. Is this speculation or known?"

"It's known, sir," Simmons replied. "Admiral, we're pressed for time. May I proceed, please?"

"Yes."

"Thank you, sir. Are you familiar with the 252 Syndicate?"

"Unfortunately, yes." Pennington nodded. "They are coming up more and more these days."

"Yes, sir." Simmons nodded in sympathy. "The night before last, one of their mid-level bosses suddenly appeared at Miami International after flying in from Grand Cayman. He was immediately tagged when passing through customs, and we put a tail on him until we could get a snatch team together. We bagged him in his hotel room just before dawn yesterday and interrogated him here."

"Why you? Why not the FBI?" Pennington asked.

"The 252s are a TCO operating outside the U.S.—that puts them in our lane. We didn't want him to get away while the Bureau and we were locked in a jurisdictional turf war, so we went ahead and grabbed him. Anyway, he was the lead 252 man for their South America operations, working out of a converted Offshore Petroleum Support Vessel in Venezuela. This ship doubled as a mobile laboratory for the 252s' chemical weapons development program.

"The 252s have been in the contract killing business since they were formed. They recently started using a line of Novichok knock-offs to support that. The Russians persuaded them to abandon that particular horror and develop their own line since we naturally associate any Novichok deaths with Moscow. The 252s hired a biochemical genius with a psychopathic streak and located the lab outside Europe to avoid tangling with the Bear. Things got interesting when the Colombian Army clobbered the 252s' cocaine vendor in Colombia, and they went looking for a new one. According to the 252 man, he struck a deal with the Salinas Cartel for a significant load," he paused as Pennington rolled his eyes. "I see you have heard of them, sir."

"Yes, they're the new kids on the block in the Western Caribbean. What they lack in brains and organization, they make up for in arms and sadistic violence. It's surprising the 252s would have anything to do with them."

"This 252 guy we picked up did not strike me as one of their rocket scientists, and, true to form, the Salinas mob double-crossed them as soon as their ship pulled into Barbello. At last report, they had killed the security guys and were holding the crew and the biochemist heading the lab for ransom."

Pennington looked around the table. "I don't know about you folks, but I'm having a hard time seeing a downside here. The 252s got a black eye, and the Salinas crowd is about to get an education in choosing your enemies."

"Well, sir," Simmons said. "I would agree with you. It's hard to get worked up about 252s and Salinas killing each other. However, the problem is that the resident genius has cooked up a new super-lethal nerve agent in the lab and the prototype rig for mass production. It has the lethality, safe handling, and self-cleaning characteristics that make it highly marketable as a large-scale battlefield munition rather than just an assassination weapon."

"Wait a minute," Pennington said. "The 252s already have this thing, right? I can see the worry, but what can we do at this point?"

"No, sir." Simmons shook his head. "The 252s were seriously afraid of the Russians, so they isolated everything on the boat. Even the lab's computers are air-gapped. Apparently, our 252 guy thought the cocaine pipeline was his primary mission and moved the boat closer to the source of supply. That would be a sound business approach with sane vendors, but it was a big mistake with the Salinas crowd. He knows this now and is singing like a canary to us, trying to stay alive. The bottom line is all the 252 eggs are in that basket, and they need it back. Within a few days, they'll have enough force gathered to go in and get it, and they won't give a damn about hostage casualties or collateral damage.

"But that isn't even the worst case. We also have to consider what would result if the 252's attack fails. The Salinas survivors would certainly turn on the biochemists and extract the secret of the nerve agent. What then? They are even more vicious than the 252s, and the possibilities of them wielding a WMD are too horrific to think about."

As Simmons paused, Pennington looked over at Miller. "It sounds like we need to blow that ship to Hell, sir," he said. "That's more your lane than mine."

Miller shook his head. "No, Harry. Besides the foreign relations disaster of our pounding a nominally friendly country with an airstrike, we can't take a chance on releasing that agent. Imagine a mass casualty event involving both chemical weapons and our bombs. Even if they are all cartel scumbags, we'd be international pariahs. There has to be another way."

Pennington's face quickly shifted to disbelief. "Sir, it sounds like you are talking about a cutting-out operation." He looked around the table. "What do you think this is, the War of 1812? Have any of you seen the charts on Barbello? I read through everything we have on the way here. It's impossible! Nothing we have bigger than a PB could get within half a mile of that rock, and the Salinas's weapons' coverage of the only entrance into the harbor is solid. They'd pick up on anything we send in before it got within a mile. Even if we could get an assault team in there without getting detected, they would get swarmed as soon as they lit off the diesels on that ship. Success would require a high-firepower assault that would be no different from an airstrike, except a lot of our guys would probably get killed."

"And if you had an asset with stealth capability?" Miller pressed.

Pennington scoffed, "Sir, if I had something with a low radar cross-section that was silent and could tow that ship out of RPG range before the need to start its engines, it might be possible. But I know of nothing like that anywhere, much less in theater."

Miller turned to Brown. "Fred?"

"Harry," Brown began. "We have an asset available that might meet your requirements."

"You're not serious!"

"I am. I'll let Jane explain. It's her baby."

"Do tell, Captain," Pennington said warily.

"Yes, sir," Mercier began. "You might recall about a year and a half ago when *Kauai* had that mishap during the last Cuban migrant surge?"

"Yes, her CO and XO were relieved for cause."

"The CO was, sir. The XO went out on a medical because of injuries during the mishap. We took a long look at the unit to see if it was better to salvage it or just bump up her scheduled decommissioning a couple of years. The hull was in good shape, and she had the gun the new patrol boats are getting, so we hung on to her. We identified some solid command cadre and rushed them on board. Things were turning around nicely, so we went all-in on an experimental Special Ops capability. If it didn't work out, no harm, no foul. So, we stacked the deck with the crew and ended up with a very smart unit.

"So, fast forward to January. You remember that sailboat drug seizure that happened north of the Keys?"

"Yes, I remember that." Pennington acknowledged the information. "It was almost a record seizure. Wrecked in a storm was the story."

"Yes, sir. That was the cover story. It was actually a 252 smuggling boat, wrecked when a nuclear-tipped Russian Kinzhal hypersonic missile impacted right next to it."

"*What?* The Russians launched on us?"

Mercier nodded to Simmons, who said, "It was an accident, sir. Do you recall how tense things were over Kaliningrad back then? They were saber-rattling with a Backfire off Miami when it got bumped by an F-16, triggering an uncommanded launch. We lost track of the missile almost immediately. We knew it hadn't detonated and did not know where it ended up other than it did not impact on land. Needless to say, it was in everyone's best interest to pretend nothing happened, but also to keep an eye out for anything unusual along the missile's track. The 252 boat got creamed by the kinetic energy of the impact, but the product it was carrying in sealed containers kept the wreck afloat. It drifted for about three days before being spotted by an HC-144 flying out of Miami and then boarded by *Kauai*'s crew.

"*Kauai* provided a very detailed description of the wreck's condition that immediately drew our attention. Within a day, I confirmed that this was an artifact of the impact. Admiral Brown had already detached *Kauai* from her drug patrol to help search for the warhead. Thanks to a clever off-label application of the SAROPS search planning tool suggested by the boat's XO, we narrowed down the search target list. After a focused, hard-target search for a few more days, we located the impact site just off Resolution Key. Unfortunately, the 252s picked up our trail, and we had to shoot it out with them."

"Let me guess," Pennington began. "That 'F-22 Crash' on Resolution was another cover story?"

"Yes, sir." Simmons nodded. "It provided an excellent account for the fire and smoke and subsequent restricted area. We picked up the warhead and any missile fragments we could find offshore, sanitized any trace of the fight with the 252 men, and salted the site with a few banged-up and scorched F-22 parts 'missed by the search' in case someone was curious enough to dig around. As far as we know, it worked. There is nothing in the news, and we have seen nothing online other than the usual 'tinfoil hat brigade' ravings that go with any plane crash."

"Impressive duplicity. You were obviously the right people for the job," Pennington said, then turned to Mercier. "So, how does that incident play into this discussion, Captain?"

"It was pure luck, *Kauai* being the one to find that wreck, sir. If it hadn't been her, we would have gotten her underway to take over. Anyway, there were about a dozen ways that the crew could have fouled up on that mission, but they performed perfectly. The officers, in particular, carried off some brilliant and gutsy moves."

"I'll second that, Admiral, if you'll excuse the interruption, Captain," Simmons said. "I was there throughout the mission, and I wouldn't be here now if it weren't for them. No one could've done that one better."

"Thank you, Doctor." Mercier nodded again. "The Director of National Intelligence agreed and invested about fifty million dollars on upgrades to move *Kauai* from a proof of concept to a standing special operations capability. We rushed her through a yard period that replaced her main plant with electric motors, high-capacity generators, and battery bank using the new Lithium-ion batteries the Japanese are using in their latest *Soryu*-class subs. She can do up to twenty knots with no sound other than the props for two hours. We also upgraded the Bridge and sensors, added composite armor resistant up to fifty-caliber, and cut her radar cross-section to about what you'd see on a Response Boat, Small."

Pennington was incredulous. "How did you manage that?"

"Mainly coatings, sir. But we also replaced the mast with a composite design."

"And this capability is available now?"

"Yes, sir." Mercier nodded. "She's just finishing workups and fine-tuning at AUTEC. I can get her moving this morning, and she can be off Barbello in as little as two-and-a-half days."

"What about the crew? This shindig will not be a day at the regatta. We're talking about close combat, even if everything goes right."

"We'll get a SEAL team to handle the assault," Miller interjected. "*Kauai* will need to tow the boat out of range."

"Yes, sir," Mercier continued. "Plus, we put the XO, two boatswain mates, and the gunner's mate through the boat assault team course at Quantico and Little Creek while *Kauai* was in the shipyard. Whoever we send over can look after themselves and do the ship-handling on the target vessel while the SEALs do the heavy lift neutralizing the opposition."

"Sounds like you have this all figured out," Pennington said with resignation. "What do you need me for?"

"They'll be under your command, Harry," Miller said. "Barbello is a law enforcement concern, and, as far as everyone outside this room is concerned, it stays that way. DoD has practically nothing on the Salinas Cartel and nothing at all on the ground on Barbello.

We need you to work your Drug Enforcement and Customs people to provide the Intel prep."

"What about our Honduran liaison? Do I bring him in on this?" Pennington asked.

Miller shook his head firmly. "Absolutely not. No foreign nationals are to have even a hint that this op is going on, and keep it to the absolute minimum among our guys. Do whatever you need to do to make sure of that. If you feel the need to move the op out of your HQ because of all the foreign presence, Fred assures me Sector Key West can fix you up."

Pennington said, "OK, sir. Now, other than this wonder boat, what can you give me?"

Miller nodded, "We'll have twenty-four-hour Global Hawk coverage and one Rivet Joint sortie monitoring emissions each night until the assault to generate a pattern of life. For the op itself, we'll have the RJ for Command and Control, an MQ-9 for EO/IR, and a SEAL team for the actual assault—they'll be flying into Key West this afternoon to meet with your staff to work out the plan. If they go in with *Kauai*, they can board when she's topping off in Key West. Otherwise, they can launch from there."

"Any chance of naval support, sir?" Pennington asked. "I lost my last destroyer about a week ago."

"Nothing I can get down there in time," Miller replied. "What's your situation with the Coast Guard cutters?"

"Three two-seventies and one two-ten are in theater. Not much help in this situation compared to a destroyer, but better than nothing." Pennington smiled ruefully. "While we are on the subject, sir, where are we supposed to sail this thing, assuming we can cut her out?"

"An interesting question," Miller replied. "Over to you, Jenn." He looked at Irving.

"Admiral, your orders are to sail her north until you cross the five-hundred-fathom line of the Cayman Trench and then scuttle her," Irving said.

"What?" Pennington said in astonishment.

"This comes straight from the president. With everything else going on, he doesn't want that boat turned into a cause célèbre. That location's deep enough so that no one can get at her or what's onboard without a major, obvious effort. Our intel is that the precursors of the agent are harmless and water-soluble. Even if they get mixed somehow on the way down, they'll hydrolyze quickly. Dr. Simmons will accompany the assault team to ensure any documents and computer data are destroyed. If the creator is still alive, he'll take him into custody. Hopefully, we can drop the boat at night before anyone gets any pictures."

"But what about the data on the agent? Are we just going to let that go?" Pennington sputtered.

Irving nodded. "Admiral, this is something we wouldn't dare use or even study. The costs of keeping it secret are immense, and if it got loose, the consequences would be catastrophic. Far better to be rid of it."

"Hmm. Did I miss something? What happens with casualties? Barbello is eight hundred miles from any of our bases, and there's nothing more than a battle dressing station and a single health services petty officer on our ships. We need combat medical support standing by."

"That's an unnecessary security risk. We don't expect anything that can't be handled locally." Irving waved a hand dismissively. "These are SEALs we are sending in, after all."

"Oh, for God's sake, Admiral!" Pennington responded with open irritation. "The Salinas crowd are nuts. If they once pick up on that operation, they'll unload everything they have on it with a religious fury. If that happens, there will be wounded, regardless of how awesome the SEALs are." He turned to Miller. "I won't throw away lives, sir!"

"What do you suggest, Harry?" Miller tilted his head. "We don't have any carriers available, and the air force Jollies can't reach that far, even with tanking. This is one of those times we may have to roll the dice."

"I don't accept that, sir." Pennington shook his head. "What about the Special Ops Ospreys up at Hurlburt Field?"

Miller shook his head. "Sorry, Harry, no time to get them lined up and down there through the usual channels, and we can't fast track anything without blowing the cover on this op. Even if we could, it would be a miracle to pull it off in two days."

Pennington turned to Brown. "Give me two of the Jayhawks out of Clearwater, Fred, and I can lily-pad them down and back on the two-seventies. It's risky, but a helluva lot better than just writing off the casualties."

"Consider it done." Brown nodded.

"I'll call up to Fort Benning after we adjourn and get a combat surgeon and a couple of surgical medics on a plane to Key West, and they can ride down on *Kauai*," Miller added.

"Good." Pennington looked at his folder. "Good." After a few seconds, he looked up again at Miller. "Is that all, sir?"

"Yes, Harry. I'm putting my J3 staff at your disposal. They'll coordinate the DoD stuff and iron out any wrinkles. Can I offer you my Blackhawk for the trip back? An hour flight is better than three more hours on the road."

Pennington thought briefly, then replied, "Thank you, General. Mind if I use it to get to AUTEC instead?"

Miller sat back. "OK, if that's what you want." He gave Pennington a stern look. "Are you sure that's a good idea?"

Pennington nodded. "If I'm going to send those kids into a buzzsaw, I will give it to them face-to-face. The staffs can handle any planning without my kibbitzing, and my EA can hang around here to provide a direct liaison with your J3." He smiled sadly and turned to Mercier. "Besides, I'm curious about this wonder boat and would like to see what it can do firsthand. They'll have to stage out of Key West—I'll just ride over with them."

"OK, Harry," Miller said. "I don't suppose it would take if I gave you any advice about getting too personal."

"No, sir."

"Didn't think so." He looked around the table. "Well, let's get'r done then." As Miller rose, the rest of them followed and stood at attention. "Carry on, thank you."

The group filed out after handshakes all around, with Pennington bringing up the rear. He stopped at the desk and motioned Keener over, and he turned to the standing administrative assistant. "Chief, any chance of getting a private office with a secure phone?"

"Yes, sir," Shipley replied. "The general thought you might need one. Specialist Folsom here will escort you and get it set up. When would the admiral like the helicopter to be ready to depart?"

"An hour from now?" Pennington responded with a raised eyebrow.

"Very good, sir. Is there anything else I can do for the admiral?"

"No, thank you, Chief." He turned to the saluting specialist. "Thank you. Lead on, please."

As the specialist led them out, Keener turned to Pennington. "Helicopter, sir?"

"Yes, I'll be heading to AUTEC. The bad news is you still have a three-hour car ride back to the office. The good news is I'm sparing you a fifteen-hour boat ride," Pennington said, his gaze fixed ahead as they walked.

"Yes, sir."

10

Return on Investment

USCG Cutter *Kauai*, AUTEC Weapons Range, off Andros Island, Bahamas
10:04 EDT, 3 April

Ben

When the message arrived, *Kauai* was nearing the turning point at the end of the radar sensor range. Ben had the OOD watch with Zuccaro monitoring navigation and sensors and, by default, the message center on the FC3 console. "XO, incoming operational immediate message."

"Right, standby." Ben waited another minute to clear the southernmost buoy, then turned to the helmsman. "Left ten degrees rudder, steady on three-five-three, belay passing headings."

"Left ten degrees rudder, steady on three-five-three, belay passing headings, aye, sir."

Kauai listed slightly to the right in the gentle left turn, and Ben took one last scan to port as a final safety check, then strode to the FC3 console to read the message. Sent by the Seventh District Commander in Miami, it immediately ended the testing operation and transferred *Kauai*'s operational control to JIATF-South. If that were not surprising enough, they were to return to port at AUTEC at once and meet Admiral Pennington himself at the AUTEC Command Building and transport him to Key West. With raised eyebrows, he lifted the telephone and called Sam. “Captain, we received incoming immediate tasking you will not believe. Could you come to the Bridge, please, sir?”

“On the way,” Sam replied. He arrived on the Bridge a minute later and walked straight over to the console.

“Captain on the Bridge,” Ben announced.

“Thank you, carry on, please.” Sam sat at the console to read the message as Ben resumed his OOD duties. When Sam finished, he walked over to Ben for a quiet conversation. “The DARPA guys won’t like this one bit.”

“From the tone of that message, I don’t think we’ll be high-fiving either, sir.”

“Well, it is what it is. Let’s set the Special Sea Detail and return to port. Now that we’re suspending testing, who’s in the rotation for the mooring?”

“Bondurant, sir. He was planning to let Lee try with him over-the-shoulder.”

"Sorry, but not today," Sam said as he glanced back at the console. "Get things rolling while I break the news to the head geek." As he strode aft, he stopped and turned with a smile. "And when you contact Harbor Control, be sure to say *please*."

Ben smiled back as he picked up the microphone for the 1MC public address system. "It's what I live for, Captain!" He keyed the microphone. "Now, discontinue all testing and secure test gear. Set the Special Sea Detail for entering port."

****

An hour-and-a-half later, Sam, Ben, and Hopkins were hurrying toward the Command Building in fresh, tropical blue uniforms. If it hadn't left them disheveled and sweaty, they would have been running—junior officers and chiefs do not keep admirals waiting longer than necessary.

There was no question Pennington had arrived. An army helicopter made several orbits of *Kauai* on her way in, and there was a two-star admiral's flag flying on the flagpole near the building. Hopkins had left Lee and Zuccaro rummaging through *Kauai*'s flag locker to rig a similar display once the admiral came aboard. The three quickly passed through the reception desk to the center's sensitive compartmented information facility and were ushered in by a navy sailor. They stood at attention as Pennington came around the table to greet them.

"Carry on, please. Hoppy, is that you?" Pennington asked with a smile. "My God, what a terrific surprise. How are you?" He stepped up and shook her hand.

"I'm fine, thank you, Admiral."

Pennington turned to Sam and held out his hand. "I hope you'll forgive the breach of protocol, Lieutenant. But Hoppy and I were shipmates on the *Escanaba*. Do you go by Sam or Samuel?"

Sam shook Pennington's hand. "Sam, sir. May I present my XO, Ben Wyporek?"

Pennington shook Ben's hand, "Pleased to meet you, Ben. I've heard some pretty amazing things about both of you guys."

"Likewise, sir," Ben said.

"Come over here and sit down, please." Pennington beckoned to the table. "Before we start, I will be talking at the Top Secret level." He directed a glance toward Hopkins.

"We are all cleared and read in, sir," Sam said.

"Outstanding. Well, your old friends, the 252 Syndicate, have been very naughty. They have been employing a converted offshore petroleum supply vessel as a lab to create chemical weapons. They were doing a good job keeping a low profile until a couple of days ago. Then they got themselves in a jam—landed in the middle of a drug war, and now the boat and their lead chemist are hostages. The boat is being held in Barbello, just north of Roatan." He pulled a high-resolution chart from a leather case on the table, and they all stood to look at it. "The island is an ancient volcanic caldera, with the remaining topography roughly crescent-shaped. It has an almost enclosed lagoon, with the buildings and quay here." He pointed at the center of the interior shoreline. "It's all shoal water except for a channel leading into the lagoon, passing a quarter-mile south of this point."

Sam looked at the chart in deep thought. "Yes, sir, I remember. When I was assigned to *Spencer*, we staked it out for a few days. Good harbor, not much else. We thought it was a drug transshipment point, but nothing came of it." He looked at Pennington again. "Who grabbed them, sir?"

"An outfit called the Salinas Cartel."

"Are they new, sir? I don't remember hearing that name."

"Yes, they're oozing up to the top in Honduras and Guatemala. They're really bad news. Think of a gang of a hundred guys too sadistic for MS-13 standing up a drug-funded death cult. Anyway, they are about to get some genuine experience in total war. The 252s don't take insults or prisoners."

"Sir, why us?" Sam asked. "I mean, Delta Force or the SEALs would be the right choice for a rescue mission."

"It's not a rescue, Sam. I wouldn't lift a finger to save those bastards, much less risk your lives. The problem is they have come up with a particularly nasty nerve agent, and we can't let that loose. We are sending you in there to tow it to deep water and scuttle it. What happens to any 252 scientists is incidental."

"I don't understand, sir. Surely, the 252s have everything now. What would it accomplish if we succeeded?"

"Great question." Pennington nodded. "They don't have it, according to the defector that brought us the news. They had run afoul of the Russians earlier, using knock-offs of their Novichok agents for assassinations. To keep the development a secret from them, they confined everything to the boat, even air-gapping the computers."

"Excuse me, Admiral," Sam interrupted. "Why not bomb the boat?"

"No, Sam, it's in Honduras territory. We can't launch an airstrike against a Central American country without provocation. Neither can we run a search and destroy commando raid that leaves a sunken ship at the dockside. And if that agent got loose and slimed the island, we would really be in trouble, even if we could prove we didn't create it."

"Sir, stealing a ship violates sovereignty too."

"Only if we're caught, Sam. The Hondurans ceded that island to the cartel—they have no presence there. We go in at night, steal the ship from a criminal organization who stole it from another criminal organization and dispose of it. We'll claim it held a classified weapon of mass destruction if called on it, which is perfectly true. Even if the Hondurans figure out it was us, a nasty problem is solved, and they still have plausible deniability. The 252s will hit that place and leave no one alive, anyway."

"Admiral, I suppose we could get in there undetected if we waited until moonset and used the batteries. But as soon as we hit that ship, all hell will break loose. We'll have a running fight from the moment we board until we clear the harbor. Assuming we aren't sunk before then."

"Sam, you think I would send you in alone?" Pennington shook his head. "There's a SEAL team en route to Key West as we speak. As you guys glide in there, they'll have taken the ship and discreetly knocked out any lighting on the quay. A Rivet Joint plane is heading in tonight and tomorrow night to read the pattern of life, patrols, and radio comms. During your penetration, they'll be there to control the ground force and keep you advised of any hostile activity. Your biggest challenge will be running the gauntlet of this point of land here." He pointed at the chart. "It's fortified and has an armed watch. But if you clear it before first light, there's a good chance you can slip by unseen and unheard." Pennington paused and scanned the faces across the table. They all focused on the chart before them and were long with worry. "Anything else?"

After a second, Sam looked up with a stony expression. "Yes, sir. What about casualties? It will be a miracle if no one is wounded. Given what you've told us, we can hardly cruise into a nearby port to put them in the hospital, and it's seven hundred miles easy to a US facility."

"You'll be taking an army combat surgeon and two medics on *Kauai*. I'm pre-positioning *Thetis* with a

Clearwater H-60 twenty miles away and *Northland* off Cozumel as a lily pad. It's five hours of flying from Barbello to the nearest trauma center in Miami, but the surgeon will stabilize any casualties before they're lifted."

"Yes, sir." Sam nodded, then continued. "Admiral, suppose the worst case happens, and they pop open our hull with a couple of RPGs. What's the contingency plan? I need to know my crew won't be sacrificed for nothing."

Pennington gave a solemn look. "In Key West, you will also take on board a pair of DIA agents who will destroy the agent precursors with thermite charges."

Sam scowled. "One of those DIA agents wouldn't be Peter Simmons, would it, sir?"

"Yes, I understand he was with you on the Resolution mission."

"That he was, sir," Sam continued. "He damn near got Ben killed twice. The second time I had to drive *Kauai* at flank speed through fog and shoal water to save Ben's and his asses and shoot up two civilian SUVs on U.S. soil to do it! He's not my number one favorite guy, sir."

Pennington nodded. "I understand, Sam. I assume I can rely on your professionalism to overcome your personal feelings regarding Dr. Simmons. Am I in error?"

"No, sir, I can do the job. I just need you to be aware of the nature of our relationship." He glanced at the others and then continued. "Admiral, can we take these charts out of the SCIF? We'll need them to devise approach and departure strategies."

"Yes, they're unclassified. But you need to keep them out of sight until you leave Key West."

"Yes, sir. Admiral, I would like a chance to discuss the op with Ben and Chief Hopkins, so they can begin planning. Could we keep the SCIF for half an hour?"

A sad smile spread across Pennington's face. He knew Sam's question was a politely coded request to get the hell out so they could talk openly about the load of crap just dumped on them. "Not a problem, Sam. It's mine for as long as I need it. I'll just have a chat with the CO while you're working. When you're done, send someone to fetch me."

"Yes, sir. You still want to ride with us to Key West?"

"Definitely." Pennington nodded. "I'm interested in a hands-on tour of your new setup."

"Sir," Sam said as he, Ben, and Hopkins stood at attention.

"Carry on, please. Thank you," Pennington said as he walked out and closed the door.

Sam turned to the others, who gazed back in silence. "Folks, things just got very, very real. Comments before we start?" Ben and Hopkins both shook their heads. "OK. We need to develop an approach doable in complete darkness using GPS and night-vision goggles only. Then we need an egress plan with a one-hundred-fifty-ton vessel in tow. Chief, that's yours."

"Yes, Captain."

"It handicaps us not knowing exactly where the ship is moored or its orientation, so have alternatives for both north and south."

"Yes, sir."

Sam turned to Ben. "Number One, your job will be planning the actual assault. We'll put that combat training to use now. I want you to pick your boarding team with the assumption that your guys will have to handle getting the tow rigged and casting off all mooring lines and shore ties. You might get help from the SEALs, but I wouldn't plan on it."

"Yes, sir. Should I bring an engineer to try lighting off the mains?" Ben asked.

"You can, as long as it's Brown. You'll need a lot of muscle to pull up the towing hawser. The engines can't be started anyway until we clear the harbor—can't take a chance on them being heard. They probably won't be available even then. If I were one of the cartel guys, I would sabotage the mains or remove a critical part so that the crew couldn't try anything.

"Yes, sir. It will be hard to plan anything before getting a sense of the boat's size and layout and its orientation on the quay. Maybe the admiral can help?"

"Definitely. I'll tell him we can't plan without it. Now, here's the deal as far as the rest of the crew goes. I'll pull COB aside and give him the bones of the plan so he can help us squelch any rumors. I know it's not our usual way, but I don't want any discussion of our destination or mission until after we leave Key West. We need to determine what everyone else will do before we finalize our role, and I don't want the crew to work themselves up on speculation. I expect a full mission briefing at JIATF-South, and it will be at least a day to Barbello, so we have plenty of time to fill everyone in en route. One benefit of hauling a flag officer around is everyone will focus on that rather than why we are hauling ass to Key West." He smiled as he looked at them. "Questions?"

"No, sir," both Ben and Hopkins said in reply.

"OK. I'll grab the admiral and meet you guys by the flagpole." He then turned and left.

Ben looked at Hopkins with a smile. "You continue to surprise, *Escanaba* shipmate!"

"Hey, I know people too, XO." She smiled back as she stuffed the charts into the leather case on the table.

Pennington

The Coast Guard party left the Command Building in a brisk walk toward the piers, with Sam and Pennington side-by-side in the lead and Ben and Hopkins behind them. When they reached *Kauai*, Pennington was piped aboard with proper ceremony by Drake and Bondurant. After a brief tour of the new engineering plant, he settled into the captain's chair on the Bridge. After an uneventful departure, the cutter set a north-northeast track toward the Northeast Providence Channel. They would follow it and then the Northwest Providence Channel into the Florida Straits off Fort Lauderdale. It was a lengthy roundabout route, but the only way available because of the vast shoals of the Great Bahama Bank west and north of Andros Island.

As soon as they cleared the harbor and set the regular watch, Sam took Pennington around the Bridge to point out the recent overhaul upgrades. He left the FC3 station's presentation to Williams, who provided a proud, hands-on demonstration of its capabilities. Finally, Sam ordered the diesel engines to shut down to show the electric motors using only battery power. As *Kauai* glided along at twelve knots, the only sound being a very slight hiss of the passing water, Pennington shook his head and turned to Sam.

"Amazing. It gives me the shivers scooting along like this without a sound or any vibration."

Sam chuckled. "Yes, sir. That was the common feeling for us the first couple of times." He then ordered up the full battery speed of twenty knots. *Kauai* was no longer silent as the intensity of the propeller thrumming sound and vibration increased.

"Full speed is definitely audible, but still pretty quiet. How far away can it be heard, Captain?" Pennington asked.

"On the surface, it's audible to the unaided ear at a maximum of one-hundred-fifty yards, sir," Sam said. "With an enhanced audio sensor, about five times that. Underwater, the blade beat carries much further, but we're still about as stealthy as you can be for a powered vessel."

"Remarkable. Can we adjourn to the cabin for a private chat? I'm interested in hearing a firsthand account of your adventure at Resolution."

"Yes, sir. Can you excuse me for a moment, please?"

"Of course."

Sam stepped over to Bondurant, who had the OOD watch, gave some last instructions, and returned. "Could you follow me, please, sir?"

"Right behind you."

After reaching the cabin, Sam shut the door, and they sat down facing each other. Sam led the discussion. "Sorry, sir. I'm sure we're more cramped than what you are used to."

"Nonsense. My first command was a PB."

"Really, sir? Which boat?"

"The good ship *Kauai*. I was the old girl's first CO." He paused as Sam's jaw dropped in silence. "No way I was passing up the chance for another ride."

"That's incredible, sir. I did not know. Is it bringing back memories?"

"Some. Mostly good ones, although a pre-commissioning detail has plenty of headaches."

"Yes, sir." Sam paused in thought. "Is there anything in particular you wanted to discuss, sir?"

"Yes. I wanted to avoid putting you on the spot in front of Ben and Hoppy, but I'm interested in your assessment of the mission and chances of success."

"Um, is this one of those 'tell truth to power' moments, sir, or would you prefer the rainbows and unicorns version?"

Pennington rocked his head back in a hearty laugh. "I guess I had that coming, Captain. I hope you can trust me enough to give me the former."

“Very good, sir.” Sam nodded. “A lot depends on where that ship is, exactly, and the defense measures the cartel guys are using. My sense is that they aren’t military geniuses, so they probably just have armed guards and a roving watch. If I were them, I’d put down an anchor. That would be game over for what we’re planning—we wouldn’t have time to weigh it or cut the chain before they swarmed us. But they’re not seamen, and they’re expecting either a payoff or a gunfight from the 252s, not a smash and grab. We’ll need up-to-date intel with visuals ASAP, sir.”

“We’re working that as we speak. Please continue.”

“Yes, sir. Then it depends on the SEALs. They must take out any cartel guys in the immediate area without raising the alarm. I don’t know how in hell they’ll do that, but I’ll take it on faith they’ll find a way. My guys can’t help. They’ll have their hands full for the first fifteen minutes, rigging the tow and unmooring the ship. A lot can happen in fifteen minutes, sir.

“So, assuming everything goes right, it will be about ninety minutes from ingress to egress. That is cutting it close on my battery charge life at full power, sir. Just saying.”

“I hear you, Captain. Do you think it might be prudent to light off at least one of your diesels after clearing the quay?”

“No, sir. I think I’ll push my luck. Anyone awake in that harbor would hear our starters, given the topography. I can light them all off quickly enough if things go south. We have drilled this pretty hard to knock down the time needed, and our last trial had it down to thirty-three seconds."

"I see. So, what's the bottom line here?"

"Sir, if we can work up to full speed on the tow without detection, we should get through, even if we have to shoot it out with that sentry post."

"And if you're detected before that?"

"In that case, I think the Servicemembers Group Life Insurance will make a pretty big payout this month, sir," Sam replied with a crooked smile. "But we'll buy enough time to torch that lab."

Pennington looked down for a moment. Then he looked up, leaned forward, and rested his right hand lightly on Sam's shoulder. "Thank you, Captain."

11

Assemble and Sortie

USCG Cutter *Kauai*, Moored, Truman Annex, Naval Air Station, Key West, Florida
08:33 EDT, 4 April

Ben

Berthing at the Truman Annex was a novel experience for *Kauai*—they usually moored half a mile to the northeast at the Coast Guard Sector at Trumbo Point. However, they carried the Director of JIATF-South himself, and his office was here, so the accommodation was made. At least, that was the story. One of the most secret pre-mission briefings in history was about to occur, involving various *Kauai* crew members and the JIATF-South staff, among others. Proper operations security argued against a lot of traveling back and forth.

Once Pennington was piped ashore, *Kauai* started the regular activities for a mid-patrol in-port period. Ben cleared paperwork and personnel issues and met and settled the first of their guests, army Major Shane Roberts, the combat surgeon, and his team of two surgical nurses and their equipment. They showed no concern about *Kauai*'s messdeck's close quarters as the operating room's venue. Ben suspected, correctly, that they had seen much worse in Southwest Asia. He left them in the capable hands of Bryant, who was a former army combat medic himself.

Drake supervised the topping off of the cutter's diesel fuel and water supplies, then moved on to the special mission preparations Sam had ordered. The Squid launcher unit, useless for the task to come, was detached and stored ashore for their return in a few days. The gasoline for the RHIB, stored on deck in a jettisonable fifty-five-gallon drum to reduce the risk of an internal fire, was also put ashore. Sam did not expect any small boat operations, and the gasoline was a dangerous source of fire and illumination if hit by hostile gunfire. Guerrero supervised the replacement of the twenty-five-millimeter ammunition they had expended at AUTEC and the rest of their solid rounds with high-explosive shells. These were more suitable for suppressing the small arms and rocket-firing opposition they expected to encounter. Along with the *Kauai*'s two junior seamen, Bondurant and Lee managed the special towing hawser's on-load and layout for the mission.

By 11:30, the preparations were complete, and the crew took a breather. This was accompanied by a surprise as a taxi pulled up to *Kauai's* berth and deposited Seaman Juan Lopez, freshly graduated from the Maritime Law Enforcement Specialist School in Charleston, South Carolina. Lopez was a solid hand before he left, and Sam and Ben were delighted to have him back aboard for the challenging mission. Ben led the greetings. "Glad to see you back, Lope, but I think you might regret not hanging around for the graduation blow-out."

"Sir, you don't think I'm going to be OK sitting around drinking beer while you guys are headed into action?"

Sam's face froze in a half-smile. "What makes you think that?"

"Captain, I've seen the towing hawser. You've also offloaded that net cannon and the gasoline—no reason to do that before a normal patrol. Finally, you've pulled in here instead of Trumbo Point, where we always stage. Something very unusual is going on here."

Sam looked at Ben. "I guess we should have pulled in and out in the dark. I'll keep that in mind for the next one." He looked back at Lopez and smiled. "I can't confirm or deny anything, but do me a favor and keep it to yourself for now. We'll give everybody the full story once we're underway."

Lopez smiled and saluted. "Aye, aye, sir!" After the officers returned the salute, he picked up his bags and headed inside the boat.

Sam looked at Ben and shook his head. "Operations Security. It's not the leaks; it's the signs that get you. Well, can't be helped now."

"Yes, sir," Ben replied. "I just got a call from the JIATF office. Final planning conference in the secure conference room at 13:00, sir."

"So much for beers over at Sloppy Joe's," Sam said with a smile. "I can't wait to hear what you and Hoppy have in store for us."

Briefing Room, JIATF-South Headquarters, Key West, Florida
12:58 EDT, 4 April

Ben

The Briefing Room at JIATF-South was not large—even a planning session as restricted as this one created quite a crowd. Sam, Ben, and Hopkins were sitting together on one side of the room. Also present were the navy lieutenant leading the SEAL team effort, a DEA representative, and two air force captains, one an electronic warfare specialist and the other a meteorologist. Simmons arrived to take his seat with one minute to go, receiving a friendly nod from Ben, icy glares from Sam and Hopkins, and studied indifference from the remaining attendees.

Ben understood why Sam, Hopkins, and Drake disliked Simmons. In their minds, he was a reckless fool who put himself and Ben in a situation that required Sam to break all the rules and risk his command to save their lives. But this was one of the very few issues on which Ben and his shipmates parted company. He didn't know if it was the one-on-one time he had had with the DIA officer, that they had stood, or rather, kneeled shoulder-to-shoulder through that shootout, or the genuine possibility the man could end up being a quasi-brother-in-law. Ben liked Peter Simmons and enjoyed talking with him, even if they didn't see eye-to-eye on what the agent casually referred to as "Risk Management."

The door opened, and the navy lieutenant called out, "Attention on deck!" as Pennington entered the room. Everyone came to their feet, and the military attendees stood at attention as Pennington took the podium.

"Carry on. Be seated, please," Pennington said. After they all sat down, he continued, "Ladies and gentlemen, we are here to set up a mission of extreme importance. I will express my regrets that some details are so sensitive they will need to be withheld, and I ask for your patience. There is to be no outside discussion of what we say here, and I remind you all that you signed a non-disclosure memo.

"Bottom line up front: there is a weapon of mass destruction mounted on the commercial vessel *Carlos Rojas* moored in the harbor of Barbello, Honduras, and under control of the Salinas drug cartel. To our knowledge, they are unaware of what they have. A second criminal organization is moving to seize the *Carlos Rojas* and its cargo within three days. We will prevent that, and because the vessel is within the sovereign territory of a foreign nation, we will go in covertly, with a dangerously light footprint. These are top-level decisions and not open to discussion. Your purpose here is to complete a plan of action to execute those decisions. Now, before I yield the floor, does anyone have questions?"

"Sir." Sam stood.

"Yes, Lieutenant Powell?"

"I respectfully request an explicit statement of our rules of engagement, Admiral."

Pennington smiled. "Yes, I thought you would." His smile disappeared as he looked around the room. "This is a national defense mission, and you will employ whatever deadly force is needed without warning to overcome any resistance."

"Thank you, sir," Sam said and then sat.

"Any other questions? Very well. Dr. Simmons, you have the floor." He left the podium and took a seat in the front row beside one of the air force captains.

Simmons stood, took the podium, and said, "Thank you, Admiral. Ladies and gentlemen, as the admiral has said, there is a WMD capability on the *Carlos Rojas* that, if copied and distributed, could cause mass casualties, if not global nuclear war. Our primary goal will be to board and seize the *Carlos Rojas*, remove her from the harbor, and sink her in deep water. Once aboard, I and another operative will rig everything we can find related to the weapons for destruction with thermite charges. We will wait to activate those charges until just before the *Carlos Rojas*'s scuttling if our extraction of the vessel is successful. In the event of a successful counterattack, we will activate the charges at once. Does anyone have questions?" Many of the participants exchanged looks, but none had questions. "Thank you. I believe you are next, Lieutenant Powell." He sat down.

Sam stood and took the podium while Ben and Hopkins stood alongside. "Admiral, ladies and gentlemen, I'm CO of the Coast Guard Cutter *Kauai*, for those who don't know me. We have modified her from the original Island Class design to diesel-electric-battery propulsion, allowing near-silent operations for brief periods. We will use this capability to enter the harbor undetected, lay alongside the *Carlos Rojas*, and put over a boarding party who will unmoor and rig her for towing. My XO, Lieutenant Junior Grade Wyporek, will lead the boarding party and command *Carlos Rojas* during the egress. *Kauai* will tow her clear of the harbor using battery power to avoid detection. We will switch to diesel power when clear and continue the tow, or escort, if the *Carlos Rojas*'s engines prove serviceable, to the five hundred-fathom line of the Cayman Trench. There, we will evacuate all aboard using our RHIB, then sink her using explosive charges. If they detect us, we will light off our diesels and use twenty-five-millimeter and fifty-caliber machine gun fire to enable our escape, if possible. If not, we will delay the counterattack long enough for Dr. Simmons to destroy the weapons and associated materials.

"Our intelligence from the DEA agent on the scene is that the Salinas gang has a large stockpile of small arms and RPGs. We can assume that these will be available at the fortified position on the point of land defining the entrance and on small boats. My chief concern in terms of a firefight is the KPV our overflights observed on that promontory. They'd be pretty lucky to tag us in a vulnerable spot with an RPG from five hundred yards, but they have a good chance of roughing us up with the KPV. Therefore, we'll be throwing everything we have at it if it comes to a fight." The presence of the Russian KPV heavy machine gun had been terrible news. It fired 14.5mm armor-piercing rounds that could punch through *Kauai*'s light plating even from a quarter-mile away. There were worried looks and murmurs around the room before Sam continued. "I'll pause for questions before yielding to Chief Petty Officer Hopkins, who will brief the approach and egress."

There were no questions, and Hopkins replaced Sam at the podium and activated a projection showing Barbello harbor beside an overhead diagram of a ship. "Admiral, everyone, there is a single, narrow channel leading into the harbor just beyond this point of land to the north and shoals and islets to the south," she said, pointing at the display. "Moonset is at 00:56 local time, and we plan to pass through 'the gate,' as we call it, at 01:10. Once inside, as you can see, we have a large area of good water we can use to set up the approach. The *Carlos Rojas* is moored heading north along the quay as shown here, and we will approach from the southeast. As soon as we touch, Mr. Wyporek's boarding party and the DIA men will cross over. We will stay alongside until the towing hawser is passed and rigged to the vessel's anchor windlass here on the bow." She pointed at a co-projected diagram of the *Carlos Rojas*. "When Mr. Wyporek signals the vessel is unmoored, we will tow her eastward, through the gate, and then turn north once we are out of weapons range of this point." She pointed at the small point of land making up the northern side of the gate. "We estimate twenty minutes in the ingress, fifteen to rig the tow and unmoor the vessel, and forty-five to fifty-five minutes to clear the gate. We will keep a short tow inside the harbor for better navigational control and keep us in range to provide suppressive fire on that point, if needed." She looked at Pennington. "Any questions, Admiral?"

"None, thank you, Chief."

As Hopkins stepped aside and Ben took the podium. "Admiral, ladies and gentlemen, I will board the *Carlos Rojas* with three other men. We will be occupied with the towing hawser until we rig it. It weighs over ten pounds per linear foot and will need all of us to lift it to and through the bullnose in the bow. As soon as we rig the tow, I will lead a seaman along the ship's port side and throw off any mooring line or shore tie we encounter, leaving a man on the bow to stand by the hawser. Once the moorings are clear, we will move to the Bridge and stay there throughout the exfil. We will be armed with carbines and suppressed pistols for self-defense, but we will be occupied and unable to aid in *Carlos Rojas*'s seizure. Once the tow is stabilized, we can contribute to the vessel's defense, but I must stay on the Bridge. Do you have questions, Admiral?"

"No, thank you, Lieutenant."

"Sir. Anyone else? OK, Lieutenant Davis?" *Kauai's* personnel sat as Davis, the navy SEAL officer, stood and took the podium.

"Admiral, ladies, and gentlemen, I have a nine-man detachment loading up at Virginia Beach as we speak. They will fly to Barbello and execute a jump into the water west of the island at 01:45 tomorrow morning. They will rendezvous with the DEA man on the scene and execute a covert reconnaissance of the harbor facilities and opposing forces over the day and evening. At or around 00:45 on the 6th, they will take the *Carlos Rojas* by force, secure the vessel and the adjoining quay, and await *Kauai's* arrival. My men will signal the Rivet Joint aircraft when the target has been secured. If practicable, they will sabotage the power to the lighting on the quay in the ship's vicinity. That one they must play by ear—if they can't make it look like an ordinary failure, it may tip off the enemy to the assault later. After departing the quay, they will rig explosive charges at key points in the hull to ensure the ship's rapid scuttling. They will then prepare fortified positions along the port side in case there is a firefight on the way out. Do you have questions, Admiral?"

"No questions, thank you, Lieutenant."

"Sir," he said, sitting down.

"Captain Landry?" Pennington said.

The air force electronics specialist got to her feet and took the podium. "Yes, sir. Admiral, Chief, and gentlemen, the Rivet Joint aircraft has been conducting electronic surveillance in international airspace just east of Barbello for the past two nights. We collected enough data to identify every emitter on the island and establish a pattern of life. We will revisit tonight to look for any changes. During the assault, the aircraft will carry Lieutenant Davis, who will oversee the ground forces until *Kauai*'s arrival. We can jam every communications device on that island. Still, I recommend holding off on that capability until the SEAL assault is underway to avoid premature disclosure. We will transmit updates on request starting at midnight on the 6th and stay thirty minutes after *Kauai*'s departure to watch for any pursuit.

"The downside is we have forecasted weather in the area that will negate the MQ-9—it can't handle the wind shears at low level and won't be of much use up high. So, no EO/IR or close support will be available. Do you have questions of me, Admiral?"

"No. Thank you, Captain."

"You are welcome, sir. I will hand off to Captain Fergus for the weather brief." The other air force captain stood, made his way to the podium, and switched the display to a meteorological map as Landry returned to her seat.

"Admiral, ladies, and gentlemen, as Captain Landry pointed out, we have a low-pressure area moving over the Northwestern Caribbean that will generate unstable air across the region. This pattern is very unusual for the season—it's usually dry there. I am forecasting persistent scattered cumulonimbus cells throughout the area, moving east to west for the operational period's duration, with lightning and locally heavy rain and wind. The storms' scattered nature and general lack of prevailing winds should cause calm to light seas in the area. Are there questions?"

Sam stood. "Admiral, I have a question." At Pennington's nod, he continued. "Can we predict when a cell might come over the island, Captain?"

"Perhaps thirty to forty-five minutes beforehand, no earlier," Fergus replied.

"What are you thinking, Lieutenant?" Pennington asked.

"Sir, these storms could help or hurt us. If I can ride in and out during one of them, that would be an immense advantage remaining covert, assuming we aren't struck by lightning." He paused as the attendees chuckled. "On the other hand, they might see us coming in with no rain and lightning strobing. I recommend we keep a little flexibility in the timetable in case we have an opportunity or hazard to deal with. Can you support that, Mr. Davis?"

"While I am in contact with the ground force, there should not be a problem."

"Good," Sam said and turned to Pennington. "Sir, with your permission, we'll keep flexible in terms of the timetable."

"Granted. That's good thinking." After Sam and Fergus sat, Pennington turned to Bartlett, the DEA man. "Agent Bartlett?"

Bartlett stood in place and said, "Thank you, Admiral. Folks, we have a man undercover on Barbello named Dominguez. He's not deep in the gang, just posing as a mechanic among the day workers they employ. I expect to hear from him in a couple of hours for a regular check-in, during which I'll brief him to expect the SEALs and prepare for their arrival. I want him to come off with your guys, Lieutenant," he said to Davis. "Once you snatch that ship, there's no way to predict the gang's reaction, and I don't want him around then."

"We'll get him off with us, sir," Davis replied.

"Good. Now let me tell you about the Salinas gang. It's more of a cult, with its own death-worship features that make MS-13, Al Qaeda, and ISIS look like a church choir by comparison. They recruit young boys from the barrios of Honduras and Guatemala and brainwash them with some truly vile initiation rituals or kill them in the process. Lieutenant Powell asked earlier about rules of engagement. If you encounter someone carrying a gun on Barbello, that is a Salinas soldier. He may be as young as fourteen, but rest assured, that meeting will end with one of you being killed. Make sure it's him." He paused to let that grim thought sink in before continuing. "Questions?" After waiting to scan all the participants, he said, "Thank you, Admiral," then sat.

Pennington scanned the room. "Does anyone have anything to add?" After pausing briefly, he continued. "Folks, I think we have the best plan available under the circumstances. I want to emphasize that once on the scene, I expect you to evaluate the situation and adjust if needed according to your best judgment. Do what you think is necessary to carry out the primary mission and get your people home. You have my full trust and support, come what may. I will be in my office if any of you need me. I wish you good luck and a safe return." As he rose, the other attendees came to their feet, with the military people coming to attention. "Carry on, thank you, everybody." He then turned and left the room.

After Pennington departed, Sam turned to Ben and said, "Number One, I'll leave you to link up with our DIA friend. Find out about this other guy he's bringing along and what sort of handling arrangements they need for the thermite. The only thing I know about it is that I don't want it anywhere inside the ship."

"Yes, sir," Ben responded. After Sam and Hopkins left, Ben walked over to Simmons. "Good to see you again, Pete." He shook Simmons's hand.

"Same here, Ben." He glanced toward the door. "I perceive I'm still *persona non grata* among your shipmates?"

"I'm afraid so. Don't worry; they won't let it impede the mission." When Simmons looked back in his direction, he continued. "I need to ask you who you are bringing along. We don't have any bona fides on him."

"You will shortly. His name is Billy, William Gerard. He was around during the Resolution op, but you guys didn't meet up. He's solid as they come."

"Good to hear. So how did you get mixed up in this mess?"

"After Resolution, I went back to my actual job—poking the 252s in the eye. I found they were stirring up trouble in Colombia, grabbing up such large amounts of cocaine that their vendor was getting out of the box the government likes those people to stay inside. So, I called in Victoria the Data Jedi, re-tasked some satellite surveillance effort, and *Voila*! I have a nice, tight target package I can bring to the Colombians. They run a raid and end up clobbering the 252's vendor. Good news, right?

"Well, because the Law of Unintended Consequences must be obeyed, this sent the local 252 knothead scurrying for another vendor. His choice of the Salinas mob would have been serendipitous had it not been for the fact the boat he lost to them was carrying a particularly nasty WMD. Said knothead legged it when he realized he was holding the bag for a colossal foul-up and came to Miami to turn himself in to the FBI. We spotted him at the airport, tailed him to his hotel, and grabbed him before he could get tangled up with Hoover's boys."

"Not exactly good form."

"Perhaps not, but if he had turned himself into them, they'd still be processing the paperwork just to talk to him. Besides, TCOs like the 252s are in our lane, not FBI or CIA's."

"OK. One other question. I was a little surprised there was no discussion of protective equipment, you know, suits and respirators. Won't we need that if this thing gets loose?"

Simmons frowned as he looked back. "You don't want to be wearing that when we assault. You'd get tagged by even the dumbest Salinas goon because you'd never be able to see him or hear him. Besides, with this thing, all the MOPP gear and atropine in the world won't help you. The good news is it will be quick—one whiff will stop your heart within five seconds."

Ben swallowed hard. He had been worried about getting shot, but the possibility of dying from a chemical agent filled him with horror. He had a taste of being on the receiving end of a chemical attack at Resolution when he was hit with a paralytic agent employed by the 252s. Simmons had saved him with the antidote, but Ben still had nightmares from the experience. It was an effort to keep his voice steady.

"Right. We shove off at 18:00. I need you guys on board and settled in by 17:30, but don't show up before 17:00. It will take time to prepare the ground with Sam."

"Understood. See you at 17:00!"

"Can't wait," Ben said and turned to the door for the short walk back to *Kauai*. On the way, he came to terms with his fear. *Dead is dead, whether it's from a bullet or a gas. At least this one kills quickly.*

Once in his room, he stared longingly at Victoria's picture and considered calling her for one last chat before the mission, but it was too early in the day. She could not bring her cellphone into the office because of security concerns, and he didn't want to put her on the spot by calling on her office line. Besides, the timing would trigger a lot of questions from her. He did not want to get her on the phone, upsetting her routine, and then dump a load of "sorry, can't tell you" answers on her. Ben knew it was the right thing to do, but he was still down that it would be at least two, perhaps three, days before he could hear her voice again. He compromised and sent her a text message. "V, going offline for a few days, but thinking of U as always. Pls set aside Apr 12–16 for me. Can't wait to see U again. B." He then shut off the phone, locked it in his desk, and left for pre-sail preparations on the Bridge.

12

Gaze Long into the Abyss

Isla de Barbello, Honduras
16:03 EDT, 4 April

Dominguez

Jorge Dominguez walked carefully through the heavily forested hills above the harbor. The trail he had set up was a compromise between something he could remember and follow in most daylight conditions and one that his "associates" would be unlikely to stumble across or be able to follow to his storage place. The man knew what would happen then: they would kill him. In that case, the only question would be whether it would be a merciful bullet in the back of his head or a matter of him joining the ranks of the *No Consagrado*, the poor wretches crucified and left to die of thirst outside the main hacienda. He was sure it would be the latter—as an undercover agent of the US

Drug Enforcement Agency, he would be considered among the most unholy by the Salinas leaders.

The trail led to a hidden cache of weapons, ammunition, MREs, satellite phones, and spare batteries. This store was his last line of defense if things went wrong. Hide out, call in the cavalry, survive. It was also a link to the real world. Once per week, if practicable, his orders were to call in and report his status. It was not the usual procedure for a UC, but the Salinas Cartel was new, deep, and dark, and his bosses needed as much current information as possible about them and their new stronghold on Barbello. In his earlier days, he would have been infuriated by this "management" level and its risks. Now Dominguez was nonchalant about the dangers, almost bordering on indifferent. He had been in the field too long and seen too many horrors in his UC assignments. So much so that this pack of animals' depredations could not make much of an impression.

Dominguez should have rotated out of the field more than a year ago. Still, he had remarkable skills with language and was a genius as an engine mechanic—always a marketable skill to drug gangs in need of reliable transport. These factors meant he could always work his way into the targeted gang, and he was just too valuable to spare. Now, however, even his controls at the agency could see that he was pushing over the edge. Dominguez had the DEA equivalent of combat fatigue, and, like the military version, it could only lead to mistakes that endangered his life. Or worse. His supervisors had decided.

Although he didn't know it yet, Barbello would be Dominguez's last field assignment, and it would end soon.

Dominguez stopped suddenly and turned. He could have sworn he heard something, a rustle of the grass. Although he was probably hearing things, he opted for safety. He turned right off the trail on the next viable path and picked up the pace. When he was sure he was out of sight of anyone who could follow, he broke into a trot, veered left into a cul-de-sac in the jungle, and concealed himself, looking and listening.

After about twenty minutes of sitting in silence, Dominguez shook his head. *OK, I guess you've been paranoid enough this day.* He stood up and started retracing his path to the trail. After a few minutes' trek, he regained the main trail and turned to follow it to the end. After another ten minutes, he had reached the cache and was booting up one of the satellite phones. He made a satellite link, and after a brief delay, he had established a connection with his boss and executed the usual security kabuki.

"Dom! I'm relieved to hear your voice. How are things there?"

"Mostly same-old/same-old, but we had some excitement a few days ago when my masters went Barbary Pirates on one of their customers."

"That was one thing I wanted to talk to you about. Tell me what you know."

"Well, this offshore oil service boat pulled in, there was some shooting, a few bodies dropped, and a couple of fresh faces showed up on the crucifix field. My masters sent me on board to disable the main engines so that no one would get any ideas. That night, the local *jefe* announced that the boat owners had disrespected the Salinas's holy order and been assessed for tribute. It serves the damn fools right, sailing into a bottle like this. You need me back on board to get eyes on the inside?"

"No. We can't risk you right now. Dom, we're pulling you off this one."

"What? Do you know what it took me to get in here? What the hell, man?"

"I know, I know. The thing is, the Salinas cartel just poked the bear and is about to be crushed. When it's done, we don't expect to see anyone left alive on Barbello. So, you are coming off. You said you disabled the engines on that boat. Is that permanently disabled, or can you fix them?"

"I just took out the control cabling for the starters. I can have them up and running again in twenty minutes."

"Good, good. We are sending in some sailors to take that boat out of the harbor, and they'll need your help to get it running. They'll also need the latest on forces and dispositions. Do you have a suitable spot picked out where you can hole up and observe?"

SEALs? Shit, what the hell is on that boat? "Naturally. When should I expect company?"

"About 02:00 tomorrow morning. They'll be dropping in the drink and coming ashore on the island's west side. I need you to set up a rendezvous point and safe approach to the harbor. Call me when you have that. You'll be remaining with them once they arrive and giving them whatever help they need. Questions?"

"No," Dominguez replied, his bitterness plain.

"Don't take this wrong, Dom. This operation comes right from the top, and you're a critical part. We need you to stay clear and stay safe from here on out. No contact or reconnoitering on your own, clear?"

"Got it." Dominguez shook his head. What the hell was the matter with him? This was good news—he was to be pulled out of hell on earth, and he wasn't leaving a job undone. "I'll call you in two or three hours once I scout the west beach."

"Roger that. Stay out of trouble until then."

"Will do. Talk to you soon. Out." He had just turned off the phone when he froze at the sound of a soft crack behind him. Someone had stepped on a fallen palm branch and snapped it. Pretending not to hear, he put the phone back into the storage bin, extracted a silenced Glock, quietly inserted a magazine, and chambered a round. Keeping the gun out of sight, he locked the container, then walked a short distance away from the sound's direction and crouched where he could monitor the cache site unseen. After about five minutes, a figure emerged from the brush and walked over to the site, moving slowly with his head swiveling, looking for the owner. Satisfied, he kneeled to examine and try the lock.

Dominguez recognized the visitor. He was one of the adolescents recruited, or sometimes snatched, from the barrios of Honduras and Guatemala as small boys and brought up within the Salinas gang's brutal faith. Basically, it was a twenty-first-century version of the Hitler Youth, only much worse. Those of average intelligence furnished the muscle and fodder for gang operations, while the smart ones were refined and groomed to enter the gang's leadership. This was not one of the smart ones.

Moving quietly, Dominguez stole behind the youth undetected, bringing the gun up and sighting it on the back of his head. *Do it! One less monster in the world. It's not like you have a choice!* His hands began shaking, and he realized he couldn't just shoot the young man, not like this. He lowered the gun and said, "*Hola, amigo.* What are you doing here?" The youth startled and stood, drawing a large bowie knife from his belt. Dominguez fought the urge to laugh when the thought of "bringing a knife to a gunfight" flashed across his mind.

"I saw you! I heard you, *traidor*! *Espía*! I'll see you dead today!"

"Alright, let's pause and think a bit. I have a pistol; you have a knife. If I die today, you won't live to see it." He paused as he could see the youth's jaw working, his eyes darting, looking for some advantage. "Come on. Put the knife down. I give you my word, short incarceration. Then I'll let you go unharmed." He pressed that point. "Come on, son. There is nothing here worth dying for." The youth's eyes widened, and a snarl curled his mouth. *Oh, shit!*

"I AM NOT YOUR SON!" He charged Dominguez and took two shots in the center of his chest before falling on his face well short of his quarry.

Dominguez stepped forward carefully, his gun sighted on the fallen young man while checking his pulse. Nothing. Dominguez sat down heavily and stared at the body for a full five minutes. It wasn't the first time he had killed an opponent, but the futility of the youth's attack troubled him more than any earlier time. *Why? Why did you do that, kid? What did you think you would accomplish?* He finally shook himself out of his stupor and reopened the storage case. He retrieved a couple of phones, batteries, water bottles, and a few magazines for the pistol and placed them in a shoulder bag. After locking up the case, he walked over, picked up the body, and slung it over his shoulder—he would drop it off in the jungle en route to the western beach. *I'm sorry, kid, you got a shit deal and deserve a decent burial, but this thing is bigger than either of us.* He moved off down a trail he had scouted leading west.

Two hours later, Dominguez reached the western side of the island and found a stretch of beach reasonably free of rocks suitable for the SEALs to come ashore. He scouted out a good hideout and made notes of the trail leading down so they could make their way back in darkness early the next morning. Once he had set everything up, he called in again on the satellite phone.

"Dom, good to hear from you. What have you got?"

"I have a nice, isolated beach, a solid trail leading east, and a suitable spot to lie up for the day tomorrow. I have the lat-long when you're ready to copy."

"Sweet. Send it, please." After Dominguez had provided the coordinates, his boss continued. "OK, the master plan is still coalescing right now, but the basic gist is that you will help the SEALs get on board and then fix the engines."

"Um, you know, as soon as we start an engine, they'll be on us like flies on shit. It'll be Little Bighorn II."

"I'm told that will be taken care of. I'm sorry to be so cryptic, but you need to take it on faith that we will get you guys out of there."

"OK. Still on for oh-two-hundred?"

"Yep. Just lie low until 01:45, then turn on your beacon. The visitors will have Blue Force Trackers and will contact you. Authentication combo is Stake-Tent."

"Got it. Anything else?"

"No. Stay safe, and I'll see you when you get back. Out."

"Roger that." He switched off the phone. *God willing.*

USCG Cutter *Kauai*, Florida Straits, twenty nautical miles southwest of Key West, Florida
18:58 EDT, 4 April

Ben

Kauai cleared the harbor of Key West and passed the sea buoy about thirty minutes previously. Sam had called for a meeting of the dozen crew not on watch and the embarked army personnel on the open afterdeck at 19:00. He usually held meetings on the messdeck, where people could sit comfortably, but there were far too many attendees today.

Rumors were flying since they started heading southwest after clearing the sea buoy instead of the expected easterly course back to the homeport of Port Canaveral, Florida. Sam chafed under the need to keep their mission a secret and was eager to brief the crew on those aspects he could share. As the appointed hour approached, Drake gathered the crew into ranks and settled the army personnel to the side. When Sam stepped out onto the afterdeck with Ben a step behind, Drake shouted, "Attention on Deck!" The crew came to attention, and when Sam halted before them, Drake saluted and said, "Crew present or accounted for, sir."

After he and Ben returned the salute, Sam said, "Thank you, Chief. Fall out and gather 'round everybody!" Sam continued as the crew formed a semicircle in front of the officers. "I'm sure most of you have heard that we will take the scenic route back to Port Canaveral. I wanted to get you the good news that the Coast Guard is providing this Caribbean holiday completely free!" He waited for the laughing to subside and then continued. "More on that later. Right now, we have some important business to attend to. Seaman Juan Lopez, front and center!" Lopez stepped forward and came to attention. "Carry on, please. Everybody, I'm pleased to announce that we have a brand-new graduate of the Maritime Law Enforcement Specialist School in our midst. Congratulations, Seaman Lopez!" Sam led the crew in applause and held up his hand after a few seconds. "As the TV commercial says: But wait! There's more! Normally, when someone goes to A-school from a patrol boat, they move on to another unit on graduation. We are lucky enough to get Lope back with us, but he seems to be out of uniform!" Sam smiled at Lopez's concerned look and said, "Chief Drake, would you assist me, please?"

"With pleasure, Captain," Drake said as Ben handed him and Sam each a third-class petty officer's collar insignia.

After the two men had pinned them on Lopez's collar, they stepped back, and Sam announced. "Crew of *Kauai*, I have the pleasure of presenting Maritime Law Enforcement Specialist Third Class Juan Lopez!" He stepped forward and shook Lopez's hand as the crew cheered and pounded his back. After allowing a couple of minutes for congratulations, Sam raised his hand, and the crew went silent and stepped forward.

"OK, folks, that was the fun part. Now, I'm going to fill you in on what we're going to be doing for the next few days. I know some of you wondered why our trip to AUTEC was cut short and what the hell a two-star admiral was doing riding with us to Key West. I'm sure you also recognized our old friend Dr. Simmons when he came aboard, and those of you who surmised that meant we are going into action are correct." He paused for a few murmurs, then raised his hand again.

"We are heading down through the Yucatan Channel to an island off the coast of Honduras called Barbello. Now that place is the stronghold for a drug gang called the Salinas Cartel. They have seized an offshore supply vessel from another criminal organization and are holding it for ransom. I know your first reaction is the same as mine: 'who cares?' Unfortunately, that OSV is also carrying a weapon of mass destruction, and we cannot let that go. So, tomorrow night we'll sneak in under battery power, hook up a towing hawser, and tow that boat out of there. Once we clear the harbor, we'll either tow or escort the boat up to the deep water north of the island and scuttle her." Once more, there were murmurs, and Sam paused briefly before raising his hand.

"Now, obviously, the Salinas gang might have some objections to our planned activities, but you'll be happy to know that we have a team of Navy SEALs on their way down there right now. They will take the boat and enough pier space for us to do our job without raising the alarm. The tricky part will come on the way out, as the only usable channel comes within five hundred yards of a promontory the Salinas gang has fortified. If we're lucky, we'll slip past them in the dark. But even if we're not lucky and they spot us, we have enough firepower between our twenty-five-millimeter and fifty-caliber and the SEAL's weapons to muscle our way through. While I'm confident we'll get through without casualties, we are shipping an army combat medical unit with us, just in case." He looked over to the army personnel and said, "Everyone, this is Major Roberts, combat surgeon and specialists Langley and Rabin, who will live on our messdeck for the trip. Please do your best to welcome them aboard and help them as needed. Now, does anyone have questions?" There were more indistinct murmurs, but no one stepped up.

"OK, thank you all. If I were a gambler, Petty Officer Lopez, I'd bet you wish you were back in Charleston sucking down beers at your graduation party right now!"

"You'd lose that bet, sir!" Lopez replied with a smile, generating a fresh round of laughter.

"Happy to hear that!" Sam nodded with a smile. "OK, one last thing. Dr. Simmons brought a specialist with him to help find and deal with that WMD aboard the boat. Much of what they do is super-secret, so any conversation with them is likely to be uncomfortable for everyone. By mutual agreement, we will suspend our normally friendly and hospitable behavior in their case. Just don't talk with them and keep your distance. Any questions? OK, since this will be a night job and in honor of our new petty officer, *Kauai* will be on holiday routine until tomorrow at midnight. Get all the sleep you can when you're not on watch." He turned to Drake. "That's all, Chief."

Drake said, "Yes, sir. Attention on Deck!" Then rendered a salute as the crew came to attention.

Sam and Ben returned the salute, and then Sam said, "Thank you, Chief. Carry on, please." He and Ben then turned and left as the crew drifted over to talk with Lopez and the army personnel. As they walked forward, Sam said, "The same goes for you, Number One. I want you well-rested for tomorrow night. Lay off whenever you can."

"Yes, sir." They stopped before the entry door, and Sam looked back at the afterdeck in grim silence. After a moment, Ben said, "It will be alright, Captain. We all knew what we were signing on for."

"Yes." Sam nodded. "Yes." Then he turned and went inside, Ben a step behind.

4527 Sangamore Road, Apt. B23, Bethesda, Maryland
21:06 EDT, 4 April

Victoria

Victoria shut down her PC and then looked at Benjamin's text again. "Can't wait to see U again." She was disappointed when she read it after picking up her phone outside the office on the way home. He had only sent the message half an hour before, and she called back at once, hoping to catch him before he left. The call rolled over to voice mail, and she hung up immediately—she could not risk leaving a foolish-sounding message she could not erase. It worried her all the way home that Benjamin would see the missed call without a voice mail and wonder what was wrong with her. As soon as she got home, she sat down and laboriously composed a reply. This was important, and she had to be sure not to make any mistakes. "Benjamin, I will request leave for 12-16 April. I tried to call you back without success. I will miss talking to you. Please call me as soon as it is convenient. Victoria." She had initially put "as soon as you can," then "as soon as you return," before settling on the needy-neutral version she sent.

Regardless of the message, she observed the nightly ritual at her desk. There was always a chance of a change allowing Benjamin to call, and she needed to be able to answer. Regardless, the pictures and her eidetic replay of the events of their two dates were comforting for her.

Isla de Barbello, Honduras
02:16 EDT, 5 April

Dominguez

Dominguez was startled when he heard the click of a weapon safety coming from the water's direction. "Stake!"

"Tent!" came the reply, and nine figures rose from the surf and waded ashore carrying equipment.

Dominguez walked to meet them. “Howdy, boys. The name’s Dominguez, but you can call me Dom.”

The leader shook his hand. “Glad to meet you. Senior Chief D’Agostino, plus eight. Give us a minute to get into traveling gear. How far to the observation point?”

“Two-and-a-half, three hours, tops. But it’s a little tricky in total darkness.”

“Not an issue for us. Have you ever used the ANVS-9 night vision goggles?”

“Nope.”

“Parker here will hook you up.”

The junior petty officer extracted a spare set of goggles and harness and fitted the device to Dominguez’s head. The capability was startling to the agent, who had only used hand-held scopes before. “This is amazing!” he whispered.

“Take it easy, small steps, and let one of us lead. You call the trail. The resolution is pretty good, but your depth perception will stink, so be careful,” D’Agostino said. “OK, we’re ready to move. Parker will lead; you keep your hand on his shoulder and tell him where to go.”

The party of ten set off quietly, with Dominguez calling the turns in a whisper. It was almost dawn when they pulled up on Dominguez’s cache hideout. After shedding their goggles, the team made their way through the jungle to the ridge overlooking the harbor and took cover. D’Agostino sent two groups of three men each to the opposite ends of the ridge to hunker down and observe. He turned to Dominguez. "Tell me about the boat."

"Pulled in four days ago, looking for an on-load. As soon as she was tied up with the engines shut down, the Salinas hitters boarded and capped all the guards and about half the crew. The other half they strung up on crucifixes outside the main hacienda."

"Dead?"

"Unfortunately for them, no. They will be soon, though."

"Shit!"

"Yeah, that's the word. There are two left onboard still alive, and I think they're passengers or sponsors or some damn thing the *Jefe* thinks can bring in some money. You guys here to rescue them?"

"Nope. Couldn't give a rat's ass if they live or die. There's something on the boat that means we have to sink it and sink it in deep water."

"Wow. What is it, some sort of weapon of mass destruction? I didn't see anything unusual when I was on there."

"Brother, all I know is that we take that boat, wait for one of ours to tow it out of here, and then sink it into the Cayman Trench."

"They're crazy! They bring a tugboat there, and it will wake up every Salinas hood on the island. I've seen their armory—they have enough RPGs to blow a damn Aegis Cruiser out of the water. A tugboat won't get to first base!"

"It won't be a conventional tugboat. All I know is it will be quiet, almost invisible at night, and it will tow us out. They catch on to us, and we'll light off the engine and fight our way out. That boat and whatever's on it needs to be destroyed. I understand you disabled the engines. How long to get them running?"

"Fifteen minutes, twenty tops."

D'Agostino nodded. "That should do. Now tell me about the lights on the pier and where they get their power."

13

The Gift of the Magi

USCG Cutter *Kauai*, Yucatan Channel, thirty nautical miles southwest of Cape San Antonio, Cuba 11:48 EDT, 5 April

Ben

"I relieve you, sir," Lee said as she rendered a crisp salute.

"I stand relieved," Ben replied. "On the Bridge, Petty Officer Lee has the Deck and Conn!"

"Aye!" replied everyone on the Bridge.

Ben turned back to Lee, now taking a visual sweep of the horizon with the OOD binoculars. Something was off that he could not quite put his finger on. "Are you OK, Shelley?" he whispered.

Lee, startled, turned to look at him and hesitated briefly before whispering back. "Um, I'm a little worried about tonight, XO."

“Just a little? I envy you. What are you worried about?”

She looked down again. “I’ve never been a towmaster before, sir. I mean, I’ve done a few tows of sailboats or pleasure craft, but nothing this big or important. If I screw it up, that’s the ballgame.” She looked up at Ben with an anxious expression.

Ben smiled back. “I have some worries too, and your role in this is definitely not among those. In fact, knowing you’ll be the one setting up and tending to the towline that will save my ass is a considerable comfort to me.”

“No shit?”

“No shit. You’ll do fine, believe me. We’ll all get through this.” He leaned in with a broad grin. “I have too many ‘blue’ jokes left for anything bad to happen.”

Lee rolled her eyes and smiled. “Well, when you put it that way....” She nodded again. “Thanks, XO.”

“You’re welcome. Have a nice watch, and I’ll see you later.”

Ben stepped over to stand beside Sam, saluted, and said, “Captain, I’ve been relieved by Petty Officer Lee. Request permission to lay below for lunch.”

Sam stood and returned the salute. “Very well, thank you. Can I keep you company?”

“My pleasure, sir.”

“Right.” He turned and headed down, with Ben following. Once they were off the Bridge, he said over his shoulder, “Everything OK with Lee?”

“No worries, Captain.”

"Good. No sign of a reprieve, I'm afraid. How's it going with your team?"

"As well as it can be, sir. We've studied the latest pictures, what-if-ed, and talked everything pretty much to death. I finally think I've pried the smile off of Lopez's face with the reality of it."

"You're not bringing him along to talk down any Salinas guys, I hope. If so, I'll be happy to re-clarify the rules of engagement for you."

"No, sir, but there might be some crew left alive, and my Spanish just isn't up to it."

"OK, good thinking." Sam nodded as they stepped onto the messdeck. Regular cooking was out of the question with the crowd of visitors aboard *Kauai*, so Sam and Ben raided the freezer for microwave meals. Ben looked around as they waited. The two army specialists were working on setting up an autoclave in the corner. Jenkins was sitting at one table chatting with Bondurant over a meal, and Gerard and Simmons were sitting in silence at the other. Sam and Ben moved over to the table with the boatswain's mates when their meals were cooked, Sam waving his hand as the two petty officers moved to stand. "Relax, guys."

"Thank you, sir," Bondurant replied. "Anything new?"

"Nope. Still heading south, no change in plans," Sam said as he opened his meal. "The SEALs are on the island now. At least we know that much."

"That puts things in perspective," Bondurant said. "Don't know if I could jump into a nest of armed psychos hoping someone would sneak in and pick me up."

After that preamble, the conversation was mainly light with a discussion of kids, the latest basketball news, and the new baseball season's start. By unspoken agreement, anything but what awaited them that night. After working through the meal, Ben excused himself and headed for his stateroom. In the passageway, he saw Hopkins and called out, "Hey, Chief, got time for a question?"

"Yes, sir."

After they stepped into his stateroom, he asked, "I noticed Williams, Zuccaro, and Bunting seem to be on an odd schedule with the FC3 watch. Anything I should know about?"

"No, sir, nothing you need to know about officially."

"OK, I'm officially not listening. Now, what's up?"

"I'm trying to keep Natalia and Shelley from standing watch together."

Ben frowned and said, "Um...."

"Relax, XO, it's nothing like that. Shelley found out Natalia was getting ogly-eyed with Joe while she was up north, and they had words. There are still hard feelings, and I'm trying to keep them undistracted while on watch, which translates to they shouldn't be on watch together. I put a stop to ogly-eyeing after Natalia tried it on you when you got back. Fortunately, you were impervious to her attempt."

"More like oblivious. What the hell does ogly-eyed mean? I'll bet there's no such word."

"Is so! It's been about ten years for me, but allow me to demonstrate." Hopkins took off her glasses, opened her eyes wide, looked at him from the side, tilted her head, and said in a throaty voice, "Oh, sir! You just *slayed* those drug guys. I would have been *soooo* scared." She batted her eyelashes at the last sentence, then put her glasses back on and resumed her expressionless look. "Ogly-eyed. Got it?"

"Got it. Wow, I must have been wicked tired. I don't remember anything like that."

"She was more subtle. I was exaggerating for demonstration purposes. Anyway, Shelley's still mad, though no longer homicidal, and I'm just trying to keep the temperature down. Welcome to chief stuff, sir."

"Actually, it's a relief to know that normal life is still happening. Joe and Shelley? How long has that been going on?"

"Sir, you are just adorable, you know that? Try about a year. And again, no need for you to worry. Nothing physical is happening on the boat. COB and I made it clear to both of them that we would kill them if they crossed that line."

"Does the captain know about this?"

"Nope. You need to tell him?"

"Not as long as it stays like this. Any change, and I need to get the word, please."

"Naturally, sir. The chiefs of *Kauai* will always ensure the officers know everything they need to know." She winked.

Doing his best imitation of Hopkins's ogly-eyed shtick, Ben said, "Oh *Chief*, you and COB are just *soooo* Mom and Dad!"

Hopkins smiled and shook a finger at him. "Now, careful, sir. You know I can straighten out commissioned officers just as thoroughly as third-class petty officers!"

Ben laughed. "That I do. Thanks, Chief." As she turned and walked away, Ben recalled the respectful but scathing dressing down she had given him for not putting a stop to Simmons's recklessness during their last encounter. Although Sam never spoke to him about it, Hopkins had made it clear that Ben had put their lives and careers in danger. It was a turning point for Ben in his view of personal responsibility.

Simmons appeared at the end of the passageway, and as they passed, Hopkins delivered a cold nod. "Doctor."

"Chief," Simmons replied with a smile.

When he reached Ben's door, he said, "Can we have a private chat, please?"

"Come in," Ben replied. Simmons shut the door, and they sat in the cramped room.

"Brrrrr. I guess I have a way to go before I get on her good side."

"A man's reach should exceed his grasp, or what's a heaven for?"

"Browning, no less. Well played, sir!" Simmons smiled, then leaned forward. "You looked pretty worried yesterday. We're pretty well supported on the ground this time."

"Shit, ya! If that KPV gets into the game, it will cut us to pieces. Where in the hell did a bunch of looney dopers lay their hands on ordnance like that?"

"Bought it in Nicaragua, probably. A nice leftover from the Sandinista days. Everyone's a capitalist now." He looked at the pictures on the bulkhead over Ben's shoulder. "I'd like to continue on a more personal note, if you don't mind."

"Personal? I wonder what that could be about," Ben said with a raised eyebrow.

"I think you know."

"Well, I think your worries about Victoria were unfounded. I'm a goner for her, but it's not mutual. We have built up a strong friendship, but that's it, as far as she's concerned."

"Is that what she told you?"

"No, I didn't ask her straight out, but she's an open book. If she felt something beyond that, she'd tell me. She doesn't hold back on anything. I was going to take leave to pitch my case with her when we got back from AUTEC, but then we got assigned to this op, and I'm having second thoughts."

"Why? You love her, right? That's what you mean by goner, isn't it?"

"Yes, but it's complicated."

"Complicated? With Victoria? She's the most straightforward person I've ever known. You've told me yourself you could talk to her about anything. Explain, please."

"It's because of this," Ben said, sweeping around with his right arm. "I don't mind telling you, I'm pretty scared about what we're going into tonight, but I wouldn't even think about being anywhere else when my family here is heading for a fight. And this won't be our last one. Captain Mercier made that clear when she put the question to us—we're the go-to guys for 'dangerously light footprint,' as the admiral put it. You told me Victoria doesn't take loss well. How can I lay something like that on her and then run off whenever there's a call?"

"I think you misinterpreted what I said. Victoria's bad experiences were because of being discarded, not from a loss. Let me explain: her last emotional attachment was an analyst in another office up in Bethesda who thought he was God's gift to women. He wanted to have his cake and eat it with her—when she told him she was in love with him, he told her she was 'too clingy' and dumped her. Can you imagine what that did to her?"

"Bastard!"

"Indeed. It gets worse. He had the nerve to hit on her again after she recovered, intimating that 'word might get around' about her if she didn't consent."

"Is he still alive?" Ben asked in complete seriousness.

"Yes, but after I learned of it, well, let's just say Lashon and I paid him a visit at his apartment. He became convinced that he would end up doing a federal prison term in a wheelchair if he continued to pursue anything like that course of action. Being hung upside-down by your ankles off your sixth-floor balcony by Lashon Bell can really focus your attention."

Ben nodded. Bell was a former US Marine Recon Sergeant and one of the DIA team present when Ben had first met Victoria. The day after that meeting, he single-handedly tackled and captured a 252 fugitive after being shot twice. You did not want to get on the wrong side of Lashon Bell.

"So, you can see the difference between the risks associated with your job and what that scumbag did. Let me ask you this. If the roles were reversed and Victoria had a dangerous job, would you want to be with her?"

"Yes."

"Even if it meant she might not come back one day? You could accept that loss?"

"It would kill me, but yes. I would take that risk to be with her, even if it was only for a while."

"Then how can you justify taking that choice away from her?"

Ben looked at Simmons intently. "That's not the choice. The choice is whether I want to win her over. To make her need me and then not be there when she does."

Simmons put on an icy scowl. "Wow, you really are a *noble* son of a bitch, aren't you? You could flip on your charm and have her fall at your feet anytime, but you want to spare her poor little broken heart when you strap on that body armor and sail away. What an *awesome* guy you are!"

"Screw you!"

"You need to get over yourself, boy. Do you think you can manipulate her like that? Why? Because she is not 'neurotypical?' Do you think so little of her?"

Ben was shocked into silence. Simmons had just held up a mirror, and Ben was ashamed of what he saw. "No, I don't think that. The fact is that I've gone from being worried about hurting her to worrying that she might have passed me by because I didn't reach out."

Simmons's face softened into a smile. "Now there's the Ben I remember. Sorry, friend, but I needed to show you are overthinking things. She needs to know how you feel, and she needs to hear it from you. And you don't need to worry about her passing you by."

"Thank you for saying that, but I have a tough road ahead. Victoria would have told me if she felt that way, and she hasn't."

"I wouldn't be so sure of that if I were you."

"What are you telling me?"

"That you should not conclude she is not in love with you. She's not a robot, you know. There are some things even she would hold back." He glanced at the picture on the bulkhead. "That picture of you two together on the Mall in DC—how did you feel about her when it was taken?"

"That was the day that removed any doubts for me."

"I see the same thing in her face. It's not wishful thinking. Look at the picture!"

"But if that were true, why doesn't she tell me? She shares everything else, good and bad."

“Think of what happened the last time she told someone she loved him.”

“She can’t think I would do *that*!”

“No, no, I’m sure she knows you would let her down kindly if you didn’t feel the same. But you have to see her dilemma: she would be afraid of driving you away if she led the disclosure. And she *does* feel something for you.” He pointed at the DC Mall picture. “I have it on good authority that she had that picture on her desk at work for a time, and then she took it home because it was too distracting for her to work.” He shook his head, still smiling. “I think we have two people in love with each other but afraid they’ll drive the other away if they admit it. Remarkable.”

“I am glad you’re so amused, Obi-Wan,” Ben said with a frown. “Can you find a point somewhere among the laughs?”

“My point, young padawan, is that you need to pick up my satellite phone this evening after I accidentally dial her number and tell her how you feel. Don’t worry about the mission; you’re going to come back. I was right when I told you that on Resolution, and we were in much deeper shit there than we will be tonight. And in the tiny chance that you stub your toe or something over there, she will remember that you told her you loved her. Not somebody else. I had only one regret with Julie about this topic: I didn’t tell her sooner.”

“I’ll bet you picked an extraordinary place, just the right time, and took a lot of prep with the setup, didn’t you? Would you care to explain how to do that on a satellite phone, please?”

"No, actually, I didn't. The moment came when we were waiting outside of a seminar. Do you know what Julie said after I blurted it out? 'Took you long enough! I love you too.' Now, the marriage proposal, you need to put some effort and prep into that baby.

"This is one of those situations where Victoria's condition will work for you. She couldn't give a rat's ass about music, bluebirds, or fancy restaurants. She will assess value in every additional second she knows your genuine feelings."

Ben knew this was all correct. He was thinking of flowers and another trip to the Mall to get the mood just right when all that would only be a distraction. Ben would at least have liked to hold her hand and look in her eyes when he said it, but he knew Simmons was right. He had to take what he could get. "Alright, you win. But it will need to wait until 19:00. We have an arrangement to call between 19:00 and 21:00, and I want to stick to that."

"Good call. I'll see you then," Simmons said, standing up and walking out of the room.

4527 Sangamore Road, Apt. B23, Bethesda, Maryland
19:06 EDT, 5 April

Victoria

Victoria's phone rang, but it wasn't Benjamin's callback number. Instead, the caller ID said, "INMARSAT Unk." She was annoyed. What if

Benjamin were to call while she was tied up with this person? She willed herself to settle down. *I will keep the call short, and if Benjamin calls, I will switch over to him or call him back.* Now it was past the third ring and approaching the fourth! *No, no, no!* She picked up the phone and said, "Hello?"

"Hello, Victoria, it's me."

Benjamin! What is he doing? Why isn't he using his cell phone?

"Hello, Benjamin. I am astonished it is you. I almost did not answer the phone."

"Yes, I'm sorry about that, Victoria, but we are at sea, and I can't use my mobile. One of the people we are working with has a satellite phone and was gracious enough to offer it up so I could call you."

"Oh, how wonderful!"

"Yes, so, let's return to normal. Hello, Victoria. How was your day?"

After about ten minutes of her chatting on the details of the day, she turned the call over to him as usual. "So, Benjamin, you are at sea. Can you tell me about your mission?"

"No, I'm sorry. It's one of those that I can't discuss. I would like to talk about something very important, though.

"Of course, whatever you like."

"Are you at your desk where you can see the pictures of our day together?"

"Yes. I always sit here when I am talking to you."

"Good. I'm outside of my room. The satellite phone must be in the open air to work, but I'm holding the picture of the two of us on the Mall that day. I would like to be there with you right now to hold your hand and look into your eyes, but this picture will have to serve as a proxy for me. Could you please pick one of your pictures and do the same?"

What is happening? Why is he saying this? Is he breaking up with me?

"Victoria, are you still there?"

"Yes, Benjamin." She looked at the single picture of him, the beautiful blue eyes and the smile. "I am looking at your picture now."

"Good. I love you, Victoria Carpenter."

She gasped. "What did you say?"

"I said, I love you, Victoria. I know it's wrong to tell someone the first time over the phone instead of in person. But I couldn't wait any longer. I hope you will forgive me for that."

"Forgive you? Oh, Benjamin! I have been in love with you since that day we spent together." Her eyes welled up. *Oh, no, no, no! I cannot choke up, not now!* "I was so afraid to tell you because I thought it might drive you away."

"Well, it was earlier for me than that day, but I had the same fear. It's just incredible. I thought we could talk about anything, yet an entire month went by because I was afraid to say it. I feel like the biggest fool on Earth."

"No, no, no. Please do not say that." She wiped away her tears and went on. "I wanted to tell you too, but it is so hard for me to tell how people feel, even you, and it was too important for me to get it wrong. Can you forgive *me*?

"Every day Monday through Saturday and twice on Sundays!"

Victoria laughed. "That is funny. I did not expect you to say that."

His voice became more subdued. "I love the way you laugh. It's beautiful, like everything else about you."

"Oh, Benjamin!"

"Victoria, I'm sorry, but these satellite calls are obscenely expensive, and I have to go. We have a lot to talk about when I get up there. I can't wait to see you and hold you and, well, you know."

"Benjamin, I love you. It feels so good to say that to you, and I cannot wait until you get here."

"Goodnight, my love. I used to say that after every phone call since our wonderful day. I'm glad I can say it to you now. Goodnight, my love."

"Goodnight, my dearest Benjamin!"

The line disconnected, and Victoria sat in the chair, gazing at Benjamin's picture, replaying the conversation in her mind like a video clip on loop playback. After an hour, she got up, brushed her teeth, changed into her nightshirt of the day, and went to bed. Victoria would not fall asleep thinking of mathematical algorithms tonight. She would not fall asleep thinking of mathematical algorithms ever again.

USCG Cutter *Kauai*, Caribbean Sea, ninety nautical miles north of Isla de Barbello, Honduras
19:33 EDT, 5 April

Ben

Ben ambled up to Simmons on the messdeck and handed him the satellite phone. His expression was inscrutable, and eventually, Simmons couldn't take it any longer.

"Well?"

"You called it. She's been in love with me since that day on the Mall. We're all set; God help us."

"Good for you, both of you!" He clapped Ben on the arm. "Now you can relax and get on with the job. I know it's tough, but try to get some sleep. Every bit will help."

"Right. I'll see you in a few." He turned and headed for his stateroom. The most important issue of his life had been resolved. Now on to the most urgent.

14

What the Day Demands

Isla de Barbello, Honduras
23:08 EDT, 5 April

D'Agostino

Shortly after sunset, the SEALs rallied at Dominguez's base camp to share intelligence and finalize the attack plan. The weather had deteriorated throughout the day, ending in rain showers that passed over and around the island. The rain made for a miserable existence in the already hot and humid jungle environment. Operationally, it was a significant boon as the Salinas men were disinclined to spend time out in the rain. Dozens of individual decisions opting to limit discomfort had a significant overall cumulative effect of gutting security. D'Agostino wished he had access to whatever the Honduran equivalent of the Weather Channel was called so that he could plan his marches to occur in the middle of a rain shower. As it was, they were frequent enough for his men to return in about half the time expected.

After consulting with his men, D'Agostino checked in with his command via satellite communications. The operation was still on. Not only that, but the patrol boat CO had seen the potential in the weather forecast to leverage the rain showers and was adjusting accordingly. Although they'd never met, D'Agostino was beginning to like this guy. If they could execute the takedown and exit when most of the dopers were hunkering down in the rain, that would be a massive reduction in mission risk. He hoped that boat jockey wouldn't wait for the perfect rainstorm and launch too late.

The other thing on D'Agostino's mind was the four speedboats the Salinas gang had tied up at the dock. If they got those babies spun up during the retreat, it could be dreadful news. There was some question about whether low-trained thugs could hit moving vessels with RPGs fired from the promontory five hundred yards away. But they couldn't miss from a speedboat a few dozen yards away.

D'Agostino looked across at Parker. "P, we need those boats disabled. How many dopers were on guard at the marina?"

"Just one, Boss. And that was before the rain. There may be nobody there now."

"OK. Take your squad down there and cut the fuel lines. Tap anyone you see and hide the bodies. And by cut, I don't mean just slice it and leave an easy splice; take a big section out of it. When you're done, head for the IP; we'll meet you there."

"Aye, aye, Senior Chief!" Parker replied as he stood and motioned his men to follow.

****

D'Agostino's forces had completed the infiltration and sabotage, raising no alarm, and were now positioned at opposite ends of the quay, ready to converge on the *Carlos Rojas*. The rain showers in the area had provided a mixed blessing: almost perfect cover for movement when a storm was overhead, but playing hell with their NVGs otherwise. His force was equally split. Parker, his three men, and Dominguez were with D'Agostino, while Banks and his three men were poised on the other side. It had been forty-five minutes since the last storm's passing, and the Salinas men were at their posts. One was about fifty yards ahead of the ship on the quay, another about fifty yards behind, with one walking around on the ship's large well deck. Those three men were about to die. D'Agostino took no pleasure in it. Neither did he have any qualms after looking at the corpses and soon-to-be corpses strung up on the crosses before the hacienda. It was just another mission.

Another rain shower was arriving, and D'Agostino decided this was the one. "Cadillac Two Three, this is Greenman One, over."

"Greenman One from Cadillac Two Three, go ahead." replied the Rivet Joint, or "RJ" aircraft, an air force electronic warfare version of the venerable Boeing 707 passenger jet orbiting twenty-five thousand feet overhead.

"Cadillac Two Three, Greenman One, is Orchid on station? We are about to step off, over."

"Greenman One, Cadillac Two Three, affirmative. Orchid is holding at the IP now."

"Cadillac Two Three, Greenman One, roger, we are going dark, starting assault in two minutes. Over."

"Greenman One, Cadillac Two Three, roger, out."

D'Agostino switched his radio over to the team net. "All Greenmen, launch in two mikes. I expect the watch to duck under cover in the same spots as before. Take them first. Drop anyone else you see moving."

"Roger One," Banks acknowledged on the radio, while Parker just patted his shoulder twice.

As the rain's intensity increased, the guard on the quay stepped under an overhang of a building. D'Agostino keyed his radio. "Greenmen, GO!" Two pops sounded behind him as Parker's marksman fired his noise-suppressed SR-25 rifle, dropping both the man by the building and the man on the ship within three seconds. The five men stood as one and trotted on the boat, linking up with Banks's group by the boarding port and stepping aboard. Parker's group split in two, each of two men moving along the outside of the ship to take out any other guards. D'Agostino led Banks's group inside the main entry. This group also split in two, with D'Agostino leading two men along the main deck in the ship's interior and Parker with two men and Dominguez headed for the engineering spaces.

The first pass resulted in five Salinas dead, all taken by surprise, either sitting or lying down. D'Agostino's men then began a thorough sweep of all compartments. The senior SEAL himself burst into the room holding the two hostages, who immediately went to their knees with their hands raised. D'Agostino bound both men and left one of his men as a sentry. He met up with Parker in the passageway.

"Main Space secured, boss. Dominguez is working on the engines, now," Parker said.

"Right," D'Agostino replied. He switched his radio back to the tactical frequency. "Cadillac Two Three, Greenman One, objective secured, no casualties."

"Greenman One, Cadillac Two Three, roger that. Well done, guys. Orchid is through the gate, ETA three mikes, over."

"Roger, out." He looked at Parker. "Let's go up and welcome the cavalry."

USCG Cutter *Kauai*, Caribbean Sea, four nautical miles east of Isla de Barbello, Honduras
01:58 EDT, 6 April

Sam

Kauai had gone to General Quarters Condition One when they reached the final departure point around ten nautical miles east of "the Gate" at Barbello at one a.m. The patrol boat was buttoned up and at darken ship—doors were closed and dogged down to prevent the spread of flooding and fire in case of damage. Before reporting to the Bridge, Ben had made an inspection tour to ensure no light sources were exposed. The crew had been briefed and took the warnings to heart, but sometimes fasteners or covers worked themselves loose, and even a sliver of light could alert and draw fire from their opponents.

The fact was that despite these precautions and the selective armor enhancements on the Bridge and engineering spaces, *Kauai* was extraordinarily vulnerable to any weapons larger than small arms simply because, unlike larger warships, she didn't have the space to absorb punishment. Sam was quite correct in his warning to Pennington about RPGs—she would be lucky to survive one hit along or below the waterline, and two would do her in for sure.

Everyone on the Bridge and working on the weather decks, as the ship's exterior was known, was in full battle gear: body armor, anti-flash garments, and Enhanced Combat Helmets. The Bridge was crowded, with the FC3 console fully manned by Williams, Zuccaro, and Bunting. Pickins was on the helm, Hopkins OOD, and, of course, Sam was there in his role as commanding officer. During the initial approach through the Gate, Ben would also be on the Bridge as a supernumerary, ready to take over if Hopkins or Sam were hit and disabled. Once they cleared the Gate and were maneuvering within the harbor, Ben would join his team below to be ready for the assault.

The plan remained as briefed in Key West. Hopkins would conn *Kauai* into contact with *Carlos Rojas*. Ben and his team of Bondurant, Lopez, and Machinery Technician Third Class Dave Brown would jump on board, along with Simmons and Gerard. Ben, Bondurant, and Lopez would carry suppressed pistols besides carbines in case they encountered any Salinas soldiers missed by the SEALs on the way to *Carlos Rojas*'s bow, while Brown carried the messenger line. The messenger line was an ordinary rope attached to the heavy hawser *Kauai* would use to tow the other ship. The hawser weighed ten pounds per linear foot, and it would take all four of Ben's team to pull it up the thirty feet from *Kauai*'s afterdeck to *Carlos Rojas*'s bow and manhandle it into position for the tow. On *Kauai*, Lee would supervise the deck party of the junior boatswain's mate Jenkins and the three medical technicians to handle the hawser on her end.

As predicted, the weather was stormy, and Sam hoped one of the transient rain showers would give him a ticket in, unseen by whoever might be watching on the promontory. *Kauai*'s refit had included installing a new multi-mode radar capable of both surface search for navigation and tracking targets and weather mapping for tracking precipitation. It was in the latter mode now, and Sam stood behind Zuccaro, watching the blobs representing rain showers come and go. There had been two promising candidates in the last hour that fizzled, but a strong one was forming now that offered some promise. Regardless of how this one turned out, Sam was determined to head in—they simply couldn't wait any longer.

Under standard navigation rules, you waited for storms or anything else restricting visibility to pass before entering harbor. The Global Positioning System-enabled navigation management system was accurate to within fifteen feet and agnostic to environmental conditions. Still, it was prudent to use visual and radar fallbacks to improve the margin of safety. However, on this occasion, the benefits of being obscured on the journey outweighed the risks. Sam nodded in satisfaction at the screen as their storm firmed up and moved toward the island. He turned to Hopkins. "This looks like the one, Chief. Start your approach."

"Very good, sir. Helm, come left, steer two-six-five," Hopkins ordered as she moved the engine thrust setting up to ten knots. At this rate, they would enter the rear of the storm about half a mile outside the Gate and penetrate about halfway through by the time they reached the quay.

"Chief, my heading is two-six-five."

"Very, well. Zuccaro, shift to surface search range four on the radar and bring up navigation mode on screen three."

"Aye, Chief, switching to surface four on radar and nav mode on screen three," the petty officer repeated.

Hopkins pressed the transmit button on the intercom. "Main Control, conn, shift to battery and shut down diesels. Prepare for emergency restart."

"Conn, Main Control, shift to battery complete, placing all engines in Bravo-Zero."

"Conn, aye," Hopkins said, then stood back as the low growl of the diesel engines went silent.

Sam put on his headset and switched to the common tactical frequency on the encrypted radio. "Cadillac Two-Three, this is Orchid, over."

"Go ahead, Orchid from Cadillac Two Three."

"Cadillac Two Three, we are starting our approach into the harbor, ETA eighteen minutes. Request update on OpFor, please."

"Orchid, Cadillac Two Three. Roger, no radar emitters are currently operating. Reading a normal pattern of life on all communications. Greenman is beginning assault now, will report when the objective is achieved. Buzzer is coming on, over."

"Cadillac Two Three, Orchid, roger, out." Sam took off his headset and switched to the speaker on the tactical radio. He was relieved to hear that the Salinas mob was not operating any radars, although it would be nearly impossible for them to pick up *Kauai* through the rain with her stealth coatings. Greenman was the SEALs, now beginning their effort to seize control of the ship and its immediate vicinity along the quay. Buzzer referred to the radio jammer the RJ would employ to disable the gang's communications. The RJ had mapped out every transmitter on the island during the previous nights' flights and would render them all useless with the flip of a switch. The trick was to do this early enough to disrupt any counterattack, but not so early as to warn the opposition an attack was imminent. Since the attack was underway, now was the time.

They were catching up to the storm now. The patter of the large raindrops quickly sped up to a low roar. Sam keyed his tactical radio again, "Overwatch, Actual, might as well come in out of the rain. You won't be able to see anything out there, anyway. You too, Mount 51."

"Roger, sir, coming down," Guerrero's voice replied. Half a minute later, there was a thud from aft, then Guerrero came in the bridge door with his sniper rifle slung on his shoulder and Hebert right on his heels. "Thanks, Captain. Whew! It's really coming down out there."

"Captain, I'm losing both EO and infrared on the Gate," Williams announced.

"Very well. Shift forward and report when you have the quay," Sam said.

The loss was expected, since the rain would work both ways. Sam stepped aside to allow Hopkins to reposition behind the console, using the navigation screen to conn the patrol boat since she no longer had visual references. Sam's stomach tightened as he watched the electronic map representation of Barbello's entrance channel close in from both sides of the pipper in the center that stood for *Kauai*. He jumped when a sudden flash of light illuminated the Bridge, followed almost at once by a clap of thunder. *Shit! I never thought I would ever say, Thank God, it's only lightning.* He was glad he had issued orders for hands to stay inside during the approach, as the lightning moved the concern from simple discomfort to the safety of life. He glanced over at Hopkins and noted the intense expression on her face in the glow of the screens as she issued helm commands to keep *Kauai* in the center of the channel.

As they cleared the Gate and the area of good water broadened around them, Ben stepped up to Sam and said, "By your leave to lay below, Captain?"

Sam turned and gazed into his eyes, then shook his hand firmly and said quietly, "Very well. Godspeed, Ben."

"Thank you, Captain."

Hopkins, the tension of the passage through the channel over, turned and gave him a hug, whispering, "Take care, sir."

"I'll be back directly, Chief," Ben said as he returned the hug.

Williams turned from his screen and bumped fists with Ben. "Give 'em hell, XO."

"Thanks, Joe. Keep them off my back, will ya?"

"Same as always, sir."

Ben nodded to everyone, then turned and went below.

Ben

The messdeck was far more crowded than the Bridge between the three-man army medical team, plus Bryant, Lee, and Jenkins, Ben and his three teammates, and, finally, Simmons and Gerard. Standard white lighting was turned off in favor of the red illumination that preserved night vision. The conversation was very subdued as everyone contemplated the upcoming mission, with only the near-silent electric motors and drumming of the rain on the decks providing background noise.

Ben slung his carbine and touched the three spare magazines in his vest by force of habit. He then clipped the night vision goggles onto his helmet, plugged in the battery, and checked them for focus and operation, flipping them up to the off position when he finished. Finally, Ben picked up the suppressed nine-millimeter pistol, checked the magazine and chamber, and slipped it into his holster. His checklist complete, he turned to his teammates, already rigged for action. “Any last-minute issues or questions, guys?”

“No, sir,” Bondurant said. “Let’s get it done.”

“Roger that.” He pressed the transmit button on his radio. “Orchid, Alpha-One, Alpha Team ready.”

“Alpha-One, Orchid,” Bunting’s voice said. “Roger, that. Break, break. All teams, Orchid. Man positions, ETA five minutes, over.”

“Alpha-One, roger, out,” Ben said.

“Towmaster, roger, out,” Lee said.

“Alright, let’s do it, everybody!” Ben announced. “Dr. Simmons, you and your man stick with me until we get on board.”

“Yes, sir,” Simmons said, picking up and slinging his Uzi. He turned to Gerard and said, “Ready, Billy?”

Gerard nodded and stood. “Let’s do it.”

Ben turned to Lee and put out his hand. “Be careful, Shelley.”

She shook his hand, looked up at him, and nodded grimly. "You too, sir."

After Simmons and Gerard joined him, Ben led the way out of the messdeck and into the rain, flipping down his NVGs to turn them on. He immediately realized they were useless in the rain and flipped them back up. Ben was sodden within a few steps and could barely see the details of the afterdeck as he led his group to the rail and crouched. Nothing was visible off the patrol boat's side, just the large fenders hanging alongside and a curtain of rain.

Ben continued to sweep his view from side to side as *Kauai*'s silent approach continued. The knowledge that they were moving at five knots in zero visibility near land and other vessels was unnerving to a trained mariner like Ben.

"Alpha-One, Orchid, fifty yards. Cleared to board at discretion."

"Orchid, Alpha-One, roger, out," Ben said.

Finally, Ben could make out details off the port side. First, the quay and its buildings and then, the *Carlos Rojas* herself, looming forward of the beam. He could hear the soft starting and stopping of the electric motors as Hopkins "walked" *Kauai* sideways into the other vessel. Two figures appeared on the *Carlos Rojas*'s afterdeck, and Ben was reaching for his pistol when one gave the "safe" hand signal. *Kauai* finally made contact, and the fenders compressed with a loud squeak that made Ben's hair stand up.

"Alright, let's go!" Ben whispered and jumped over to the other vessel, followed by Simmons, Gerard, and the rest of his team. He stopped briefly to talk to the two men whose appearance left no doubt they were SEALs. "Lieutenant J.G. Wyporek, Cutter *Kauai*."

"Welcome aboard, Lieutenant. Senior Chief D'Agostino, Petty Officer Parker," D'Agostino said. "Please put these clips on your left shoulder. They're keyed to our NVGs. We're still doing a sweep and don't want to tap you guys by mistake." He handed each team member one clip, which they attached to their vests. "There's a DEA guy in plain clothes down below trying to get the engines working. Please don't shoot him."

"Thanks, Senior Chief. This is Simmons of DIA. He and his man here will deal with the device."

"Roger that, gents, follow me," D'Agostino said, then turned and walked off, followed by Simmons, Gerard, and Parker.

"OK, let's go," Ben said, drawing his pistol and moving forward. The four men stepped carefully forward—the decks were running with water in the rain, and a slip and fall was a particular hazard for men carrying loaded weapons. They quickly reached and climbed the ladder leading to the foredeck. Brown then continued to the bow, carrying the messenger line. After threading it through the bullnose in the bow, the four men started pulling on the line, taking in the slack. After they had boarded, *Kauai* crept forward to put her afterdeck directly alongside *Carlos Rojas*'s bow to shorten their distance to lift the hawser. Finally, the messenger line was paid out, and Alpha Team started pulling up the hawser. More and more of the heavy line came off *Kauai*'s deck, and the grunts and panting among the four men reached a peak just as the hawser's eye went through the bullnose. As the other men continued to pull in the hawser, Ben took the end and dragged it to the capstan. "Lope!" he whispered.

Lopez broke off from the group and helped Ben wrap the heavy line around the capstan with three loops, then tied off the end to a mooring bitt.

"OK, guys, we're done," Ben panted. "Boats, you stay here. Lope and Brown follow me." They went first to the mooring line leading from the bow, removed it from its bitt, and dropped it overboard. They moved aft, repeating the process with every line and cable connection they encountered. When he was satisfied they had cleared everything, Ben turned and said, "Brown, get down to the engine room and see if you can help that DEA guy. Remember, do not start any engines, or do anything else noisy without an order from me. Clear?"

"Yes, sir," the engineer replied.

"Lope, we're heading to the Bridge."

"Right behind you, sir."

As they made their way to the Bridge, Ben caught a last glimpse of *Kauai* as she disappeared into the rain, and *Carlos Rojas* drifted off the dock. Ben stopped and kneeled as he saw a shadow move in the bridge door window, and Lopez crouched behind him. *SEAL or Salinas?* Ben thought as he sighted his pistol on the figure. Finally, the figure turned, and Ben could see he was not in military gear and was carrying an

AK-47. "Pop-pop" went his pistol with a tinkle of glass from the broken window, and the figure dropped to the deck. Ben and Lopez quietly opened the door and crept inside, sweeping the interior through their pistol sights. Nothing. Lopez leaned over and checked for a pulse. "He's dead, XO."

"Right. Help me figure out the helm," Ben said as he pulled out the NVG flashlight. He could see the rudder indicator, and it was rudder amidships; thank God. Ben had feared the crew had left the rudder hard over to port or starboard, a condition which would have made the *Carlos Rojas* impossible to tow without being corrected. He keyed his radio. "Orchid, Alpha-One, hawser secured, all moorings cast off, ship ready for towing."

"Alpha-One, Orchid, roger. We've lost sight of you in the rain. Advise us when heading is right of zero-seven-five."

"Orchid, Alpha-One, WILCO, out."

Within seconds, they felt more movement as the towline alternated between tightening and loosening. Somewhere out of sight in the rain, *Kauai* was applying small bursts of thrust to pull *Carlos Rojas* off the quay and get her lined up and moving. They had to start slowly, pivoting the ship to alignment with the towline before applying full thrust or risk parting the hawser or destroying the tow points on the bow. It was essential, but it took time, and Ben knew that the time available for hiding under this squall was running out. He checked the compass—it read zero-two-zero, basically north-northeast, and was inching slowly to the right. The bow had to swing past zero-seven-five, roughly east-northeast, before the side loading on the towline was low enough for *Kauai* to pull in earnest.

After two minutes, which seemed to stretch to two hours, the compass finally swung past zero-seven-five. "Orchid, Alpha-One, passing zero-seven-five, still swinging right."

"Alpha-One, Orchid Actual, roger, hang on back there," Sam's voice said. "We are coming out of the squall now, out."

Ben grimly accepted that last bit of news. The storm that allowed them to slip in unseen and begin the tow had been a godsend, and it was too much to hope that it would also cover them on the way out. Now things could get interesting. He keyed his transmit button again. "Alpha-Two, Alpha-One, Orchid's taking a strain on the tow now. Leave it and report to the SEAL commander, over."

"Alpha-One, Alpha-Two, WILCO, out," Bondurant said.

There was no sense having Bondurant stay on the bow, as the tow line's tension would prevent any slippage from the windlass or bitt. He needed to be back where he could help or be helped as required if shooting were to start. Ben looked forward through the bridge windows and saw the formerly solid curtain of rain was wavering. They were coming out of the storm. And safety.

Simmons

As Ben and the rest of Alpha Team made their way toward the foredeck, D'Agostino and Parker led Simmons and Gerard below to the living quarters. The ship's interior was dark—Dominguez had shut down the generator to prepare for their silent departure. D'Agostino used his red-lensed flashlight to lead the way, and Simmons took out his for immediate use.

"You guys both DIA?" D'Agostino asked.

"Yup," Simmons said.

"Right," D'Agostino said with a scowl, turned, and continued down the passageway. As they rounded a corner, Simmons could see three bodies dressed in civilian clothes spread along the corridor floor and a SEAL standing casually beside a door. "OK, we've got it. Head back to the well deck," D'Agostino said.

"Roger, Boss," the man said and moved past them toward the vessel's rear.

D'Agostino opened the door and shined in the light, and the two occupants startled and sat up.

"They say anything to you, Senior Chief?" Simmons asked.

"Negative, not a peep."

"OK, we'll take it from here, thanks."

D'Agostino gave them another sour look. "You sure?"

"Yes, thank you. It's all on me."

"Suit yourself. P, let's get going." The two men turned and moved briskly back down the corridor as

Simmons turned on his flashlight, led Gerard into the room, and shut the door.

Simmons shined the flashlight back and forth between the two men and asked, “Which one of you is Gronkowsky?”

The man on the right looked at the other man, who stood. “I am Gronkowsky.”

Simmons stepped forward, cocked his Uzi with purposeful menace, and turned slightly toward Gerard, keeping his eyes on the two men. “Take a good look, Billy. Behold a genuine mad scientist.” He turned to face the two men. “There are only two possible outcomes from this encounter, gentlemen. One is that you comply with our orders instantly and completely and live to take your chances in an American court. The other is that I kill you without hesitation or remorse. What is it going to be?”

“I want to live, of course,” Gronkowsky replied.

“I agree,” Dorshak answered sullenly.

“Good choice. Now for some ground rules. Know that the assault force has killed everyone on board this ship except you two. Calling for help will only get you a broken jaw, and running will get you shot in the back. Let’s move out to the lab.”

Dorshak nodded and stood. Simmons led the way out the door, with Gorshak and Gronkowsky following, and Gerard bringing up the rear. As their procession wound down the ladder and into the production lab, Simmons noted the vessel was moving. Ben and his team had gotten it underway and clear of the quay.

The lab was dark, and the lack of any sound other than the distant creaks of the slowly moving vessel lent an ominous gloom to the compartment. Simmons gestured to two chairs at one of the tables. "Pull those chairs into that corner and sit down," Simmons said to the two prisoners. Simmons continued to Gerard as they complied. "OK, Billy, get to work."

Gerard nodded and started exploring. The computer set was relatively compact and concentrated on the desks on one side of the room. He started tracing network cables to ensure every external storage device was identified for destruction. Simmons noted two large tanks, positioned on either side of the room, with control devices mounted at the top and piping leading to large, complicated apparatuses sitting atop two of the tables.

"This is it? All the equipment?" Simmons asked Gerard.

"If the info we got from Holtz is legit, yes," Gerard replied.

"OK, rig the computers with thermite first, then the gizmos on the tables and the tanks." As Simmons continued to guard the prisoners, Gerard went to work. He had just finished laying out the thermite charges on the second table-mounted apparatus when a loud whirring sound erupted from behind them, followed by the familiar grumble of a diesel engine start. It worked up to speed within a few seconds, and the lights came on.

"Thank God! We're through!" Gerard said with relief.

Simmons shook his head. "No. It's too soon. We're in trouble." His words were followed by more whirring and an abbreviated grumble, indicating a second diesel engine had failed to start. A few seconds elapsed, then a second failed start try, and Simmons could now hear gunfire from topside. "Right, rig the tanks!" he said.

15

The Nearest Run Thing

USCG Cutter *Kauai*, Underway, Departing Harbor, Isla de Barbello, Honduras
02:18 EDT, 6 April

Sam

"Orchid, Towmaster, Alpha Team away, messenger line passed, recommend slow ahead," Lee passed to the Bridge.

"Towmaster, Orchid, roger," Bunting said.

"Rudder amidships," Hopkins said as she pushed both thrust levers just forward of the "Stop" detent. After five seconds, she moved both thrust levers back to Stop, as *Kauai*'s momentum allowed her to continue to creep slowly forward.

"Orchid, Towmaster, twenty feet to go…ten feet to go… Recommend stop."

Hopkins pulled the thrust levers back to provide a small burst of reverse thrust and then moved them to Stop. The silent kabuki between *Kauai* and *Carlos Rojas* continued for about five minutes. Lee issued guidance from the afterdeck, and Hopkins used engines and rudder to hold the patrol boat in position while the tow was rigged.

"Position is good. Hold," Lee transmitted, then provided a running report of the operation. "Messenger line paying out. Hold position. Messenger line is out. Hawser is going up. Hold position. Hawser is on board. Hold position. Alpha Team signaling hawser is rigged. Standing by."

"Towmaster, Orchid, payout six hundred feet and then hold."

"Helm, right ten degrees rudder, steer zero-four-five," Hopkins ordered.

"Chief, my rudder is right ten degrees, coming to zero-four-five," Pickins responded.

Hopkins moved both thrust levers just forward of Stop, and *Kauai* crept forward, turning slowly to the right. Within one minute, *Carlos Rojas* was lost from sight in the rain. After two more minutes, Ben's voice burst from the radio speaker.

"Orchid, Alpha-One, hawser secured, all moorings cast off, ship ready for towing."

As Bunting responded, Hopkins moved the thrust levers forward to a slightly higher power setting. "Bunting, I need an update on the towline," Hopkins said.

The petty officer nodded, "Towmaster, Orchid, say status."

"Orchid, Towmaster, six hundred feet paid out, hawser secured to towing bitt. Hawser is taking the load. Hawser lifting."

Hopkins pulled the thrust levers back to Stop.

"Hawser steady, hawser settling," Lee reported.

And so it went for the next five minutes. Hopkins applied bursts of thrust to pull the *Carlos Rojas* into alignment on a due east course out of the harbor. The deluge of rain was tapering off, and visibility was improving ahead when Ben's voice finally reported again.

"Orchid, Alpha-One, passing zero-seven-five, still swinging right."

Sam stepped forward and put his hand on Bunting's shoulder. "I'll take this." He pressed his radio transmit button.

"Alpha-One, Orchid Actual, roger, hang on back there. We are coming out of the squall now," Sam said as Hopkins moved the thrust levers forward to the ahead one-third position.

As quickly as it had come, the storm passed on, and *Kauai* was in clear air with *Carlos Rojas* just coming into view behind. Sam's heart sank as the visibility increased to virtually unlimited, and flashes of lightning from other storms to the south and east were strobing at a rate of several strikes per minute. *OK, not ideal, but we've been lucky so far.* He looked over in the promontory's direction. *Stay asleep, you bastards, and we'll all live through this.* "Williams,

Surface Action Port. Load high explosive incendiary. Find that KPV emplacement and put the gunsight on it. Weapons tight."

"Aye, Captain, searching," Williams said as he cued the EO/IR camera in the general direction they had recorded. He selected another control, and the main gun issued a series of clanks as the autoloader chambered a round. "Gun loaded with H.E., still searching for the target."

"Very well," Sam said and turned to Guerrero. "Up you go, Gunner."

"Yes, sir. On the way," Guerrero said, then turned and left the Bridge.

"You want me on Mount 52, Captain?" Hebert asked.

"No, you hang out here. That promontory is too far for effective fifty-caliber fire, and you'll be too exposed on the mount. If we tangle with small boats, I'll cut you loose."

"Yes, sir," Hebert said with some relief.

"Captain, I have movement on the promontory with the infrared camera," Williams said. "Looks like two individuals."

"Stay on them," Sam said. *Come on, don't look this way.* He winced as more lightning flashed off their starboard side. "Zuccaro, what's our battery status and speed of advance?"

"Forty-one percent and four knots, sir," the young petty officer replied after checking the figures.

It's going to be close. From their testing, Sam knew the battery figure was deceptive. Power output from the battery bank dropped precipitously at levels below five percent. They had another fifteen minutes before he had to start the diesels. A series of lightning flashes erupted from the south as if on cue.

"Orchid, Cadillac Two Three, I'm getting calls from the peninsula. They may have seen you, over."

Sam grabbed the handset. "Cadillac Two Three, Orchid. Can you confirm they have us?"

"Orchid, Two Three, negative. They are just trying to get through to the primary base. We are still jamming. This behavior is unusual—they do not have a regular call schedule."

"Two Three, Orchid, roger out." Sam replaced the headset and keyed his tactical radio. "Overwatch, Actual, you are weapons-free. Any searchlights swinging our way or gunfire, and you're cleared to fire."

"Understood, sir. Out," Guerrero responded.

They were a little under a quarter-mile from the Gate; they would be abeam in three minutes at this speed. Another series of lightning flashes strobed off to starboard, and suddenly the bright beam of a searchlight stabbed into the darkness and hastened toward them.

"Crack!" went Guerrero's rifle.

The searchlight went out at once, and gunfire erupted from the promontory. A rocket launched two seconds later and sped far overhead, sparks spewing from its tail. There was a loud pop, and then both ships were silhouetted in the blinding white light of a parachute flare. Hopkins keyed the intercom, "Main

Control, Conn, Emergency Engine Start Sequence, now!"

"Williams, target on last known GPS coordinates for the KPV. Lay down a pattern. Suppressive fire, Batteries Release, Commence Fire!"

As the first diesel engine whirred to life, the main gun barked out three targeting shots, then started automatic fire on the hidden gun emplacement at two rounds per second, each shell a mini grenade exploding on contact. A series of pops distinct from the intensifying gunfire sounded from the nearby land. Within half a minute, all three diesel engines were operating and supplying power to the motors. Hopkins pushed the thrust levers forward to ahead two-thirds speed—now was the time to push the towline to the limit. She keyed her radio. "Towmaster, Conn, how's the towline?"

"Conn, Towmaster, towline is taught. Almost no catenary, but it's holding. I don't think there's much left!" Lee replied.

"Roger, stay under cover until further notice!"

"WILCO, out!" Lee said.

Sam's primary worry, the KPV, had so far failed to materialize. The automatic fire from small arms was mainly falling short, with the occasional thump of a strike on the hull. He looked back at *Carlos Rojas*—the SEALs were returning fire with their squad automatic weapons. He unconsciously winced as he heard two objects hiss past the Bridge in the darkness. RPGs! There wasn't anything more he could do about that threat except hope the long odds against a hit held. "Zuccaro, speed and position."

"Six knots, sir. We are through the gate. *Carlos Rojas* is coming abeam now."

Sam was about to reply when an enormous crash sounded just behind the Bridge, shattering the port bridge door window and almost throwing Sam and Hopkins off their feet. Standing back up, Sam shook his head to clear it. *Shit, so much for the odds!* "Everyone OK?" After receiving a thumbs up from the bridge crew, he keyed his radio. "All stations, RPG hit aft of the Bridge, report status. Williams, keep firing!"

"Yes, sir!" He had released the trigger in the shock of the hit. A moment later, the gun was banging away again.

"Conn, Towmaster, one casualty," Lee's voice said. "Jenkins is wounded and being moved inside now. Towline is holding. Hit appears to have been on the boat deck. No fire, over."

Jenkins! Sam's jaw clenched at the thought, but he had to put the young boatswain out of his mind for now. "Roger. Overwatch, report."

"My ears are ringing. Otherwise, OK, sir. Over," Guerrero reported.

"Conn, Main Control, systems normal, no damage, no casualties," Drake reported over the intercom.

"Conn, aye," Hopkins said.

"Hebert, Lee's on her own. Get down to the afterdeck and help her!" Sam said.

"Aye, aye, sir!" Hebert said, then turned and ran back off the Bridge.

Sam winced again as a second flare burst over the scene just as the first burned out. Dammit, that guy knows his job! The flare was far behind them but was almost overhead the *Carlos Rojas*, and the gunfire was shifting to follow. Almost immediately, two explosions in close succession sounded from the towed vessel, followed a couple of seconds later by a sound like a cannon shot, and *Kauai* lurched forward.

"Conn, Towmaster, the towline has parted!" Lee reported.

As Hopkins brought the thrust levers to Stop, Sam hung his head and unconsciously pounded his right fist on his thigh. "Towmaster, Captain, cut the line!"

"Aye, aye, sir!"

Williams's jaw tightened as he tried to concentrate on laying down fire. They had to cut the hawser—it was useless now and, dragging over the stern, was an extreme risk to *Kauai* during maneuvering. Unfortunately, "cut the line" meant Lee had to take the sharpened ax and chop through ten inches of strengthened fiber out in the open air of the afterdeck in an environment alive with gunfire and rockets. Hopkins glanced down and saw Williams's expression and reached down to give his shoulder a light squeeze.

"Alpha-One, Orchid Actual, prepare to abandon ship. We'll be dropping back to pick you up."

"Orchid, Alpha-One, roger, sir. We may have engines shortly, will advise."

After a minute, which seemed like an eternity to Sam, Lee came on the radio again. "Captain, Towmaster," she panted. "Towline cut and clear!"

Thank God! "Well done, Lee! Get inside now!"

"Chef and I <pant> are already <pant> there, sir!"

Williams let out his breath, and Hopkins released her hold on his shoulder with a soft pat.

OSUV *Carlos Rojas*, under Tow, Isla de Barbello Harbor, Honduras
02:53 EDT, 6 April

Ben

Like Sam over on *Kauai*, Ben had to suppress the urge to jump every time lightning flashed out on the starboard side. The rain had passed entirely, and visibility was nearly perfect. Ben and Lopez had nothing to occupy their attention as the ships slowly moved out of the harbor, unlike their shipmates on the other vessel. He was thoroughly frightened and deduced Lopez was in the same state.

"So, Lope, when we were debriefing after the last one, Captain Mercier told us you would get some 'special' attention over at Law Enforcement School. Did that come to pass?"

"Oh, yeah, sir. While everyone else in my class was living the good life in Charleston every weekend, I was getting advanced small arms and personal defense training shoved up my ass!"

"I hear ya. I got the same thing up in Quantico. Like to freeze my ass off on that small arms range all day." He winced again in the darkness as a long series of lightning flashes strobed across the starboard side.

It was actually quite beautiful, the bolts weaving up from the surface of the Caribbean and then winding through and lighting up the clouds from within. He wished he could enjoy the view. "Quite a show."

"No shit, sir," Lopez said in a measured voice. "I'd prefer to see this movie in the next showing, though."

Ben laughed, then looked forward in alarm as a searchlight lanced into the darkness from the promontory, followed by the sound of gunfire. "Shit!" He keyed his radio. "Alpha-Four, One, light off now!"

"Alpha-One, Four, roger, lighting off!" Brown replied.

As the first flare burst off to starboard, a muffled whirring sounded deep in the hull, followed by the rattling rumble from the smokestacks as the ship's generator fired. The main engines needed a lot more power to turnover than the batteries could provide, so step one was getting a generator running. As the generator's noise topped out, a second, louder whirring came up from the engine spaces. Ben's heart sank when the initial rumble of the large engine died away. A second main engine start sequence sounded a few seconds later, with the same result. Ben was about to key his radio, then thought better of it. An inquiry at this point would just distract Brown from his work. The sound of automatic gunfire came up from the well deck—the SEALs joined the fight with their heavy machine guns.

The fight between *Kauai* and the promontory was heating up, and Ben could hear the 'thumps' every half-second from the main gun and see the tracers streak across the water. Williams was doing a good job keeping the pressure on. So far, nothing more than small arms fire was being thrown their way. Suddenly, a flash followed by an enormous boom came from *Kauai*, and the main gun ceased firing. "Shit, shit, shit!" Ben exclaimed, pounding his fist on the helm console. After a few seconds, the rapid thumping and twenty-five-millimeter tracer streaks returned, and Ben let out an enormous sigh of relief.

Ben was about to comment on a second flare that had appeared almost overhead when an enormous blast threw him onto the deck. One moment he was standing there; the next, he was flat on his face, covered in broken glass. "Lope!"

"Here, sir! I'm OK!" the young petty officer said as he got to his knees.

Ben looked behind the Bridge. The rocket had apparently hit the port smokestack, which was now shredded. He had just gotten to his feet and pulled Lopez up when the second rocket hit the foredeck. This time, the forward windows shattered, and the two men were thrown down again. Worse, shrapnel from the explosion sliced through some outer strands of the towing hawser. Given the enormous strain the line was under, there could be only one result: the cascade of individual strand failures in milliseconds merged into one loud "Bang." The two new ends shot away from the breakpoint, one slamming into *Carlos Rojas*'s superstructure with a loud "clang" and the other falling into the water just short of *Kauai*.

Ben looked forward in shock as they got to their feet again, then keyed his tactical radio. "Alpha-Four, Alpha-One, we just lost the towline. We need main engines now, or we're dead!"

"Almost there, sir! We've fixed the problem and are closing up now!"

"For God's sake, hurry!"

"Yes, sir!"

Ben's command radio came alive. "Alpha-One, Orchid Actual, prepare to abandon ship. We'll be dropping back to pick you up."

"Orchid, Alpha-One, roger, sir. We may have engines shortly, will advise." He turned to Lopez. "Lope, get down to the well deck and tell the SEALs to evacuate as soon as *Kauai* comes alongside, then find Simmons and tell him to light the torch."

"Yes, sir!" the young man said, then made for the door with his feet crunching on the shattered glass covering the deck.

"Alpha-Four, One, we'll be abandoning in about two minutes!"

"Yes, sir. Attempting start on starboard engine now!"

The whirring of the start sequence sounded again, but this time, the rattling grumbles continued and built up volume and tempo. *Yes! Go, baby!*

"Alpha-One, Alpha-Four, starboard engine on the line and ready to answer all bells!"

"Well done, Dave!" He moved the right thrust lever forward, watching with satisfaction as the propeller pitch and r.p.m. increased. "Orchid, Alpha-One, starboard engine online, and we're making way!"

"Well done, Alpha Team! Follow us." Sam's voice responded.

Ben reminded himself that they were not out of the woods as a few stray rounds from shore pinged off a windowsill. "Alpha-Three, One, we're sticking with it for now. Get back to the Bridge."

"One from Three, on the way, sir," Lopez said.

Ben looked at the panel. At two-thirds speed on the starboard engine, they were making eight knots. They would have to follow *Kauai* to navigate as the rockets' explosions had knocked out the compass. The whirring sound returned, signaling a start attempt on the port engine. This one was successful.

"Alpha-One, Alpha-Four, port engine ready to answer all bells."

"Four, One, roger, out." He was advancing the left thrust lever to match the right when Lopez came through the bridge door. The firing was tapering off as the pit log steadied at twelve knots. "Feel like taking the helm? You need to stay on *Kauai*'s tail—the compass is shot to hell."

"I've got it, sir," Lopez said, stepping over to the helm.

"Thanks. I'm heading down to see what's going on."

"Right, sir."

Ben crunched over to the door and headed to the well deck. When he arrived, he noted two men were down being tended by a medic and froze in his tracks. "John!"

"Over here, sir," came a voice from his right.

Ben almost cried out with relief. "Glad to see you in one piece."

"Yes, sir, you too. It was pretty hot down here, but I about shit myself when those rockets hit forward. How are things back at home?"

"*Kauai* took a rocket hit behind the Bridge. I heard on the command net that Jenkins went down. Shelley was on her own for a while. She's the one who axed the towline after it broke."

"Shit! Any word on the kid?" Bondurant's face was a mask of concern.

"Hang on a minute. Senior Chief D'Agostino?"

"Here, Lieutenant."

"How are your men?"

"I've got two with minor wounds, but they're both ambulatory."

"That's good news. We're making twelve knots, but the dopers could still catch up with us in the boats we saw."

"Not happening, sir. We cut all their fuel lines before we took the ship, and we also have their only mechanic below us now. This one's over."

"It's a distinct pleasure dealing with professionals, Senior Chief," he said as he offered his hand.

"Likewise, sir," D'Agostino said as he shook it. "If you'll excuse me, sir, I need to get back to my guys."

"Certainly." He keyed his command radio. "Orchid, Alpha-One, Alpha Team is all OK. Greenman has two casualties, both minor wounds. Do you have any report on Jenkins? Over."

"Alpha-One, Orchid Actual, roger. He took some shrapnel in the arm and thigh. He's out for this round, but should recover."

"That's a relief, sir. We have both engines online, but the Bridge is beaten up. We'll need to follow you to the dumpsite."

"Roger that. Two hours at present speed."

"Thank you, sir." He turned to Bondurant. "Jenkins took some shrapnel from the rocket hit, but he'll be OK."

"OK. Thank you, sir," Bondurant said with his head down.

"Hey, we're not done yet. Could you head up to the Bridge and keep Lope on the straight and narrow for me?"

"On the way, sir." The big boatswain shouldered his carbine as he headed forward.

Ben turned and went inside to find Simmons and Gerard. According to the briefing, the lab was just forward of the engineering spaces in a medium-sized compartment. As Ben neared the room, he could hear a muffled conversation. He knocked when he reached the door and called out, "Wyporek!"

The door opened. Gerard stepped out and nodded for Ben to enter. As Ben walked into the room, he noted Simmons guarding two men in the corner. Gerard stepped in behind him and started gathering up some loose gear in the center of the compartment.

"I presume we survive to fight another day," Simmons quipped.

"It was close, but yes, we're clear," Ben said. He glanced at the two tanks. "Is that it?" he asked as a chill ran through him.

"Yes. It's a binary compound. Each component is safe on its own," Simmons answered. "We have the computers and hard drives rigged with thermite and just finished un-rigging the product generators and tanks. Don't want to take any chances."

"Right. Well, I have to get back to it. We've got a couple of hours to go before we get to the dump point," Ben said.

"I'm afraid to ask, but what was the final bill?" Simmons asked.

"*Kauai* took an RPG just aft of the Bridge, and Jenkins was hit by shrapnel, but he'll pull through. Two of the SEALs are down, but D'Agostino says they'll be OK. It could have been a hell of a lot worse."

"Jenkins? Dammit! I really like that kid. I hope he bounces back."

"Time will tell. OK, you need any help down here?"

"No, we've got it. Please give me a heads up when we're ready to leave. We don't want to activate the thermite until we are ready to step off. It will burn through the tables and go right on through the deck."

"Got it. I'll see you soon."

Ben left the men in the room and walked back to the well deck. It felt good to get back into the open night air, and he indulged himself for about a quarter of an hour, watching the lightning arcing through the distant rain clouds. Then he headed back to the Bridge for the rest of the transit.

16

The Last Gasp

OSUV *Carlos Rojas*, Underway, Caribbean Sea, four nautical miles east of Isla de Barbello, Honduras 05:17 EDT, 6 April

Ben

"Alpha-One, Orchid, we've reached the location. Heave to and shut down. Over."

"Orchid, Alpha-One, WILCO, out." Ben pulled both thrust levers back to Stop, and the noise of the main engines drew back to idle. He keyed the transmit button on his team radio and said, "Alpha-Four, One, that's it for this one. Secure all engines and come up."

"Roger, sir," Brown said.

"OK, guys, I'll meet you on the well deck," Ben said to Bondurant and Lopez. After they had crunched away, Ben stood briefly looking around the Bridge.

"You did good, old girl," he said, patting the helm. Then he turned and left the Bridge for the ladder.

When he reached the well deck, the SEALs were gathering in one corner, and his team, plus one man in civilian clothes, were chatting in the other. As Ben walked over, Brown spoke up, "XO, this is Mr. Dominguez, DEA. He's the one who got the engines running."

Ben grabbed his outstretched hand and shook it warmly. "I don't know how to thank you, sir. You saved all our asses for sure back there."

"Believe me, Lieutenant, it was my pleasure. Couldn't have done it without Dave here." Dominguez nodded toward Brown.

"Noted. Thank you," Ben said. He turned to Bondurant. "Boats, how about you guys check with the SEALs and see if they need any help with their wounded guys or gear?"

"On it, sir. C'mon, guys," Bondurant said, leading the other two petty officers to the SEAL group.

Ben watched as *Kauai* swung around *Carlos Rojas*'s stern in the pre-dawn twilight. Since the rocket hit on the boat deck had wrecked the RHIB, *Kauai* would have to come alongside to take them off. *The paperwork on that one is going to be a nightmare.* Ben smiled to himself. *How do you know you're safe? When the paperwork is your chief worry.*

Dominguez stepped up beside him. "I heard she took an RPG hit. It looks like she came out OK."

"Yes, it definitely could have been worse. Changed our plans for getting off using the small boat. It's a little riskier for her to come alongside, but at least the seas are calm. Should be pretty quick."

"Right," Dominguez said. "This will be my first time on a Coast Guard cutter."

Ben was about to reply when his vision exploded in stars and then went black.

Sam

"All hands, prepare for a direct approach to the vessel, rig fenders on the port side," Hopkins announced over the PA and replaced the microphone. She set the patrol boat up for a shallow approach to *Carlos Rojas*'s starboard side, pressing the vessels together just long enough to disembark everyone. The sense of relief on the Bridge was pervasive. They had all come through, and now only one last detail to carry out.

She glanced over to ask Zuccaro for a position report when the sound of gunfire, first one, then several guns, erupted from the other vessel. In shock, Hopkins froze for a moment, then pulled the thrust levers back to Stop. "Captain!"

Sam keyed his radio. "Alpha-One, Orchid Actual." He paused as the gunfire came to a stop. "Alpha-One, Orchid Actual, report!"

"Orchid, Alpha-Two, XO is down, repeat, XO is down," Bondurant's voice came from the speaker.

Sam's mouth opened in silence. A gigantic icy ball had formed in his stomach. *No! That can't be right.* He blinked and looked around the Bridge—everyone was looking at him. He keyed the radio again. "Alpha-Two, Orchid Actual, roger, report, over."

"Orchid, Alpha-Two, one of the gang bangers must have been hiding out somewhere. He just opened up with an AK. The SEALs shredded him. I'm going to the XO now. The DEA man is down, too."

"Alpha-Two, Orchid, roger, see to them and report when able."

"Roger, sir, standby."

Ben

"XO, XO!" Bondurant's voice echoed from a distant place.

Ben could feel hands on him, and he was being shaken gently. He slowly opened his eyes and had a brief bout of panic as he saw only a faint light. *What's wrong? Why is it dark?* He relaxed as he remembered. *Because it's night, dumbass!* His head felt like it was exploding. "Wha...What happened?"

"Lie still, sir. The medic's coming," Bondurant said.

Ben turned toward the voice when his head exploded in pain again. "Shit!"

There was some movement, and another voice said, "Freeze, Lieutenant, let me check you out." Gradually, his head and vision cleared, and the voice continued. "OK, sir. It looks like you took an AK round off your helmet. I don't see any wounds. Can you tell me how you feel?"

"Bad headache. It's fading, though. No other pain and I can feel everything." Ben wiggled his toes to make sure.

"Orchid, Alpha-Two, XO is OK, just got his bell rung," Bondurant reported. "Yes, sir. Yes, sir, I will."

He's talking to the captain. Why can't I hear it? Oh, my helmet is off.

The medic leaned over. "Right, I want to see if you can sit up. Don't push it. We'll stop if something doesn't work or there's too much pain."

"OK," Ben said. He felt hands under his shoulders lift him, and he sat up. Another wave of pain passed over him, and then he said, "So far, so good."

"Alright, we're going to help you to your feet now. No heroics, sir. If you can't make it or the pain gets too much, say so."

"WILCO," Ben said. Then hands helped pull him up. "I'm a little dizzy, but I think I can stand OK."

"That's enough for now, sir. You lean on your shipmate for a while."

"OK," Ben said. His head was still clearing, and he would not argue. "Boats?"

"Yes, sir," Bondurant said.

"What happened?"

"One doper just popped up. He must have been holed up in a hidden compartment. No one saw him until he opened up with an AK. Then the SEALs took him out."

"Anyone besides me get hit?" At Bondurant's silence, he continued. "Tell me."

"Sir, the DEA man, Dominguez. He's dead. Took one right through the head. The rest of us are OK."

"Son of a bitch!" Ben hung his head, his headache returning. "He saved our lives, and I don't want him left behind. That's an order."

"Yes, sir, I've seen to that. We are putting him in a litter we took from the ship's sickbay."

I should have known. "Sorry, Boats. I'm not at the top of my game right now."

"No worries, sir. *Kauai*'s coming alongside now. We'll get you on board and have the doc look you over."

"Don't fuss over me, Boats. See to the rendezvous. Get a headcount and make sure everyone gets off OK."

"Yes, sir. Dr. Simmons, could you look after him, please?"

"Yes, John, I've got him," Simmons said, taking Bondurant's place at Ben's side. Whispering to Ben, he said, "You scared the shit out of me, friend! I thought I would have to make 'that call' to Victoria."

"How the hell did a cartel guy get by the sweep?" Ben asked.

"It was one of their 'Hitler Youth.' He couldn't have been over thirteen. He was probably hiding in a cabinet somewhere. Unbelievable."

"I had time. I should have searched. Dominguez…" he shook his head.

"Don't go there. This is not on you. It's not on anybody. These things happen, particularly on wild-ass ops like this." He looked over as *Kauai* snugged up against the side. "Let's go, partner. We've got a fire going on the computers downstairs that will light up this barge in a minute."

Ben nodded, started to bend over to pick up his helmet, then stopped and stood up as another wave of pain washed over him. "Ahhh," he said, putting his hand to his head. "Can one of you guys bring that helmet, please? The NVGs alone are worth nine grand."

"I've got it, Lieutenant," Gerard said as he picked up the helmet.

Ben was still a little dizzy and had an intense headache, but with Simmons's help, he made it to the side and over the rail onto *Kauai*'s afterdeck, with additional support from Bondurant and Lopez.

"Everyone accounted for, sir," Bondurant reported.

"Thank you, Boats, carry on, please."

"Yes, sir."

Bondurant stepped aside as Lee trotted up. She took a deep breath as she looked into Ben's eyes, then snapped a crisp salute. "Welcome home, sir."

Ben returned it. "Glad to see you in one piece, Shelley."

"Same here, sir. The bastards broke my boat, sir!" she blurted out.

Ben glanced up at the mess on the boat deck, smiled, and turned back to her. "Don't worry. The taxpayers will buy you a new one."

"I suppose. But I had this one all tuned up!" She grinned back.

Ben put his hand on her shoulder, gave it a soft squeeze, and watched as *Kauai* pulled away from the other vessel. D'Agostino walked up and got his attention.

"We're ready to blow her, sir."

"How is she rigged, Senior Chief?"

"I've got charges right above the bilges in each compartment. Give the word, and I'll blow her bottom out."

"Boats? Call the Bridge and tell them we are ready to scuttle on their order."

"Yes, sir," Bondurant said, then keyed his radio. "Conn, afterdeck, seized vessel ready to scuttle. Very good, sir." He looked at Ben. "Let'r rip, sir."

After getting a nod from Ben, D'Agostino announced, "Fire in the hole!" Then he pressed a button on a hand-held controller.

Seven quick thuds sounded from the *Carlos Rojas*, and the ship settled, slowly at first. As the bow sank level to the sea, the vessel rolled left and quickly plunged out of sight, leaving a spreading patch of white foam and debris.

"Now, I think you should head in to see the doc," Simmons said.

"I'll let him finish with men who are actually bleeding before I go to him for a headache," Ben said. He turned back and looked at *Carlos Rojas*'s grave as his head started pounding again. "You should be elated. Another win for the good guys."

Simmons shook his head. "They'll just be another one when I get back. 'Tomorrow, and tomorrow, and tomorrow, creeps in this petty pace from day to day.'"

Ben closed his eyes to another wave of pain and struggled to think. "Man, you're not pulling a Mac…Mac…." He tried to move to the rail but ended up falling to his knees and throwing up on the deck. The pain was blinding, all-consuming. He couldn't see, just heard shouting.

"John! Help me get him inside!"

Strong arms lifted him off the deck and carried him like a baby. It had to be Bondurant, but he couldn't see. He struggled to think. Pain! He felt himself being put down gently on the mess table.

"What were his symptoms?" A new voice. That army doctor. What is his name?

"He's had a headache, and he collapsed and threw up."

"Was he unconscious after the injury?"

"Yes, for a couple of minutes."

"Shit! Where's his helmet? Find it!"

"Why do you need that?"

"Don't argue with me, goddammit! Get me his helmet! Rabin, I need an IV stat and pump in forty milligrams of propofol as soon as it's running. Langley, get the craniotome bit into the autoclave and wipe down the ultrasound wand."

Ben felt a hand on his face, then a blinding light and what felt like a knife in his eye. "AHHH!"

"I know it hurts. I'm sorry, Ben. Right pupil, normal and reactive, left, fixed and dilated."

"Here it is, sir!" *John's voice again.*

"Yes, yes. OK, there it is."

"Propofol going in, Doctor."

"Thank you." The voice became louder. "Ben, you have a type of brain injury that is causing a bleed inside your skull, and I have to knock you out so I can treat it." The voice became distant. "Is he married?"

"No, but his girl's name is Victoria." *Pete's voice.*

Louder again. "Ben, you'll be going to sleep now. I want you to think about Victoria. You'll see her soon."

The pain was subsiding, and he was back in Bethesda. The apartment door opened, and she was standing there looking so beautiful, more beautiful than he ever imagined—*Victoria!* Then the vision narrowed to blackness.

Sam

Sam had just finished watching *Carlos Rojas*'s last moments. He had expected to feel happy or at least satisfied, but he just felt drained. *Is that all I have, the absence of despair? I guess it beats the alternative.* He had been quite close to complete despair twice in the last few hours. First, when the towline parted, then when the report came that Ben had been gunned down. Each moment had been resolved with a seeming miracle, and Sam wondered how much longer his luck would hold. He shook himself. *Take the win. Let's go home.* "Chief, Port Canaveral via Key West, twenty-four knots, if you please."

"Very good, Captain," Hopkins responded, advancing the thrust levers to the required power setting.

Sam lifted the microphone to contact the Coast Guard Cutter *Thetis* and tell her to stand down the helicopter on alert for MEDEVAC when the phone rang.

"Bridge, Bunting," the young technician said. "Standby. Captain, it's Doc, urgent."

Sam took the phone. "Captain."

"Captain, Bryant here. The XO has collapsed. It looks like some sort of TBI. We've just moved him onto the table. I recommend you get the MEDEVAC helo spun up, sir."

"I'm coming down." He hung up the phone without waiting for a response. "Bunting, contact *Thetis* and get that MEDEVAC bird in the air ASAP. Chief, the XO just went down with a head injury. I'm heading down, but I'll be on the headset if you need me. Stay on your present course, but call flight quarters as soon as the helo calls airborne and get on a good course and speed for hoisting when they are inbound."

"Yes, sir," Hopkins said.

Sam ran to the rear of the Bridge and slid down the railing of the ladder without his feet touching a rung, the dad's voice in the back of his mind hoping none of the junior enlisted members saw him. He pulled up to the messdeck door, crowded with crew members gazing in with worry. "Gangway," he said, and they stepped aside.

Ben was stretched out on the mess table, unmoving, an IV in his arm and an oxygen mask over his face. The surgeon moved a small held-held device over Ben's head, watching a monitor and making an occasional mark with a sharpie pen. Sam stood silently, watching as the surgeon finished his exploration with the device.

"Rabin, Betadine everything within two inches of the X." He turned, saw Sam, and stepped over. "Captain, the lieutenant was shot in the head. His helmet kept the bullet out, but the impact was akin to a hammer blow to the side of his head. He has a severe bleed inside his skull. I'm going to do a stopgap procedure to keep him alive, but he needs to be medevac-ed to one of the Miami trauma centers as soon as possible."

"I've got a helo spooling up on a cutter about twenty miles away."

"Good. I'll need about twenty minutes to get it done. Then it's a race against time to get him to surgery."

"What are you going to do?"

Roberts looked at him for a second, then pulled him away from the other crew. When they were out of earshot, he continued. "I'm going to drill a hole in his skull and drain out the excess blood, Captain," he whispered.

Sam's mouth hung open briefly. "My God!"

"I know how that sounds, but if I don't do it, he'll be dead before he gets halfway to Miami."

"I understand. Is there anything I can do, anything you need?"

"Yes. As you can imagine, this is about as delicate a procedure as it gets. Anything you can do to dampen down the deck motion would help."

"Of course," Sam replied and keyed his microphone. "Conn, Captain."

"Conn aye, sir," Hopkins replied immediately.

"Chief, Major Roberts needs to perform…a surgical procedure on the XO. Get the speed down and maneuver as required to get the lowest pitch and roll possible. Do you copy?"

"Affirmative, sir. Throttling back now."

The engine noise reduced, and Sam felt *Kauai* come down from the semi-planing mode as her speed slackened. "Good, keep her as steady as possible from now through the helo hoist. Maneuver at discretion."

"Understood, Captain."

Sam shut off his microphone. "Doctor, it will probably take Chief Hopkins a minute or two to find a sweet spot."

"That's fine, thank you, Captain."

"Doctor, we're ready," Langley said.

"Right. Captain, I need you and everyone else out of here. I know he's a buddy, but you can't help and won't be able to unsee this."

"Yes, yes." Sam turned and said, "Everyone out, now!" As he followed them out the door, he looked back and said, "Good luck, Doctor."

17

The Golden Hour

USCG Cutter *Thetis*, Underway, Caribbean Sea, twenty nautical miles northeast of Isla de Barbello, Honduras
06:15 EDT, 6 April

Becker

The ship had been at Flight Quarters Condition Three (Modified) since 02:00 to prepare for rapid turn-up and launch of the embarked MH-60T helicopter. Firefighting and rescue equipment were readied and laid out. The flight deck crew were attired in their color-coded flash-protection gear, and the Helicopter Control Station was manned. The helicopter crew had "cocked" the aircraft on the flight deck, pre-flighted the airframe, removed all engine and sensor covers, and taken off all tie-downs other than the primary chocks and chains.

The aircraft commander, Lieutenant Commander Stephanie Becker, was in *Thetis*'s Combat Information Center, following the latest information on the mission and keeping a keen eye on the weather. Her crew, consisting of her copilot, Lieutenant Keith Holmgren, Flight Mechanic, Petty Officer Nikita Harris, and Rescue Swimmer, Petty Officer Greg Daniels, were lounging by the aircraft parked on the flight deck, ready to jump in and complete an expedited start at a moment's notice.

The rainstorms providing a welcome sanctuary for *Kauai* during her approach had proven quite a challenge for *Thetis*. Her flight deck was barely broad and long enough to support the landing of the MH-60, and her hangar was far too small to house the large helicopter. With a vulnerable aircraft parked on the open air of her flight deck, *Thetis* had to be kept clear of thunderstorms, with their powerful shearing winds and lightning. Occasionally, an anxious OOD had to pour on full speed to dodge a rapidly building storm.

Becker was about ready to call it a day. Reports from the cutter involved in the mission, callsign Orchid, showed a few minor wounds in action, nothing justifying the risks of a helicopter hoist and long flight back to the States. She was gathering up her charts and kneeboard when an urgent call came over the command net: "*Thetis*, this is Orchid, request immediate assistance. Require MEDEVAC for one patient with traumatic brain injury and one medical attendant, over."

So much for calling it a day. Becker quickly jotted down the latitude, longitude, course, and speed of the cutter and headed back to the flight deck as the announcement to set Flight Quarters Condition One reverberated through the ship. By the time she reached the aircraft, Holmgren had already started the APU, a small jet engine providing power to start the main engines and run the electronics, and was carrying out the pre-flight checks. The flight crew had reached an agreement with the ship's captain that they could start the APU independently without waiting for the ship's fire parties to man up fully during an emergency launch like this.

When *Thetis* reached full readiness at all flight quarters stations, the yellow-shirted Landing Signal Officer, or LSO, gave the pilots a thumbs up. Holmgren keyed his radio. "*Thetis*, Six-Zero-Two-Three, request permission to start engines and engage rotors."

"Six-Zero-Two-Three, *Thetis*, permission granted to start engines and engage rotors. Amber deck."

"Six-Zero-Two-Three, roger."

After starting the two main engines and getting the rotors up to full speed, Becker and Holmgren completed the last cockpit checks, called for a takeoff, and received a reply. "Six-Zero-Two-Three, *Thetis*, cleared for takeoff to port, take signals from the LSO. Green deck."

Holmgren gave the "remove tie-downs" hand signal to the LSO, who dispatched the aircraft's tiedown crew. They removed the wheel chocks and tiedown chains from the helicopter and scurried forward clear of the flight deck. The LSO kneeled for one last visual check, then stood, waved his hand in a circle, and pointed off to the ship's port side. Becker lifted the helicopter into a brief hover over the flight deck, then slid left clear of the ship and began an acceleration and climb. Once clear and climbing, Holmgren keyed the radio again. "*Thetis*, Six-Zero-Two-Three, flight operations normal, over."

"Six-Zero-Two-Three, *Thetis*, roger, maintain guard with me for now. Good luck. Out." Becker glanced at the aircraft's clock: 06:30, thirteen minutes from callout to airborne, very respectable, especially considering the shipboard launch.

The flight from *Thetis* to *Kauai*'s position was a short nine minutes. In the last five, the cutter's officer of the deck discussed the operation with Holmgren to complete plans and decrease the helicopter's time overhead. There would be two hoists: the first of the cutter's health services technician, the medical attendant for the flight, then the litter containing the patient. On arrival, Becker slowed the helicopter and said, "Complete rescue checklist part one for direct delivery of the rescue strop." Harris slid the cabin door open and attached the strop to the hoist hook.

"Rescue check part one complete," Harris announced. She keyed the intercom again as the helicopter pulled into a hover alongside *Kauai*. "Holy Shit! Look at the boat!" A large black smudge stretched across most of the rear of *Kauai*'s superstructure, the boat crane's arm was severed, and the tubes on the RHIB were shredded and deflated.

"OK, let's stick to business. Complete rescue check part two," Becker responded.

Harris snapped out of her awe and completed the check. "Rescue check part two complete."

"Orchid, Six-Zero-Two-Three, ready for hoist."

"Two-Three, Orchid, cleared to hoist."

The medical technician and his go-bag came up first. Once he and it were safely aboard, Harris and Daniels hauled out the litter and sent it down. After a minute, the patient was positioned in the litter and hoisted aboard. Harris shut the cabin door, and as the helicopter climbed and accelerated away, Daniels handed the medical technician a flight helmet and plugged it into an intercom cord.

"Can you hear me?" Daniels asked after the technician had put on the helmet.

"Loud and clear," the technician responded.

"I'm Greg, and this is Mikita," Daniels said. "Anything we can do to help?"

"Not right now, thanks. The name's Mike Bryant."

"OK. What's in the bag?"

"Two IV bags, two units of O-negative, medical disposal bags, and a lot of towels."

"Towels? You expecting rain?" Daniels quipped.

"No, blood. A lot."

"What the hell?"

"The patient has a brain bleed. The surgeon made a burr hole and installed a drain. I have to keep it clear until they get him to surgery, or he'll die. So, we're going to have bleeding.

"Shit, what happened down there?"

"Sorry, that's classified."

"Did he get it when the boat was hit?"

"Again, sorry. Can't discuss it."

"OK." Bryant's reticence would have probably put off the average person, but Daniels was not to be denied and said, "Who is he, anyway?"

"He's our XO."

"Oh, well, you guys won't have to worry about shoeshines and haircuts for a while."

Becker cringed and was about to put a stop to the conversation when Daniels hurriedly said, apparently to a reaction from Bryant, "Hey, I'm kidding!"

"Kid about something else, asshole!" Bryant shouted.

"Daniels, how about you stick to business and give everyone a break?" Becker interrupted. "We've got a long trip ahead of us."

"Yes, ma'am," Daniels said contritely. "Sorry, man."

"Forget about it," Bryant said. "Can you give me a hand with the towels here?"

"You've got it."

Office of the Director, Joint Interagency Task Force South, Key West, Florida
06:45 EDT, 6 April

Pennington

"We have a report from Orchid, sir," Commander Keener called on the intercom.

"Bring it in, please," Pennington responded. After realizing that he was thoroughly demoralizing his staff by hovering in the situation room, Pennington had confined himself to his office. His relief on hearing that both *Kauai* and *Carlos Rojas* had cleared Barbello harbor and were en route to the dump point with only three casualties was immense. None of the wounded required medevac, even better. He was happy to be proven wrong, even if it was by that callous DIA asshat.

There was a knock on the door, and then Keener came in holding a clipboard with a TOP SECRET cover on it, closing the door behind him. "Here it is, sir."

"Read it." Pennington took off his glasses and rubbed his eyes. He had gotten about five hours of sleep in the last three days and could barely see his desk, much less read message text.

"*Carlos Rojas* sunk at 10:12 Zulu and gives a position." He paused with his mouth open.

Pennington looked up with concern. "What is it?"

"Revised casualty list, sir. There was a Salinas stowaway on the *Carlos Rojas*, and he opened fire as the boarding party was gathering to disembark." He paused again.

"Well?"

"One killed, Dominguez, DEA agent. One serious injury, Lieutenant J.G. Wyporek. He's just been hoisted from *Kauai*. His condition is listed as an epidural hematoma. It's some kind of traumatic brain injury."

Pennington pressed his palms against his eyes. They punched through that gauntlet of machine guns and RPGs and then got blindsided by a nut job with an AK? How does that make sense? "Where is the helo going?"

"Miami. He'll need a neurosurgeon and a trauma center, sir."

"We know which one?"

"Um. No, sir."

Pennington took his hands from his eyes and put on his glasses. "What do you mean, no? Do you expect them to make arrangements via INMARSAT? For God's sake, Dan, give them some help. I don't care which one it is, but I want a top-flight neurosurgeon scrubbed and ready to cut when that helo touches down. Get on it! If I need to bust Fred Brown's or General Miller's balls to make that happen, you tell me! Move!"

"Yes, sir!" Keener said, then fled the room.

Pennington stared at the door after it closed. Ben, we'll get you right if I have to chew up every commander, captain, admiral, or general from here to DC. We owe you and your crew that much!

National Intelligence University, Bethesda, Maryland
07:32 EDT, 6 April

Victoria

Victoria was walking on air as she made her way to the office. She only had a few hours of sleep, excited as she was after her phone call with Benjamin the previous evening. This would have left her tired, grumpy, and unproductive on a typical day. Not today. She felt like she could solve P versus NP if she put her mind to it. After locking up her bag and cellphone, she cheerfully presented her badge and almost skipped through the metal detector at the security checkpoint. It was just a short walk to the Data Analysis Division and her cubicle.

Debbie was away from her desk, which was typical, as she usually had administrative housekeeping tasks piled up at the start of each day. Victoria sat in her cubicle, booted her computer, and started the login process. A knock on the wall behind her startled her. She turned and smiled when she saw it was Debbie—she couldn't wait to tell her about the phone call. The smile quickly faded. Something was wrong. Mr. Fletcher, the office director, was standing behind Debbie, and they both looked.... What? Her brain searched for the correct term. Grim. Yes, that was it. She must have done something very wrong.

"Dear, could you come with us, please? There's something we need to talk to you about," Debbie said.

"Yes," Victoria said, standing up. The situation was alarming. So much so that she almost left her Common Access Card plugged into her computer, which would have been a serious security violation on top of whatever faux pas she had committed. She followed them silently into Mr. Fletcher's office and sat down at the table next to Debbie while Mr. Fletcher sat on the edge of his desk.

"Victoria, this is about that young Coast Guard officer you've been seeing. His name is Ben Wyporek, is that right?" Mr. Fletcher asked.

I cannot be in trouble for that, can I? Benjamin is a commissioned officer with the highest security clearance, not a foreigner. "Yes, Mr. Fletcher. Is there a report I should have submitted for that?"

"No, it's nothing like that. I…, I just…."

"Sir, may I, please," Debbie interrupted on seeing his distress. At his nod, she continued. "Dear, I got a call from Peter Simmons this morning right after I got to work."

"Yes?" Victoria was confused. *What did Peter have to do with this?*

Debbie reached over and took her hand. "He was with Ben last night. I don't know how to say this, but Ben was badly hurt."

Her vision seemed to close into a tunnel centered on Debbie's face, and the sound echoed in her head. She felt like she couldn't breathe and squeezed Debbie's hand. All that came out was, "No. No, no, no. He's not…not…."

"He's not dead, Victoria, but he was badly hurt. They have taken him off his ship by helicopter, and he is on the way to a hospital in Miami. He should arrive there around one o'clock."

"Miami?" Her brain was spinning, but math quickly took hold. Over six hours by helicopter, average speed one-hundred-fifty miles per hour, eight hundred miles. They would bring him to the closest hospital trauma center in the US, so eight hundred miles from Miami. "What was he doing in the Caribbean?"

Debbie and Mr. Fletcher looked at each other in surprise. "I'm sorry, dear, we don't have that information," she said.

"How was he hurt?"

"Peter said it was a head injury. Something called an epidural hematoma."

"Oh, no!" An eidetic memory like Victoria's could be a gift or a curse. Just now, it was the latter. She had read about epidural hematomas and knew that if Benjamin did not receive immediate neurosurgery, he could die or be permanently disabled. Five hours did not equal "immediate" in her mind. "I must go to him. Mr. Fletcher, I need to take leave. I am sorry. I know I am supposed to submit a request for leave two weeks in advance."

Mr. Fletcher shook his head. "Victoria, that is not a problem. But are you sure you want to go right now? I'm told he could be unconscious...indefinitely with these things."

“Mr. Fletcher, he will either wake up in one to two days, or he will die.” She nodded firmly. “I need to be there when he wakes up.” Victoria knew Mr. Fletcher was right. She did not bring any knowledge or skills to bear that could influence the outcome in the slightest. However, as irrational as it seemed, while Benjamin’s life hung in the balance, she was determined to be with him. She turned to Debbie. “Can you help me find a flight to Miami? I do not have time to learn how.”

“Yes, I’d be happy to, dear,” Debbie replied with tears in her eyes.

“I’ll see if we have anyone headed down that way who can escort you,” Mr. Fletcher added.

“Thank you, Mr. Fletcher. I will go in any case, but having someone I can trust along would be very helpful.”

“Good. I’ll let you two move along to make arrangements while I make some phone calls. Victoria, I’m very sorry about Ben, and I pray he will be OK. If there is anything we can do, I hope you will call us.”

“I certainly will. Thank you, Mr. Fletcher.”

USCG Cutter *Kauai*, Underway, Caribbean Sea, eighty-five nautical miles north of Isla de Barbello, Honduras
08:52 EDT, 6 April

Sam

Sam looked across the messdeck at Simmons as he sat, head down, staring at his hands resting on the table. Sam's attitude toward the DIA man had fluctuated considerably since their first meeting almost three months ago. What started as a wary acceptance and understanding of a man with an enormous challenge had ended in white-hot anger when Simmons had carelessly blundered into an ambush and dragged Ben with him. At the end of the last mission, he had told Captain Mercier in no uncertain terms that there would be a reckoning if he and Simmons ever crossed paths again.

That moment had come. The anger had faded in the interval, but the distrust and dislike remained. That Ben had a cordial, almost friendly attitude toward the man who had so flippantly risked his life was a great mystery to Sam and one of the few issues on which he and Ben disagreed. He supposed you could not stand under fire with another man without developing some attachment. There was also Simmons's young protégé, admittedly quite beautiful, and with whom Ben was utterly smitten.

Sam had to admit that the current crisis was not a result of anything Simmons had done. They had all performed their duty, took appropriate actions, and did their best to minimize the risks. Ben's injury was a matter of bad luck, not recklessness this time. Sam swallowed hard and walked over to the table. "Doctor, are you alright?"

Simmons looked up at Sam, who was surprised to see actual pain in the man's face. "No, Captain, I'm really not. For the second time in three months, I've set events in motion that may finish, if not kill, the finest man I've ever known. I just made a call up to Bethesda so Victoria's boss can share with her the wonderful news that the man she loves may die today. How can I possibly be alright?"

"Doctor, you know I'm not your biggest fan. So, you can believe me completely when I say that this situation is not your fault. Even I am good enough at math to know the butterfly effect theory is bullshit. No act of yours long ago and thousands of miles away had any influence on events here. And, by the way, Ben is not finished yet. Roberts says all the factors line up on his side."

"Yes, sir. I hear what you're saying, but I'd like to continue to wallow in self-contempt for a time, if you don't mind. At least until we get some good news."

"Suit yourself. I'm not here to console you, but I need to use your satellite phone to arrange for my wife to see to things back in Miami. I will, of course, pay for any charges incurred."

"Don't be ridiculous, Captain. I will not bill you for that."

"Yes, you will. I want no favors from you, and I won't have any pencil-necks hanging an ethics charge on me down the road."

"OK," Simmons said, pulling the phone out of his bag. "Do you know how to use one of these?"

2035 SW 14th Terrace, Miami, Florida
09:17 EDT, 6 April

Joana

Joana Mendez Powell was juggling three balls this morning. Her two children, Robbie and Danni, were, naturally, her most important and demanding ball. Fortunately, new birthday toys from Robbie's namesake, Sam's mentor, Bobby Moore, held their attention for a while. The second demand on her time was working up the chain to find *someone* who knew *something* about the household goods move coming up in a couple of weeks. It drove her crazy that a move of two hundred miles from Miami to Patrick Air Force Base proved more difficult than one of *five thousand miles* from Honolulu to Miami! How her parents managed eight of these during her father's navy career and kept their sanity was a wonder to her. The final and least urgent was the book cover she had contracted to design for a self-published author. She still had a couple of weeks to finish that, but he was nice, and she wanted to deliver early, if possible.

Joana hit save on her computer when the phone rang, grabbed it, and moved to a position where she could monitor the kids while she talked. She had learned that at least one sensor had to be trained on the children continuously, or mayhem would shortly ensue. The caller ID simply said INMARSAT Unk—it was probably from Sam. Who else would call using the International Maritime Satellite service? "Hello?"

"Hi, sailor."

"Well, my beloved captain, to what do I owe the surprise of an INMARSAT call? Did you forget my birthday or something?"

"Jo, I…"

Joana's blood went cold. This was going to be bad. "OK, darling, let's have it."

"It's Ben. We just medevac-ed him. He's on the way to Miami now and should get there about one o'clock."

"Oh, My God! How bad is it?"

"Very. He has a head injury, a kind of brain bleed."

Tears welled up, and her hands shook. Ben was not just another shipmate for Sam, but his closest friend and the brother he never had. And it didn't end with Sam. Joana was closer to Ben than her brother Eddie in many respects. She took a deep breath and tried to steady her voice. "Is he going to make it?"

"Jo, I want to tell you yes in the worst way. I don't know. The doc we have with us says he has the best shot we can give him, but there's just no way to tell with this sort of thing.

She wiped her eyes and took a deep breath. "OK, what do I need to do? Do you want me to call his parents?"

"No. Ben and I discussed this situation as a possibility when we took the new job. He didn't want them freaked out when there was nothing they could do. The service has to do the notifications anyway—protocol.

"I need you to be at the hospital when Ben gets there. The JIATF guys are working on it and will call you when they get one locked in. Mike Bryant is attending him on the flight and could use some help. Also, Ben's girl has been contacted by her people and is probably on the way down."

Oh, God! The math geek? What can I say to her? "OK, I'll do my best. Is anyone else hurt? You damn well better not be holding out on me that you're bleeding somewhere!"

"No, my love, I'm fine except for an acute case of the guilts. We had one other guy catch a hit, Brian Jenkins, but he'll be OK."

As hard as it was for her, she knew the responsibility factor would crush Sam. He would normally lean on Ben for help with that, but now Ben was the one in danger. "I wish I was there to hold you. Promise me you'll get Emilia to help you. And don't worry about anything here; I've got it covered."

"Jo, I… I don't have the words."

"Don't worry, my captain, I'm an artist; I know all the words."

"I love you, *querida*. I'll see you in a couple of days."

"Come home safe, *mi amor*."

The call disconnected, and she put the phone down. Robbie had come over and was looking up at her with the most profound concern a three-year-old could conjure.

"You're crying, Mommy. Do you have an owey?"

She picked him up and hugged him tightly as she blinked away the tears. "I'll be OK. Thank you, my little man!"

USCG Cutter *Kauai*, Underway, Caribbean Sea, 107 nautical miles north of Isla de Barbello, Honduras 09:47 EDT, 6 April

Lee

Drake stepped onto the Bridge and walked over to Lee. "You got the OOD?"

"Yes, COB."

"How's he doing?" Drake said, nodding toward Sam, sitting in his captain's chair.

"Don't know. He hasn't said a word since I reported the relief." *If he's anything like me, he's a wreck.* Lee had been frightened when the towline had broken, but the urgency of cutting away that loose end had pushed back the fear. But that had been nothing compared to the horror she felt when Mr. W suddenly just collapsed in front of her, writhing in pain on the deck.

The relief Lee experienced on hearing that he was OK after being shot had been overpowering. She had almost hugged him when he stumbled back aboard, getting hold of herself at the last second and firing off a salute instead. Mere minutes later, John carried him into the medical station while she was doing all she could not to scream.

"OK." Drake nodded. then walked behind Sam's chair and said, "Captain?"

Sam turned slowly to him. "Yes, COB?"

"Sir, we have set up a makeshift ward for the wounded in the forward port berthing area. We've cleaned up the messdeck and cleared it out sufficiently for Chef to maneuver. He would like permission to resume normal meal preparation."

"Yes, that's a good idea." Sam nodded. "We have almost twice the compliment on board. Can he prepare enough food for everyone?"

"I think he's got gumbo and primavera planned for the next two meals. They should stretch OK."

"That's fine. Make it so."

"Yes, sir." He turned to leave, then hesitated. "You know, the XO will be OK, sir."

Sam turned to him and said, "Yes, he will."

Drake nodded, turned, and departed. A minute later, Roberts came through the door. "Permission to enter the Bridge? I would like to talk to the captain, please."

"Permission granted, sir," Lee said. She didn't know if she was supposed to listen to the conversation, but she would stay close enough to hear unless the captain told her to get lost. She stepped over to the FC3 console next to the captain's chair and pretended to concentrate on the navigation and radar screens.

Roberts walked over to Sam, who stood up to greet him. As Sam extended his hand, he said, "Doctor, I can't thank you enough for your work today."

"All part of the job. Heard anything from the helo?"

"Not from them, which I'm hoping is good or, at least, not bad news. The guys at JIATF South lined up a surgeon at Dadeland Hospital in Miami. Ben should go straight in."

Roberts nodded. "That's good. I'm pretty sure he'll make it to Miami. After that, it's up to them. And Dadeland's one of the best."

"Good to hear. And how are your other patients? Do I need to arrange another airlift?"

"No, they're stable where they are. Getting knocked around in a helo hoist would do more harm than good at this point. They can hold out fine until we pull into Key West."

"OK. May I ask what you were doing with that wand when I came into the surgery this morning?"

"That 'wand,' as you call it, is an ultrasound transducer. I was mapping the hematoma to find the best location for the burr hole."

"I thought you needed MRIs or CAT scans to treat these things."

"You do, and he'll get one first thing in Miami. Understand, Captain, I wasn't fixing anything this morning. I was applying the neurosurgical equivalent of a tourniquet."

"Yes. I'm impressed you'd have tools available for this sort of thing."

"It's a different environment in combat medicine now. Twenty years ago, we didn't have a lot of injuries like that. That bullet would have gone straight through the helmet and killed him on the spot. The good news with the new materials is fewer immediate deaths; the bad news is more traumatic injuries. We found out quick that head bangs can be as deadly as bullet wounds, so I added a craniotome to the kit."

"I see. What are Ben's chances?"

"You can never tell with the brain; everyone's different. I wish he'd come to me as soon as he got on board. He had a huge bleed, which is why his symptoms progressed so quickly. That said, all the risk factors and medical resources coming in are on his side. If I had to make a bet, I'd say he'll be fine if there are no other issues on the way."

"Well, I'm certainly glad you were with us on this trip. If you or your guys need anything, let me know."

"Will do. Thanks, Captain."

"Thank *you*, doctor."

After Roberts had departed, Sam stepped over to Lee. "Lee, I'm heading below. Before I go, I just wanted to say what you did last night was one for the books. We probably wouldn't be here right now if it weren't for you."

Lee blushed and looked down. "Just doing my job, Captain." After a second, she looked up at Sam with an almost pleading expression. "Mr. Wyporek will be alright, won't he, sir?"

Sam smiled and lightly patted her shoulder. "Like the doctor just said, I'd bet on it. Have a good watch."

"Thank you, sir." Lee watched Sam leave, then walked to the windows for a visual scan outside. *I don't know if we can rely on what that army guy said, but it picked the captain up a bit, Thank God.*

Hopkins

Hopkins was sitting in her stateroom, just completing a good fifteen-minute cry. She was utterly drained by the intense cycling of emotions since yesterday evening, starting with the fear of the extreme danger facing the crew. The battle itself was a fog except for that moment of sheer terror when the towline parted, and it seemed they were all lost. Then the relief of getting through, followed by the devastating report the XO had been shot, then he was OK, then at death's door again.

Hopkins thought the world of Ben Wyporek. He and the captain had come in together and turned what was a complete shitstorm into not just the best unit she had ever been assigned, but the best she'd ever *heard of.* They were both good, kind, and professional men she admired. Thank God she hugged the XO before he departed. It was the second time she had done that; the first was the mission back in January when that bastard Simmons almost got him killed. It was a serious breach of protocol for an enlisted member to hug an officer, but screw it. She never forgave herself for failing to hug her husband Brad before he left on the day he was killed on a search and rescue case. They had had a ridiculous snit that morning over something she couldn't even remember. She would not make that mistake again with someone special to her.

She looked at the picture on the wall of her two sons, with her and Fritz standing behind them. It was a Soccer Saturday from a couple of months ago, and Fritz was down from Cape Cod on a two-week leave. Fritz was a wonderful addition to her life. A tall Avionics Electrical Technician First Class stationed at Coast Guard Air Station Cape Cod, Massachusetts, Erich "Fritz" Deffler was a master Unmanned Aerial Vehicle pilot who had deployed with them briefly last January.

Hopkins had vowed never to get involved with another Coast Guardsman after her husband's tragic death. Yet, she found herself drawn to Fritz during their time together on the deployment, and they arranged to see each other afterward. He was a divorced father of two young girls living with their mother in Hawaii and had immediately clicked with her two pre-teen sons. She loved his quiet confidence and sense of humor; he was one of the few people she knew who could regularly make her laugh aloud. Her smile faded, and the pain returned when she remembered that Ben Wyporek was another of those very few people. *God, I wish I could talk to Fritz right now, just to hear his voice.*

The knock on the door startled her. She wiped her eyes and took a deep breath. "Yes?"

"Emilia, it's me," came Drake's deep baritone voice. "Got a minute?"

"Sure, come in, Jim."

The door opened, and Drake stuck in his head. "I was just passing by and thought I'd ask how you are holding up."

"Maintaining an even strain, thank you. Just needed to pop in here for a minute to re-cage the gyros."

"I get it. This getting banged-up shit is becoming a regular thing with the XO. You and I ought to sit him down and straighten him out when he gets back," he said with a sad smile.

"Yeah, junior officers. What are we going to do with them?"

"Don't know. This is one of the few times I don't know a guy to see about the problem. Look, if you're up to it, I was hoping you could join me on a walkabout. I sense the kids are reeling after everything that's happened. We should help take some of the load off the skipper."

"I'm with you." She stood. "You know, it's ironic. The XO was just joking with me yesterday that me and you were soooo mom and dad."

Her tears welled up again, and Drake stepped in, shut the door, and hugged her. "He's going to be alright. Believe that."

After a few moments, she nodded and said, "I'm OK. Let's go."

USCG MH-60T 6023, Airborne, eighty nautical miles southwest of Key West, Florida
10:48 EDT, 6 April

Becker

Becker loosened her restraint harness and lifted herself slightly out of her seat. The slight pain in her upper thighs shifted to a much sharper pain in her coccyx. Being a pilot of a helicopter held several advantages over being a crewmember. As a commissioned officer, you were much better paid, of course. Then there was the matter of control—you drove in front and rode in the back. One significant disadvantage was that you were planted in a seat built for survival rather than comfort for hours at a time. The crewmen could get up and move around during the flight, but not so the pilots. Becker had what she called a "four-hour ass," meaning things really started to ache about four hours into a sortie. She was four and a half into this one, with two hours to go. *Ouch.*

The refueling operation aboard the Cutter *Northland* had gone without a hitch. *Northland* was a sister ship of the *Thetis*, and the similar configurations and procedures made the approach and landing easier. They employed "hot refueling" on this visit, accepting a slightly higher risk to save time and avoid the chance of problems during shutdown and start. The fuel hose was laid out along the deck edge before the helicopter arrived. After the landing and applying chocks and tie-downs, a refueling crew appeared and hooked up the single-point fueling nozzle to the aircraft. The process was reversed after pumping in enough fuel to top off all tanks. The crew disconnected the fuel hose, removed the chocks and tie-downs, and the helicopter was once more on its way to Miami, a mere twenty-two minutes after landing. They now had ample fuel to reach Dadeland Memorial Hospital in Miami, perhaps even enough to continue all the way home to Clearwater without refueling again after dropping off the patient. They would decide on that later.

There were no repeats of Bryant and Daniels's earlier hostility; the latter had learned his lesson for this trip. Neither was there much conversation, which was fine as far as Becker was concerned. Even in the relatively quiet long en route segments like this one, the crew should have their heads in the game and eyes outside looking for trouble. This was doubly true of Daniels—he was a good man and an excellent rescue swimmer. Still, he was also one of the most empathically dyslexic individuals she had ever known. It wasn't the first time she had to intervene to prevent an actual fight in the cabin because of his mouth. She made a mental note to talk with his chief about it when they returned to Clearwater.

United Air Lines Flight 1990, Airborne over Myrtle Beach, South Carolina, en route Miami International Airport
11:53 EDT, 6 April

Victoria

Victoria appreciated the minor miracle that Debbie and Mr. Fletcher had achieved this morning. She was sitting in Seat A of the last row of the Airbus A319, her sometimes teammate Lashon Bell was seated in Seat C, and Seat B was empty. No one was sitting behind her, kicking or jostling her seat, and no stranger was seated next to her, *touching* her throughout the flight. There were two exit doors directly behind her, and Lashon was steady enough to handle any emergency. It was a direct, non-stop flight, so there were only two horror-filled airport terminals to deal with instead of three, and they would arrive only fifteen minutes after Benjamin was scheduled to land at the hospital. It would take them at least an hour to deplane, get the rental car and drive over, but at least she would be nearby. Anyway, she was sure Benjamin would be rushed in for an MRI and from there into surgery—it would be several hours before she could see him, even if she were at the hospital when he arrived.

Bell focused on reading a book he had brought, his eyes coming up and scanning the cabin at regular intervals. Victoria knew Lashon was very reticent and would be content to go the entire flight without speaking. She respected that and tried to keep herself occupied by reading the latest data science literature on her tablet, but she could not get her mind to focus. Victoria was still reeling from this morning's emotional upheaval of going from as happy as she could ever recall to this terrible fear of losing everything. She finally gave up and pulled up the two pictures of Benjamin from their day together, along with the others he had sent of his shipboard friends, and looped through them on her tablet. Each one told a wonderful story in her mind that pushed back some fear, at least a little.

Victoria never had a family or close friends in the conventional sense. Her parents were killed in an automobile accident when she was eight years old. Her sister Julie had raised her through high school and the beginnings of college. When her genius and autism revealed themselves after her parents' deaths, it became too difficult for her to interact with other children. So, she turned inward, focusing on her studies, which sped her through school but left her lonely. When Julie died, she thought her world had ended, but Julie's fiancé Peter came to the rescue. She completed her schooling with his help and was soon a vital part of the DIA team, but still without family or anyone she could call a friend, except Debbie. When Victoria saw the faces in Ben's pictures, even she could read the affection and trust they had for each other. His stories connecting those images were warm and funny, and she lived her dreams of a family vicariously through them. They were a great comfort to her just now.

About an hour later, they began their approach to Miami and Victoria raised the window's shade. Usually, she kept the shade open since seeing the outside helped her deal with the aircraft cabin's confined space. But with the sun on that side of the aircraft, she needed to reduce the glare on her tablet. Victoria was fascinated by the processes that went into flight and watched intently through the window as the wing's high-lift devices deployed, and they wallowed in to a soft touchdown on the runway. She was curious why the pilot retracted the flaps and slats after landing when they would be used again for the next takeoff. *Benjamin's father is an airline pilot; I can ask him when we meet.* Then reality retook hold, and she fought back the urge to cry. *If we meet.*

As they were waiting for the other passengers to deplane, Victoria turned on her phone and checked her voice mail and text messages. There was no news of Benjamin's condition, but Debbie had sent a text message that he would go to Dadeland Memorial Hospital and provided an address. She showed it to Bell, who nodded and typed it into his phone to use for navigation after they rented the car. The trip through the terminal was loud and terrifying, and Victoria hung tightly onto Lashon's arm throughout the long walk and the wait in the car rental line. She did not mind being thought of as "clingy" today.

Finally, they were through the line, driving to the hospital. The weather was pleasant, sunny, and warm. The traffic was moderately heavy for mid-day. Benjamin had mentioned that traffic here was among the worst he had seen, although he admitted he had never driven around DC during rush hour. It took the better part of an hour to drive the ten miles from the airport to the hospital in University Park. As Victoria walked to the door with the stoic Bell, her apprehension increased with every step. She had never been in a hospital waiting room before but was sure it would be frightening and very lonely.

18

A Confluence of Souls

Dadeland Memorial Hospital, Miami Florida
14:21 EDT, 6 April

Victoria

After signing the visitors' log at the trauma center, Victoria and Bell headed for the waiting room. She was almost praying that seats were available away from other people, where she could hear her thoughts without distraction. When they came to the door and started looking around, an attractive, dark-haired woman noticed them and came over.

"Excuse me, are you Victoria Carpenter?"

"Yes, I am," Victoria answered, wondering how this strange woman could know her name.

"I'm pleased to meet you," she said with a smile. "I'm Joana Powell. My husband is Ben's commanding officer."

Victoria almost fainted with relief. Benjamin had described Joana Powell as one of the finest women he had ever met and considered her a close friend. He shared many stories of her warmth and kindness, and Victoria had been looking forward to meeting her. "Oh, Mrs. Powell, I am so happy to meet you! Benjamin speaks of you so often." She smiled as she looked her up and down. "He was correct; you are very beautiful." Joana gasped, and her eyes filled with tears. *Oh, no! I made her cry! Why can I never say the right thing at times like this?* "Mrs. Powell, I am very sorry. I did not mean to upset you," Victoria said hastily.

"No, please don't think that!" Joana said, then took a breath and wiped her eyes. "You could not have said anything more right just now. I know we've just met, but I want very much to hug you. Do you mind?"

"Oh, not at all!" Victoria answered and then gave her a warm hug. When they separated, she continued. "This is Lashon Bell. He escorted me down from Bethesda."

Joana held out her hand and said, "I'm pleased to meet you, Mr. Bell."

"Likewise, Ma'am," Bell said, shaking her hand.

"If you'll follow me, I have staked out seats for us over here. And I wish you two would call me Joana."

As they approached the empty seats, a young man with short hair in surgical scrubs and wire-rimmed glasses stood up.

"Victoria Carpenter, Lashon Bell, this is Mike Bryant. He's the Health Technician on *Kauai* and attended Ben on the flight," Joana said.

"Oh, yes. Benjamin has told me about you as well. How are you, Michael?" Victoria asked, holding out her hand.

"I'm well, thank you, Miss," Bryant replied, awkwardly shaking her hand.

"Oh, good. You are wearing surgical garments. Are you going to assist with the procedure?"

"No, Miss, they loaned me these after we got here. My uniform was...dirty." In fact, his uniform was covered with blood, but he did not want to mention that detail.

"Oh, I see. Can you tell me what is happening?"

"Yes, Miss. It would be better if we sat down, I think." After they were seated, he continued. "What have you been told?"

"Benjamin suffered a head injury that resulted in an epidural hematoma. He was evacuated by helicopter from his ship and flown directly here."

Bryant relaxed a little. "That's right, Miss. Do you know what an epidural hematoma is?"

"I have read about it." She recited the definitions and details she had read on the MedlinePlus site.

Bryant was clearly impressed. "Wow. OK, after the lieutenant collapsed, the army surgeon we were carrying had a look and called the condition. He, um, did an initial treatment to remove the excess blood and relieve the pressure. Then we were hoisted by the helicopter and taken here. They took the lieutenant straight in for an MRI while I briefed Dr. Chaudhri, the surgeon, on how he got hurt and the steps we'd taken so far. He went into surgery about half an hour ago."

"Oh, I see. I am sorry to ask all these questions, but I am very nervous. Benjamin told me you were a heroic medic in the army before you came into the Coast Guard. Can you tell me from your experience what we can expect?"

Bryant's mouth hung open briefly, then he said, "He told you *that*? Um, well, it's like this, Miss…." He then engaged in a serious discussion with the young woman for over thirty minutes.

The exchange astounded Joana. She and Sam had had Bryant over for dinner, along with a couple of other crew members. Despite their considerable talents at putting people at ease, they had barely gotten five words in a row out of him. This young woman had him excitedly telling his life's story minutes into their first meeting. Joana's turn came next.

"Joana, I hope you do not mind answering questions, but I am still very nervous and am hoping for a distraction while we await news of Benjamin's operation. He told me you do computer graphic design. I am comfortable working with computers, and I enjoy art, but I struggle with the concept of how they can be put together. Would you mind explaining how you do that, please?"

"My pleasure, Victoria," Joana answered. They went into a lively back and forth about raster graphics and bitmaps, 3D modeling, rendering, and the various other tools and techniques she used. Victoria's voracious interest in her work was so captivating that Joana could gratefully lose herself in the conversation and put aside, for a time, the crushing worry that brought them here.

A few minutes into the conversation, Bell realized what was happening, got up, and walked to Bryant. "Come on, kid. Let me buy you a cup of coffee," he said. Bryant nodded and followed him out of the waiting room. Once in the hallway, Bell said, "Don't take it personally. She has a one-person lock-on function."

An hour-and-a-half later, they were all together again when a staff member came into the room and announced, "Michael Bryant."

Bryant looked at the others and said, "This is it. I listed myself on the check-in form." They all stood and walked over to the woman calling his name. "I'm Bryant."

The woman looked at the others and said, "Are all these people family?"

"The women are cleared," Bryant said. He turned toward Bell. "I'm sorry, Lashon, you're not on the list."

"Not a problem. I'll hang out here."

"Thanks." He turned back to the woman. "After you."

The woman led them to a small room with a table and four chairs. "Wait here, please. The doctor will be here shortly."

After they all sat down, Victoria's mind was racing. Why did they move us in here? Is it because it is bad news? Are they afraid we are going to make a scene?

Joana looked at her and must have realized she was upset. She reached over and took her hand. "Don't go crazy, Victoria. The privacy laws prevent them from saying anything about Ben's condition in public, and that's why they moved us here."

"Thank you, Joana. I was worried about that."

There was a knock, and a tall, dark-skinned man with eyeglasses pushed up on his forehead stepped in and closed the door as Victoria, Joana, and Bryant stood. "Hello, I'm Rajesh Chaudhri. I already met Mike. You are?"

"Doctor, this is Victoria Carpenter and Joana Powell. The patient has cleared both on his releases."

"Oh, good, please sit down."

When they had settled, Victoria's hands were shaking. Joana put her right arm around Victoria's shoulder and put out her left hand for Victoria to hold.

"I have good news. The procedure went very well." Chaudhri paused when Victoria exhaled. "I closed up the damaged artery with a very small craniotomy. He will be in recovery for another hour, and then we will move him to the ICU."

"So, when will he wake up?" Victoria blurted out. *Why did you say that? Give the man a chance!* "I am sorry, Doctor. I am very nervous."

"That's perfectly understandable." Chaudhri reached out and patted her hand. "I would not expect him to come out of the coma for at least twenty-four hours, possibly as much as seventy-two."

Victoria took a deep breath. "He will be alright then, correct?"

"There is every chance of that. I didn't see any damage to the brain structures, either on the MRI or when we had him open, but it was a huge bleed. We won't know for sure until he awakens, and we can do some tests."

Victoria closed her eyes. "I need to be with him."

"We can certainly arrange that once he is settled in the ICU, but honestly, he won't be conscious again for at least a day."

"I need to be with him, Doctor. I can talk to him. Would that help?"

"I don't know. I'm sure it wouldn't hurt."

"That is it, then. I am staying."

Chaudhri smiled and patted her hands again. "Very well, I'll see to it. If you'll excuse me, I need to look after another patient." They all stood and shook hands, then Chaudhri left the room.

"I need to get down to Key West to meet the ship if I can," Bryant said. "Lashon is heading down there, and I thought I could bum a ride off of him."

"I can stay here with you if you like, Victoria," Joana said.

"No, you need to attend to your children. I would be very grateful if you could wait with me until Benjamin is in his room."

"Absolutely. Mike, do you need anything before you go?"

"No, thanks, Mrs. P. I'll be fine."

"Well, I guess we can go rejoin the world then."

They moved back into the waiting area and met up with Bell.

"Victoria, I need to get on to Key West to meet Pete. I think they will be in a little after dawn, so I need to head down tonight. Will you be OK here?" Bell asked.

"Lashon, I'll take care of her," Joana said. "You and Mike hit the road before it gets too crazy."

"OK, if you're sure," Bell said.

"I am sure, Lashon. Thank you very much for taking care of me!" Victoria said as she hugged the agent.

"OK, let me bring up your bag, and then we'll roll."

The two men left after retrieving her bag, and Victoria and Joana sat down again. "Joana, may I ask you a personal question?"

"Naturally. What's on your mind?"

"I do not know if I am right for Benjamin. I was so frightened, and I am still so frightened about what happened to him. Does it go away?"

"No, it doesn't. You can learn to live with it, but it's always there. When Sam is out and the phone rings, my heart is in my throat until I find out it's not bad news. It might be a little easier for me than for some other spouses. My dad was a Navy submariner, and we never knew where he was or what he was doing. We learned how to live with the fear."

"Have you thought about asking Samuel to stop and do something else?"

"I have. And he could, too. He turned his back on a lucrative Wall Street career to join the service long before we met. If I were to push hard and make it a choice between the Coast Guard or me, I know he would resign his commission. To provide for us, he would go cap-in-hand to his father and, after a suitable period in scut jobs to atone for his previous career mistake, be welcomed back into the fold, start making big money and be home every night. Cool, right? The problem is he wouldn't be Sam anymore, just another soulless suit commuting in every day and doing anything, everything to make more money because that's all they live for.

"So, I hold my breath when the phone rings and treasure every day he's home with us. He's worth it."

"Do you think Benjamin is worth it?"

Joana looked at Victoria and raised her eyebrow. "That's a question only you can answer. I can tell you that Ben is certainly a close second to the finest man I've ever known. I am friends with Emilia Hopkins, and she swears there isn't anyone in the crew who wouldn't take a bullet for him. But I can't tell you he's worth being a Coast Guard spouse. I can only assure you that there's no one else who would be more worth it."

"I see," Victoria said with a furrowed brow. "Do you think I would be good for him?"

"Victoria, I've only known you for a couple of hours, but I think you're wonderful. I know Ben is crazy about you. But, besides the sudden death thing, which is admittedly quite big, there's the career thing. I work from home and am very happy with that. Sam could be assigned to Kodiak, Alaska, and I'd be OK with living there, as long as they have the Internet. Would you? If you want a top-flight career, moving up the corporate ladder, you need to find someone else because there will eventually be a collision. Then it's either a breakup or someone compromises big time, which probably still ends in a breakup. Just saying, better now than later."

"Oh, I have no aspirations toward a career. I am not good with people at all. There is a...a *problem* that hinders my understanding of affect, so I could never cope with being a manager. I like to do mathematical analysis, and I am very good at it. I think I can find that work anywhere. Perhaps I could even do that online, like you. But I am worried about the fear and if I can handle it."

"So, here's your test, girl. This is almost as bad as it gets. You'll have your answer when it's over."

Victoria turned to face her. "It could be worse than this?"

Joana nodded, thinking of Hopkins's experience. "Yes. You can get the final news without the wait." She put her arm around Victoria's shoulder. "But you'll always have your Coast Guard family to help you."

Victoria was settling in to contemplate that last point when the hospital staffer appeared again and came over to their location. "Miss Carpenter? Mr. Wyporek has been moved to his room in the ICU, and you can see him now."

"Yes. Thank you. Please go ahead." Victoria grabbed the handle of her rollaboard, and she and Joana followed the woman through several hospital corridors before arriving at the door. Victoria froze at the door, locked in an internal conflict of desperately wanting to be with Benjamin and a mind-numbing fear of what she would see when she walked into the room.

After a few seconds, the staffer remarked with some annoyance, "You can go in now, Miss Carpenter."

"Thank you, that will be all. We can handle it from here," Joana responded with even more annoyance. After the staffer wheeled and strode off, Joana took Victoria's free hand and whispered, "There's no hurry at all. We can go in whenever you are ready."

Victoria took a deep breath, nodded, and said, "Thank you, Joana. We can go in now." They walked through the door together. Victoria went slightly weak in the knees at her first sight of Benjamin, then recovered when Joana put her arm around her and steadied her. Victoria carried out the process she had planned while they were waiting. She positioned her rollaboard against the wall, pulled up a small chair, sat, and took Benjamin's left hand in both of hers. His hand was warm but limp, and she held it to her cheek briefly as she looked at his face. His eyes were closed like he was asleep, and his head had a small bandage on the right side. He was breathing silently and steadily through a nasal cannula, connected by a clear tube to a bubble humidifier. Several tubes and wires led from under his blanket to a monitor station displaying pulse, blood pressure, respiration, temperature, and O2 saturation. Victoria observed with relief that all these readings appeared to be within the normal range from what she had read.

Joana kneeled beside the chair and asked. "Are you OK? Is there anything I can do for you?"

Victoria put her arm around Joana's shoulders and said, "No. You have done so much for me already. I was really frightened when I arrived, and I was so relieved that I could meet and talk to you while I was waiting. Benjamin is fortunate to have friends like you."

Joana brushed away a fresh tear and said, "Thank you." She handed Victoria a note. "This is my cell phone number. I'll be in tomorrow, but if you need anything or just want to talk, it doesn't matter what time you call me. OK?"

"Thank you, Joana. I will see you tomorrow," Victoria said and turned back to Ben.

Joana stood, leaned over, kissed Ben lightly on the forehead, then turned and did the same to Victoria before leaving the room.

"Benjamin," Victoria began. "I do not know if you can hear me. But if you can, I want you to know I am here and waiting for you to return." She held his hand to her cheek again. "I love you so much, Benjamin. Please come back to me."

USCG Cutter *Kauai*, Underway, Yucatan Channel, fifty-seven nautical miles south-southwest of Cape San Antonio, Cuba
16:48 EDT, 6 April

Hopkins

The smell of the primavera was very inviting. Hopkins knew Chef was putting his heart into this meal, appreciating the opportunity it furnished to restore some balance after the mayhem. Sam had requested everyone not on watch muster on the afterdeck as they had the day they left Key West. The mood was subdued—everyone was thinking of the wounded men, especially the XO.

"Attention on Deck!" Drake shouted as Sam appeared. He stopped in front of the assembled group and returned Drake's salute. "All present or accounted for, sir."

"Thank you, COB. Fall out and gather round, please!"

Hopkins made her way to stand behind Sam as the crew moved forward. All looked concerned, as they knew some important news had arrived. Hopkins noticed that even Lee, usually solid as a rock, seemed almost fearful and held Williams's arm with both hands as they moved forward.

"Folks, I have some good news. We just got word from JIATF South: Mr. Wyporek's surgery was successful, and he has been moved into recovery."

There were a few gasps, then a chorus of cheers and clapping. Hopkins, holding her breath, exhaled and shared a look with Drake, who nodded and mouthed, "Told ya."

Sam held his hand up, and the celebration subsided. "Definitely cause to celebrate, but he may be out for a while. The next couple of days will tell the tale. I want to call out Major Roberts and Specialists Rabin and Langley, who no shit saved the XO's life and did some fine work to make Brian Jenkins and our other wounded guests as comfortable as possible. Let's hear it for our army guests." There was more clapping and nods to Roberts and his aides. "Sadly, we are carrying back the remains of Jorge Dominguez, the DEA agent. He saved the mission and most of our lives by getting *Carlos Rojas*'s engines operating at that most critical time and fell alongside the XO in that last firefight. Let's remember him always as one of our shipmates." There was more subdued clapping and a few nods.

"I want to finish with a personal thank you from me for the terrific job you have done on this mission. I can't give you much in the way of details, but I can assure you it was of supreme importance to the country. Alright, I don't want to keep you from Chef's culinary masterpiece any longer. We will pull into Key West for a fuel stop tomorrow at 09:00, and I'll pass along anything I hear about the XO. Questions?" After a brief pause, he continued. "Chiefs, hang around for a bit. Everyone else, dig into that primavera!"

"Attention on Deck!" Drake shouted, and everyone came to attention.

"Carry on, thank you!" Sam said.

As the crew turned and wandered toward the door to the messdeck, Hopkins moved over to Drake, and together they went to see Sam. He was talking with one of the SEALs and turned as they stepped over.

"Chief Drake, Chief Hopkins, have you met Senior Chief D'Agostino?"

After greetings and handshakes, Sam continued. "We will obviously be tight for space. Fortunately, it will be a quick trip. COB, get Major Roberts set up in the XO's stateroom, then you and Chief Hopkins work with the senior chief to find a spot for his guys." He turned to D'Agostino. "I'm sorry, Senior Chief, but the best we can offer until Key West is some deck space for each man."

"We've had worse, Captain."

"Yes, I'm sure you have. Anyway, please see COB here if there's anything you need. Thank you, Senior Chief, and I'll see you later." After returning D'Agostino's salute, he turned to Drake and Hopkins. "Chiefs, we need to keep a lid on this mission. I need you to do a personal sit down with every crew member and emphasize what classified means and what can happen to them if they spill to anyone. Read me?"

"Yes, sir," Drake and Hopkins said in unison.

"OK, let's head in before Chef runs out of chow."

Sam

The arrival at Truman Annex was a solemn event. As soon as *Kauai* moored, the wounded were taken off and placed in ambulances for the local hospital trip. Admiral Pennington and his command staff were standing in ranks on the mole and came to attention and saluted when Dominguez's body was brought ashore. The seven unwounded SEALs carried the body as an impromptu honor guard as Bondurant blew the salute on his Boatswain's Pipe, and *Kauai*'s crew rendered honors in tropical blue uniforms. Everyone stood at attention until the body had been turned over to Agent Bartlett and placed in the hearse standing by on the mole.

When the hearse had driven off, Sam came ashore, walked over to Pennington, came to attention, and saluted. Pennington returned the salute and shook Sam's hand. "Congratulations on a magnificent job and bringing your crew back safely, Sam."

"Most of them, sir. But thank you."

"Yes, I can't tell you how sorry I am about Ben. I inquired over there before I came down—no change. But it's still early, and I think we can count on him being back with us soon."

"Yes, sir," Sam nodded. "Beyond the personal stuff, he's left quite a hole Hopkins and I are struggling to fill."

"I know, I know," Pennington said, then turned and looked at *Kauai*'s crane and boat damage. "Our beautiful Orchid got a bit roughed up. I'm relieved you had as few casualties as you did. Listen, I know you're beat, but can you take me around and give me a personal report?"

"Of course, sir. Do you want me to hold off on refueling until after you leave?"

"No, no. Please have the crew carry on with the work. We need to get you all home ASAP."

"Yes, sir," Sam said tiredly. "If you could follow me, please."

Dadeland Memorial Hospital, Miami, Florida
14:38 EDT, 7 April

Victoria

It had been a long, mostly sleepless night for Victoria. The nursing staff had provided her with sheets and pillows she could use in the room's recliner, and she made the best of it. However, besides the new surroundings and general discomfort of the chair, the monitor station beeped loudly after recording Ben's blood pressure at fifteen-minute intervals. Her brain's rational part acknowledged the beeping was a normal part of the hospital environment, and there was no reason for alarm. Yet, that tiny, less rational part saying, "Yes, but what if this time there is?" always won out, waking her up and forcing her to check for herself.

For most of the day, Victoria talked to Benjamin and read to him from a Patrick O'Brian adventure novel she had downloaded to her tablet. She knew he enjoyed the sound of her voice and had expressed his enjoyment of the historical fiction genre in one of their talks. Victoria hoped she was reading it correctly—the authenticity of the language O'Brian employed was very challenging for her. By mid-afternoon, fatigue won out, and Victoria put her head down on the bed next to Benjamin's hand and slept.

It was that wonderful day again, back on the DC Mall. The weather was perfect, and she was walking close to Benjamin, feeling his warmth, feeling totally safe in his presence. They stopped outside the Metro station, and she looked up into those beautiful eyes, blue as the sky, while he pushed her hair back and stroked her temple. She loved the feeling as his fingers gently caressed her hair. Then the wonderful dream faded away.

But not the gentle stroking of her temple.

Victoria's eyes flew open, and she bolted upright. Benjamin's hand fell away as she sat up, so she reached out and grasped it with both of hers. He looked at her with those beautiful eyes and a slight smile on his stubble-covered face. *I am not still dreaming, please; I am not still dreaming!* "Benjamin!"

He was trying to say something, but was too hoarse to speak. Finally, he mouthed, "Water, please." Victoria put his hand down carefully and poured a cup of ice water. Her hands were shaking as she moved the cup to his lips until his hands closed over and gently steadied them. After a few sips, he nodded, and she placed the cup back on the table, then returned and took both his hands in hers. He smiled more broadly at her and squeezed her hands softly.

"Hello, Victoria," he said in a creaky voice. "How was your day?"

She could not find the words to speak, could not even find the thoughts to think. She just leaned over, gripped Benjamin's shoulders, buried her face in his chest, and quietly sobbed as he gently stroked her hair.

19

The Reckoning

USCG Cutter *Kauai*, Moored, Truman Annex, Naval Air Station Key West, Florida
15:49 EDT, 7 April

Hopkins

They were just completing sailing preparations, and Sam was discussing some last-minute details in his cabin with Hopkins. "I just saw Major Roberts and his crew off an hour ago. Has Dr. Simmons left yet, Chief?"

"Yes, sir. He and his pal slithered off while you were tied up with the admiral. Good riddance."

Sam sat back and rubbed his eyes. "I know how you feel and would like to pile on, but the man was just doing his job this time around. He can't be blamed for what happened. I also talked to him afterward, and he's pretty twisted up about the XO. You might want to cut him some slack."

"With respect, sir, not going to happen."

"OK, just a thought," Sam said and stood up when his cell phone rang. Hopkins recognized the ring tone as belonging to Joana and said, "I can step out, Captain."

"No, please stay." He picked up the phone and pressed the speaker button. "Hello, sailor. I'm here with Emilia, and I hope you have some good news."

"Better than that, hang on," Joana said, followed by a ruffling sound.

"Hello, skipper." It was Ben's voice, a little raspy sounding but clear.

"Ben!"

"Yes, sir, back from the dead. Sorry to give you such a rough time."

Sam tried to say something but couldn't get the words to come out. Hopkins, blinking back tears herself, noted his struggle and gently took the phone from his shaking hand. "XO, is that really you?" she said.

"Chief? Yes, it's me. Is the captain alright?"

"He's… temporarily indisposed. How are you, sir?"

"Still a little loopy from the drugs and all, but everything seems to work."

"I'm so glad to hear that! Hang on, the captain's back." She handed the phone back to Sam, who had just finished wiping his eyes.

"Ben, words fail me. We didn't expect you awake for another day or so."

"Oh, Captain, you know Wyporeks are too ornery to follow the rules."

"So it would seem. Truthfully, you can't imagine how relieved I am to hear your voice. Is there anything you need?"

"Captain, Victoria is here holding my hand and smiling at me. I can't think of a single thing I could add to that, but thank you. Before I hand the phone back to the captain's spouse, do you have any orders for me, sir?"

"Yes. I order you to take it easy, mend, and enjoy your time with your lady. Clear?"

"Aye, aye, sir! Here's Jo."

More shuffling, then Joana's voice returned. "OK, my captain, I've stepped out of the room. How are you?"

"Absolutely exhausted and deliriously relieved. How did this come about?"

"I was on my way and almost at the hospital when I got the call from Victoria. When I got to the room, the scene was one for the ages."

"Wow, I wish I could have seen that. What do you think of her?"

"Victoria? She had me crying like a baby within a minute of meeting her. She's amazing! If Ben doesn't marry her, I'll ditch you and marry her myself."

"I'm crushed!"

"It's not personal. Men are just soooo overrated," she teased. "Seriously, I can see why Ben is so bowled over by her and hope they can make it work."

"OK. Emilia is pointing at her watch, and I need to get us underway for home. I'll call you when we are snugged down at PC."

"Do it safely, please, and get some rest. I'll see you soon, my captain."

"Goodbye, my love." After hanging up, Sam turned off the phone and dropped it in his desk drawer. "Chief, it looks like we have a pre-sailing announcement that should put some spring in everybody's step."

"That we do, Captain!"

"Well, let's get it done. Set the Special Sea Detail, and I'll see you on the Bridge.

"Very good, sir."

Isla de Barbello, Honduras
04:23 EDT, 8 April

The attack began with a twelve-man assault team landing just north of the fortified position of the Gate and pushing south. They used silenced pistols to kill anyone they met and were guided by observations of a small, infrared camera-equipped UAV hovering overhead. Resistance was surprisingly light, but even had it been heavy, it would have made no difference—former Spetsnaz soldiers trained and led the team while their opponents barely knew how to aim and pull the trigger. They had pushed to the water's edge within fifteen minutes, leaving no survivors. After setting remote-controlled and booby-trapped demolition charges on the heavy machine gun and in the ammunition magazine, they reembarked on their rubber boats to rejoin the main force.

The assault on the quay was carried out by a twenty-man party split into equal groups and landing at opposite ends. The operation proceeded much like the landing at the Gate: the two groups swept inward from each end, silently dispatching any person they encountered until finally converging in the center. It was here that the men discovered that their target, OSV *Carlos Rojas*, was missing. The only evidence of her presence was the discarded mooring lines still hanging in the water from the quay. The assault team leader quickly changed the rules of engagement to kill only armed persons on sight—he needed prisoners to interrogate. Now augmented by the twelve-man team, the primary force spread out to assault the hacienda and dormitories.

The main assault was almost anticlimactic. Two ten-man teams each took a dormitory while the twelve-man team attacked the hacienda. The guards' dispatch was the last silent operation of the day—the teams used grenades and automatic rifles for the buildings' forced entry, since there was no further need for stealth. True to form, the Salinas members resisted to the last, futilely, as their opponents hopelessly over-matched them. At the end of the assault, only a couple dozen day workers remained alive. These were interrogated and then penned up while the team leader called in for instructions.

"Boss, this is Piotr," the leader said, once his satellite phone achieved a connection.

"Yes, Piotr. Give me some good news," Crețu responded.

"Sir, the good news is the assault on the port was completely successful. We have liquidated all Salinas members on Barbello."

"I am awaiting the news of the boat."

"There is no news, sir. The boat is gone."

"What?"

"It apparently sailed two nights ago. The day workers we took said there was a big firefight off the point. The mooring lines we found dangling off the dock suggest that someone came in and took the boat out from under the Salinas's noses."

"Who in the hell would have the resources to do something like that? What did those workers see?"

"Practically nothing, sir. The fighting occurred off the point at the entrance to the harbor. None of these people could see anything in detail in the dark or with the storms at that distance. We found that heavy machine gun emplacement beat to hell and picked up a couple of dud M792 rounds lying around it."

"What is an M792?"

"Sir, the M792 is a high-explosive round fired by the American Bushmaster cannon. The Americans and Canadians are the only ones in this hemisphere who use them. My conclusion is the American navy came in under cover of darkness and extracted the vessel."

"Shit!"

"What do you want me to do, sir?"

"Alright. We can at least complete the punitive aim of this raid. Search the warehouses for product. If you find a worthwhile amount, use the day workers to load it on the command vessel. Then blow up any magazines and arms or munitions and burn every building to the ground."

"Shall I dispose of the day workers when we are done?"

"No. Kill any who resist or refuse to work, but leave the rest alive with any food and water you find. Make sure they know you are with the 252 Syndicate. We want this object lesson to be shared far and wide. Report back when you are done. Questions?"

"No, sir."

"Get on with it. I want all our men off that island by sunset. Out." The call disconnected.

USCG Cutter *Kauai*, Moored, Trident Wharf, Port Canaveral, Florida
08:03 EDT, 8 April

Sam

"Captain, quarterdeck here. There's a captain headed this way with another lady officer, sir."

Sam cringed, then said, "Right, I'm on my way. And Connally, there are no 'lady officers,' just 'officers.' OK?"

"Yes, sir," the young fireman replied.

Sam hung up the phone and grabbed his cap. "Another lady officer" implied the captain was female, and a female captain was almost certainly his boss, Captain Mercier. That was quick—they'd only secured from mooring stations about half an hour ago. With her crane and boat destroyed and possible structural damage from the rocket hit, *Kauai* was in no shape to go out again, thank God. So, he wondered what mischief would put the Seventh District's Chief of Response on a three-hour car trip up from Miami instead of just picking up the phone. Fortunately, Sam was well rested for the encounter after six good hours of sleep—exhaustion, relief, and a thorough but respectful browbeating from Hopkins and Drake had seen to that.

Sam made his way to the quarterdeck and stepped over onto the pier. He saw it was Captain Mercier and a female lieutenant he did not recognize, and Sam rendered a crisp salute as they approached. "Good morning, Captain."

"Good morning, Sam," Mercier said as she and the lieutenant returned the salute. She shook hands, saying, "I'm delighted to see you back in one piece." She turned to her companion. "This is Lena Huang from SFLC Norfolk, and she's here to have a look at your damage and get the ball rolling on repairs."

"Lena, Sam. Pleased to meet you," Sam said, shaking her hand.

"Same here."

"Ma'am, if you'll follow me, please." Sam led the other two officers past *Kauai*'s bow, stopping when they were alongside and could see the damage clearly.

"Holy shit!" Huang said. "What happened?"

Sam looked at Mercier, who said, "The action is classified. Sam will share whatever aspects are needed to complete repairs, but the location and nature of the mission are 'need to know' only."

"I understand, Captain," Huang said. "Sam?"

"We were hit by a rocket in the crane's arm. As you can see, it's severed. My chief engineer says the boat has had it—the console is smashed, and the hull tubes are shredded. We have minor shock damage on the rear superstructure and, I suspect, the deck below the crane and boat, and the windows of the port bridge wing door are blown in. We haven't done a thorough assessment yet."

"Right," Huang looked at him in wonder. "Did you have casualties?"

"Just one from this hit. Shrapnel wound. He'll recover."

"Wow. I'm glad to hear that," Huang said.

"Sam, could Chief Drake take Lena around for the inspection? There are some things I need to discuss with you in private."

"Yes, ma'am. Excuse me, please." Sam stepped over to the quarterdeck and picked up the phone. Within a minute, Drake had come ashore and rendered the proper greeting. "COB, Lieutenant Huang is from the Surface Force Logistics Center, and she's here to do an assessment for repairs."

"Glad to have you, Lieutenant," Drake said. "I hope you brought something to crawl around in besides tropical blue."

"What engineer would leave home without coveralls, Chief?" Huang smiled, patting her gym bag.

"Ma'am, I think this is the beginning of a beautiful friendship. Will you follow me, please?" Drake said.

As they walked off in deep discussion, Sam said, "Well, I guess 'he knows a guy' up at SFLC now."

****

Sam had finished providing his action report, recorded on an encrypted audio recorder Mercier had brought. They had moved on to award recommendations. "I want the Silver Star for Ben and Lee."

"That's a pretty tall order. It will be hard to push that through without going public on a lot of stuff," Mercier said.

"That's my recommendation, ma'am. I understand I'm not the last word, but there it is."

"OK, I'll do my best. But Lee? Are you sure?"

"Ma'am, do I need to remind you she went out into the open, under rocket and automatic gunfire, and single-handedly cut away the towline wreckage with an ax, saving the ship and mission? They should name a Fast Response Cutter after her, for God's sake."

"Touché. Next?"

"Bronze Stars for Hopkins, Bondurant, and Williams. Also, for Roberts, if you can push it through the army."

"Those should be doable. Anyone else?"

"Yes, Commendation Medals for Drake, Bryant, Brown, and Lopez. Achievement Medals for Hebert and Jenkins. Oh, yes, Purple Hearts for Jenkins and Ben if we can swing it."

"I'll do what I can."

"I appreciate that, ma'am."

"That was fun. Now on to the hard stuff. I've combed the lists for a good J.O. to send up here, and I'll need your opinion on some candidates."

Sam's face darkened, and he said coldly, "Why, ma'am?"

"I think you know why."

"It will be at least a month before we're repaired and operational again. Ben will be back in a couple of weeks."

"You don't know that, Sam. The initial report looks promising, yes. But I read up on this type of injury. We have to come to terms with the fact that he might be finished. In that case, we need to have a replacement in the pipeline."

"It's only been one day, ma'am. I'm not ready to just write him off like that!"

"We haven't written him off, Sam. Believe me, if he can come back, he will. But you need to face reality here. If he can't return, you need to have an XO who can do the job. If nothing else, you'll have help to put things back together while Ben is healing up." She paused as Sam's head sank. "C'mon, you know I'm right about this."

Sam squeezed his eyes closed for a few seconds. He was so relieved and happy Ben was awake that he had not considered the long-term implications. Now, that realization had come home with a vengeance. "Yes, I understand, ma'am. I'll look at whoever you decide to send up."

"Thank you, Sam. Do you want me to swing by the hospital and tell him when I get back?"

Sam looked up and shook his head. "No, ma'am. That's my responsibility. I'll head down there as soon as I have things squared away here."

"I'm sorry about this, Sam. Is there anything I can do for you? Anything you need?"

"I guess I'll know better when Lena is done with her inspection. I'll let you know, ma'am."

Secure Conference Room 6A, National Security Agency Headquarters, Fort Meade, Maryland 15:35 EDT, 8 April

Simmons

Simmons looked around the table at the select committee's assembled members, and his thoughts went back to the last such mission debriefing he had attended, sitting in the hot seat with Sam Powell and Ben Wyporek. Those poor men thought they would be hanged as they went into that meeting—keeping the secret that they were already acquitted was very distasteful to him. *At least I'm on my own this time, right where I belong.* Kevin Welles, the Director of National Intelligence, led the committee. It included the Chairman of the Joint Chiefs of Staff, the Directors of the CIA and NSA, and Vice Admiral Irving, the DIA Director.

"Dr. Simmons, we have your report," Welles said. "And we would like to ask a few follow-up questions. Do you have questions before we start?"

"No, sir."

"Good. Admiral Irving?"

"Thank you, sir. Dr. Simmons, did you have difficulty understanding your orders before this mission?"

"No, ma'am."

"In that case, why didn't you follow them?"

"I am not aware of any breach of my orders, Admiral."

"You were ordered to secure Dr. Gronkowsky and his research materials. Yet, you destroyed the latter."

"My orders, Admiral, were to secure Dr. Gronkowsky and all his research materials, *if practicable,* and ensure their destruction otherwise. It was practicable to grab and extract Gronkowsky, but his research and data were all stored on air-gapped computers without removable hard drives. I could not ascertain a practicable means of extracting the data, so I ensured its destruction." *Which I would have done, anyway. My God! Don't we have enough of this crap already?*

"I find it difficult to believe that a man of your intelligence, learning, and skills could not find a means in the time available."

"I am neither a computer scientist nor an IT engineer, Admiral. I do not have the learning and skills to crack into a cyber-protected computer."

"You had plenty of manpower available between the SEAL team and Coast Guard personnel. You could easily have physically extracted the computers to the Coast Guard cutter."

"And when they asked me, 'What's this?', what was I to tell them? That they risked their lives and violated Honduran sovereignty to be accessories in a violation of the Chemical Weapons Convention? I remind you that you gave your word to General Miller and Admiral Pennington that this horror would be destroyed, and I doubt they would have agreed to this mission otherwise."

"Don't pretend you're an idiot, Doctor. You could have told them what you needed to in order to complete your mission. You serve the nation best by seizing opportunities, not catering to the sensibilities of people outside the community."

So that's how it is. You were trying to build brownie points with the President with a fait accompli over-delivery on the mission. You knew Miller and Pennington would raise a stink over something like this, so you lied to them.

"I think the nation is best served by adhering to core principles that separate us from rogue nations and criminal syndicates. If you wanted someone without scruples on this mission, Admiral, you should have sent one of your toadies, not me."

"You insolent bastard! I'll...."

"Enough!" Welles said as he slammed the table with his fist. Then he looked back and forth between them. "What the hell is the matter with you two?"

Simmons took a breath, then said, "I apologize for my outburst, sir."

Irving glared at Simmons and said, "If I can continue...."

"No!" Welles said. "I move we rule that Dr. Simmons complied with his orders and table further discussion of that point. In favor?" All committee members except Irving raised their hands. "Carried." Welles looked around the table. "Does anyone else have questions? No? Then I guess we can adjourn this one. Thank you, everyone." As everyone at the table rose, he continued. "Dr. Simmons, can I have a moment with you, please?"

"Yes, sir," Simmons replied. Irving glared at him as she picked up her notebook and walked out.

When only the two of them remained, Welles said, "Have a seat, please." After they sat down, he continued. "I take it Admiral Irving did not discuss her issues with you beforehand."

"No, sir."

"How do you assess your present situation?"

"I not only failed to rid the king of the turbulent priest, but I also flipped him off for good measure. I don't think I'm much of a contender for employee of the month over at DIA."

The older man chuckled. "You really are a wiseass. What do you plan to do?"

"I think I'll be looking for something else. This last one did it for me. Going down there with one hand tied behind our back sucked, sir! It ended up with one good man dead, four wounded, and the numbers would have been the other way around if Irving had had her way. She would have sent us in without medical support if Pennington hadn't stood up to her. Did you know that?"

"No, I didn't."

"After tonight, I can't work for her. She'll be looking for payback, and I don't need to be worrying about that, along with everything else. I guess I can fall back on the original career, maybe teach. I don't know."

"I understand, but I have to ask you for a favor. We really can't spare you from the committee work. Let me set up a detail position for you to work directly for me. That way, you can stay in DIA but be out of her reach. The DIA Director is a temporary appointment, and you can think about moving back once she moves on. You won't have the reachback into the organization you're used to, but it will keep you in the game."

Simmons was silent for a moment. "Give me a couple of days to think about it, but I'm inclined to accept. Thank you, sir."

"I'm glad to hear it. I'll get the ball rolling on my end. Let me know as soon as you can."

"Yes, sir."

They both stood, and the older man offered his hand. "Take it easy, Pete. Hope to hear from you soon."

Simmons shook his hand firmly. "Thank you, sir. You will."

20

Coda

Ben

Ben remained in the ICU for a day after recovering consciousness and had just completed a move to a standard room for three more days of observation before his eventual release. He and Joana worked on Victoria all day to get her to go somewhere where she could get some good sleep. She elected to take a room at the hotel across the street from the hospital while Ben was still an inpatient. She also insisted on being with him at his apartment for the two weeks he was "Sick in Quarters," what the Coast Guard called sick leave, to complete whatever rehab he needed. Fortunately, Ben still had his Miami apartment—between the shipyard, his training up in Virginia, and *Kauai's* relentless shakedown and operational schedule, there wasn't time to close out his lease and clear out the place.

Ben was delighted but visibly nervous about learning of Victoria's decision to stick around after his discharge. When she left the room to call her office to give them an update, Ben turned to Joana with a worried look. "Jo, can I use your cell, please?"

"Sure, here you go," she said as she handed it to him.

Ben hurriedly dialed the number of his apartment management office. "Janie, Ben Wyporek. Well, been better, but OK. Yes, do you have a cleaning service that can do a quick turnaround on my place? Yes, everything from bottom to top. As soon as possible. Tomorrow? Yes! That will be fine. Could you let them in, pleeeeease? Thank you, Ma'am!" After hanging up, he looked at the ceiling and said, "Thank God!"

Joana took her phone back and said, "Are you freaking kidding me? You're out of a coma one day, and your biggest worry is a dirty apartment?"

"Jo, it may just be because I got my bell rung, but I can't remember whether I left dirty skivvies on the floor in the bathroom." He peered hard at the door. "This situation was not on the list of possibilities the last time I left! What? Did you think I was some kind of neatnik?"

Joana shook her head sadly and said, "No, just dreading what I can expect when Robbie hits puberty!"

Victoria returned with a smile a couple of minutes later with the news that they had approved her leave. Sam and Hopkins, both in civilian clothing, came in almost on Victoria's heels, with Sam drawing a tender hug and passionate kiss from Joana before moving to

Ben's warm handshake. Then Hopkins received a hug and handshake.

"Victoria, this is my CO, Lieutenant Sam Powell," Ben said as Sam stepped forward to take Victoria's hand.

"Oh, Lieutenant Powell, Benjamin has told me so much about you!" She turned to Hopkins. "And you are Chief Petty Officer Emilia Hopkins! Benjamin has also told me much about you. I am so glad to meet you!"

"Victoria, we are all on first names off the ship. You can call me Sam if you like."

"I think she would prefer Samuel, dear," Joana corrected him.

"Yes, and please call me Emilia," Hopkins jumped in with a smile. "What a treat to meet you at last." She turned to Ben. "Here's your keys and phone, XO," she said as she handed them to him.

"So, what do you think of driving the Camaro?" Ben asked.

"A bit too much horsepower for a mom like me. And I don't want one anywhere near Chris when he gets his license in a few years!"

"Aw, MOM!" Ben quipped to a smile from Victoria and laughs from everyone else.

After more laughs and conversation, Sam turned to Joana. "Dear, would you mind giving Emilia a ride over to her place, please? I need to discuss something with Ben."

"On it, my captain. I'll see you when you get home." She turned to Ben, shook her head with a smile, and walked out of the room.

Hopkins walked over and shook his hand again. "I'm thrilled you're OK, sir. I can't wait for you to get back and take over the inbox again! Victoria, it was wonderful to meet you, and I hope to see you again soon."

"Thank you, Emilia!" After Hopkins left, Victoria turned to Sam. "Do you need me to leave, Samuel?"

Sam gave Ben a more sad look, and Ben said, "No, Victoria, please stay. Sam is about to explain that my injury may keep me from coming back to *Kauai*."

Victoria's smile disappeared, and she sat next to Ben and took his hand in hers.

"Well, so much for breaking it to you gently," Sam began. "I want to emphasize that we will do everything we can to get you back, but the boat is off-limits for you for two weeks, at least. That's why I had Hoppy bring your stuff. After that, you'll need a full physical with a special neurological workup. Don't ask me what that means; it was just what they told me. If that clears you, you're in."

"Then I guess I had better study!" Ben said lightheartedly. On the inside, he was quite worried. It was a wait-and-see situation, and there was little he could do to affect the outcome. Victoria turned to him with a tragic expression, and he gently squeezed her hand and said, "It will be alright." He turned back to Sam. "Will you be able to get someone in there to help, sir? I can't stand the thought of all my work being dumped on Hoppy and COB."

"Captain Mercier has put together a slate of candidates for a temp slot, and I'll be giving her feedback first thing tomorrow."

"OK, sir. Whoever gets picked, please have them see me before they head over. I'd like to set them up as best I can."

Sam nodded and said, "I knew you would say something like that. You're a class act, Ben."

"I've been the understudy for the best, sir." Ben offered his hand, and Sam shook it briefly, then pulled him into a hug.

He rose again and blinked a few times before continuing. "I need to get back home and administer some hugs. I'll swing by tomorrow before Hoppy and I head back to the boat. Is there anything I can bring you?"

"I'm good, sir. Please give R & D a hug from Uncle Ben!"

"Will do. Goodbye, Victoria. I wish we could have met on a happier occasion."

"Thank you, Samuel."

After he left, Victoria turned to Ben with tears in her eyes. "Oh, Benjamin! I am so sorry! I do not know what to do!"

He caressed her face, wiping away one of her tears. "Hey, I'm not out of the game yet. And what you have done, what you are doing.... When I came to yesterday and saw you sleeping next to me, I thought I was hallucinating. I didn't want to wake you, but I had to touch you to make sure you were real. When I brushed your hair back, you smiled in your sleep. Then when you woke up, it was finally real; you were really here. Can you even imagine what that meant to me?

"But I'm worried about you. Victoria, I love you so very much, but maybe you need to consider your interests now."

"What are you saying, Benjamin? I love you."

"Yes, but look at where we are. I will either be out of a job soon or return to the job that put me here. No matter which way this turns out, what do I have to offer you?" Victoria looked at him, and her face slowly changed into a soft smile. "What?" Ben asked.

"You provide exactly what I need, Benjamin."

Ben looked back in befuddlement. *She is saying this like it has some profound meaning. It is from something.... What?* Then he remembered. *Oh, THAT!* He smiled back and held his arms open. Once she had snuggled in, he said, "Victoria Carpenter, you are a very foolish woman." She hugged him tightly, and he kissed the top of her head. "We'll figure this out somehow."

****

Ben was a few days out of the hospital, but still reporting daily for testing and physical therapy. Victoria was doing what she could to help, driving him to and from the clinic, cooking and cleaning up, standing firm against Ben's resistance to the doctor's orders prohibiting such activities until they were sure his balance and depth perception were up to it. She had never been so assertive before with another person, which both found surprising and pleasing.

This night, they were headed to Sam and Joana's for what Joana called a "House Cooling Party"—a celebration of her finally besting the bureaucratic dragon and securing the household goods move to Canaveral. The only other guests were Emilia Hopkins and Fritz Deffler, who was down on leave from Massachusetts. Ben was nervous, despite the small gathering, as this was the first social occasion he had attended with Victoria, and he wasn't sure how she or they would react.

He needn't have worried. Joana met them at the door, gave each a warm hug, and then led Victoria to the kitchen, where Emilia was already waiting with wine. As Ben started to follow, Joana turned and said, "Whoa, sailor. We're going in for girl talk. You can join your mates in the den."

Ben forced a smile and dutifully joined Sam and Fritz in the friendly technical discussion they were having in the den. After a few minutes, several bursts of raucous laughter, including Victoria's, were drifting in. Sam and Ben paused, directing puzzled looks at the kitchen. Looking back and forth at the two men, Fritz smiled and said, "Gentlemen, you're being dished up in there. Em and I haven't been together long enough for her to have any stories that funny about me."

The dinner and the rest of the evening went swimmingly. Emilia and Fritz announced that he had been given orders to the new UAV unit standing up at the Coast Guard aviation deployment center in

Jacksonville with a promotion to chief petty officer. They all celebrated that Fritz and Emilia's separation distance had shrunk from a two-and-a-half-day drive to one of two-and-a-half hours. Not cohabitation, but an improvement. The evening came to a pleasant end, with Victoria sharing warm, tearful hugs with Joana and Emilia as she and Ben left. The drive home was quiet—Ben did not want to distract Victoria as she drove home at night in a strange place and car. However, even back at the apartment, she was pensive, and Ben finally had to say something. "Are you alright, Victoria? Did someone say something to upset you?"

"No, Benjamin. On the contrary, I am very sad I will have to leave. Joana and Emilia are so wonderful and welcoming. I know I am very different from everyone else in the way I think and talk, but they made me feel like I belong. I have never felt that way before tonight. Between them, the pictures you sent me, and stories you told about your shipmates and their families, I long to be a part of this world."

"Why don't you then?"

She gave Ben a puzzled look. "I do not understand."

Ben swallowed hard. "Why don't you become part of this world? Assuming I pass the physical and get back in the game, why don't you move down here?"

"Benjamin, are you suggesting we live together?" Victoria replied in astonishment.

"Yes, I am. I love you, Victoria. I'm probably not the easiest guy to live with, but I want to be with you."

"Benjamin, I…." She looked down. "I have issues that would be difficult for you to deal with, things you do not know about that do not come out in phone conversations or sporadic dates. It is not as easy as you think."

"Victoria, with respect, I think you are selling me short. Do you love me?"

She looked up into his eyes. "You know I do."

"I probably have quirks you haven't seen or thought of. Would you discard me without at least trying to accommodate them?"

"No, certainly not."

He took her hands. "I can't imagine anything about you that would make me not want to be with you. On my honor, I promise you I would not give up on us without the fight of my life. I know this is a big decision, and I don't expect you to answer right now, not until this medical thing sorts itself out, but please consider living with me."

Victoria blinked away tears, put her arms around Ben's neck, and pulled him into the most passionate kiss either had experienced. When she pulled back, she cupped his face in her hands, looked into his eyes, and said, "I will live with you, medical issues notwithstanding." She broke into a playful smile. "You are a very foolish man, Benjamin Wyporek." Then she hugged him tightly. "We will figure this out somehow."

Victoria

Victoria sat anxiously in the waiting room of the Patrick Air Force Base Medical Center. In the two weeks since his discharge from Dadeland, Benjamin had completed his week of physical therapy and several consults, culminating in a cranial MRI. This final consult with the neurologist was the last step in determining whether Benjamin would return to duty on *Kauai* or begin processing out of the Coast Guard with a medical discharge.

They had spent the last week at a local hotel with Benjamin meeting with medical professionals, Victoria interviewing with local scientific consulting firms, and looking at apartments together. Victoria was confident that Benjamin would be cleared for duty, but increasingly discouraged by what she felt was a series of failed interviews. Benjamin had the opposite view. While he was worried about his medical issue, he confidently expected Victoria would connect with a company that could see past her abbreviated people skills and leverage her genius with data science.

Every time Victoria had left Benjamin to go inside for an interview, he had given her a passionate kiss "for luck." When his name had been called in the waiting area, she stood with him and gave him an equally passionate kiss. "For luck," she said.

"Hopefully, you are better at passing it on than I seem to be," he said with a rueful smile.

That had been almost an hour ago. Victoria was flipping through apartment photos on the Internet to get her mind off the current situation, trying to find one that optimized their combined travel time to Port Canaveral for Ben and Melbourne, where the firms she interviewed with were located. Her decision to leave the DIA was not an easy one—it was the only job she had ever held, and she knew she would miss Debbie and Peter. She was surprised when Peter encouraged her decision to leave, given how he had always been so protective of her, and wondered if it had something to do with his new special assignment to the Director of National Intelligence's staff. Regardless, he expressed his delight that she was getting together with Benjamin and giving living together a test before they took things further.

Victoria was still pondering this and the many things she had to take care of starting her new life when the door opened and Benjamin emerged. She almost jumped out of her chair to go to him. He was smiling, an excellent sign. "Benjamin, please tell me!" she pleaded.

"Fit for Duty!" he exclaimed happily. "They will monitor me for a while, and I am to avoid…." He opened the folder and read, "'Elective activities associated with a high risk of head injury.' So, no skydiving, boxing, or other contact sports for me."

"Oh, Benjamin, I am so happy for you!"

"Thank you, Victoria, for being here. I don't know how I could have gotten through it without you. Now let's get lunch, and then we'll get you to that next interview. I'm feeling very lucky right now, and I'm sure some will rub off on you!"

Ben

They had just returned to the hotel room from the last interview. Like the others, Victoria was convinced that she had bombed, based on the interviewers' questions and her perceived reactions, and she was inconsolable. Ben was frustrated with himself for not finding something to say or do that could help her. He was about to suggest they go out, perhaps to the Space Center Visitor's Complex, anything to get her mind off it, when her cellphone rang.

"It is them! It is them!" Victoria said after checking the caller ID.

"OK. Do you want me to leave while you talk to them?"

"No! No, no, no. Please stay and hold my hand."

"Alright, I'm here for you." He took her left hand with his right and held up crossed fingers on his left as she answered the phone.

Victoria took a deep breath to control her voice, then answered the phone. "Hello? Yes, it is. Yes, I have time to talk now." The conversation lasted for about ten minutes, but Ben could tell it was excellent news after two. "Yes, that would be acceptable. That is correct. Very good. I look forward to receiving them. Goodbye." She hung up the phone and squealed, which stunned Ben, given her voice's typically low pitch. "I have the job!" They both jumped up, hugged, and then kissed.

"Congratulations, my love!" Ben gushed. "I knew it was just a matter of finding the company that had brains. When do you start?"

"It will be in the package they are sending me, but I have so much to do!"

"I'll be there to help. I guess we really do need to pick out an apartment," Ben finished with a smile.

"Not yet! I have something else in mind right now!" Victoria said with a mischievous grin that surprised Ben.

"By all means, lead on, My Lady!"

"Heroic Airline Crew Awarded Queen's Commendation for Valuable Service in the Air," *The Times*, 7 June.

The Queen's Birthday Honors list published yesterday included the award of the Queen's Commendation for Valuable Service in the Air to each of the six crewmembers of the Pan-Commonwealth Airways flight downed by adverse weather over the North Atlantic Ocean last March.

PCA Flight 403, originating from London Heathrow to Nassau Lynden Pindling International via Bermuda on March 26th, encountered unforecast severe thunderstorms with hail on approach to the Bahamas, resulting in complete loss of power. Unable to reach land, the Airbus A321LR was forced down in the open Atlantic Ocean over 100 miles (169 km) from

Nassau. The crew managed what was described in official reports as "an extraordinarily difficult power-off open sea landing of the crippled aircraft and subsequent evacuation of the 120 passengers on board without loss of life or serious injury." A U.S. Coast Guard Cutter rescued the passengers and crew within hours.

The flight crew, Captain Emma Taylor, 42, Pilot; First Officer Samesh Patel, 36, Co-pilot; Chief Steward Richard Burgess, 53, Senior Flight Attendant; Ms. Nancy Hamilton, 43, Flight Attendant; Ms. Bryony Weaver, 33, Flight Attendant; Mr. Naveen Ashkani, 24, Flight Attendant, were cited for exceptional skill, judgement, and perseverance in the award. The crew's noteworthy performance had been previously mentioned in the official Department of Transport, Air Accidents Investigation Branch report on the incident released on May 13th.

Asked for comment, PCA Chief Executive Officer Ralph Desmond said, "We are, of course, proud, pleased, and extremely grateful to Her Majesty for her recognition of this magnificent crew. A 'dead stick' landing of a large airliner at sea and evacuation of its passengers afterward is one of the worst situations imaginable. Captain Taylor and her crew provided a shining example of how skill, professionalism, and teamwork can overcome this most daunting challenge. It is a great privilege to include people of this calibre among the PCA family."

Captain Taylor was characteristically modest, commenting simply, "I was serving with the best crew in the world and did what PCA trained me to do. We were lucky in the end, with both a benign sea and rescue close at hand. I want to extend my most sincere gratitude to the crew of the U.S. Coast Guard Cutter *Kauai*, who plucked us from the sea and storm at substantial risk to themselves and carried us safely to Nassau."

Author's Notes

None of the characters in this book represents any real person, living or dead. However, some of *Kauai*'s fictional crew members' best qualities were inspired by many of the fine people with whom I had the honor and pleasure to serve while I was a part of the Coast Guard.

USCGC *Kauai* is fictional. There is no "D Class" of the 110-foot patrol boat series, and the last of those built was USCGC *Galveston Island* (WPB-1349). I created a fictitious D-Class to buy some extra margin of verisimilitude and get the nit-pickers off my back. The medium endurance cutters *Dependable*, *Northland*, and *Thetis* are real and currently in service as of this writing. The "Fast Response Cutters" referred to by Sam Powell in Chapter 18 are an actual class of patrol vessels and a-building of this work's writing. They are each named for a Coast Guard enlisted member of historical note.

Pan-Commonwealth Airways is fictional. However, the mishap depicted is a fictional composite of two real-life incidents:

- USAir Flight 1549, an Airbus A320 with 150 passengers and five crew, on January 15, 2009: the aircraft collided with a flock of geese and lost power on both engines shortly after takeoff from La Guardia Airport. Unable to reach La Guardia or any other airport, Captain Chesley Sullenberger made a forced landing in the Hudson River west of

New York City and successfully evacuated all passengers and crew.

- Garuda Indonesia Flight 421, a Boeing 737-300 with fifty-four passengers and six crew, on January 16, 2002: the aircraft entered a severe thunderstorm and lost power on both engines due to rain and hail ingestion. Unable to reach an airport, Captain Abdul Rozaq made a forced landing in the Bengawan Solo River in Central Java, Indonesia. One flight attendant died of injuries received in the crash, but the remaining crew and all passengers survived.

The dialog between the Coast Guard people and in radio transmissions depicted in this story has much more "plain language" than what you would hear during actual operations. Including all the acronyms, jargon, and formal protocols vital for clarity and brevity in real life would have been more authentic. However, it would also be a great deal more tedious or confusing for the average reader. I ask all veterans and any other purists forgiveness for this compromise for the sake of readability.

MAYDAY, MAYDAY – Request Assistance!

First of all, thank you for purchasing *Caribbean Counterstrike*! I know you could have picked any number of books to read, but you chose this book, and for that, I am incredibly grateful. I hope it gave you what you were seeking, be it a little extra enjoyment or just a chance to escape the trials and tribulations of life for a while. If so, it would be really helpful if you could share this book with your friends and family by posting a mention of it on Facebook and Twitter.

If you enjoyed this story, I'd like to hear from you and hope that you could take some time to post a review or at least a rating on your bookseller's website. Your feedback and support will help me as I work on future projects, and I am very interested in hearing your thoughts. Please visit my website when you have the time to provide your feedback, find out what is new, and grab the occasional freebie:

https://www.edwardhochsmann.com

Very Respectfully,

Ed

Post a Review

Friends, we authors live and die by the ratings you provide on your bookseller's website and book discovery services such as Bookbub. If you liked this book, I ask you for one last service: please use one or more of the QRC/URL links below to give it a rating or review. Thank you so much for your attention and participation.

Bookbub:
https://www.bookbub.com/books/caribbean-counterstrike-cutter-kauai-sea-adventures-book-2-by-edward-m-hochsmann

Amazon:
https://mybook.to/CaribbeanCounterstrike

Apple:
https://books.apple.com/us/book/caribbean-counterstrike/id6442847844

The Next Book in the Series

A New Captain's First Patrol Turns into a Fight for Their Lives!

Young Coast Guard Lieutenant Haley Reardon gets her dream assignment: a patrol boat command in the red-hot operating area of South Florida and the Caribbean. She has not even gotten her feet on the ground when she finds herself and her crew supporting a dangerous covert mission. The strict protocols she has lived by in the law enforcement world are in abeyance, and there is no time for her to grow into the job. Her XO is experienced and able, but even younger than Haley and dealing with the trauma of his earlier missions and the challenge of courting a woman with special needs (a neurodiverse genius).

They must insert and retrieve a DIA operations team trying to seize a transnational criminal syndicate boss from a small Caribbean island controlled by a front company of the Chinese government and protected by a superior military force. Most importantly, they are on their own and must remain covert, and Haley has strict orders to avoid contact with the Chinese.

Can Haley avoid leaving the DIA team to their fate when attempting to rescue them could destroy her crew and boat and lead to war?

Excerpt from Bravely and Faithfully

They were within a quarter-mile now. Haley could clearly see the deck was crowded with individuals, and the ship had a visible list to port. They were still charging at full speed. *Hopkins had better hit the brakes if she doesn't want to overshoot.*

As if reading her mind, Hopkins's voice came over the 1MC, "All hands, prepare for crash-back!"

Haley observed the deck crew kneeling and grabbing a handhold. As she did the same, the bow suddenly dipped down, and the hull began the shudder Haley recognized as engines going full astern with a high forward speed. She almost fell forward in the deceleration as *Kauai* came to a halt about thirty feet off the *Miho Dujam*.

"Heaving lines, let fly!" Hebert shouted, and two small lines with weighted balls at the end streaked across the water to where Ben and Bondurant were standing. They hurriedly pulled over the two mooring lines, threading them through the hawseholes on the ship and giving a thumbs-up to indicate they had been attached. In the meantime, Hopkins was working motors and rudder to walk *Kauai* sideways into the larger vessel, with the crewmen pulling in the slack from the mooring lines. Finally, the two vessels came together with the loud squeak of compressing fenders. "Hold all lines!" Hebert shouted. "Second men, report to me!"

The second man at each position dropped his mooring line and trotted over as Hebert said, "Help Doc get the litter over there." As they assisted Bryant, Hebert turned to Haley. "Ma'am, it's gonna get mighty crowded mighty fast. Can you take them to the messdeck when we gather half a dozen? I have water bottles laid out for them."

"No problem!" Haley answered.

"Thank ya, ma'am."

The litter with the catatonic woman came across first, with Drake and Bondurant on each side handing it carefully across to their counterparts on *Kauai*, followed immediately by Bryant. The men carried it aside, laid it down on the deck for Bryant to do his work, and returned to their place on the rail. Like the litter, Drake and Bondurant handed off each survivor to the crewmen waiting on the patrol boat while Ben was herding the others into a single file for the transfer. Haley beckoned over each new arrival to keep the path clear. The fear they showed of the male crewmembers and the contrasting expressions of gratitude on their faces when they saw Haley almost made her tear up. As they huddled close to her, Haley was grateful for Bryant's gift—even in the open air, and through the Vapor Rub smear she applied under her nose, the stench of waste and old sweat and vomit was almost overpowering.

When she hit the required critical mass of six rescues, she led them aft to the open messdeck, sat them down in the chairs, and handed out water bottles. There was some concern among the women when she turned to leave, so Haley smiled, waved her hand down, and said, "*Bleib hier.*" as Bryant suggested. The few who had stood sat down again, although their looks of concern remained until Haley returned with the second half dozen survivors. Some faces were more expressive than others, but the new arrivals brought signs of relief and hope.

On her second return to the foredeck, Haley noticed Ben was no longer herding the remaining women in line. In fact, he was nowhere to be seen, and she wondered if he had returned on board while she was shuttling survivors to the messdeck. After her third run, she remained on the foredeck and watched as the last survivor came aboard. Drake and Bondurant then cast off *Kauai*'s mooring lines before jumping across. As the two vessels drifted apart, Haley went directly to Drake and asked, "Chief, where's the XO?"

"He's up looking for evidence, ma'am," Drake replied puzzledly.

"He's *what*?"

"He told us to cast off and return on board after the last survivor crossed over. He's taking the RHIB back." He and Bondurant shared a worried look.

"How much longer will that ship last?"

"Ma'am, I'm surprised she's still upright."

Haley hated stepping in, but things seemed to be getting out of hand. "Chief, call the RHIB!"

"*Kauai*-One, COB, is the XO with you?"

"Negative," Lee's voice replied.

Drake lifted his radio again, but before he could speak, a series of loud bangs erupted from the *Miho Dujam*, and she quickly rolled to the left. He keyed the radio and shouted, "*Kauai*, COB, XO is still on board!"

The ship continued to roll with a cacophony of bangs and crashes and, within twenty seconds, had completely capsized with only her hull bottom visible. Haley, Drake, and Bondurant were transfixed in shock until the 1MC jolted them into motion.

"Man Overboard Port Side, repeat Man Overboard Port Side! This is no drill!"

Check Out the First Book in the Series

An obsolescent patrol boat is all that stands between the world and nuclear annihilation!

The world is on the brink of war, with NATO mobilizing to counter a Russian threat to Poland and Lithuania and leaders openly discussing war options. In the midst of the crisis, a Russian bomber collides with a U.S. fighter off Florida, causing the accidental launch of a nuclear-tipped hypersonic missile.

A Coast Guard cutter finds a drug-laden sailboat smashed and adrift north of the Florida Keys. The boat's damage is from a near miss by the Russian missile, which had not flown harmlessly deep into the Gulf of Mexico as initially thought, but crashed somewhere in the keys.

The Coast Guard crew is racing against a vicious and powerful international crime syndicate to find and recover the Russian nuke before its discovery can trigger a nuclear war.

Excerpt from *Dagger Quest*:

USCG Cutter *Kauai*, one nautical mile west of Resolution Key, Florida
07:27 EST, 19 January

Sam

"Conn, Mount 51, sound of gunshots zero-four-zero relative, no visual target!" Hebert shouted through the bridge door from his position on the starboard machine gun.

"Conn, aye!" Hopkins replied.

Sam watched the scene ashore unfold in real-time in the video feed from the orbiting Puma. His heart pounded, and he felt rising nausea as he watched the SUVs split apart and then stop. Figures emerged from both vehicles.

"*Kauai*, Shore-One, we are taking fire; repeat, we are taking fire. Request immediate assistance!" Ben's voice burst from the radio.

"Conn, Mount 51, sound of continuous gunfire zero-five-zero relative, no visual target!" came the redundant report.

"Conn, aye! Captain, one point seven miles to shoal water."

Hopkins had called down to Drake at the two-mile point, and Sam saw the engine speed back down slightly to "normal" emergency ahead in response.

"Very well, prepare for crash back. Williams?"

"Nothing yet, Captain, sorry," Williams said, shifting in his seat.

Hopkins announced, "Captain, one and a half miles to shoal water." Into the telephone, she said, "Chief, stand by for crash back."

"Very well, stand by," Sam responded.

On the Puma's video display, Sam saw Bill take the fatal hit and fall back dead. His heart was in his throat until he leaned forward to peer at the screen, then a wave of relief when he saw the long hair and beach clothing, apparent even in the low-resolution image. It must be the prisoner. He noted a pause in the action and saw the figures behind the westernmost vehicle aim a mortar-like device and fire it. The camera picked up a flash of a small object, then a burst overhead Ben and Simmons's redoubt. Either Ben or Simmons—from the camera aspect and mist, he couldn't tell which—fast-crawled to the other briefly, then returned to his position. Sam was unconsciously pounding his right fist on his thigh as the scene played out before him.

"Getting something," Williams said. "Yes! Two targets on long-wave IR."

Sam leaned in. "Surface action starboard, train on the target on the far left and standby. Deffler, illuminate the hostile vehicle farthest west." Standing up, he shouted, "OOD, Crash Back Now!" He keyed his handheld radio. "Pickins, haul ass back to the boat deck now!"

Hopkins shouted into the telephone, "Main Control, Conn, Crash Back, all back full!"

"Unmasked," Deffler piped up. "Target illuminated."

Sam held on to the safety rail as the patrol boat pitched down and violently shuddered while shedding speed quickly in the emergency stop. He watched the firing resume on the screen, and the figures started moving from behind the vehicles and closing on Ben and Simmons's position.

"Main Control, Conn, All Stop!" Hopkins shouted into the phone when the speed dropped to zero. The roar of the engines immediately died away.

"Conn, Mount 51, more continuous gunfire bearing zero-six-zero relative, no visual target!"

"Conn, aye!"

"Target identified, target confirmed, on target and tracking!"

"Batteries release. Commence fire!"

Short Story—Ben Saves a Family

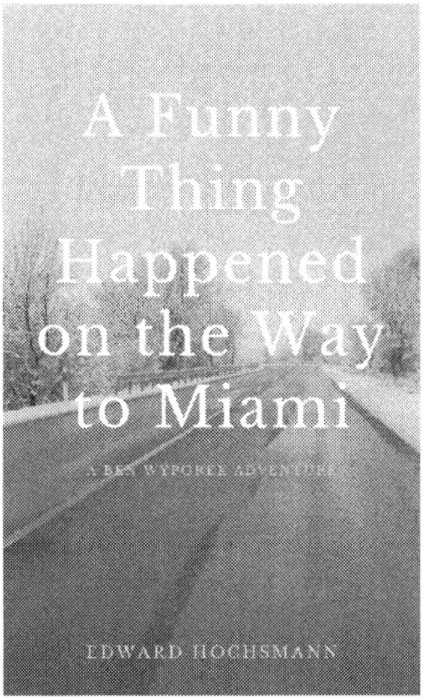

An ice storm had just passed on that frigid January morning in Southern Virginia as Lieutenant Junior Grade Ben Wyporek made his way to his new assignment aboard USCG Cutter *Kauai* in Miami. Little did he know that icy roads were about to become the least of his worries.

Read "A Funny Thing Happened on the Way to Miami" exclusively on Amazon Kindle.

https://mybook.to/FunnyThingMiami

Made in the USA
Columbia, SC
09 January 2024

29431635R00209